03/12

D0726196

SKETCHES OF
YOUNG GENTLEMEN

Charles Dickens

NONSUCH

First published 1838
Copyright © in this edition Nonsuch Publishing, 2007

Nonsuch Publishing
Cirencester Road, Chalford, Stroud, Gloucestershire, GL6 8PE

Nonsuch Publishing (Ireland)
73 Lower Leeson Street, Dublin 2, Ireland

www.nonsuch-publishing.com

Nonsuch Publishing is an imprint of NPI Media Group

For comments or suggestions, please email the editor of this series at:
classics@tempus-publishing.com

British Library Cataloguing in Publication Data.
A catalogue record for this book is available from the British Library.

ISBN 978 1 84588 240 2

Typesetting and origination by Nonsuch Publishing Limited
Printed in Great Britain by Oaklands Book Services Limited

CONTENTS

INTRODUCTION TO THE MODERN EDITION

CHARLES DICKENS, GENERALLY REGARDED AS the foremost literary figure of his age, scarcely needs an introduction; to describe him as a household name would be to damn his memory with faint praise. He is perhaps second only to Shakespeare in the literary consciousness, certainly in terms of those writing in the English language. Roman Polanski's recent film adaptation of *Oliver Twist* thrust Dickens firmly into the modern spotlight, introducing him to a generation who may have been surprised to find that nestled beneath the frightening weight of his reputation lay a storyteller who could thrill, able to excite even today's media-savvy youth. *Sketches of Young Gentlemen* is a less well-known work, a collection of the author's shorter pieces from the beginning of his career, but fundamentally important in terms of what was to follow; 'The Mudfog Papers', for instance, one of the sketches included in the present volume, provided the basis for what was later to become *Oliver Twist*.

The circumstances of Dickens' early life can be clearly seen to have shaped the tenor of his writing. He read voraciously by all accounts, with a particular taste for the classics and the works of Smollet and Fielding. His family life was initially comfortable; his father, John, was a clerk in the Naval Pay Office who liked to entertain. John Dickens' means were to prove insufficient to support his social ambitions, however, and led him inexorably towards Marshalsea Debtors' Prison. At this point, the young Charles, then twelve years of age, was to be shown a darker side of life. He was put to work at Warren's Blacking Factory, a traumatic experience which was made even worse by the fact that, after the family's finances improved, his mother insisted that her son continue in the job. *David Copperfield*, which is considered to be his most autobiographical work, describes his feelings best:

> I had no advice, no counsel, no encouragement, no consolation, no assistance, no support, of any kind, from anyone, that I can call to mind, as I hope to go to heaven.

If there was one silver lining in this blackened cloud it was that it gave Dickens an insight into the conditions of life for London's poor, an insight that was given full expression over the course of his writing career. Few authors could be seen to have combined commercial success in their lifetime with such a strident and ultimately effective call for change.

At fifteen Dickens became a legal clerk, which was a route through which he might have progressed to become a lawyer, if he did not hold the profession in such low esteem. He left this post to become a court stenographer, and then a journalist covering Parliamentary debates, at which he excelled. He began to publish his sketches and observations under the pen-name 'Boz'. It was not long until his first novel, *The Pickwick Papers*, was published. It was a tremendous success and at this point Dickens nailed his colours to the mast and became a full-time novelist. Few today would argue with his decision.

His literary output over the course of his lifetime was prolific; perhaps not on the scale of Anthony Trollope or his formidable mother, but his commitment to the enterprise was clear. When one considers that among the list of titles he penned stand such epic works as *David Copperfield*, *Bleak House*, *Hard Times* and *Great Expectations* there can be little doubt of the timeless quality of his writing, or the impact that he has had on the canon of English literature.

The essence of the Nonsuch Classics series has always been to focus on those titles which have slipped through the net of popular recognition, victims of a fickle posterity. From the tales of Sam Slick in *The Clockmaker* to Cuthbert Bede's *Adventures of Mr Verdant Green*, there is a great array of works which are well known to the few and hidden from the many, and it is with a very great pleasure that these works are brought back into the light, where they have always deserved to be. *Sketches of Young Gentlemen* is a fine example of such a work, and is one that will continue to delight for as long as it continues to be read.

Sketches of Young Gentlemen

Sheweth,—

That your Dedicator has perused, with feelings of virtuous indignation, a work purporting to be "Sketches of Young Ladies"; written by Quiz, illustrated by Phiz, and published in one volume, square twelvemo.

That after an attentive and vigilant perusal of the said work, your Dedicator is humbly of opinion that so many libels, upon your Honourable sex, were never contained in any previously published work, in twelvemo or any other mo.

That in the title page and preface to the said work, your Honourable sex are described and classified as animals; and although your Dedicator is not at present prepared to deny that you are animals, still he humbly submits that it is not polite to call you so.

That in the aforesaid preface, your Honourable sex are also described as Troglodytes, which, being a hard word, may, for aught your Honourable sex or your Dedicator can say to the contrary, be an injurious and disrespectful appellation.

That the author of the said work applied himself to his task in malice prepense and with wickedness aforethought; a fact which, your Dedicator contends, is sufficiently demonstrated, by his assuming the name of Quiz, which, your Dedicator submits, denotes a foregone conclusion, and implies an intention of quizzing.

That in the execution of his evil design, the said Quiz, or author of the said work, must have betrayed some trust or confidence reposed in him by some members of your Honourable sex, otherwise he never could have acquired so much information relative to the manners and customs of your Honourable sex in general.

That actuated by these considerations, and further moved by various slanders and insinuations respecting your Honourable sex contained in the said work, square twelvemo, entitled "Sketches of Young Ladies", your Dedicator ventures to produce another work, square twelvemo, entitled "Sketches of Young Gentlemen", of which he now solicits your acceptance and approval.

That as the Young Ladies are the best companions of the Young Gentlemen, so the Young Gentlemen should be the best companions of the Young Ladies; and extending the comparison from animals (to quote the disrespectful language of the said Quiz) to inanimate objects, your Dedicator humbly suggests, that such of your Honourable sex as purchased the bane should possess themselves of the antidote, and that those of your Honourable sex who were not rash enough to take the first, should lose no time in swallowing the last,—prevention being in all cases better than cure, as we are informed upon the authority, not only of general acknowledgment, but also of traditionary wisdom.

That with reference to the said bane and antidote, your Dedicator has no further remarks to make, than are comprised in the printed directions issued with Doctor Morison's pills; namely, that whenever your Honourable sex take twenty-five of Number 1, you will be pleased to take fifty of Number 2, without delay.

And your Dedicator shall ever pray, &c.

The Bashful Young Gentlemen

SKETCHES OF YOUNG GENTLEMEN

THE BASHFUL YOUNG GENTLEMAN

WE FOUND OURSELF SEATED AT a small dinner-party the other day opposite a stranger of such singular appearance and manner, that he irresistibly attracted our attention.

This was a fresh-coloured young gentleman, with as good a promise of light whisker as one might wish to see, and possessed of a very velvet-like, soft-looking countenance. We do not use the latter term invidiously, but merely to denote a pair of smooth, plump, highly-coloured cheeks of capacious dimensions, and a mouth rather remarkable for the fresh hue of the lips than for any marked or striking expression it presented. His whole face was suffused with a crimson blush, and bore that downcast, timid, retiring look, which betokens a man ill at ease with himself.

There was nothing in these symptoms to attract more than a passing remark, but our attention had been originally drawn to the bashful young gentleman, on his first appearance in the drawing-room above-stairs, into which he was no sooner introduced, than making his way towards us who were standing in a window, and wholly neglecting several persons who warmly accosted him, he seized our hand with visible emotion, and pressed it with a convulsive grasp for a good couple of minutes, after which he dived in a nervous manner across the room, oversetting in his way a fine little girl of six years and a quarter old—and shrouding himself behind some hangings, was seen no more, until the eagle eye of the hostess detecting him in his concealment, on the announcement of dinner, he was requested to pair off with a lively single lady, of two-or three-and-thirty.

This most flattering salutation from a perfect stranger would have gratified us not a little as a token of his having held us in high respect, and for that reason been desirous of our acquaintance, if we had not suspected from the first that the young gentleman, in making a desperate effort to get through the ceremony of introduction, had, in the bewilderment of his ideas, shaken hands with us at random. This impression was fully confirmed by the subsequent behaviour of the bashful young gentleman in question, which we noted particularly, with the view of ascertaining whether we were right in our conjecture.

The young gentleman seated himself at table with evident misgivings, and turning sharp round to pay attention to some observation of his loquacious neighbour, overset his bread. There was nothing very bad in this, and if he had had the presence of mind to let it go, and say nothing about it, nobody but the man who had laid the cloth would have been a bit the wiser; but the young gentleman in various semi-successful attempts to prevent its fall, played with it a little, as gentlemen in the streets may be seen to do with their hats on a windy day, and then giving the roll a smart rap in his anxiety to catch it, knocked it with great adroitness into a tureen of white soup at some distance, to the unspeakable terror and disturbance of a very amiable bald gentle man who was dispensing the contents. We thought the bashful young gentleman would have gone off in an apoplectic fit, consequent upon the violent rush of blood to his face at the occurrence of this catastrophe.

From this moment, we perceived, in the phraseology of the fancy, that it was "all up" with the bashful young gentleman, and so indeed it was. Several benevolent persons endeavoured to relieve his embarrassment by taking wine with him, but finding that it only augmented his sufferings, and that after mingling sherry, champagne, hock, and moselle together, he applied the greater part of the mixture externally, instead of internally, they gradually dropped off, and left him to the exclusive care of the talkative lady, who, not noting the wildness of his eye, firmly believed she had secured a listener. He broke a glass or two in the course of the meal, and disappeared shortly afterwards; it is inferred that he went away in some confusion, inasmuch as he left the house in another gentleman's coat, and the footman's hat.

This little incident led us to reflect upon the most prominent characteristics of bashful young gentlemen in the abstract; and as this portable volume will be the great text-book of young ladies in all future generations, we record them here for their guidance and behoof.

If the bashful young gentleman, in turning a street corner, chance to stumble suddenly upon two or three young ladies of his acquaintance, nothing can exceed his confusion and agitation. His first impulse is to make a great variety of bows, and dart past them, which he does until, observing that they wish to stop, but are uncertain whether to do so or not, he makes several feints of returning, which causes them to do the same; and at length, after a great quantity of unnecessary dodging and falling up against the other passengers, he returns and shakes hands most affectionately with all of them, in doing which he knocks out of their grasp sundry little parcels, which he hastily picks up, and returns very muddy and disordered. The chances are that the bashful young gentleman then observes it is very fine weather, and being reminded that it has only just left off raining for the first time these three days, he blushes very much, and smiles as if he had said a very good thing. The young lady who was most anxious to speak, here inquires, with an air of great commiseration, how his dear sister Harriet is to-day; to which the young gentleman, without the slightest consideration, replies with many thanks, that she is remarkably well. "Well, Mr. Hopkins!" cries the young lady, "why, we heard she was bled yesterday evening, and have been perfectly miserable about her." "Oh, ah," says the young gentleman, "so she was. Oh, she's very ill, very ill indeed." The young gentleman then shakes his head, and looks very desponding (he has been smiling perpetually up to this time), and after a short pause, gives his glove a great wrench at the wrist, and says, with a strong emphasis on the adjective, "*Good*-morning, *good*-morning." And making a great number of bows in acknowledgment of several little messages to his sister, walks backward a few paces, and comes with great violence against a lamp-post, knocking his hat off in the contact, which in his mental confusion and bodily pain he is going to walk away without, until a great roar from a carter attracts his attention, when he picks it up, and tries to smile cheerfully to the young ladies, who are looking back, and who, he has the satisfaction of seeing, are all laughing heartily.

At a quadrille party, the bashful young gentleman always remains as near the entrance of the room as possible, from which position he smiles at the people he knows as they come in, and sometimes steps forward to shake hands with more intimate friends: a process which on each repetition seems to turn him a deeper scarlet than before. He declines dancing the first set or two, observing, in a faint voice, that he would rather wait a little; but at length is absolutely compelled to allow himself to be introduced to a partner, when he is led, in a great heat and blushing furiously, across the room to a spot where half-a-dozen unknown ladies are congregated together.

"Miss Lambert, let me introduce Mr. Hopkins for the next quadrille." Miss Lambert inclines her head graciously. Mr. Hopkins bows, and his fair conductress disappears, leaving Mr. Hopkins, as he too well knows, to make himself agreeable. The young lady more than half expects that the bashful young gentleman will say something, and the bashful young gentleman feeling this, seriously thinks whether he has got anything to say, which, upon mature reflection, he is rather disposed to conclude he has not, since nothing occurs to him. Meanwhile, the young lady, after several inspections of her bouquet, all made in the expectation that the bashful young gentleman is going to talk, whispers her mamma, who is sitting next her, which whisper the bashful young gentleman immediately suspects (and possibly with very good reason) must be about *him*. In this comfortable condition he remains until it is time to "stand up," when murmuring a "Will you allow me?" he gives the young lady his arm, and after inquiring where she will stand, and receiving a reply that she has no choice, conducts her to the remotest corner of the quadrille, and making one attempt at conversation, which turns out a desperate failure, preserves a profound silence until it is all over, when he walks her twice round the room, deposits her in her old seat, and retires in confusion.

A married bashful gentleman—for these bashful gentlemen *do* get married sometimes; how it is ever brought about is a mystery to us— a married bashful gentleman either causes his wife to appear bold by contrast, or merges her proper importance in his own insignificance. Bashful young gentlemen should be cured, or avoided. They are never hopeless, and never will be, while female beauty and attractions retain their influence, as any young lady will find, who may think it worth while on this confident assurance to take a patient in hand.

THE OUT-AND-OUT YOUNG GENTLEMAN

Out-and-out young gentlemen may be divided into two classes—those who have something to do, and those who have nothing. I shall commence with the former, because that species come more frequently under the notice of young ladies, whom it is our province to warn and to instruct.

The out-and-out young gentleman is usually no great dresser, his instructions to his tailor being all comprehended in the one general direction to "make that what's-a-name a regular bang-up sort of thing." For some years past the favourite costume of the out-and-out young gentleman has been a rough pilot coat, with two gilt hooks and eyes to the velvet collar; buttons somewhat larger than crown-pieces; a black or fancy neckerchief, loosely tied; a wide-brimmed hat, with a low crown; tightish inexpressibles, and iron-shod boots. Out-of-doors he sometimes carries a large ash stick, but only on special occasions, for he prefers keeping his hands in his coat pockets. He smokes at all hours, of course, and swears considerably.

The out-and-out young gentleman is employed in a city counting-house or solicitor's office, in which he does as little as he possibly can: his chief places of resort are the streets, the taverns, and the theatres. In the streets at evening time, out-and-out young gentlemen have a pleasant custom of walking six or eight abreast, thus driving females and other inoffensive persons into the road, which never fails to afford them the highest satisfaction, especially if there be any immediate danger of their being run over, which enhances the fun of the thing materially. In all places of public resort the out-and-outers are careful to select each a seat to himself, upon which he lies at full length, and (if the weather be very dirty, but not in any other case) he lies with his knees up, and the soles of his boots planted firmly on the cushion, so that if any low fellow should ask him to make room for a lady, he takes ample revenge upon her dress, without going at all out of his way to do it. He always sits with his hat on, and flourishes his stick in the air while the play is proceeding, with a dignified contempt of the performance; if it be possible for one or two out-and-out young gentlemen to get up a little crowding in the passages, they are quite in their element, squeezing, pushing, whooping, and shouting in the most humorous manner possible. If they can only succeed in irritating the gentleman who has a family of daughters under his charge, they are like to die with laughing, and boast of it among their companions for a week afterwards, adding, that one or two of them were "devilish fine girls," and that they really thought the youngest would have fainted, which was the only thing wanted to render the joke complete.

If the out-and-out young gentleman have a mother and sisters, of course he treats them with becoming contempt, inasmuch as they (poor things!), having no notion of life or gaiety, are far too weak-spirited and moping for him. Sometimes, however, on a birthday or at Christmas-time, he cannot very well help accompanying them to a party at some old friend's, with which view he comes home when they have been dressed an hour or two, smelling very strongly of tobacco and spirits, and after exchanging his rough coat for some more suitable attire (in which, however, he loses nothing of the out-and-outer), gets into the coach and grumbles all the way at his own good nature: his bitter reflections aggravated by the recollection that Tom Smith has taken the chair at a little impromptu dinner at a fighting man's, and that a set-to was to take place on a dining-table between the fighting man and his brother-in-law, which is probably "coming off" at that very instant.

As the out-and-out young gentleman is by no means at his ease in ladies' society, he shrinks into a corner of the drawing-room when they reach the friend's, and unless one of his sisters is kind enough to talk to him, remains there without being much troubled by the attentions of other people, until he espies, lingering outside the door, another gentleman, whom he at once knows, by his air and manner (for there is a kind of freemasonry in the craft), to be a brother out-and-outer, and towards him he accordingly makes his way. Conversation being soon opened by some casual remark, the second out-and-outer confidentially informs the first that he is one of the rough sort and hates that kind of thing, only he couldn't very well be off coming; to which the other replies, that that's just his case—"and I'll tell you what," continues the out-and-outer in a whisper, "I should like a glass of warm brandy and water just now,"—" Or a pint of stout and a pipe," suggests the other out-and-outer.

The discovery is at once made that they are sympathetic souls; each of them says at the same moment that he sees the other understands what's what: and they become fast friends at once, more especially when it appears that the second out-and-outer is no other than a gentleman long favourably known to his familiars as "Mr. Warmint Blake," who upon divers occasions has distinguished himself in a manner that would not have disgraced the fighting man, and who—having been a pretty long time about town—had the honour of once shaking hands with the celebrated Mr. Thurtell himself.

At supper these gentlemen greatly distinguish themselves, brightening up very much when the ladies leave the table, and proclaiming aloud their intention of beginning to spend the evening—a process which is generally understood to be satisfactorily performed when a great deal of wine is drunk and a great deal of noise made, both of which feats the out-and-out young gentlemen execute to perfection. Having protracted their sitting until long after the host and the other guests have adjourned to the drawing-room, and finding that they have drained the decanters empty, they follow them thither with complexions rather heightened, and faces rather bloated with wine; and the agitated lady of the house whispers her friends as they waltz together, to the great terror of the whole room, that "both Mr. Blake and Mr. Dummins are very nice sort of young men in their way, only they are eccentric persons, and unfortunately *rather too wild!*"

The remaining class of out-and-out young gentlemen is composed of persons who, having no money of their own and a soul above earning any, enjoy similar pleasures, nobody knows how. These respectable gentlemen, without aiming quite so much at the out-and-out in external appearance, are distinguished by all the same amiable and attractive characteristics, in an equal or perhaps greater degree, and now and then find their way into society, through the medium of the other class of out-and-out young gentlemen, who will sometimes carry them home, and who usually pay their tavern bills. As they are equally gentle manly, clever, witty, intelligent, wise, and well-bred, we need scarcely have recommended them to the peculiar consideration of the young ladies, if it were not that some of the gentle creatures whom we hold in such high respect are perhaps a little too apt to confound a great many heavier terms with the light word eccentricity, which we beg them henceforth to take in a strictly Johnsonian sense, without any liberality or latitude of construction.

THE VERY FRIENDLY YOUNG GENTLEMAN

We know—and all people know—so many specimens of this class, that in selecting the few heads our limits enable us to take from a great number, we have been induced to give the very friendly young gentleman the preference over many others, to whose claims upon a more cursory view of the question we had felt disposed to assign the priority.

The very friendly young gentleman is very friendly to everybody, but he attaches himself particularly to two, or at most to three families: regulating his choice by their dinners, their circle of acquaintance, or some other criterion in which he has an immediate interest. He is of any age between twenty and forty, unmarried of course, must be fond of children, and is expected to make himself generally useful if possible. Let us illustrate our meaning by an example, which is the shortest mode and the clearest.

We encountered one day, by chance, an old friend of whom we had lost sight for some years, and who—expressing a strong anxiety to renew our former intimacy—urged us to dine with him on an early day, that we might talk over old times. We readily assented, adding, that we hoped we should be alone. "Oh, certainly, certainly," said our friend, "not a soul with us but Mincin." "And who is Mincin?" was our natural inquiry. "Oh, don't mind him," replied our friend, "he's a most particular friend of mine, and a very friendly fellow you will find him;" and so he left us.

We thought no more about Mincin until we duly presented ourselves at the house next day, when, after a hearty welcome, our friend motioned towards a gentleman who had been previously showing his teeth by the fireplace, and gave us to understand that it was Mr. Mincin, of whom he had spoken. It required no great penetration on our part to discover at once that Mr. Mincin was in every respect a very friendly young gentleman.

"I am delighted," said Mincin, hastily advancing, and pressing our hand warmly between both of his, "I am delighted, I am sure, to make your acquaintance—(here he smiled)—very much delighted indeed—(here he exhibited a little emotion)—I assure you that I have looked forward to it anxiously for a very long time:" here he released our hands, and rubbing his own, observed, that the day was severe, but that he was delighted to perceive from our appearance that it agreed with us wonderfully; and then went on to observe that, notwithstanding the coldness of the weather, he had that morning seen in the paper an exceedingly curious paragraph, to the effect, that there was now in the garden of Mr. Wilkins of Chichester a pumpkin measuring four feet in height, and eleven feet seven inches in circumference, which he looked upon as a very extraordinary piece of intelligence. We ventured to remark that we had a dim recollection of having once or twice before observed a similar paragraph in the public prints, upon which Mr. Mincin took us confidentially by the button, and said, Exactly, exactly, to be sure, we were very right, and he wondered what the editors meant by putting in such things. Who the deuce, he should like to know, did they suppose cared about them? that struck him as being the best of it.

The lady of the house appeared shortly afterwards, and Mr. Mincin's friendliness, as will readily be supposed, suffered no diminution in consequence; he exerted much strength and skill in wheeling a large easy-chair up to the fire, and the lady being seated in it, carefully closed the door, stirred the fire, and looked to the windows to see that they admitted no air; having satisfied himself upon all these points, he expressed himself quite easy in his mind, and begged to know how she found herself to-day. Upon the lady's replying very well, Mr. Mincin (who it appeared was a medical gentleman) offered some general remarks upon the nature and treatment of colds in the head, which occupied us agreeably until dinner-time. During the meal, he devoted himself to complimenting everybody, not forgetting himself, so that we were an uncommonly agreeable quartette.

"I'll tell you what, Capper," said Mr. Mincin to our host, as he closed the room door after the lady had retired, "you have very good reason to be fond of your wife. Sweet woman, Mrs. Capper, Sir!" "Nay, Mincin—I beg," interposed the host, as we were about to reply that Mrs. Capper unquestionably was particularly sweet. "Pray, Mincin, don't." "Why not?" exclaimed Mr. Mincin, "why not? Why should you feel any delicacy before your old friend—*our* old friend, if I may be allowed to call you so, Sir; why should you, I ask?" We of course wished to know why he should also, upon which our friend admitted that Mrs. Capper *was* a very sweet woman, at which admission Mr. Mincin cried

"Bravo!" and begged to propose Mrs. Capper with heartfelt enthusiasm, whereupon our host said, "Thank you, Mincin," with deep feeling; and gave us, in a low voice, to understand that Mincin had saved Mrs. Capper's cousin's life no less than fourteen times in a year and a half, which he considered no common circumstance—an opinion to which we most cordially subscribed.

Now that we three were left to entertain ourselves with conversation, Mr. Mincin's extreme friendliness became every moment more apparent; he was so amazingly friendly, indeed, that it was impossible to talk about anything in which he had not the chief concern. We happened to allude to some affairs in which our friend and we had been mutually engaged nearly fourteen years before, when Mr. Mincin was all at once reminded of a joke which our friend had made on that day four years, which he positively must insist upon telling—and which he did tell accordingly, with many pleasant recollections of what he said, and what Mrs. Capper said, and how he well remembered that they had been to the play with orders on the very night previous, and had seen *Romeo and Juliet*, and the pantomime, and how Mrs. Capper, being faint, had been led into the lobby, where she smiled, said it was nothing after all, and went back again, with many other interesting and absorbing particulars: after which the friendly young gentleman went on to assure us that our friend had expressed a marvellously prophetic opinion of that same pantomime, which was of such an admirable kind that two morning papers took the same view next day: to this our friend replied, with a little triumph, that in that instance he had some reason to think he had been correct, which gave the friendly young gentleman occasion to believe that our friend was always correct; and so we went on, until our friend, filling a bumper, said he must drink one glass to his dear friend Mincin, than whom he would say no man saved the lives of his acquaintances more, or had a more friendly heart. Finally, our friend having emptied his glass, said, "God bless you, Mincin,"—and Mr. Mincin and he shook hands across the table with much affection and earnestness.

But great as the friendly young gentleman is, in a limited scene like this, he plays the same part on a larger scale with increased *éclat*. Mr. Mincin is invited to an evening party with his dear friends the Martins, where he meets his dear friends the Cappers, and his dear friends the Watsons, and a hundred other dear friends too numerous to mention. He is as much at home with the Martins as with the Cappers; but how exquisitely he balances his attentions, and divides them among his dear friends! If he flirts with one of the Miss Watsons, he has one little Martin on the sofa pulling his hair, and the other little Martin on the carpet riding on his foot. He carries Mrs. Watson down to supper on one arm, and Miss Martin on the other, and takes wine so judiciously, and in such exact order, that it is impossible for the most punctilious old lady to consider herself neglected. If any young lady, being prevailed upon to sing, becomes nervous afterwards, Mr. Mincin leads her tenderly into the next room, and restores her with port wine, which she must take medicinally. If any gentleman be standing by the piano during the progress of the ballad, Mr. Mincin seizes him by the arm at one point of the melody, and softly beating time the while with his head, expresses in dumb show his intense perception of the delicacy of the passage. If anybody's self-love is to be flattered, Mr. Mincin is at hand. If anybody's over-weening vanity is to be pampered, Mr. Mincin will surfeit it. What wonder that people of all stations and ages recognise Mr. Mincin's friendliness; that he is universally allowed to be as handsome as amiable; that mothers think him an oracle, daughters a dear, brothers a beau, and fathers a wonder! And who would not have the reputation of the very friendly young gentleman?

THE MILITARY YOUNG GENTLEMAN

We are rather at a loss to imagine how it has come to pass that military young gentlemen have obtained so much favour in the eyes of the young ladies of this kingdom. We cannot think so lightly of them as to suppose that the mere circumstance of a man's wearing a red coat ensures him a ready passport to their regard; and even if this were the case, it would be no satisfactory explanation of the circumstance, because, although the analogy may in some degree hold good in the case of mail coachmen and guards, still general postmen wear red coats, and *they* are not to our knowledge better received than other men; nor are firemen either, who wear (or used to wear) not only red coats, but very resplendent and massive badges besides—much larger than epaulettes. Neither do the twopenny-post-office boys, if the result of our inquiries be correct, find any peculiar favour in woman's eyes, although they wear very bright red jackets, and have the additional advantage of constantly appearing in public on horseback, which last circumstance may be naturally supposed to be greatly in their favour.

We have sometimes thought that this phenomenon may take its rise in the conventional behaviour of captains and colonels and other gentlemen in red coats on the stage, where they are invariably represented as fine swaggering fellows, talking of nothing but charming girls, their king and country, their honour, and their debts, and crowing over the inferior classes of the community, whom they occasionally treat with a little gentlemanly swindling, no less to the improvement and pleasure of the audience than to the satisfaction and approval of the choice spirits who consort with them. But we will not devote these pages to our speculations upon the subject, inasmuch as our business at the present moment is not so much with the young ladies who are bewitched by Her Majesty's livery as with the young gentlemen whose heads are turned by it. For "heads" we had written "brains"; but upon consideration, we think the former the more appropriate word of the two.

These young gentlemen may be divided into two classes—young gentlemen who are actually in the army, and young gentlemen who, having an intense and enthusiastic admiration for all things appertaining to a military life, are compelled by adverse fortune or adverse relations to wear out their existence in some ignoble counting-house. We will take this latter description of military young gentlemen first.

The whole heart and soul of the military young gentleman are concentrated in his favourite topic. There is nothing that he is so learned upon as uniforms; he will tell you, without faltering for an instant, what the habiliments of any one regiment are turned up with, what regiments wear stripes down the outside and inside of the leg, and how many buttons the Tenth had on their coats ; he knows to a fraction how many yards and odd inches of gold lace it takes to make an ensign in the Guards; is deeply read in the comparative merits of different bands, and the apparelling of trumpeters; and is very luminous indeed in descanting upon "crack regiments," and the "crack" gentlemen who compose them, of whose mightiness and grandeur he is never tired of telling.

We were suggesting to a military young gentleman only the other day, after he had related to us several dazzling instances of the profusion of half-a-dozen honourable ensign somebodies or nobodies in the articles of kid gloves and polished boots, that possibly "cracked" regiments would be an improvement upon "crack," as being a more expressive and appropriate designation, when he suddenly interrupted us by pulling out his watch, and observing that he must hurry off to the Park in a cab, or he would be too late to hear the band play. Not wishing to interfere with so important an engagement, and being in fact already slightly overwhelmed by the anecdotes of the honourable ensigns aforementioned, we made no attempt to detain the military young gentleman, but parted company with ready good-will.

Some three or four hours afterwards, we chanced to be walking down Whitehall, on the Admiralty side of the way, when, as we drew near to one of the little stone places in which a couple of horse-soldiers mount guard in the daytime, we were attracted by the motionless appearance and eager gaze of a young gentleman, who was devouring both man and horse with his eyes, so eagerly that he seemed deaf and blind to all that was passing around him. We were not much surprised at the discovery that it was our friend, the military young gentleman, but we *were* a little astonished when we returned from a walk to South Lambeth to find him still there, looking on with the same intensity as before. As it was a very windy day, we felt bound to awaken the young gentleman from his reverie, when he inquired of us with great enthusiasm whether "that was not a glorious spectacle," and proceeded to give us a detailed account of the weight of every article of the spectacle's trappings, from the man's gloves to the horse's shoes.

We have made it a practice since, to take the Horse Guards in our daily walk, and we find it is the custom of military young gentlemen to plant themselves opposite the sentries, and contemplate them at leisure, in periods varying from fifteen minutes to fifty, and averaging twenty-five. We were much struck a day or two since by the behaviour of a very promising young butcher, who (evincing an interest in the service, which cannot be too strongly commended or encouraged), after a prolonged inspection of the sentry, proceeded to handle his boots with great curiosity, and as much composure and indifference as if the man were wax-work.

But the really military young gentleman is waiting all this time, and at the very moment that an apology rises to our lips, he emerges from the barrack gate (he is quartered in a garrison town), and takes the way towards the High Street. He wears his undress uniform, which somewhat mars the glory of his outward man; but still how great, how grand, he is! What a happy mixture of ease and ferocity in his gait and carriage, and how lightly he carries that dreadful sword under his arm, making no more ado about it than if it were a silk umbrella! The lion is sleeping: only think if an enemy were in sight, how soon he'd whip it out of the scabbard, and what a terrible fellow he would be!

But he walks on, thinking of nothing less than blood and slaughter; and now he comes in sight of three other military young gentlemen, arm-in-arm, who are bearing down towards him, clanking their iron heels on the pavement, and clashing their swords with a noise, which should cause all peaceful men to quail at heart. They stop to talk. See how the flaxen-haired young gentleman with the weak legs—he who has his pocket-handkerchief thrust into the breast of his coat—glares upon the faint-hearted civilians who linger to look upon his glory; how the next young gentleman elevates his head in the air, and majestically places his arms a-kimbo, while the third stands with his legs very wide apart, and clasps his hands behind him. Well may we inquire—not in familiar jest, but in respectful earnest—if you call that nothing. Oh! if some encroaching foreign power—the Emperor of Russia, for instance, or any of those deep fellows—could only see those military young gentlemen as they move on together towards the billiard-room over the way, wouldn't he tremble a little!

And then, at the theatre at night, when the performances are by command of Colonel Fitz-Sordust and the officers of the garrison—what a splendid sight it is! How sternly the defenders of their country look round the house as if in mute assurance to the audience that they may make themselves comfortable regarding any foreign invasion, for they (the military young gentlemen) are keeping a sharp look-out, and are ready for anything. And what a contrast between them and that stage-box full of grey-headed officers with tokens of many battles about them, who have nothing at all in common with the military young gentlemen, and who—but for an old-fashioned kind of manly dignity in their looks and bearing—might be common hard-working soldiers for anything they take the pains to announce to the contrary!

Ah! here is a family just come in who recognise the flaxen-headed young gentleman; and the flaxen-headed young gentleman recognises them too, only he doesn't care to show it just now. Very well done indeed! He talks louder to the little group of military young gentlemen who are standing by him, and coughs to induce some ladies in the next box but one to look round, in order that their faces may undergo the same ordeal of criticism to which they have subjected, in not a wholly inaudible tone, the majority of the female portion of the audience. Oh! a gentleman in the same box looks round as if he were disposed to resent this as an impertinence; and the flaxen-headed young gentleman sees his friends at once, and hurries away to them with the most charming cordiality.

Three young ladies, one young man, and the mamma of the party receive the military young gentleman with great warmth and politeness, and in five minutes afterwards the military young gentleman, stimulated by the mamma, introduces the two other military young gentlemen with whom he was walking in the morning, who take their seats behind the young ladies and commence conversation; whereat the mamma bestows a triumphant bow upon a rival mamma, who has not succeeded in decoying any military young gentlemen, and prepares to consider her visitors from that moment three of the most elegant and superior young gentlemen in the whole world.

THE POLITICAL YOUNG GENTLEMAN

Once upon a time—*not* in the days when pigs drank wine, but in a more recent period of our history—it was customary to banish politics when ladies were present. If this usage still prevailed, we should have had no chapter for political young gentlemen, for ladies would have neither known nor cared what kind of monster a political young gentleman was. But as this good custom in common with many others has "gone out," and left no word when it is likely to be home again; as political young ladies are by no means rare, and political young gentlemen the very reverse of scarce, we are bound in the strict discharge of our most responsible duty not to neglect this natural division of our subject.

If the political young gentleman be resident in a country town (and there *are* political young gentlemen in country towns sometimes), he is wholly absorbed in his politics; as a pair of purple spectacles communicate the same uniform tint to all objects near and remote, so the political glasses, with which the young gentleman assists his mental vision, give to everything the hue and tinge of party feeling. The political young gentleman would as soon think of being struck with the beauty of a young lady in the opposite interest as he would dream of marrying his sister to the opposite member.

If the political young gentleman be a Conservative, he has usually some vague ideas about Ireland and the Pope which he cannot very clearly explain, but which he knows are the right sort of thing, and not to be very easily got over by the other side. He has also some choice sentences regarding church and state, culled from the banners in use at the last election, with which he intersperses his conversation at intervals with surprising effect. But his great topic is the constitution, upon which he will declaim, by the hour together, with much heat and fury; not that he has any particular information on the subject, but because he knows that the constitution is somehow church and state, and church and state somehow the constitution, and that the fellows on the other side say it isn't, which is quite a sufficient reason for him to say it is and to stick to it.

Perhaps his greatest topic of all, though, is the people. If a fight takes place in a populous town, in which many noses are broken, and a few windows, the young gentleman throws down the newspaper with a triumphant air, and exclaims, "Here's your precious people!" If half-a-dozen boys run across the course at race time, when it ought to be kept clear, the young gentleman looks indignantly round, and begs you to observe the conduct of the people; if the gallery demand a hornpipe between the play and the afterpiece, the same young gentleman cries " No" and " Shame" till he is hoarse, and then inquires with a sneer what you think of popular moderation *now*; in short, the people form a never-failing theme for him ; and when the attorney, on the side of his candidate, dwells upon it with great power of eloquence at election time, as he never fails to do, the young gentleman and his friends, and the body they head, cheer with great violence against *the other people* with whom, of course, they have no possible connection. In much the same manner the audience at a theatre never fail to be highly amused with any jokes at the expense of the public—always laughing heartily at some other public, and never at themselves.

If the political young gentleman be a Radical, he is usually a very profound person indeed, having great store of theoretical questions to put to you, with an infinite variety of possible cases and logical deductions therefrom. If he be of the utilitarian school, too, which is more than probable, he is particularly pleasant company, having many ingenious remarks to offer upon the voluntary principle and various cheerful disquisitions connected with the population of the country, the position of Great Britain in the scale of nations, and the balance of power. Then he is exceedingly well versed in all doctrines of political economy as laid down in the newspapers, and knows a great many parliamentary speeches by heart ; nay, he has a small stock of aphorisms, none of them exceeding a couple of lines in length, which will settle the toughest question and leave you nothing to say. He gives all the young ladies to understand that Miss Martineau is the greatest woman that ever lived; and when they praise the good looks of Mr. Hawkins the new member, says he's very well for a representative, all things considered, but he wants a little calling to account, and he is more than half afraid it will be necessary to bring him down on his knees for that vote on the miscellaneous estimates. At this, the young ladies express much wonderment, and say surely a Member of Parliament is not to be brought upon his knees so easily; in reply to which the political young gentleman smiles sternly, and throws out dark hints regarding the speedy arrival of that day when Members of Parliament will be paid salaries, and required to render weekly accounts of their proceedings, at which the young ladies utter many expressions of astonishment and incredulity, while their lady-mothers regard the prophecy as little else than blasphemous.

It is extremely improving and interesting to hear two political young gentlemen, of diverse opinions, discuss some great question across a dinner-table; such as, whether, if the public were admitted to Westminster Abbey for nothing, they would or would not convey small chisels and hammers in their pockets and immediately set about chipping all the noses off the statues; or whether, if they once got into the Tower for a shilling, they would not insist upon trying the crown on their own heads, and loading and firing off all the small arms in the armoury, to the great discomposure of Whitechapel and the Minories. Upon these, and many other momentous questions which agitate the public mind in these desperate days, they will discourse with great vehemence and irritation for a considerable time together, both leaving off precisely where they began, and each thoroughly persuaded that he has got the better of the other.

In society, at assemblies, balls, and playhouses, these political young gentlemen are perpetually on the watch for a political allusion, or anything which can be tortured or construed into being one; when, thrusting themselves into the very smallest openings for their favourite discourse, they fall upon the unhappy company tooth and nail. They have recently had many favourable opportunities of arguing in churches, but as there the clergyman has it all his own way, and must not be contradicted, whatever politics he preaches, they are fain to hold their tongues until they reach the outer door, though at the imminent risk of bursting in the effort.

As such discussions can please nobody but the talkative parties concerned, we hope they will henceforth take the hint and discontinue them, otherwise we now give them warning that the ladies have our advice to discountenance such talkers altogether.

THE DOMESTIC YOUNG GENTLEMAN

Let us make a slight sketch of our amiable friend, Mr. Felix Nixon. We are strongly disposed to think that if we put him in this place he will answer our purpose without another word of comment.

Felix, then, is a young gentleman who lives at home with his mother, just within the twopenny-post-office circle of three miles from St. Martin-le-Grand. He wears Indiarubber goloshes when the weather is at all damp, and always has a silk handkerchief neatly folded up in the right-hand pocket of his great-coat, to tie over his mouth when he goes home at night; moreover, being rather near-sighted, he carries spectacles for particular occasions, and has a weakish tremulous voice, of which he makes great use, for he talks as much as any old lady breathing.

The two chief subjects of Felix's discourse are himself and his mother, both of whom would appear to be very wonderful and interesting persons. As Felix and his mother are seldom apart in body, so Felix and his mother are scarcely ever separate in spirit. If you ask Felix how he finds himself to-day, he prefaces his reply with a long and minute bulletin of his mother's state of health ; and the good lady, in her turn, edifies her acquaintance with a circumstantial and alarming account, how he sneezed four times and coughed once after being out in the rain the other night, but having his feet promptly put into hot water, and his head into a flannel something, which we will not describe more particularly than by this delicate allusion, was happily brought round by the next morning, and enabled to go to business as usual.

Our friend is not a very adventurous or hot-headed person, but he has passed through many dangers, as his mother can testify: there is one great story in particular, concerning a hackney coachman who wanted to overcharge him one night for bringing them home from the play, upon which Felix gave the aforesaid coachman a look which his mother thought would have crushed him to the earth, but which did not crush him quite, for he continued to demand another sixpence, notwithstanding that Felix took out his pocket-book, and, with the aid of a flat candle, pointed out the fare in print, which the coachman obstinately disregarding, he shut the street-door with a slam which his mother shudders to think of; and then, roused to the most appalling pitch of passion by the coachman knocking a double knock to show that he was by no means convinced, he broke with uncontrollable force from his parent and the servant girl, and running into the street without his hat, actually shook his fist at the coachman, and came back again with a face as white, Mrs. Nixon says, looking about her for a simile, as white as that ceiling. She never will forget his fury that night, Never!

To this account Felix listens with a solemn face, occasionally looking at you to see how it affects you, and when his mother has made an end of it, adds that he looked at every coachman he met for three weeks afterwards, in hopes that he might see the scoundrel; whereupon Mrs. Nixon, with an exclamation of terror, requests to know what he would have done to him if he *had* seen him, at which Felix smiling darkly and clenching his right fist, she exclaims, "Goodness gracious!" with a distracted air, and insists upon extorting a promise that he never will on any account do anything so rash, which her dutiful son—it being something more than three years since the offence was committed—reluctantly concedes, and his mother, shaking her head prophetically, fears with a sigh that his spirit will lead him into something violent yet. The discourse then, by an easy transition, turns upon the spirit which glows within the bosom of Felix, upon which point Felix himself becomes eloquent, and relates a thrilling anecdote of the time when he used to sit up till two o'clock in the morning reading French, and how his mother used to say, "Felix, you will make yourself ill, I know you will"; and how *he* used to say, "Mother, I don't care—I will do it"; and how at last his mother privately procured a doctor to come and see him, who declared, the moment he felt his pulse, that if he had gone on reading one night more—only one night more—he must have put a blister on each temple, and another between his shoulders; and who, as it was, sat down upon the instant, and writing a prescription for a blue pill, said it must be taken immediately, or he wouldn't answer for the consequences. The recital of these and many other moving perils of the like nature constantly harrows up the feelings of Mr. Nixon's friends.

Mrs. Nixon has a tolerably extensive circle of female acquaintance, being a good-humoured, talkative, bustling little body, and to the unmarried girls among them she is constantly vaunting the virtues of her son, hinting that she will be a very happy person who wins him, but that they must mind their P's and Q's, for he is very particular, and terribly severe upon young ladies. At this last caution the young ladies resident in the same row, who happen to be spending the evening there, put their pocket-handkerchiefs before their mouths, and are troubled with a short cough; just then Felix knocks at the door, and his mother, drawing the tea-table nearer the fire, calls out to him, as he takes off his boots in the back parlour, that he needn't mind coming in in his slippers, for there are only the two Miss Greys and Miss Thompson, and she is quite sure they will excuse *him*, and nodding to the two Miss Greys, she adds, in a whisper, that Julia Thompson is a great favourite with Felix, at which intelligence the short cough comes again, and Miss Thompson in particular is greatly troubled with it, till Felix, coming in, very faint for want of his tea, changes the subject of discourse, and enables her to laugh out boldly and tell Amelia Grey not to be so foolish. Here they all three laugh, and Mrs. Nixon says they are giddy girls ; in which stage of the proceedings Felix, who has by this time refreshened himself with the grateful herb that "cheers but not inebriates," removes his cup from his countenance and says with a knowing smile, that all girls are; whereat his admiring mamma pats him on the back and tells him not to be sly, which calls forth a general laugh from the young ladies, and another smile from Felix, who, thinking he looks very sly indeed, is perfectly satisfied.

Tea being over, the young ladies resume their work, and Felix insists upon holding a skein of silk while Miss Thompson winds it on a card. This process having been performed to the satisfaction of all parties, he brings down his flute in compliance with a request from the youngest Miss Grey, and plays divers tunes out of a very small music-book till supper-time, when he is very facetious and talkative indeed. Finally, after half a tumblerful of warm sherry and water, he gallantly puts on his goloshes over his slippers, and telling Miss Thompson's servant to run on first and get the door open, escorts that young lady to her house, five doors off: the Miss Greys, who live in the next house but one, stopping to peep with merry faces from their own door till he comes back again, when they call out "Very well, Mr. Felix," and trip into the passage with a laugh more musical than any flute that was ever played.

Felix is rather prim in his appearance, and perhaps a little priggish about his books and flute, and so forth, which have all their peculiar corners of peculiar shelves in his bedroom; indeed, all his female acquaintance (and they are good judges) have long ago set him down as a thorough old bachelor. He is a favourite with them, however, in a certain way, as an honest, inoffensive, kind-hearted creature; and as his peculiarities harm nobody, not even himself, we are induced to hope that many who are not personally acquainted with him will take our good word in his behalf, and be content to leave him to a long continuance of his harmless existence.

THE CENSORIOUS YOUNG GENTLEMAN

There is an amiable kind of young gentleman going about in society, upon whom, after much experience of him, and considerable turning over of the subject in our mind, we feel it our duty to affix the above appellation. Young ladies mildly call him a "sarcastic" young gentleman, or a "severe" young gentleman. We, who know better, beg to acquaint them with the fact that he is merely a censorious young gentleman, and nothing else.

The censorious young gentleman has the reputation among his familiars of a remarkably clever person, which he maintains by receiving all intelligence and expressing all opinions with a dubious sneer, accompanied with a half smile, expressive of anything you please but good-humour. This sets people about thinking what on earth the censorious young gentleman means, and they speedily arrive at the conclusion that he means something very deep indeed; for they reason in this way—"This young gentleman looks so very knowing that he must mean something, and as I am by no means a dull individual, what a very deep meaning he must have if *I* can't find it out!" It is extraordinary how soon a censorious young gentleman may make a reputation in his own small circle if he bear this in his mind, and regulate his proceedings accordingly.

As young ladies are generally—not curious, but laudably desirous to acquire information, the censorious young gentleman is much talked about among them, and many surmises are hazarded regarding him. "I wonder," exclaims the eldest Miss Greenwood, laying down her work to turn up the lamp, "I wonder whether Mr. Fairfax will ever be married." "Bless me, dear," cries Miss Marshall, "what ever made you think of him?" "Really I hardly know," replies Miss Greenwood; "he is such a very mysterious person that I often wonder about him." "Well, to tell you the truth," replies Miss Marshall, "and so do I." Here two other young ladies profess that they are constantly doing the like, and all present appear in the same condition except one young lady, who, not scrupling to state that she considers Mr. Fairfax "a horror," draws down all the opposition of the others, which having been expressed in a great many ejaculatory passages, such as "Well, did I ever!" and "Lor Emily, dear!" ma takes up the subject, and gravely states that she must say she does not think Mr. Fairfax by any means a horror, but rather takes him to be a young man of very great ability; "and I am quite sure," adds the worthy lady, "he always means a great deal more than he says."

The door opens at this point of the disclosure, and who of all people alive walks into the room but the very Mr. Fairfax who has been the subject of conversation! "Well, it really is curious," cries ma, "we were at that very moment talking about you." "You did me great honour," replies Mr. Fairfax; "may I venture to ask what you were saying?" "Why, if you must know," returns the eldest girl, "we were remarking what a very mysterious man you are." "Ay, ay!" observes Mr. Fairfax; "indeed!" Now Mr. Fairfax says this ay, ay, and indeed, which are slight words enough in themselves, with so very unfathomable an air, and accompanies them with such a very equivocal smile, that ma and the young ladies are more than ever convinced that he means an immensity, and so tell him he is a very dangerous man, and seems to be always thinking ill of somebody, which is precisely the sort of character the censorious young gentleman is most desirous to establish ; wherefore he

says, "Oh, dear, no," in a tone obviously intended to mean, "You have
me there," and which gives them to understand that they have hit the
right nail on the very centre of its head.

When the conversation ranges from the mystery overhanging the
censorious young gentleman's behaviour to the general topics of the
day, he sustains his character to admiration. He considers the new
tragedy well enough *for* a new tragedy, but Lord bless us—well, no
matter; he could say a great deal on that point, but he would rather not,
lest he should be thought ill-natured, as he knows he would be. "But
is not Mr. So-and-so's performance truly charming ?" inquires a young
lady. "Charming!" replies the censorious young gentleman. "Oh, dear,
yes, certainly; very charming—oh, very charming indeed." After this he
stirs the fire, smiling contemptuously all the while; and a modest young
gentleman, who has been a silent listener, thinks what a great thing it
must be to have such a critical judgment. Of music, pictures, books, and
poetry, the censorious young gentleman has an equally fine conception.
As to men and women, he can tell all about them at a glance. "Now let
us hear your opinion of young Mrs. Barker," says some great believer
in the powers of Mr. Fairfax, "but don't be too severe." "I never am
severe," replies the censorious young gentleman. "Well, never mind
that now. She is very lady like, is she not?" "Lady-like!" repeats the
censorious young gentle man (for he always repeats when he is at a loss
for anything to say). "Did you observe her manner? Bless my heart and
soul, Mrs. Thompson, did you observe her manner?—that's all I ask." "I
thought I had done so," rejoins the poor lady, much perplexed; "I did
not observe it very closely perhaps." "Oh, not very closely," rejoins the
censorious young gentleman, triumphantly. "Very good; then *I* did. Let
us talk no more about her." The censorious young gentleman purses
up his lips, and nods his head sagely, as he says this; and it is forthwith
whispered about that Mr. Fairfax (who, though he is a little prejudiced,
must be admitted to be a very excellent judge) has observed something
exceedingly odd in Mrs. Barker's manner.

THE FUNNY YOUNG GENTLEMAN

As one funny young gentleman will serve as a sample of all funny young gentlemen, we purpose merely to note down the conduct and behaviour of an individual specimen of this class, whom we happened to meet at an annual family Christmas party in the course of this very last Christmas that ever came.

We were all seated round a blazing fire which crackled pleasantly as the guests talked merrily and the urn steamed cheerily—for, being an old-fashioned party, there *was* an urn, and a teapot besides—when there came a postman's knock at the door, so violent and sudden that it startled the whole circle, and actually caused two or three very interesting and most unaffected young ladies to scream aloud and to exhibit many afflicting symptoms of terror and distress, until they had been several times assured by their respective adorers that they were in no danger. We were about to remark that it was surely beyond post-time, and must have been a runaway knock, when our host, who had hitherto been paralysed with wonder, sank into a chair in a perfect ecstasy of laughter, and offered to lay twenty pounds that it was that droll dog Griggins. He had no sooner said this than the majority of the company and all the children of the house burst into a roar of laughter too, as if some inimitable joke flashed upon them simultaneously, and gave vent to various exclamations of—To be sure it must be Griggins! and How like him that was! and What spirits he was always in! with many other commendatory remarks of the like nature.

Not having the happiness to know Griggins, we became extremely desirous to see so pleasant a fellow, the more especially as a stout gentleman with a powdered head, who was sitting with his breeches buckles almost touching the hob, whispered us he was a wit of the first water, when the door opened, and Mr. Griggins being announced, presented himself, amidst another shout of laughter and a loud clapping of hands from the younger branches. This welcome he acknowledged by sundry contortions of countenance, imitative of the clown in one of the new pantomimes, which were so extremely successful that one stout gentleman rolled upon an ottoman in a paroxysm of delight, protesting, with many gasps, that if somebody didn't make that fellow Griggins leave off, he would be the death of him, he knew. At this the company only laughed more boisterously than before, and as we always like to accommodate our tone and spirit if possible to the humour of any society in which we find ourself, we laughed with the rest, and exclaimed, "Oh! capital, capital!" as loud as any of them.

When he had quite exhausted all beholders, Mr. Griggins received the welcomes and congratulations of the circle, and went through the needful introductions with much ease and many puns. This ceremony over, he avowed his intention of sitting in somebody's lap unless the young ladies made room for him on the sofa, which being done, after a great deal of tittering and pleasantry, he squeezed himself among them, and likened his condition to that of love among the roses. At this novel jest we all roared once more. "You should consider yourself highly honoured, Sir," said we. "Sir," replied Mr. Griggins, "you do me proud." Here everybody laughed again; and the stout gentleman by the fire whispered in our ear that Griggins was making a dead set at us.

The tea-things having been removed, we all sat down to a round game, and here Mr. Griggins shone forth with peculiar brilliancy, abstracting other people's fish, and looking over their hands in the most comical manner. He made one most excellent joke in snuffing a candle, which was neither more nor less than setting fire to the hair of a pale young gentleman who sat next him, and afterwards begging his pardon with considerable humour. As the young gentleman could not see the joke, however, possibly in consequence of its being on the top of his own head, it did not go off quite as well as it might have done; indeed, the young gentleman was heard to murmur some general references to "impertinence," and a "rascal," and to state the number of his lodgings in an angry tone—a turn of the conversation which might have been productive of slaughterous consequences, if a young lady, betrothed to the young gentleman, had not used her immediate influence to bring about a reconciliation: emphatically declaring in an agitated whisper, intended for his peculiar edification but audible to the whole table, that if he went on in that way she never would think of him otherwise than as a friend, though as that she must always regard him. At this terrible threat the young gentleman became calm, and the young lady, overcome by the revulsion of feeling, instantaneously fainted.

Mr. Griggins's spirits were slightly depressed for a short period by this unlooked-for result of such a harmless pleasantry, but being promptly elevated by the attentions of the host and several glasses of wine, he soon recovered, and became even more vivacious than before, insomuch that the stout gentleman previously referred to assured us that, although he had known him since he was *that* high (something smaller than a nutmeg-grater), he had never beheld him in such excellent cue.

When the round game and several games at blind man's buff which followed it were all over, and we were going down to supper, the inexhaustible Mr. Griggins produced a small sprig of mistletoe from his waistcoat pocket and commenced a general kissing of the assembled females, which occasioned great commotion and much excitement. We observed that several young gentlemen—including the young gentleman with the pale countenance—were greatly scandalised at this indecorous proceeding, and talked very big among themselves in corners; and we observed, too, that several young ladies, when remonstrated with by the aforesaid young gentlemen, called each other to witness how they had struggled, and protested vehemently that it was very rude, and that they were surprised at Mrs. Brown's allowing it, and that they couldn't bear it, and had no patience with such impertinence. But such is the gentle and forgiving nature of woman, that although we looked very narrowly for it, we could not detect the slightest harshness in the subsequent treatment of Mr. Griggins. Indeed, upon the whole, it struck us that among the ladies he seemed rather more popular than before!

To recount all the drollery of Mr. Griggins at supper would fill such a tiny volume as this,★ to the very bottom of the outside cover. How he drank out of other people's glasses and ate of other people's bread; how he frightened into screaming convulsions a little boy who was sitting up to supper in a high chair, by sinking below the table and suddenly reappearing with a mask on; how the hostess was really surprised that anybody could find a pleasure in tormenting children, and how the host frowned at the hostess, and felt convinced that Mr. Griggins had done it with the very best intentions; how Mr. Griggins explained, and how everybody's good-humour was restored but the child's;—to tell these and a hundred other things ever so briefly, would occupy more of our room and our readers' patience than either they or we can conveniently spare. Therefore we change the subject, merely observing that we have offered no description of the funny young gentleman's personal appearance, believing that almost every society has a Griggins of its own, and leaving all readers to supply the deficiency, according to the particular circumstances of their particular case.

The Theatrical Young Gentleman

All gentlemen who love the drama—and there are few gentlemen who are not attached to the most intellectual and rational of all our amusements—do not come within this definition. As we have no mean relish for theatrical entertainments ourself, we are disinterestedly anxious that this should be perfectly understood.

The theatrical young gentleman has early and important information an all theatrical topics. "Well," says he, abruptly, when you meet him in the street, "here's a pretty to-do. Flimkins has thrown up his part in the melodrama at the Surrey." "And what's to be done?" you inquire

---

★   In its original form

with as much gravity as you can counterfeit. "Ah, that's the point," replies the theatrical young gentleman, looking very serious; "Boozle declines it—positively declines it. From all I am told, I should say it was decidedly in Boozle's line, and that he would be very likely to make a great hit in it; but he objects on the ground of Flimkins having been put up in the part first, and says no earthly power shall induce him to take the character. It's a fine part, too—excellent business, I'm told. He has to kill six people in the course of the piece, and to fight over a bridge in red fire, which is as safe a card, you know, as can be. Don't mention it, but I hear that the last scene, when he is first poisoned, and then stabbed, by Mrs. Flimkins as Vengedora, will be the greatest thing that has been done these many years." With this piece of news, and laying his finger on his lips as a caution for you not to excite the town with it, the theatrical young gentleman hurries away.

The theatrical young gentleman, from often frequenting the different theatrical establishments, has pet and familiar names for them all. Thus Covent Garden is the garden, Drury Lane the lane, the Victoria the vic, and the Olympic the pic. Actresses, too, are always designated by their surnames only, as Taylor, Nisbett, Faucit, Honey; that talented and lady-like girl Sheriff, that clever little creature Horton, and so on. In the same manner he prefixes Christian names when he mentions actors, as Charley Young, Jemmy Buckstone, Fred Yates, Paul Bedford. When he is at a loss for a Christian name, the word "old" applied indiscriminately answers quite as well: as old Charley Mathews at Vestris's, old Harley, and old Braham. He has a great knowledge of the private proceedings of actresses, especially of their getting married, and can tell you in a breath half-a-dozen who have changed their names without avowing it. Whenever an alteration of this kind is made in the play-bills, he will remind you that he let you into the secret six months ago.

The theatrical young gentleman has a great reverence for all that is connected with the stage department of the different theatres. He would, at any time, prefer going a street or two out of his way, to omitting to pass a stage-entrance, into which he always looks with a curious and searching eye. If he can only identify a popular actor in the street, he is in a perfect transport of delight; and no sooner meets him, than he hurries back, and walks a few paces in front of him, so that he can turn round from time to time and have a good stare at his features. He looks upon a theatrical-fund dinner as one of the most enchanting festivities ever known; and thinks that to be a member of the Garrick Club, and see so many actors in their plain clothes, must be one of the highest gratifications the world can bestow.

The theatrical young gentleman is a constant half-price visitor at one or other of the theatres, and has an infinite relish for all pieces which display the fullest resources of the establishment. He likes to place implicit reliance upon the play-bills when he goes to see a show piece, and works himself up to such a pitch of enthusiasm as not only to believe (if the bills say so) that there are three hundred and seventy-five people on the stage at one time in the last scene, but is highly indignant with you unless you believe it also. He considers that if the stage be opened from the foot-lights to the back wall, in any new play, the piece is a triumph of dramatic writing, and applauds accordingly. He has a great notion of trap-doors too; and thinks any character going down or coming up a trap (no matter whether he be an angel or a demon—they both do it occasionally) one of the most interesting feats in the whole range of scenic illusion.

Besides these acquirements he has several veracious accounts to communicate of the private manners and customs of different actors, which, during the pauses of a quadrille, he usually communicates to his partner, or imparts to his neighbour at a supper-table. Thus he is advised that Mr. Liston always had a footman in gorgeous livery waiting at the side-scene with a brandy bottle and tumbler, to administer half a pint or so of spirit to him every time he came off, without which assistance he must infallibly have fainted. He knows for a fact that, after an arduous part, Mr. George Bennett is put between two feather beds, to absorb the perspiration; and is credibly informed that Mr. Baker has, for many years, submitted to a course of lukewarm toast-and-water, to qualify him to sustain his favourite characters. He looks upon Mr. Fitz Ball as the principal dramatic genius and poet of the day; but holds that there are great writers extant besides him,—in proof whereof he refers you to various dramas and melodramas recently produced, of which he takes in all the sixpenny and threepenny editions as fast as they appear.

The theatrical young gentleman is a great advocate for violence of emotion and redundancy of action. If a father has to curse a child upon the stage, he likes to see it done in the thorough-going style, with no mistake about it: to which end it is essential that the child should follow the father on her knees, and be knocked violently over on her face by the old gentleman as he goes into a small cottage and shuts the door behind him. He likes to see a blessing invoked upon the young lady, when the old gentleman repents, with equal earnestness, and accompanied by the usual conventional forms, which consist of the old gentleman looking anxiously up into the clouds as if to see whether it rains, and then spreading an imaginary tablecloth in the air over the young lady's head—soft music playing all the while. Upon these, and other points of a similar kind, the theatrical young gentleman is a great critic indeed. He is likewise very acute in judging of natural expressions of the passions, and knows precisely the frown, wink, nod, or leer, which stands for any one of them, or the means by which it may be converted into any other: as jealousy, with a good stamp of the right foot, becomes anger; or wildness, with the hands clasped before the throat, instead of tearing the wig, is passionate love. If you venture to express a doubt of the accuracy of any of these portraitures, the theatrical young gentleman assures you, with a haughty smile, that it always has been done in that way, and he supposes they are not going to change it at this time of day to please you ; to which, of course, you meekly reply that you suppose not.

There are innumerable disquisitions of this nature in which the theatrical young gentleman is very profound, especially to ladies whom he is most in the habit of entertaining with them; but as we have no space to recapitulate them at greater length, we must rest content with calling the attention of the young ladies in general to the theatrical young gentlemen of their own acquaintance.

THE POETICAL YOUNG GENTLEMAN

Time was, and not very long ago either, when a singular epidemic raged among the young gentlemen, vast numbers of whom, under the influence of the malady, tore off their neckerchiefs, turned down their shirt collars, and exhibited themselves in the open streets with bare throats and dejected countenances, before the eyes of an astonished public. These were poetical young gentlemen. The custom was gradually found to be inconvenient, as involving the necessity of too much clean linen and too large washing bills, and these outward symptoms have consequently passed away; but we are disposed to think, notwithstanding, that the number of poetical young gentlemen is considerably on the increase.

We know a poetical young gentleman—a very poetical young gentleman. We do not mean to say that he is troubled with the gift of poesy in any remarkable degree, but his countenance is of a plaintive and melancholy cast, his manner is abstracted and bespeaks affliction of soul: he seldom has his hair cut, and often talks about being an outcast and wanting a kindred spirit; from which, as well as from many general observations in which he is wont to indulge, concerning mysterious impulses, and yearnings of the heart, and the supremacy of intellect gilding all earthly things with the glowing magic of immortal verse, it is clear to all his friends that he has been stricken poetical.

The favourite attitude of the poetical young gentleman is lounging on a sofa with his eyes fixed upon the ceiling, or sitting bolt upright in a high-backed chair, staring with very round eyes at the opposite wall. When he is in one of these positions, his mother, who is a worthy, affectionate old soul, will give you a nudge to bespeak your attention without disturbing the abstracted one, and whisper with a shake of the head, that John's imagination is at some extraordinary work or other, you may take her word for it. Hereupon John looks more fiercely intent upon vacancy than before, and suddenly snatching a pencil from his pocket, puts down three words, and a cross on the back of a card, sighs deeply, paces once or twice across the room, inflicts a most unmerciful slap upon his head, and walks moodily up to his dormitory.

The poetical young gentleman is apt to acquire peculiar notions of things too, which plain ordinary people, unblessed with a poetical obliquity of vision, would suppose to be rather distorted. For instance, when the sickening murder and mangling of a wretched woman was affording delicious food wherewithal to gorge the insatiable curiosity of the public, our friend the poetical young gentleman was in ecstasies—not of disgust, but admiration. "Heavens!" cried the poetical young gentleman, "how grand; how great!" We ventured deferentially to inquire upon whom these epithets were bestowed: our humble thoughts oscillating between the police-officer who found the criminal, and the lock-keeper who found the head. "Upon whom!" exclaimed the poetical young gentleman in a frenzy of poetry, "Upon whom should they be bestowed but upon the murderer!"—and therupon it came out, in a fine torrent of eloquence, that the murderer was a great spirit, a bold creature full of daring and nerve, a man of dauntless heart and determined courage, and withal a great casuist and able reasoner, as was fully demonstrated in his philosophical colloquies with the great and noble of the land. We held our peace, and meekly signified our indisposition to controvert these opinions—firstly, because we were no match at quotation for the poetical young gentleman; and secondly, because we felt it would be of little use our entering into any disputation, if we were: being perfectly convinced that the respectable and immoral hero in question is not the first and will not be the last hanged gentleman upon whom false sympathy or diseased curiosity will be plentifully expended.

This was a stern mystic flight of the poetical young gentleman. In his milder and softer moments he occasionally lays down his neckcloth, and pens stanzas, which sometimes find their way into a Lady's Magazine, or the "Poets' Corner" of some country newspaper; or which, in default of either vent for his genius, adorn the rainbow leaves of a lady's album. These are generally written upon some such occasions as contemplating the Bank of England by midnight, or beholding Saint Paul's in a snow-storm; and when these gloomy objects fail to afford him inspiration, he pours forth his soul in a touching address to a violet, or a plaintive lament that he is no longer a child, but has gradually grown up.

The poetical young gentleman is fond of quoting passages from his favourite authors, who are all of the gloomy and desponding school. He has a great deal to say too about the world, and is much given to opining, especially if he has taken anything strong to drink, that there is nothing in it worth living for. He gives you to understand, however, that for the sake of society, he means to bear his part in the tiresome play, manfully resisting the gratification of his own strong desire to make a premature exit; and consoles himself with the reflection, that immortality has some chosen nook for himself and the other great spirits whom earth has chafed and wearied.

When the poetical young gentleman makes use of adjectives, they are all superlatives. Everything is of the grandest, greatest, noblest, mightiest, loftiest; or the lowest, meanest, obscurest, vilest, and most pitiful. He knows no medium: for enthusiasm is the soul of poetry; and who so enthusiastic as a poetical young gentleman? "Mr. Milkwash," says a young lady as she unlocks her album to receive the young gentleman's original impromptu contribution, "how very silent you are! I think you must be in love." "Love!" cries the poetical young gentleman, starting from his seat by the fire and terrifying the cat, who scampers off at full speed, "Love! that burning, consuming passion ; that ardour of the soul, that fierce glowing of the heart. Love! The withering, blighting influence of hope misplaced and affection slighted. Love did you say! Ha! ha! ha!"

With this the poetical young gentleman laughs a laugh belonging only to poets and Mr. O. Smith of the Adelphi Theatre, and sits down, pen in hand, to throw off a page or two of verse in the biting, semi-atheistical, demoniac style, which, like the poetical young gentleman himself, is full of sound and fury, signifying nothing.

THE "THROWING–OFF" YOUNG GENTLEMAN

There is a certain kind of impostor—a bragging, vaunting, puffing young gentleman—against whom we are desirous to warn that fairer part of the creation, to whom we more peculiarly devote these our labours. And we are particularly induced to lay especial stress upon this division of our subject, by a little dialogue we held some short time ago, with an esteemed young lady of our acquaintance, touching a most gross specimen of this class of men. We had been urging all the absurdities of his conduct and conversation, and dwelling upon the impossibilities he constantly recounted—to which indeed we had not scrupled to prefix a certain hard little word of one syllable and three letters—when our fair friend, unable to maintain the contest any longer, reluctantly cried, "Well; he certainly has a habit of throwing-off, but then—" What then? Throw him off yourself, said we. And so she did, but not at our instance, for other reasons appeared, and it might have been better if she had done so at first.

The throwing-off young gentleman has so often a father possessed of vast property in some remote district of Ireland that we look with some suspicion upon all young gentlemen who volunteer this description of themselves. The deceased grandfather of the throwing-off young gentleman was a man of immense possessions and untold wealth; the throwing-off young gentleman remembers, as well as if it were only yesterday, the deceased baronet's library, with its long rows of scarce and valuable books in superbly embossed bindings, arranged in cases, reaching from the lofty ceiling to the oaken floor, and the fine antique chairs and tables, and the noble old castle of Ballykillbabaloo, with its splendid prospect of hill and dale, and wood, and rich wild scenery, and the fine hunting stables and the spacious courtyards, "and—and—everything upon the same magnificent scale," says the throwing-off young gentleman, "princely; quite princely. Ah!" And he sighs as if mourning over the fallen fortunes of his noble house.

The throwing-off young gentleman is a universal genius; at walking, running, rowing, swimming, and skating, he is unrivalled; at all games of chance or skill, at hunting, shooting, fishing, riding, driving, or amateur theatricals, no one can touch him—that is, *could* not, because he gives you carefully to understand, lest there should be any opportunity of testing his skill, that he is quite out of practice just now, and has been for some years. If you mention any beautiful girl of your common acquaintance in his hearing, the throwing-off young gentleman starts, smiles, and begs you not to mind him, for it was quite involuntary: people do say indeed that they were once engaged, but no—although she is a very fine girl, he was so situated at that time that he couldn't possibly encourage the—"but it's of no use talking about it!" he adds, interrupting himself. "She has got over it now, and I firmly hope and trust is happy." With this benevolent aspiration he nods his head in a mysterious manner, and whistling the first part of some popular air, thinks perhaps it will be better to change the subject.

There is another great characteristic of the throwing-off young gentleman, which is, that he "happens to be acquainted" with a most extraordinary variety of people in all parts of the world. Thus in all disputed questions, when the throwing-off young gentleman has no argument to bring forward, he invariably happens to be acquainted with some distant person intimately connected with the subject, whose testimony decides the point against you, to the great—may we say it?—to the great admiration of three young ladies out of every four, who consider the throwing-off young gentleman a very highly-connected young man and a most charming person.

Sometimes the throwing-off young gentleman happens to look in upon a little family circle of young ladies who are quietly spending the evening together, and then indeed is he at the very height and summit of his glory; for it is to be observed that he by no means shines to equal advantage in the presence of men as in the society of over-credulous young ladies, which is his proper element. It is delightful to hear the number of pretty things the throwing-off young gentleman gives utterance to during tea, and still more so to observe the ease with which, from long practice and study, he delicately blends one compliment to a lady with two for himself. "Did you ever see a more lovely blue than this flower, Mr. Caveton?" asks a young lady who, truth to tell, is rather smitten with the throwing-off young gentleman. "Never," he replies, bending over the object of admiration, "never but in your eyes." "Oh, Mr. Caveton!" cries the young lady, blushing of course. " Indeed I speak the truth," replies the throwing-off young gentleman, "I never saw any approach to them. I used to think my cousin's blue eyes lovely, but they grow dim and colourless beside yours." "Oh! a beautiful cousin Mr. Caveton!" replies the young lady, with that perfect artlessness which is the distinguishing characteristic of all young ladies; "an affair, of course." "No; indeed, indeed you wrong me," rejoins the throwing-off young gentleman with great energy. "I fervently hope that her attachment towards me may be nothing but the natural result of our close intimacy in childhood, and that in change of scene and among new faces she may soon overcome it. *I* love her! Think not so meanly of me, Miss Lowfield, I beseech, as to suppose that title, lands, riches, and beauty can influence *my* choice. The heart, the heart, Miss Lowfield." Here the throwing-off young gentleman sinks his voice to a still lower whisper; and the young lady duly proclaims to all the other young ladies, when they go up-stairs, to put their bonnets on, that Mr. Caveton's relations are all immensely rich, and that he is hopelessly beloved by title, lands, riches; and beauty.

We have seen a throwing-off young gentleman who, to our certain knowledge, was innocent of a note of music, and scarcely able to recognise a tune by ear, volunteer a Spanish air upon the guitar when he had previously satisfied himself that there was not such an instrument within a mile of the house.

We have heard another throwing-off young gentleman, after striking a note or two upon the piano, and accompanying it correctly (by dint of laborious practice) with his voice, assure a circle of wondering listeners that so acute was his ear that he was wholly unable to sing out of tune, let him try as he would. We have lived to witness the unmasking of another throwing-off young gentleman who went out a-visiting in a military cap with a gold band and tassel, and who, after passing successfully for a captain and being lauded to the skies for his red whiskers, his bravery, his soldierly bearing and his pride, turned out to be the dishonest son of an honest linen in a small country town, and whom, if it were not for this fortunate exposure, we should not yet despair of encountering as the fortunate husband of some rich heiress. Ladies, ladies, the throwing–off young gentlemen are often swindlers, and always fools. So pray you avoid them.

THE YOUNG LADIES' YOUNG GENTLEMAN

This young gentleman has several titles. Some young ladies consider him "a nice young man," others "a fine young man," others "quite a lady's man," others "a handsome man," others "a remarkably good-looking young man." With some young ladies he is "a perfect angel," and with others "quite a love." He is likewise a charming creature, a duck, and a dear.

The young ladies' young gentleman has usually a fresh colour and very white teeth, which latter articles, of course, he displays on every possible opportunity. He has brown or black hair, and whiskers of the same, if possible; but a slight tinge of red, or the hue which is vulgarly known as *sandy*, is not considered an objection. If his head and face be large, his nose prominent and his figure square, he is an uncommonly fine young man, and worshipped accordingly. Should his whiskers meet beneath his chin, so much the better, though this is not absolutely insisted on; but he must wear an under-waistcoat, and smile constantly.

There was a great party got up by some party-loving friends of ours last summer, to go and dine in Epping Forest. As we hold that such wild expeditions should never be indulged in, save by people of the smallest means, who have no dinner at home, we should indubitably have excused ourself from attending, if we had not recollected that the projectors of the excursion were always accompanied on such occasions by a choice sample of the young ladies' young gentleman whom we were very anxious to have an opportunity of meeting. This determined us, and we went.

We were to make for Chigwell in four glass coaches, each with a trifling company of six or eight inside, and a little boy belonging to the projectors on the box—and to start from the residence of the projectors, Woburn Place, Russell Square, at half-past ten precisely. We arrived at the place of rendezvous at the appointed time, and found the glass coaches and the little boys quite ready; and divers young ladies and young gentlemen looking anxiously over the breakfast-parlour blinds, who appeared by no means so much gratified by our approach as we might have expected, but evidently wished we had been somebody else. Observing that our arrival in lieu of the unknown occasioned some disappointment, we ventured to inquire who was yet to come, when we found, from the hasty reply of a dozen voices, that it was no other than the young ladies' young gentleman.

"I cannot imagine," said the mamma, "what has become of Mr. Balim—always so punctual, always so pleasant and agreeable. I am sure I can-*not* think." As these last words were uttered in that measured, emphatic manner which painfully announces that the speaker has not quite made up his or her mind what to say, but is determined to talk on nevertheless, the eldest daughter took up the subject, and hoped no accident had happened to Mr. Balim, upon which there was a general chorus of "Dear Mr. Balim!" and one young lady, more adventurous than the rest, proposed that an express should be straightway sent to dear Mr. Balim's lodgings. This, however, the papa resolutely opposed, observing, in what a short young lady behind us termed "quite a bearish way," that if Mr. Balim didn't choose to come, he might stop at home. At this all the daughters raised a murmur of "Oh, pa!" except one sprightly little girl of eight or ten years old, who, taking advantage of a pause in the discourse, remarked that perhaps Mr. Balim might have been married that morning—for which impertinent suggestion she was summarily ejected from the room by her eldest sister.

We were all in a state of great mortification and uneasiness, when one of the little boys, running into the room as airily as little boys usually run who have an unlimited allowance of animal food in the holidays, and keep their hands constantly forced down to the bottoms of very deep trouser-pockets when they take exercise, joyfully announced that Mr. Balim was at that moment coming up the street in a hackney-cab; and the intelligence was confirmed beyond all doubt a minute afterwards by the entry of Mr. Balim himself, who was received with repeated cries of "Where have you been, you naughty creature?" whereunto the naughty creature replied, that he had been in bed, in consequence of a late party the night before, and had only just risen. The acknowledgment awakened a variety of agonising fears that he had taken no breakfast; which appearing after a slight cross-examination to be the real state of the case, breakfast for one was immediately ordered, notwithstanding Mr. Balim's repeated protestations that he couldn't think of it. He did think of it though, and thought better of it too, for he made a remarkably good meal when it came, and was assiduously served by a select knot of young ladies. It was quite delightful to see how he ate and drank, while one pair of fair hands poured out his coffee, and another put in the sugar, and another the milk; the rest of the company ever and anon casting angry glances at their watches and the glass coaches,—and the little boys looking on in an agony of apprehension lest it should begin to rain before we set out; it might have rained all day, after we were once too far to turn back again, and welcome, for aught they cared.

However, the cavalcade moved at length, every coachman being accommodated with a hamper between his legs something larger than a wheelbarrow; and the company being packed as closely as they possibly could in the carriages, "according," as one married lady observed, "to the immemorial custom, which was half the diversion of gipsy parties." Thinking it very likely it might be (we have never been able to discover the other half), we submitted to be stowed away with a cheerful aspect, and were fortunate enough to occupy one corner of a coach in which were one old lady, four young ladies, and the renowned Mr. Balim the young ladies' young gentleman.

We were no sooner fairly off than the young ladies' young gentleman hummed a fragment of an air, which induced a young lady to inquire whether he had danced to that the night before. "By Heaven then, I did," replied the young gentleman, "and with a lovely heiress; a superb creature, with twenty thousand pounds." "You seem rather struck," observed another young lady. "'Gad she was a sweet creature," returned the young gentleman arranging his hair. "Of course *she* was struck too?" inquired the first young lady. "How can you ask, love?" interposed the second; "could she fail to be?" "Well, honestly I think she was," observed the young gentleman. At this point of the dialogue, the young lady who had spoken first, and who sat on the young gentleman's right, struck him a severe blow on the arm with a rosebud, and said he was a vain man; whereupon the young gentleman insisted on having the rosebud, and the young lady appealing for help to the other young ladies, a charming struggle ensued, terminating in the victory of the young gentleman and the capture of the rosebud. This little skirmish over, the married lady, who was the mother of the rosebud, smiled sweetly upon the young gentleman and accused him of being a flirt; the young gentleman pleading not guilty, a most interesting discussion took place upon the important point whether the young gentleman was a flirt or not, which, being an agreeable conversation of a light kind, lasted a considerable time. At length, a short silence occurring, the young ladies on either side of the young gentleman fell suddenly fast asleep; and the young gentleman, winking upon us to preserve silence, won a pair of gloves from each, thereby causing them to wake with equal suddenness and to scream very loud. The lively conversation to which this pleasantry gave rise lasted for the remainder of the ride, and would have eked out a much longer one.

We dined rather more comfortably than people usually do under such circumstances, nothing having been left behind but the cork screw and the bread. The married gentlemen were unusually thirsty, which they attributed to the heat of the weather; the little boys ate to inconvenience; mammas were very jovial, and their daughters very fascinating; and the attendants, being well-behaved men, got exceedingly drunk at a respectful distance.

We had our eye on Mr. Balim at dinner-time, and perceived that he flourished wonderfully, being still surrounded by a little group of young ladies, who listened to him as an oracle, while he ate from their plates and drank from their glasses in a manner truly captivating from its excessive playfulness. His conversation, too, was exceedingly brilliant. In fact, one elderly lady assured us, that in the course of a little lively *badinage* on the subject of ladies' dresses, he had evinced as much knowledge as if he had been horn and bred a milliner.

As such of the fat people as did not happen to fall asleep after dinner entered upon a most vigorous game at ball, we slipped away alone into a thicker part of the wood, hoping to fall in with Mr. Balim, the greater part of the young people having dropped off in twos and threes, and the young ladies' young gentleman among them. Nor were we disappointed, for we had not walked far when, peeping through the trees, we discovered him before us, and truly it was a pleasant thing to contemplate his greatness.

The young ladies' young gentleman was seated upon the ground, at the feet of a few young ladies who were reclining on a bank; he was so profusely decked with scarfs, ribands, flowers, and other pretty spoils, that he looked like a lamb—or perhaps a calf would be a better simile—adorned for the sacrifice. One young lady supported a parasol over his interesting head, another held his hat, and a third his neck cloth, which in romantic fashion he had thrown off; the young gentleman himself, with his hand upon his breast, and his face moulded into an expression of the most honeyed sweetness, was warbling forth some choice specimens of vocal music in praise of female loveliness, in a style so exquisitely perfect that we burst into an involuntary shout of laughter and made a hasty retreat.

What charming fellows these young ladies' young gentlemen are! Ducks, dears, loves, angels, are all terms inadequate to express their merit. They are such amazingly, uncommonly, wonderfully nice men.

CONCLUSION

As we have placed before the young ladies so many specimens of young gentlemen, and have also in the dedication of this volume given them to understand how much we reverence and admire their numerous virtues and perfections; as we have given them such strong reasons to treat us with confidence, and to banish, in our case, all that reserve and distrust of the male sex which, as a point of general behaviour, they cannot do better than preserve and maintain—we say, as we have done all this, we feel that now, when we have arrived at the close of our task, they may naturally press upon us the inquiry, what particular description of young gentlemen we can conscientiously recommend.

Here we are at a loss. We look over our list, and can neither recommend the bashful young gentleman, nor the out-and-out young gentleman, nor the very friendly young gentleman, nor the military young gentleman, nor the political young gentleman, nor the domestic young gentleman, nor the censorious young gentleman, nor the funny young gentleman, nor the theatrical young gentleman, nor the poetical young gentleman nor the throwing-off young gentleman, nor the young ladies' young gentleman.

As there are some good points about many of them, which still are not sufficiently numerous to render any one among them eligible, as a whole, our respectful advice to the young ladies is, to seek for a young gentleman who unites in himself the best qualities of all, and the worst weaknesses of none, and to lead him forthwith to the hymeneal altar, whether he will or no. And to the young lady who secures him we beg to tender one short fragment of matrimonial advice, selected from many sound passages of a similar tendency, to be found in a letter written by Dean Swift to a young lady on her marriage.

"The grand affair of your life will be, to gain and preserve the esteem of your husband. Neither good-nature nor virtue will suffer him to *esteem* you against his judgment; and although he is not capable of using you ill, yet you will in time grow a thing indifferent and perhaps contemptible; unless you can supply the loss of youth and beauty with more durable qualities. You have but a very few years to be young and handsome in the eyes of the world; and as few months to be so in the eyes of a husband who is not a fool; for I hope you do not still dream of charms and raptures, which marriage ever did, and ever will, put a sudden end to."

From the anxiety we express for the proper behaviour of the fortunate lady after marriage, it may possibly be inferred that the young gentleman to whom we have so delicately alluded is no other than ourself. Without in any way committing ourself upon this point, we have merely to observe that we are ready to receive sealed offers containing a full specification of age, temper, appearance and condition; but we beg it to be distinctly understood that we do not pledge ourself to accept the highest bidder.

SKETCHES OF YOUNG COUPLES

An Urgent Remonstrance, &c.

To the Gentlemen of England
(being Bachelors or Widowers)

The Remonstrance of their Faithful Fellow-Subject

Sheweth,—

That Her Most Gracious Majesty, Victoria, by the Grace of God of the United Kingdom of Great Britain and Ireland Queen, Defender of the Faith, did, on the 23rd day of November last past, declare and pronounce to Her Most Honourable Privy Council, Her Majesty's Most Gracious intention of entering into the bonds of wedlock.

That Her Most Gracious Majesty, in so making known Her Most Gracious intention to Her Most Honourable Privy Council as aforesaid, did use and employ the words—"It is my intention to ally myself in marriage with Prince Albert of Saxe Coburg and Gotha".

That the present is Bissextile, or Leap Year, in which it is held and considered lawful for any lady to offer and submit proposals of marriage to any gentleman, and to enforce and insist upon acceptance of the same, under pain of a certain fine or penalty; to wit, one silk or satin dress of the first quality, to be chosen by the lady and paid (or owed) for, by the gentleman.

That these and other the horrors and dangers with which the said Bissextile, or Leap Year, threatens the gentlemen of England on every occasion of its periodical return, have been greatly aggravated and augmented by the terms of Her Majesty's said Most Gracious communication, which have filled the heads of divers young ladies in this Realm with certain new ideas destructive to the peace of mankind, that never entered their imagination before.

That a case has occurred in Camberwell, in which a young lady informed her Papa that "she intended to ally herself in marriage" with

Mr. Smith of Stepney; and that another, and a very distressing case, has occurred at Tottenham, in which a young lady not only stated her intention of allying herself in marriage with her cousin John, but, taking violent possession of her said cousin, actually married him.

That similar outrages are of constant occurrence, not only in the capital and its neighbourhood, but throughout the kingdom, and that unless the excited female populace be speedily checked and restrained in their lawless proceedings, most deplorable results must ensue therefrom; among which may be anticipated a most alarming increase in the population of the country, with which no efforts of the agricultural or manufacturing interest can possibly keep pace.

That there is strong reason to suspect the existence of a most extensive plot, conspiracy, or design, secretly contrived by vast numbers of single ladies in the United Kingdom of Great Britain and Ireland, and now extending its ramifications in every quarter of the land; the object and intent of which plainly appears to be the holding and solemnising of an enormous and unprecedented number of marriages, on the day on which the nuptials of Her said Most Gracious Majesty are performed.

That such plot, conspiracy, or design, strongly savours of Popery, as tending to the discomfiture of the Clergy of the Established Church, by entailing upon them great mental and physical exhaustion; and that such Popish plots are fomented and encouraged by Her Majesty's Ministers, which clearly appears—not only from Her Majesty's principal Secretary of State for Foreign Affairs traitorously getting married while holding office under the Crown; but from Mr. O'Connell having been heard to declare and avow that, if he had a daughter to marry, she should be married on the same day as Her said Most Gracious Majesty.

That such arch plots, conspiracies, and designs, besides being fraught with danger to the Established Church, and (consequently) to the State, cannot fail to bring ruin and bankruptcy upon a large class of Her Majesty's subjects; as a great and sudden increase in the number of married men occasioning the comparative desertion (for a time) of Taverns, Hotels, Billiard-rooms, and Gaming-Houses, will deprive the

Proprietors of their accustomed profits and returns. And in further proof of the depth and baseness of such designs, it may be here observed, that all proprietors of Taverns, Hotels, Billiard-rooms, and Gaming-Houses, are (especially the last) solemnly devoted to the Protestant religion

For all these reasons, and many others of no less gravity and import, an urgent appeal is made to the gentlemen of England (being bachelors or widowers) to take immediate steps for convening a Public meeting; To consider of the best and surest means of averting the dangers with which they are threatened by the recurrence of Bissextile, or Leap Year, and the additional sensation created among single ladies by the terms of Her Majesty's Most Gracious Declaration; To take measures, without delay, for resisting the said single Ladies, and counteracting their evil designs; And to pray Her Majesty to dismiss her present Ministers, and to summon to her Councils those distinguished Gentlemen in various Honourable Professions who, by insulting on all occasions the only Lady in England who can be insulted with safety, have given a sufficient guarantee to Her Majesty's Loving Subjects that they, at least, are qualified to make war with women, and are already expert in the use of those weapons which are common to the lowest and most abandoned of the sex.

SKETCHES OF YOUNG COUPLES

THE YOUNG COUPLE

THERE IS TO BE A wedding this morning at the corner house in the terrace. The pastry-cook's people have been there half-a-dozen times already; all day yesterday there was a great stir and bustle, and they were up this morning as soon as it was light. Miss Emma Fielding is going to be married to young Mr. Harvey.

Heaven alone can tell in what bright colours this marriage is painted upon the mind of the little housemaid at number six, who hardly slept a wink all night with thinking of it, and now stands on the unswept door-steps leaning upon her broom, and looking wistfully towards the enchanted house. Nothing short of omniscience can divine what visions of the baker, or the green-grocer, or the smart and most insinuating butterman, are flitting across her mind—what thoughts of how she would dress on such an occasion, if she were a lady—of how she would dress, if she were only a bride—of how cook would dress, being bridesmaid, conjointly with her sister "in place" at Fulham, and how the clergyman, deeming them so many ladies, would be quite humbled and respectful. What day-dreams of hope and happiness—of life being one perpetual holiday, with no master and no mistress to grant or withhold it—of every Sunday being a Sunday out—of pure freedom as to curls and ringlets, and no obligation to hide fine heads of hair in caps—what pictures of happiness, vast and immense to her, but utterly ridiculous to us, bewilder the brain of the little housemaid at number six, all called into existence by the wedding at the corner!

We smile at such things, and so we should, though perhaps for a better reason than commonly presents itself. It should be pleasant to us to know that there are notions of happiness so moderate and limited, since upon those who entertain them, happiness and lightness of heart are very easily bestowed.

But the little housemaid is awakened from her reverie, for forth from the door of the magical corner house there runs towards her, all fluttering in smart new dress and streaming ribands, her friend Jane Adams, who comes all out of breath to redeem a solemn promise of taking her in, under cover of the confusion, to see the breakfast table spread forth in state, and—sight of sights!—her young mistress ready dressed for church.

And there, in good truth, when they have stolen up-stairs on tiptoe and edged themselves in at the chamber door—there is Miss Emma "looking like the sweetest picter," in a white chip bonnet and orange flowers, and all other elegancies becoming a bride (with the make, shape, and quality of every article of which the girl is perfectly familiar in one moment, and never forgets to her dying day)—and there is Miss Emma's mamma in tears, and Miss Emma's papa comforting her, and saying how that of course she has been long looking forward to this, and how happy she ought to be—and there too is Miss Emma's sister with her arms round her neck, and the other bridesmaid all smiles and tears, quieting the children, who would cry more but that they are so finely dressed, and yet sob for fear sister Emma should be taken away—and it is all so affecting, that the two servant-girls cry more than anybody; and Jane Adams, sitting down upon the stairs, when they have crept away, declares that her legs tremble so that she don't know what to do, and that she will say for Miss Emma, that she never had a hasty word from her, and that she does hope and pray she may be happy.

But Jane soon comes round again, and then surely there never was anything like the breakfast table, glittering with plate and china, and set out with flowers and sweets, and long-necked bottles, in the most sumptuous and dazzling manner. In the centre, too, is the mighty charm, the cake, glistening with frosted sugar, and garnished beautifully. They agree that there ought to be a little Cupid under one of the barley-sugar temples, or at least two hearts and an arrow ; but, with this exception, there is nothing to wish for, and a table could not be handsomer. As they arrive at this conclusion, who should come in but Mr. John! to whom Jane says that it's only Anne from number six ; and John says *he* knows, for he's often winked his eye down the area, which causes Anne to blush and look confused. She is going away, indeed, when Mr. John will have it that she must drink a glass of wine, and he says never mind it's being early in the morning, it won't hurt her: so they shut the door and pour out the wine; and Anne drinking Jane's health, and adding, "and here's wishing you yours, Mr John," drinks it in a great many sips,—Mr. John all the time making jokes appropriate to the occasion. At last Mr. John, who has waxed bolder by degrees, pleads the usage at weddings, and claims the privilege of a kiss, which he obtains after a great scuffle; and footsteps being now heard on the stairs, they disperse suddenly.

By this time a carriage has driven up to convey the bride to church, and Anne of number six prolonging the process of "cleaning her door," has the satisfaction of beholding the bride and bridesmaids, and the papa and mamma, hurry into the same and drive rapidly off. Nor is this all, for soon other carriages begin to arrive with a posse of company all beautifully dressed, at whom she could stand and gaze for ever; but having something else to do, is compelled to take one last long look and shut the street-door.

And now the company have gone down to breakfast, and tears have given place to smiles, for all the corks are out of the long-necked bottles, and their contents are disappearing rapidly. Miss Emma's papa is at the top of the table; Miss Emma's mamma at the bottom; and beside the latter are Miss Emma herself and her husband,—admitted on all hands to be the handsomest and most interesting young couple ever known. All down both sides of the table, too, are various young ladies, beautiful to see, and various young gentlemen who seem to think so; and there, in a post of honour, is an unmarried aunt of Miss Emma's, reported to possess unheard-of riches, and to have expressed vast testamentary intentions respecting her favourite niece and new nephew. This lady has been very liberal and generous already, as the jewels worn by the bride abundantly testify, but that is nothing to what she means to do, or even to what she has done, for she put herself in close communication with the dressmaker three months ago, and prepared a wardrobe (with some articles worked by her own hands) fit for a Princess. People may call her an old maid, and so she may be, but she is neither cross nor ugly for all that; on the contrary, she is very cheerful and pleasant-looking, and very kind and tender-hearted: which is no matter of surprise except to those who yield to popular prejudices without thinking why, and will never grow wiser and never know better.

Of all the company though, none are more pleasant to behold or better pleased with themselves than two young children, who, in honour of the day, have seats among the guests. Of these, one is a little fellow of six or eight years old, brother to the bride,—and the other a girl of the same age, or something younger, whom he calls "his wife." The real bride and bridegroom are not more devoted than they: he all love and attention, and she all blushes and fondness, toying with a little bouquet which he gave her this morning, and placing the scattered rose-leaves in her bosom with nature's own coquettishness. They have dreamt of each other in their quiet dreams, these children, and their little hearts have been nearly broken when the absent one has been dispraised in jest. When will there come in after-life a passion so earnest, generous, and true as theirs; what, even in its gentlest realities, can have the grace and charm that hover round such fairy lovers!

By this time the merriment and happiness of the feast have gained their height; certain ominous looks begin to be exchanged between the bridesmaids, and somehow it gets whispered about that the carriage which is to take the young couple into the country has arrived. Such members of the party as are most disposed to prolong its enjoyments affect to consider this a false alarm, but it turns out too true, being speedily confirmed, first by the retirement of the bride and a select file of intimates who are to prepare her for the journey, and secondly by the withdrawal of the ladies generally. To this there ensues a particularly awkward pause, in which everybody essays to be facetious, and nobody succeeds; at length the bridegroom makes a mysterious disappearance in obedience to some equally mysterious signal, and the table is deserted.

Now, for at least six weeks last past it has been solemnly devised and settled that the young couple should go away in secret; but they no sooner appear without the door than the drawing-room windows are blocked up with ladies waving their handkerchiefs and kissing their hands, and the dining-room panes with gentlemen's faces beaming farewell in every queer variety of its expression. The hail and steps are crowded with servants in white favours, mixed up with particular friends and relations who have darted out to say good-bye; and foremost in the group are the tiny lovers arm in arm, thinking, with fluttering hearts, what happiness it would be to dash away together in that gallant coach, and never part again.

The bride has barely time for one hurried glance at her old home, when the steps rattle, the door slams, the horses clatter on the pavement, and they have left it far away.

A knot of women servants still remain clustered in the hall, whispering among themselves, and there of course is Anne from number six who has made another escape on some plea or other, and been an admiring witness of the departure. There are two points on which Anne expatiates over and over again, without the smallest appearance of fatigue or intending to leave off; one is, that she "never see in all her life such a—oh, such a angel of a gentleman as Mr. Harvey."—and the other, that she "can't tell how it is, but it don't seem a bit like a work-a-day, or a Sunday neither—it's all so unsettled and unregular."

The Formal Couple

The formal couple are the most prim, cold, immovable, and unsatisfactory people on the face of the earth. Their faces, voices, dress, house, furniture, walk, and manner, are all the essence of formality, unrelieved by one redeeming touch of frankness, heartiness, or nature.

Everything with the formal couple resolves itself into a matter of form. They don't call upon you on your account, but their own; not to see how you are, but to show how they are: it is not a ceremony to do honour to you, but to themselves,—not due to your position, but to theirs. If one of a friend's children die, the formal couple are as sure and punctual in sending to the house as the undertaker; if a friend's family be increased, the monthly nurse is not more attentive than they. The formal couple, in fact, joyfully seize all occasions of testifying their good-breeding and precise observance of the little usages of society; and for you, who are the means to this end, they care as much as a man does for the tailor who has enabled him to cut a figure, or a woman for the milliner who has assisted her to a conquest.

Having an extensive connection among that kind of people who make acquaintances and eschew friends, the formal gentleman attends from time to time a great many funerals, to which he is formally invited, and to which he formally goes, as returning a call for the last time. Here his deportment is of the most faultless description; he knows the exact pitch of voice it is proper to assume, the sombre look he ought to wear, the melancholy tread which should be his gait for the day. He is perfectly acquainted with all the dreary courtesies to be observed in a mourning-coach; knows when to sigh, and when to hide his nose in the white handkerchief; and looks into the grave and shakes his head when the ceremony is concluded with the sad formality of a mute.

"What kind of funeral was it?" says the formal lady, when he returns home. "Oh!" replies the formal gentleman, "there never was such a gross and disgusting impropriety; there were no feathers." " No feathers!" cries the lady, as if on wings of black feathers dead people fly to heaven, and, lacking them, they must of necessity go elsewhere. Her husband shakes his head; and further adds, that they had seed-cake instead of plum-cake, and that it was all white wine. "All white wine!" exclaims his wife. "Nothing but sherry and madeira," says the husband. "What! no port?" "Not a drop." No port, no plums, and no feathers! "You will recollect, my dear," says the formal lady, in a voice of stately reproof, "that when we first met this poor man who is now dead and gone, and he took that very strange course of addressing me at dinner without being previously introduced, I ventured to express my opinion that the family were quite ignorant of etiquette, and very imperfectly acquainted with the decencies of life. You have now had a good opportunity of judging for yourself, and all I have to say is, that I trust you will never go to a funeral *there* again." "My dear," replies the formal gentleman, "I never will." So the informal deceased is cut in his grave; and the formal couple, when they tell the story of the funeral, shake their heads, and wonder what some people's feelings *are* made of, and what their notions of propriety *can* be!

If, the formal couple have a family (which they sometimes have), they are not children, but little, pale, sour, sharp-nosed men and women; and so exquisitely brought up that they might be very old dwarfs for anything that appeareth to the contrary. Indeed, they are so acquainted with forms and conventionalities, and conduct themselves with such strict decorum, that to see the little girl break a looking-glass in some wild outbreak, or the little boy kick his parents, would be to any visitor an unspeakable relief and consolation.

The formal couple are always sticklers for what is rigidly proper, and have a great readiness in detecting hidden impropriety of speech or thought, which by less scrupulous people would be wholly unsuspected. Thus, if they pay a visit to the theatre, they sit all night in a perfect agony lest anything improper or immoral should proceed from the stage; and if anything should happen to be said which admits of a double construction, they never fail to take it up directly, and to express by their looks the great outrage which their feelings have sustained. Perhaps this is their chief reason for absenting themselves almost entirely from places of public amusement. They go sometimes to the Exhibition of the Royal Academy;—but that is often more shocking than the stage itself, and the formal lady thinks that it really is high time Mr. Etty was prosecuted and made a public example of.

We made one at a christening party not long since, where there were amongst the guests a formal couple, who suffered the acutest torture from certain jokes, incidental to such an occasion, cut—and very likely dried also—by one of the godfathers; a red-faced elderly gentleman, who, being highly popular with the rest of the company ,had it all his own way, and was in great spirits. It was at supper time that this gentleman came out in full force. We—being of a grave and quiet demeanour—had been chosen to escort the formal lady downstairs, and, sitting beside her, had a favourable opportunity of observing her emotions.

We have a shrewd suspicion that, in the very beginning, and in the first blush—literally the first blush—of the matter, the formal lady had not felt quite certain whether the being present at such a ceremony, and encouraging, as it were, the public exhibition of a baby, was not an act involving some degree of indelicacy and impropriety; but certain we are that when that baby's health was drunk, and allusion were made, by a gray-headed gentleman proposing it, to the time when he had dandled in his arms the young Christian's mother,—certain we are that then the formal lady took the alarm, and recoiled from the old gentleman as from a hoary profligate. Still she bore it; she fanned herself with an indignant air, but still she bore it. A comic song was sung, involving a confession from some imaginary gentleman that lie had kissed a female, and yet the formal lady bore it. But when at last, the health of the godfather before mentioned being drunk, the godfather rose to return thanks, and in the course of his observations darkly hinted at babies yet unborn, and even contemplated the possibility of the subject of that festival having brothers and sisters, the formal lady could endure no more, but, bowing slightly round, and sweeping haughtily past the offender, left the room in tears, under the protection of the formal gentleman.

THE LOVING COUPLE

There cannot be a better practical illustration of the wise saw and ancient instance, that there may be too much of a good thing, than is presented by a loving couple. Undoubtedly it is meet and proper that two persons joined together in holy matrimony should be loving, and unquestionably it is pleasant to know and see that they are so; but there is a time for all things, and the couple who happen to be always in a loving state before company are well-nigh intolerable.

And in taking up this position we would have it distinctly understood that we do not seek alone the sympathy of bachelors, in whose objection loving couples we recognise interested motives and personal considerations. We grant that to that unfortunate class of society there may be something very irritating, tantalising, and provoking, in being compelled to witness those gentle endearments and chaste interchanges which to loving couples are quite the ordinary business of life. But while we recognise the natural character of the prejudice to which these unhappy men are subject, we can neither receive their biased evidence, nor address ourself to their inflamed and angered minds. Dispassionate experience is our only guide; and in these moral essays we seek no less to reform hymeneal offenders than to hold out a timely warning to all rising couples, and even to those who have not yet set forth upon their pilgrimage towards the matrimonial market.

Let all couples, present or to come, therefore profit by the example of Mr. and Mrs. Leaver, themselves a loving couple in the first degree.

Mr. and Mrs. Leaver are pronounced by Mrs. Starling, a widow lady who lost her husband when she was young, and lost herself about the same time—for by her own count she has never since grown five years older—to be a perfect model of wedded felicity. "You would suppose," says the romantic lady, "that they were lovers only just now engaged. Never was such happiness! They are so tender, so affectionate so attached to each other, so enamoured, that positively nothing can be more charming!"

"Augusta, my soul," says Mr. Leaver. "Augustus, my life," replies Mrs. Leaver. "Sing some little ballad, darling," quoth Mr. Leaver. "I couldn't, indeed, dearest," returns Mrs. Leaver. "Do, my dove," says Mr. Leaver. "I couldn't possibly, my love," replies Mrs. Leaver; "and it's very naughty of you to ask me." "Naughty, darling!" cries Mr. Leaver. "Yes, very naughty, and very cruel," returns Mrs. Leaver, "for you know I have a sore throat, and that to sing would give me great pain. You're a monster, and I hate you. Go away!" Mrs. Leaver has said "go away," because Mr. Leaver has tapped her under the chin: Mr. Leaver not doing as he is bid, but on the contrary, sitting down beside her, Mrs. Leaver slaps Mr. Leaver; and Mr. Leaver in return slaps Mrs. Leaver, and it being now time for all persons present to look the other way, they look the other way, and hear a still small sound as of kissing, at which Mrs. Starling is thoroughly enraptured, and whispers her neighbour that if all married couples were like that, what a heaven this earth would be!

The loving couple are at home when this occurs, and maybe only three or four friends are present, but, unaccustomed to reserve upon this interesting point, they are pretty much the same abroad. Indeed upon some occasions, such as a picnic or a water-party, their lovingness is even more developed, as we had an opportunity last summer of observing in person.

There was a great water-party made up to go to Twickenham and dine, and afterwards dance in an empty villa by the river-side, hired expressly for the purpose. Mr. and Mrs. Leaver were of the company; and it was our fortune to have a seat in the same boat, which was an eight-oared galley, manned by amateurs, with a blue striped awning of the same pattern as their Guernsey shirts, and a dingy red flag the same shade as the whiskers of the stroke oar. A coxswain being appointed, and all other matters adjusted, the eight gentlemen threw themselves into strong paroxysms, and pulled up with the tide, stimulated by the compassionate remarks of the ladies, who one and all exclaimed that it seemed an immense exertion—as indeed it did. At first we raced the other boat, which came alongside in gallant style; but this being found an unpleasant amusement, as giving rise to a great quantity of splashing, and rendering the cold pies and other viands very moist, it was unanimously voted down, and we were suffered to shoot ahead, while the second boat followed ingloriously in our wake.

It was at this time that we first recognised Mr. Leaver. There were two firemen-watermen in the boat, lying by until somebody was exhausted; and one of them, who had taken upon himself the direction of affairs, was heard to cry in a gruff voice, "Pull away, number two—give it her, number two—take a longer reach, number two—now, number two, Sir, think you're winning a boat." The greater part of the company had no doubt begun to wonder which of the striped Guernseys it might be that stood in need of such encouragement, when a stifled shriek from Mrs. Leaver confirmed the doubtful and informed the ignorant; and Mr. Leaver, still further disguised in a straw hat and no neckcloth, was observed to be in a fearful perspiration, and failing visibly. Nor was the general consternation diminished at this instant by the same gentleman (in the performance of an accidental aquatic feat, termed "catching a crab") plunging suddenly backward; and displaying nothing of himself to the company but two violently struggling legs. Mrs. Leaver shrieked again several times, and cried piteously—"Is he dead? Tell me the worst. Is he dead?"

Now, a moment's reflection might have convinced the loving wife, that unless her husband were endowed with some most surprising powers of muscular action, he never could be dead while he kicked so hard; but still Mrs. Leaver cried, "Is he dead? is he dead?" and still everybody else cried—"No, no, no," until such time as Mr. Leaver was replaced in a sitting posture, and his oar (which had been going through all kinds of wrong-headed performances on its own account) was once more put in his hand, by the exertions of the two firemen-watermen. Mrs. Leaver then exclaimed, "Augustus, my child, come to me;" and Mr. Leaver said, "Augusta, my love, compose yourself, I am not injured." But Mrs. Leaver cried again more piteously than before, "Augustus, my child, come to me;" and now the company generally, who seemed to be apprehensive that if Mr. Leaver remained where he was, he might contribute more than his proper share towards the drowning of the party, disinterestedly took part with Mrs. Leaver, and said he really ought to go, and that he was not strong enough for such violent exercise, and ought never to have undertaken it. Reluctantly, Mr. Leaver went, and laid himself down at Mrs. Leaver's feet, and Mrs. Leaver stooping over him, said, "Oh Augustus, how could you terrify me so?" and Mr. Leaver said, "Augusta, my sweet, I never meant to terrify you ;" and Mrs. Leaver said, "You are faint, my dear;" and Mr. Leaver said, "I am rather so, my love;" and they were very loving indeed under Mrs. Leaver's veil, until at length Mr. Leaver came forth again, and pleasantly asked if he had not heard something said about bottled stout and sandwiches.

Mrs. Starling, who was one of the party, was perfectly delighted with this scene, and frequently murmured half-aside, "What a loving couple you are!" or "How delightful it is to see man and wife so happy together!" To us she was quite poetical (for we are a kind of cousins), observing that hearts beating in unison like that made life a paradise of sweets; and that when kindred creatures were drawn together by sympathies so fine and delicate, what more than mortal happiness did not our souls partake! To all this we answered "Certainly," or "Very true," or merely sighed, as the case might be. At every new act of the loving couple the widow's admiration broke out afresh; and when Mrs. Leaver would not permit Mr. Leaver to keep his hat off, lest the sun should strike to his head, and give him a brain fever, Mrs. Starling actually shed tears, and said it reminded her of Adam and Eve.

The loving couple were thus loving all the way to Twickenham, but when we arrived there (by which time the amateur crew looked very thirsty and vicious) they were more playful than ever, for Mrs. Leaver threw stones at Mr. Leaver, and Mr. Leaver ran after Mrs. Leaver on the grass, in a most innocent and enchanting manner. At dinner, too, Mr. Leaver *would* steal Mrs. Leaver's tongue, and Mrs. Leaver *would* retaliate upon Mr. Leaver's fowl; and when Mrs. Leaver was going to take some lobster salad, Mr. Leaver wouldn't let her have any, saying that it made her ill, and she was always sorry for it afterwards, which afforded Mrs. Leaver an opportunity of pretending to be cross, and showing many other prettinesses. But this was merely the smiling surface of their loves, not the mighty depths of the stream, down to which the company, to say the truth, dived rather unexpectedly, from the following accident. It chanced that Mr. Leaver took upon himself to propose the bachelors who had first originated the notion of that entertainment, in doing which he affected to regret that he was no longer of their body himself, and pretended grievously to lament his fallen state. This Mrs. Leaver's feelings could not brook, even in jest, and consequently, exclaiming aloud, "He loves me not, he loves me not!" she fell in a very pitiable state into the arms of Mrs. Starling, and, directly becoming insensible, was conveyed by that lady and her husband into another room. Presently Mr. Leaver came running back to know if there was a medical gentleman in the company, and as there was (in what company is there not?) both Mr. Leaver and the medical gentleman hurried away together.

The medical gentleman was the first who returned, and among his intimate friends he was observed to laugh and wink, and look as unmedical as might be; but when Mr. Leaver came back he was very solemn, and in answer to all inquiries, shook his head, and remarked that Augusta was far too sensitive to be trifled with—an opinion which the widow subsequently confirmed. Finding that she was in no imminent peril, however, the rest of the party betook themselves to dancing on the green, and very merry and happy they were, and a vast quantity of flirtation there was; the last circumstance being no doubt attributable, partly to the fineness of the weather, and partly to the locality, which is well known to be favourable to all harmless recreations.

In the bustle of the scene Mr. and Mrs. Leaver stole down to the boat, and disposed themselves under the awning, Mrs. Leaver reclining her head upon Mr. Leaver's shoulder, and Mr. Leaver grasping her hand with great fervour, and looking in her face from time to time with a melancholy and sympathetic aspect. The widow sat apart, feigning to be occupied with a book, but stealthily observing them from behind her fan; and the two firemen-watermen, smoking their pipes on the bank hard by, nudged each other, and grinned in enjoyment of the joke. Very few of the party missed the loving couple; and the few who did heartily congratulated each other on their disappearance.

THE CONTRADICTORY COUPLE

One would suppose that two people who are to pass their whole lives together, and must necessarily be very often alone with each other, could find little pleasure in mutual contradiction; and yet what is more common than a contradictory couple?

The contradictory couple agree in nothing but contradiction. They return home from Mrs. Bluebottle's dinner-party each in an opposite corner of the coach, and do not exchange a syllable until they have been seated for at least twenty minutes by the fireside at home, when the gentleman, raising his eyes from the stove, all at once breaks silence—

"What a very extraordinary thing it is," says he, "that you *will* contradict, Charlotte!" "*I* contradict!" cries the lady, "but that's just like you." "What's like me?" says the gentleman, sharply. "Saying that I contradict you," replies the lady. "Do you mean to say that you do *not* contradict me?"

retorts the gentleman; "do you mean to say that you have not been contradicting me the whole of this day? Do you mean to tell me now that you have not?" "I mean to tell you nothing of the kind," replies the lady, quietly; "when you are wrong, of course I shall contradict you."

During this dialogue the gentleman has been taking his brandy and on one side of the fire, and the lady, with her dressing-case on the table, has been curling her hair on the other. She now lets down her back hair, and proceeds to brush it, preserving at the same time an air of conscious rectitude and suffering virtue, which is intended to exasperate the gentleman—and does so.

"I do believe," he says, taking the spoon out of his glass, and tossing it on the table, "that of all the obstinate, positive, wrong-headed creatures that were ever born, you are the most so, Charlotte." "Certainly, certainly, have it your own way, pray. You see how much *I* contradict you," rejoins the lady. "Of course, you didn't contradict me at dinner-time—oh no, not you!" says the gentleman. "Yes, I did," says the lady. "Oh, you did," cries the gentleman; "you admit that?" "If you call that contradiction, I do," the lady answers; "and I say again, Edward, that when I know you are wrong, I will contradict you. I am not your slave." "Not my slave!" repeats the gentleman bitterly; "and you still mean to say that in the Blackburns' new house there are not more than fourteen doors, including the door of the wine-cellar!" "I mean to say," retorts the lady, beating time with her hair-brush on the palm of her hand, "that in that house there are fourteen doors and no more." "Well then—" cries the gentleman, rising in despair, and pacing the room with rapid strides. "By G—, this is enough to destroy a man's intellect, and drive him mad!"

By and by the gentleman comes to a little, and passing his hand gloomily across his forehead, reseats himself in his former chair. There is a long silence, and this time the lady begins. "I appealed to Mr. Jenkins, who sat next to me on the sofa in the drawing-room during tea—" "Morgan, you mean," interrupts the gentleman. "I do not mean anything of the kind," answers the lady. "Now, by all that is aggravating and impossible to bear," cries the gentleman, clenching his hands and looking upwards in agony, "she is going to insist upon it that Morgan is Jenkins!" "Do you take me for a perfect fool?" exclaims the lady; "do you suppose I don't know the one from the other? Do you suppose I don't know that the man in the blue coat was Mr. Jenkins?" "Jenkins in a blue coat!" cries the gentleman, with a groan; "Jenkins in a blue coat! a man who would suffer death rather than wear anything but brown!" "Do you dare to charge me with telling an untruth?" demands the lady, bursting into tears. "I charge you, Ma'am," retorts the gentleman, starting up, "with being a monster of contradiction, a monster of aggravation a-a-a-Jenkins in a blue coat!—what have I done that I should be doomed to hear such statements!"

Expressing himself with great scorn and anguish, the gentleman takes up his candle and stalks off to bed, where feigning to be fast asleep when the lady comes up-stairs drowned in tears, murmuring lamentations over her hard fate and indistinct intentions of consulting her brothers, he undergoes the secret torture of hearing her exclaim between whiles, "I know there are only fourteen doors in the house, I know it was Mr. Jenkins, I know he had a blue coat on, and I would say it as positively as I do now, if they were the last words I had to speak!"

If the contradictory couple are blessed with children, they are not the less contradictory on that account. Master James and Miss Charlotte present themselves after dinner, and being in perfect good-humour, and finding their parents in the same amiable state, augur from these appearances half a glass of wine apiece and other extraordinary indulgences. But unfortunately Master James, growing talkative upon such prospects, asks his mamma how tall Mrs. Parsons is, and whether she is not six feet high; to which his mamma replies, "Yes, she should think she was, for Mrs. Parsons is a very tall lady indeed; quite a giantess." "For Heaven's sake, Charlotte," cries her husband, "do not tell the child such preposterous nonsense. Six feet high!" "Well," replies the lady, "surely I may be permitted to have an opinion; my opinion is, that she is six feet high—at least six feet." "Now you know, Charlotte," retorts the gentleman, sternly, "that that is *not* your opinion—that you have no such idea—and that you only say this for the sake of contradiction." "You are exceedingly polite," his wife replies; "to be wrong about such a paltry question as any body's height would be no great crime ; but I say again, that I believe Mrs. Parsons to be six feet—more than six feet; nay, I believe you know her to be full six feet, and only say she is not, because I say she is." This taunt disposes the gentleman to become violent, but he checks himself, and is content to mutter, in a haughty tone, "Six feet—ha! ha! Mrs. Parsons six feet!" and the lady answers, "Yes, six feet. I am sure I am glad you are amused, and I'll say it again—six feet." Thus the subject gradually drops off, and the contradiction begins to be forgotten, when Master James, with some undefined notion of making himself agreeable, and putting things to rights again, unfortunately asks his mamma what the moon's made of; which gives her occasion to say that he had better not ask her, for she is always wrong and never can be right ; that he only exposes her to contradiction by asking any question of her; and that he had better ask his papa, who is infallible, and never can be wrong. Papa, smarting under this attack, gives a terrible pull at the bell, and says, that if the conversation is to proceed in this way, the children had better be removed. Removed they are, after a few tears and many struggles; and Pa, having looked at Ma sideways for a minute or two with a baleful eye, draws his pocket-handkerchief over his face, and composes himself for his after-dinner nap.

The friends of the contradictory couple often deplore their frequent disputes, though they rather make light of them at the same time: observing, that there is no doubt they are very much attached to each other, and that they never quarrel except about trifles. But neither the friends of the contradictory couple, nor the contradictory couple themselves, reflect, that as the most stupendous objects in nature are but vast collections of minute particles, so the slightest and least considered trifles make up the sum of human happiness or misery.

The Couple who Dote upon their Children

The couple who dote upon their children have usually a great many of them: six or eight at least. The children are either the healthiest in all the world, or the most unfortunate in existence. In either case, they are equally the theme of their doting parents, and equally a source of mental anguish and irritation to their doting parents' friends.

The couple who dote upon their children recognise no dates but those connected with their births, accidents, illnesses, or remarkable deeds. They keep a mental almanac with a vast number of Innocents'-days all in red letters. They recollect the last coronation, because on that day little Tom fell down the kitchen stairs; the anniversary of the Gunpowder Plot, because it was on the fifth of November that Ned asked whether wooden legs were made in heaven and cocked hats grew in gardens. Mrs. Whiffler will never cease to recollect the last day of the old year as long as she lives, for it was on that day that the baby had the four red spots on its nose which they took for measles: nor Christmas Day, for twenty-one days after Christmas Day the twins were born; nor Good Friday, for it was on a Good Friday that she was frightened by the donkey-cart when she was in the family-way with Georgiana. The movable feasts have no motion for Mr. and Mrs. Whiffler, but remain pinned down tight and fast to the shoulders of some small child, from whom they can never be separated any more. Time was made, according to their creed, not for slaves but for girls and boys; the restless sands in his glass are but little children at play.

As we have already intimated, the children of this couple can know no medium. They are either prodigies of good health or prodigies of bad health; whatever they are, they must be prodigies. Mr. Whiffler must have to describe at his office such excruciating agonies constantly undergone by his eldest boy, as nobody else's eldest boy ever underwent; or he must be able to declare that there never was a child endowed with such amazing health, such an indomitable constitution, and such a cast-iron frame, as his child. His children must be, in some respect or other, above and beyond the children of all other people. To such an extent is this feeling pushed, that we were once slightly acquainted with a lady and gentleman who carried their heads so high and became so proud after their youngest child fell out of a two-pair-of-stairs window without hurting himself much, that the greater part of their friends were obliged to forgo their acquaintance. But perhaps this may be an extreme case, and one not justly entitled to be considered as a precedent of general application.

If a friend happen to dine in a friendly way with one of these couples who dote upon their children, it is nearly impossible for him to divert the conversation from their favourite topic. Everything reminds Mr. Whiffler of Ned, or Mrs. Whiffler of Mary Anne, or of the time before Ned was born, or the time before Mary Anne was thought of. The slightest remark, however harmless in itself, will awaken slumbering recollections of the twins. It is impossible to steer clear of them. They will come uppermost, let the poor man do what he may. Ned has been known to be lost sight of for half an hour, Dick has been forgotten, the name of Mary Anne has not been mentioned, but the twins will out. Nothing can keep down the twins.

"It's a very extraordinary thing, Saunders," says Mr. Whiffler to the visitor, "but—you have seen our little babies, the—the—twins?" The friend's heart sinks within him as he answers, "Oh yes—often." "Your talking of the Pyramids," says Mr. Whiffler, quite as a matter of course, "reminds me of the twins. It's a very extraordinary thing about those babies—what colour should you say their eyes were?" "Upon my word," the friend stammers, "I hardly know how to answer."—the fact being, that except as the friend does not remember to have heard of any departure from the ordinary course of nature in the instance of these twins, they might have no eyes at all for aught he has observed to the

contrary. "You wouldn't say they were red, I suppose?" says Mr. Whiffler.
The friend hesitates, and rather thinks they are; but inferring from
the expression of Mr. Whiffler's face that red is not the colour, smiles
with some confidence, and says, "No, no! very different from that."
"What should you say to blue?" says Mr. Whiffler. The friend glances
at him, and observing a different expression in his face, ventures to say,
"I should say they *were* blue—a decided blue." "To be sure!" cries Mr
Whiffler, triumphantly, "I knew you would! But what should you say
if I was to tell you that the boy's eyes are blue and the girl's hazel, eh?"
"Impossible!" exclaims the friend, not at all knowing why it should be
impossible. "A fact, notwithstanding," cries Mr. Whiffler; "and let me tell
you, Saunders, *that's* not a common thing in twins, or a circumstance
that'll happen every day."

In this dialogue Mrs. Whiffler, as being deeply responsible for the
twins, their charms and singularities, has taken no share; but she now
relates, in broken English, a witticism of little Dick's bearing upon the
subject just discussed, which delights Mr. Whiffler beyond measure, and
causes him to declare that he would have sworn that was Dick's if he
had heard it anywhere. Then he requests that Mrs. Whiffler will tell
Saunders what Tom said about mad bulls; and Mrs. Whiffler relating
the anecdote, a discussion ensues upon the different character of Tom's
wit and Dick's wit, from which it appears that Dick's humour is of
a lively turn, while Tom's style is the dry and caustic. This discussion
being enlivened by various illustrations, lasts a long time, and is only
stopped by Mrs. Whiffler instructing the footman to ring the nursery
bell, as the children were promised that they should come down and
taste the pudding.

The friend turns pale when this order is given, and paler still when
it is followed up by a great pattering on the staircase (not unlike the
sound of rain upon a skylight), a violent bursting open of the dining-
room door, and the tumultuous appearance of six small children, closely
succeeded by a strong nursery-maid with a twin in each arm. As the
whole eight are screaming, shouting, or kicking—some influenced by

a ravenous appetite, some by a horror of the stranger, and some by a conflict of the two feelings—a pretty long space elapses before all their heads can be ranged round the table and anything like order restored; in bringing about which happy state of things both the nurse and footman are severely scratched. At length Mrs. Whiffler is heard to say, "Mr. Saunders, shall I give you some pudding?" A breathless silence ensues, and sixteen small eyes are fixed upon the guest in expectation of his reply. A wild shout of joy proclaims that he has said "No, thank you." Spoons are waved in the air, legs appear above the tablecloth in uncontrollable ecstasy, and eighty short fingers dabble in damson syrup.

While the pudding is being disposed of Mr. and Mrs. Whiffler look on with beaming countenances, and Mr. Whiffler, nudging his friend Saunders, begs him to take notice of Tom's eyes, or Dick's chin, or Ned's nose, or Mary Anne's hair, or Emily's figure, or little Bob's calves, or Fanny's mouth, or Carry's head, as the case may be. Whatever the attention of Mr. Saunders is called to, Mr. Saunders admires of course; though he is rather confused about the sex of the youngest branches and looks at the wrong children, turning to a girl when Mr. Whiffler directs his attention to a boy, and falling into raptures with a boy when he ought to be enchanted with a girl. Then the dessert comes, and there is a vast deal of scrambling after fruit, and sudden spirting forth of juice out of tight oranges into infant eyes, and much screeching and wailing in consequence. At length it becomes time for Mrs. Whiffler to retire, and all the children are by force of arms compelled to kiss and love Mr. Saunders before going up-stairs, except Tom, who, lying on his back in the hall, proclaims that Mr. Saunders "is a naughty beast"; and Dick, who having drunk his father's wine when he was looking another way, is found to be intoxicated and is carried out, very limp and helpless.

Mr. Whiffler and his friend are left alone together, but Mr. Whiffler's thoughts are still with his family, if his family are not with him. "Saunders," says he, after a short silence, "if you please, we'll drink Mrs. Whiffler and the children." Mr. Saunders feels this to he a reproach against himself for not proposing the same sentiment, and drinks it in some confusion. "Ah!" Mr. Whiffler sighs, "these children, Saunders, make one quite an old man." Mr. Saunders thinks that if they were his they would make him a very old man; but he says nothing. "And yet," pursues Mr. Whiffler, "what can equal domestic happiness? what can equal the engaging ways of children? Saunders, why don't *you* get married?" Now, this is an embarrassing question, because Mr. Saunders has been thinking that if he had at any time entertained matrimonial designs, the revelation of that day would surely have routed them for ever. "I am glad, however," says Mr. Whiffler, "that you *are* a bachelor,— glad on one account, Saunders; a selfish one, I admit. Will you do Mrs. Whiffler and myself a favour?" Mr. Saunders is surprised—evidently surprised; but he replies, "with the greatest pleasure." "Then will you, Saunders," says Mr. Whiffler, in an impressive manner, "will you cement and consolidate our friendship by coming into the family (so to speak) as a godfather?" "I shall be proud and delighted," replies Mr. Saunders: "which of the children is it? really, I thought they were all christened ; or—" "Saunders," Mr. Whiffler interposes, "they *are* all christened; you are right. The fact is, that Mrs. Whiffler is—in short, we expect another." "Not a ninth!" cries the friend, all aghast at the idea. "Yes, Saunders," rejoins Mr. Whiffler, solemnly, "a ninth. Did we drink Mrs. Whiffler's health? Let us drink it again, Saunders, and wish her well over it!"

Doctor Johnson used to tell a story of a man who had but one idea, which was a wrong one. The couple who dote upon their children are in the same predicament: at home or abroad, at all times, and in all places, their thoughts are bound up in this one subject, and have no sphere beyond. They relate the clever things their offspring say or do, and weary every company with their prolixity and absurdity. Mr. Whiffler takes a friend by the button at a street-corner on a windy day to tell him a *bon mot* of his youngest boy's; and Mrs. Whiffler, calling to see a sick acquaintance, entertains her with a cheerful account of all her own past sufferings and present expectations. In such cases the sins of the fathers indeed descend upon the children; for people soon come to regard them as predestined little bores. The couple who dote upon their children cannot be said to be actuated by a general love for these engaging little people (which would be a great excuse); for they are apt to underrate and entertain a jealousy of any children but their own. If they examined their own hearts, they would, perhaps, find at the bottom of all this more self-love and egotism than they think of. Self-love and egotism are bad qualities, of which the unrestrained exhibition, though it may be sometimes amusing, never fails to be wearisome and unpleasant. Couples who dote upon their children, therefore, are best avoided.

THE COOL COUPLE

There is an old-fashioned weather-glass representing a house with two doorways, in one of which is the figure of a gentleman, in the other the figure of a lady. When the weather is to be fine the lady comes out and the gentleman goes in; when wet, the gentleman comes out and the lady goes in. They never seek each other's society, are never elevated and depressed by the same cause, and have nothing in common. They are the model of a cool couple, except that there is something of politeness and consideration about the behaviour of the gentleman in the weather-glass, in which neither of the cool couple can be said to participate.

The cool couple are seldom alone together, and when they are, nothing exceed their apathy and dulness: the gentleman being for the most part drowsy and the lady silent. If they enter into conversation, it is usually of an ironical or recriminatory nature. Thus, when the gentleman has indulged in a very long yawn and settled himself more snugly in his easy-chair, the lady will perhaps remark, "Well, I am sure, Charles! I hope you're comfortable." To which the gentleman replies, "Oh yes, he's quite comfortable—quite." "There are not many married men, I hope,"

The Cool Couple

returns the lady, "who seek comfort in such selfish gratifications as you do." "Nor many wives who seek comfort in such selfish gratifications as *you* do, I hope," retorts the gentleman. "Whose fault is that?" demands the lady. The gentleman, becoming more sleepy, returns no answer. "Whose fault is that?" the lady repeats. The gentleman still returning no answer, she goes on to say that she believes there never was in all this world so attached to her home, so thoroughly domestic, so unwilling to seek a moment's gratification or pleasure beyond her own fireside as she. God knows that before she was married she never thought or dreamt of such a thing; and she remembers that her poor papa used to say again and again, almost every day of his life, "Oh, my dear Louisa, if you only marry a man who understands you, and takes the trouble to consider your happiness and accommodate himself a very little to your disposition, what a treasure he will find in you!" She supposes her papa knew what her disposition was—he had known her long enough—he ought to have been acquainted with it, but what can she do? If her home is always dull and lonely, and her husband is always absent and finds no pleasure in her society, she is naturally sometimes driven (seldom enough, she is sure) to seek a little recreation elsewhere; she is not expected to pine and mope to death, she hopes. " Then come, Louisa," says the gentleman, waking up as suddenly as he fell asleep, "stop at home this evening, and so will I." "I should be sorry to suppose, Charles, that you took a pleasure in aggravating me," replies the lady; "but you know as well as I do that I am particularly engaged to Mrs. Mortimer, and that it would be an act of the grossest rudeness and ill-breeding, after accepting a seat in her box and preventing her from inviting anybody else, not to go." "Ah! there it is!" says the gentleman, shrugging his shoulders, "I knew that perfectly well. I knew you couldn't devote an evening to your own home. Now all I have to say, Louisa, is this—recollect that *I* was quite willing to stay at home, and that it's no fault of *mine* we are not oftener together."

With that the gentleman goes away to keep an old appointment at his club, and the lady hurries off to dress for Mrs. Mortimer's; and

neither thinks of the other until by some odd chance they find them
selves alone again.

But it must not be supposed that the cool couple are habitually
a quarrelsome one. Quite the contrary. These differences are only
occasions for a little self-excuse,—nothing more. In general they are as
easy and careless, and dispute as seldom, as any common acquaintances
may; for it is neither worth their while to put each other out of the way,
nor to ruffle themselves.

When they meet in society, the cool couple are the best-bred people
in existence. The lady is seated in a corner among a little knot of lady
friends, one of whom exclaims, "Why, I vow and declare there is your
husband, my dear!" "Whose ?—mine?" she says, carelessly. "Ay, yours,
and coming this way too." "How very odd!" says the lady, in a languid
tone, "I thought he had been at Dover." The gentleman coming up,
and speaking to all the other ladies and nodding slightly to his wife, it
turns out that he has been at Dover, and has just now returned. "What
a strange creature you are!" cries his wife; "and what on earth brought
you here, I wonder?" "I came to look after you, of *course*," rejoins her
husband. This is so pleasant a jest that the lady is mightily amused, as are
all the other ladies similarly situated who are within hearing; and while
they are enjoying it to the full, the gentleman nods again, turns upon
his heel, and saunters away.

There are times, however, when his company is not so agreeable,
though equally unexpected; such as when the lady has invited one or
two particular friends to tea and scandal, and he happens to come home
in the very midst of their diversion. It is a hundred chances to one that
he remains in the house half an hour, but the lady is rather disturbed
by the intrusion, notwithstanding, and reasons within herself,—"I am
sure I never interfere with him, and why should he interfere with me
? It can scarcely be accidental; it never happens that I have a particular
reason for not wishing him to come home, but he always comes. It's
very provoking and tiresome; and I am sure when he leaves me so
much alone for his own pleasure, the least he could do would be to do

as much for mine." Observing what passes in her mind, the gentleman, who has come home for his own accommodation, makes a merit of it with himself; arrives at the conclusion that it is the very last place in which he can hope to be comfortable; and determines, as he takes up his hat and cane, never to be so virtuous again.

Thus a great many cool couples go on until they are cold couples, and the grave has closed over their folly and indifference. Loss of name, station, character, life itself, has ensued from causes as slight as these, before now; and when gossips tell such tales, and aggravate their deformities, they elevate their hands and eyebrows, and call each other to witness what a cool couple Mr. and Mrs. So-and-so always were, even in the best of times.

THE PLAUSIBLE COUPLE

The plausible couple have many titles. They are "a delightful couple," an "affectionate couple," "a most agreeable couple," "a good-hearted couple," and "the best-natured couple in existence." The truth is, that the plausible couple are people of the world; and either the way of pleasing the world has grown much easier than it was in the days of the old man and his ass, or the old man was but a bad hand at it, and knew very little of the trade.

"But is it really possible to please the world?" says some doubting reader. It is indeed. Nay, it is not only very possible, but very easy. The ways are crooked, and sometimes foul and low. What then? A man need but crawl upon his hands and knees, know when to close his eyes and when his ears, when to stoop and when to stand upright; and if by the world is meant that atom of it in which he moves himself, he shall please it, never fear.

Now, it will be readily seen, that if a plausible man or woman have an easy means of pleasing the world by an adaptation of self to all its twistings and twinings, a plausible man *and* woman, or, in other words, a plausible couple, playing into each other's hands, and acting in concert, have a manifest advantage. Hence it is that plausible couples scarcely ever fail of success on a pretty large scale; and hence it is that if the reader, laying down this unwieldy volume at the next full stop, will have the goodness to review his or her circle of acquaintance, and to search particularly for some man and wife with a large connection and a good name, not easily referable to their abilities or their wealth, he or she (that is, the male or female reader) will certainly find that gentleman or lady, on a very short reflection, to be a plausible couple.

The plausible couple are the most ecstatic people living: the most sensitive people—to merit—on the face of the. earth. Nothing clever or virtuous escapes them. They have microscopic eyes for such endowments, and can find them anywhere. The plausible couple never fawn—oh no! They don't even scruple to tell their friends of their faults. One is too generous, another too candid; a third has a tendency to think all people like himself, and to regard mankind as a company of angels; a fourth is kind-hearted to a fault. "We never flatter, my dear Mrs. Jackson," say the plausible couple; "we speak our minds. Neither you nor Mr. Jackson have faults enough. It may sound strangely, but it is true. You have not faults enough. You know our way,—we must speak out, and always do. Quarrel with us for saying so, if you will ; but we repeat it,—you have not faults enough!"

The plausible couple are no less plausible to each other than to third parties. They are always loving and harmonious. The plausible gentleman calls his wife "darling," and the plausible lady addresses him as "dearest." If it be Mr. and Mrs. Bobtail Widger, Mrs. Widger is "Lavinia, darling," and Mr. Widger is "Bobtail, dearest." Speaking of each other, they observe the same tender form. Mrs. Widger relates what "Bobtail" said, and Mr. Widger recounts what "darling" thought and did.

If you sit next to the plausible lady at a dinner-table, she takes the earliest opportunity of expressing her belief that you are acquainted with the Clickits ; she is sure she has heard the Clickits speak of you— she must not tell you in what terms, or you will take her for a flatterer. You admit a knowledge of the Clickits; the plausible lady immediately launches out in their praise. She quite loves the Clickits. Were there ever such true-hearted, hospitable, excellent people—such a gentle, interesting little woman as Mrs. Clickit, or such a frank unaffected creature as Mr. Clickit? were there ever two people, in short, so little spoiled by the world as they are? " As who, darling?" cries Mr. Widger, from the opposite side of the table. "The Clickits, dearest," replies Mrs. Widger. "Indeed you are right, darling," Mr Widger rejoins; "the Clickits are a very high-minded, worthy, estimable couple." Mrs. Widger remarking that Bobtail always grows quite eloquent upon this subject, Mr. Widger admits that he feels very strongly whenever such people as the Clickits and some other friends of his (here he glances at the host and hostess) are mentioned; for they are an honour to human nature, and do one good to think of. "*You* know the Clickits, Mrs. Jackson?" he says, addressing the lady of the house. "No, indeed ; we have not that pleasure," she replies. "You astonish me!" exclaims Mr. Widger: "not know the Clickits! why, you are the very people of all others who ought to be their bosom friends. You are kindred beings; you are one and the same thing:—not know the Clickits! Now *will* you know the Clickits? Will you make a point of knowing them? Will you meet them in a friendly way at our house one evening, and be acquainted with them?" Mrs. Jackson will be quite delighted; nothing would give her more pleasure. "Then, Lavinia, my darling," says Mr. Widger, "mind you don't lose sight of that; now, pray take care that Mr and Mrs. Jackson know the Clickits without loss of time. Such people ought not to be strangers to each other." Mrs. Widger books both families as the centre of attraction for her next party; and Mr. Widger, going on to expatiate upon the virtues of the Clickits, adds to their other moral qualities, that they keep one of the neatest phaetons in town, and have two thousand a year.

As the plausible couple never laud the merits of any absent person, without dexterously contriving that their praises shall reflect upon somebody who is present, so they never depreciate anything or any body, without turning their depreciation to the same account. Their friend, Mr. Slummery, say they, is unquestionably a clever painter, and would no doubt be very popular, and sell his pictures at a very high price, if that cruel Mr. Fithers had not forestalled him in his department of art, and made it thoroughly and completely his own;—Fithers, it is to be observed, being present and within hearing, and Slummery elsewhere. Is Mrs. Tabblewick really as beautiful as people say? Why, there indeed you ask them a very puzzling question, because there is no doubt that she is a very charming woman, and they have long known her intimately. She is no doubt beautiful, very beautiful; they once thought her the most beautiful woman ever seen; still if you press them for an honest answer, they are bound to say that this was before they had ever seen our lovely friend on the sofa (the sofa is hard by, and our lovely friend can't help hearing the whispers in which this is said); since that time, perhaps, they have been hardly fair judges; Mrs. Tabblewick is no doubt extremely handsome,—very like our friend, in fact, in the form of the features,—but in point of expression, and soul, and figure, and air altogether—oh dear!

But while the plausible couple depreciate, they are still careful to preserve their character for amiability and kind feeling; indeed the depreciation itself is often made to grow out of their excessive sympathy and goodwill. The plausible lady calls on a lady who dotes upon her children, and is sitting with a little girl upon her knee, enraptured by her artless replies, and protesting that there is nothing she delights in so much as conversing with these fairies; when the other lady inquires if she has seen young Mrs. Finching lately, and whether the baby has turned out a finer one than it promised to be. "Oh dear!" cries the plausible lady, "you can-not think how often Bobtail and I have talked about poor Mrs. Finching—she is such a dear soul, and was so anxious that the baby should be a fine child—and very naturally, because she was very much here at one time, and there is, you know, a natural emulation among mothers—that it is impossible to tell you how much we have felt for her." " Is it weak or plain, or what?" inquires the other.

"Weak or plain, my love," returns the plausible lady, "it's a fright—a perfect little fright; you never saw such a miserable creature in all your days. Positively you must not let her see one of these beautiful dears again, or you'll break her heart, you will indeed—Heaven bless this child, see how she is looking in my face! can you conceive anything prettier than that? If poor Mrs. Finching could only hope—but that's impossible—and the gifts of Providence, you know—What *did* I do with my pocket-handkerchief!"

What prompts the mother, who dotes upon her children, to comment to her lord that evening on the plausible lady's engaging qualities and feeling heart, and what is it that procures Mr. and Mrs. Bobtail Widger an immediate invitation to dinner?

THE NICE LITTLE COUPLE

A Custom once prevailed in old-fashioned circles, that when a lady or gentleman was unable to sing a song, he or she should enliven the company with a story. As we find ourself in the predicament of not being able to describe (to our own satisfaction) nice little couples in the abstract, we purpose telling in this place a little story about a nice little couple of our acquaintance.

Mr. and Mrs. Chirrup are the nice little couple in question. Mr. Chirrup has the smartness, and something of the brisk, quick manner of a small bird. Mrs. Chirrup is the prettiest of all little women, and has the prettiest little figure conceivable. She has the neatest little foot, and the softest little voice, and the pleasantest little smile, and the tidiest little curls, and the brightest little eyes, and the quietest little manner, and is, in short, altogether one of the most engaging of all little women, dead or alive. She is a condensation of all the domestic virtues,—a pocket edition of the young man's best companion,—a little woman at a very high pressure, with an amazing quantity of goodness and usefulness in an exceedingly small space. Little as she is, Mrs. Chirrup might furnish forth matter for the moral equipment of a score of housewives, six feet high in their stockings—if, in the presence of ladies, we may be allowed the expression—and of corresponding robustness.

Nobody knows all this better than Mr. Chirrup, though he rather takes on that he don't. Accordingly he is very proud of his better-half, and evidently considers himself, as all other people consider him, rather fortunate in having her to wife. We say evidently, because Mr. Chirrup is a warm-hearted little fellow; and if you catch his eye when he has been slyly glancing at Mrs. Chirrup in company, there is a certain complacent twinkle in it, accompanied, perhaps, by a half-expressed toss of the head, which as clearly indicates what has been passing in his mind as if he had put it into words, and shouted it out through a speaking-trumpet. Moreover, Mr. Chirrup has a particularly mild and bird-like manner of calling Mrs. Chirrup "my dear"; and—for he is of a jocose turn—of cutting little witticisms upon her, and making her the subject of various harmless pleasantries, which nobody enjoys more thoroughly than Mrs. Chirrup herself. Mr. Chirrup, too, now and then affects to deplore his bachelor-days, and to bemoan (with a marvellously contented and smirking face) the loss of his freedom, and the sorrow of his heart at having been taken captive by Mrs. Chirrup—all of which circumstances combine to show the secret triumph and satisfaction of Mr. Chirrup's soul.

We have already had occasion to observe that Mrs. Chirrup is an incomparable housewife. In all the arts of domestic arrangement and management, in all the mysteries of confectionery-making, pickling, and preserving, never was such a thorough adept as that nice little body. She is, besides, a cunning worker in muslin and fine linen, and a special hand at marketing to the very best advantage. But if there be one branch of housekeeping in which she excels to an utterly unparalleled and unprecedented extent, it is in the important one of carving. A roast goose is universally allowed to be the great stumbling-block in the way of young aspirants to perfection in this department of science; many promising carvers, beginning with legs of mutton, and preserving a good reputation through fillets of veal, sirloins of beef, quarters of lamb, fowls, and even ducks, have sunk before a roast goose, and lost caste and character for ever. To Mrs. Chirrup the resolving a goose into its smallest component parts is a pleasant pastime—a practical joke—a thing to be done in a minute or so, without the smallest interruption to the conversation of the time. No handing the dish over to an unfortunate man upon her right or left, no wild sharpening of the knife, no hacking and sawing at an unruly joint, no noise, no splash, no heat, no leaving off in despair; all is confidence and cheerfulness. The dish is set upon the table, the cover is removed; for an instant, and only an instant, you observe that Mrs. Chirrup's attention is distracted; she smiles, but heareth not. You proceed with your story; meanwhile the glittering knife is slowly upraised, both Mrs. Chirrup's wrists are slightly but not ungracefully agitated, she compresses her lips for an instant, then breaks into a smile, and all is over. The legs of the bird slide gently down into a pool of gravy, the wings seem to melt from the body, the breast separates into a row of juicy slices, the smaller and more complicated parts of his anatomy are perfectly developed, a cavern of stuffing is revealed, and the goose is gone!

To dine with Mr. and Mrs. Chirrup is one of the pleasantest things in the world. Mr. Chirrup has a bachelor friend, who lived with him in his own days of single-blessedness, and to whom he is mightily attached. Contrary to the usual custom, this bachelor friend is no less a friend of Mrs. Chirrup's, and, consequently, whenever you dine with Mr. and Mrs. Chirrup, you meet the bachelor friend. It would put any reasonably-conditioned mortal into good-humour to observe the entire unanimity which subsists between these three; but there is a quiet welcome dimpling in Mrs. Chirrup's face, a bustling hospitality oozing as it were out of the waistcoat-pockets of Mr. Chirrup, and a patronising enjoyment of their cordiality and satisfaction on the part of the bachelor friend, which is quite delightful. On these occasions

Mr. Chirrup usually takes an opportunity of rallying the friend on
being single, and the friend retorts on Mr. Chirrup for being married,
at which moments some single young ladies present are like to die of
laughter; and we have more than once observed them bestow looks
upon the friend, which convinces us that his position is by no means
a safe one, as, indeed, we hold no bachelor's to be who visits married
friends and cracks jokes on wedlock, for certain it is that such men
walk among traps and nets and pitfalls innumerable, and often find
themselves down upon their knees at the altar rails, taking M. or N. for
their wedded wives, before they know anything about the matter.

However, this is no business of Mr. Chirrup's, who talks, and laughs,
and drinks his wine, and laughs again, and talks more, until it is time
to repair to the drawing-room, where, coffee served and over, Mrs.
Chirrup prepares for a round game, by sorting the nicest possible little
fish into the nicest possible little pools, and calling Mr. Chirrup to assist
her, which Mr. Chirrup does. As they stand side by side, you find that
Mr. Chirrup is the least possible shadow of a shade taller than Mrs.
Chirrup, and that they are the neatest and best-matched little couple
that can be, which the chances are ten to one against your observing
with such effect at any other time, unless you see them in the street
arm-in-arm, or meet them some rainy day trotting along under a very
small umbrella. The round game (at which Mr. Chirrup is the merriest
of the party) being done and over, in course of time a nice little tray
appears, on which is a nice little supper; and when that is finished
likewise, and you have said "Good-night," you find your self repeating
a dozen times, as you ride home, that there never was such a nice little
couple as Mr. and Mrs. Chirrup.

Whether it is that pleasant qualities, being packed more closely in
small bodies than in large, come more readily to hand than when they
are diffused over a wider space, and have to be gathered together for
use, we don't know, but as a general rule,—strengthened like all other
rules by its exceptions,—we hold that little people are sprightly and
good-natured. The more sprightly and good-natured people we have

the better; therefore, let us wish well to all nice little couples, and hope that they may increase and multiply.

THE EGOTISTICAL COUPLE

Egotism in couples is of two kinds.—It is our purpose to show this by two examples.

The egotistical couple may be young, old, middle-aged, well-to-do, or ill-to-do; they may have a small family, a large family, or no family at all. There is no outward sign by which an egotistical couple may be known and avoided. They come upon you unawares; there is no guarding against them. No man can of himself be forewarned or fore-armed against an egotistical couple.

The egotistical couple have undergone every calamity, and experienced every pleasurable and painful sensation of which our nature is susceptible. You cannot by possibility tell the egotistical couple anything they don't know, or describe to them anything they have not felt. They have been everything but dead. Sometimes we are tempted to wish they had been even that, but only in our uncharitable moments, which are few and far between.

We happened the other day, in the course of a morning call, to encounter an egotistical couple, nor were we suffered to remain long in ignorance of the fact, for our very first inquiry of the lady of the house brought them into active and vigorous operation. The inquiry was of course touching the lady's health, and the answer happened to be, that she had not been very well. "Oh, my dear!" said the egotistical lady, "don't talk of not being well. We have been in *such* a state since we saw you last!"—The lady of the house happening to remark that her lord had not been well either, the egotistical gentleman struck in: "Never let Briggs complain of not being well—never let Briggs complain, my dear Mrs. Briggs, after what I have undergone within these six weeks. He doesn't know what it is to be ill, he hasn't the least idea of it; not the faintest conception."—"My dear," interposed his wife, smiling, "you talk as if it were almost a crime in Mr. Briggs not to have been as ill as we have been, instead of feeling thankful to Providence that both he and our dear Mrs. Briggs are in such blissful ignorance of real suffering."—" My love," returned the egotistical gentleman, in a low and pious voice, "you mistake me;—I feel grateful—very grateful. I trust our friends may never purchase their experience as dearly as we have bought ours; I hope they never may!"

Having put down Mrs. Briggs upon this theme, and settled the question thus, the egotistical gentleman turned to us, and, after a few preliminary remarks, all tending towards and leading up to the point he had in his mind, inquired if we happened to be acquainted with the Dowager Lady Snorflerer. On our replying in the negative, he presumed we had often met Lord Slang, or beyond all doubt, that we were on intimate terms with Sir Chipkins Glogwog. Finding that we were equally unable to lay claim to either of these distinctions, he expressed great astonishment, and turning to his wife with a retrospective smile, inquired who it was that had told that capital story about the mashed potatoes. "Who, my dear?" returned the egotistical lady, "why Sir Chipkins, of course; how can you ask? Don't you remember his applying it to our cook, and saying that you and I were so like the Prince and Princess, that he could almost have sworn we were they?" "To be sure, I remember that," said the egotistical gentleman, "but are you quite certain that didn't apply to the other anecdote about the Emperor of Austria and the pump?" "Upon my word then, I think it did," replied his wife. "To be sure it did," said the egotistical gentle man, "it was Slang's story, I remember now, perfectly." However, it turned out, a few seconds afterwards, that the egotistical gentleman's memory was rather treacherous, as he began to have a misgiving that the story had been told by the Dowager Lady Snorflerer the very last time they dined there; but there appearing, on further consideration, strong circumstantial evidence tending to show that this couldn't be, inasmuch as the Dowager Lady

Snorflerer had been, on the occasion in question, wholly engrossed by the egotistical lady, the egotistical gentleman recanted this opinion; and after laying the story at the doors of a great many great people, happily left it at last with the Duke of Scuttlewig:—observing that it was not extraordinary he had forgotten his Grace hitherto, as it often happened that the names of those with whom we were upon the most familiar footing were the very last to present themselves to our thoughts.

It not only appeared that the egotistical couple knew everybody, but that scarcely any event of importance or notoriety had occurred for many years with which they had not been in some way or other connected. Thus we learned that when the well-known attempt upon the life of George the Third was made by Hatfield in Drury Lane theatre, the egotistical gentleman's grandfather sat upon his right hand and was the first man who collared him; and that the egotistical lady's aunt, sitting within a few boxes of the royal party, was the only person in the audience who heard his Majesty exclaim, "Charlotte, Charlotte, don't be frightened, don't be frightened; they're letting off squibs, they're letting off squibs." When the fire broke out which ended in the destruction of the two Houses of Parliament, the egotistical couple, being at the time at a drawing-room window on Blackheath, then and there simultaneously exclaimed, to the astonishment of a whole party—"It's the House of Lords!" Nor was this a solitary instance of their peculiar discernment, for chancing to be (as by a comparison of dates and circumstances they afterwards found) in the same omnibus with Mr. Greenacre, when he carried his victim's head about town in a blue bag, they both remarked a singular twitching in the muscles of his countenance; and walking down Fish Street Hill, a few weeks since, the egotistical gentleman said to his lady—slightly casting up his eyes to the top of the Monument—"There's a boy up there, my dear, reading a Bible. It's very strange. I don't like it.—In five seconds afterwards, Sir," says the egotistical gentleman, bringing his hands together with one violent clap—"the lad was over!"

Diversifying these topics by the introduction of many others of the same kind, and entertaining us between whiles with a minute account of what weather and diet agreed with them, and what weather and diet disagreed with them, and at what time they usually got up, and at what time went to bed, with many other particulars of their domestic economy too numerous to mention; the egotistical couple at length took their leave, and afforded us an opportunity of doing the same.

Mr. and Mrs. Sliverstone are an egotistical couple of another class, for all the lady's egotism is about her husband, and all the gentleman's about his wife. For example:—Mr. Sliverstone is a clerical gentleman, and occasionally writes sermons, as clerical gentlemen do. If you happen to obtain admission at the street-door while he is so engaged, Mrs. Sliverstone appears on tiptoe, and speaking in a solemn whisper, as if there were at least three or four particular friends up-stairs all upon the point of death, implores you to be very silent, for Mr. Sliverstone is composing, and she need not say how very important it is that he should not he disturbed. Unwilling to interrupt anything so serious, you hasten to withdraw, with many apologies; but this Mrs. Sliverstone will by no means allow, observing, that she knows you would like to see him, as it is very natural you should, and that she is determined to make a trial for you, as you are a great favourite. So you are led upstairs—still on tiptoe—to the door of a little back room, in which, as the lady informs you in a whisper, Mr. Sliverstone always writes. No answer being returned to a couple of soft taps, the lady opens the door, and there, sure enough, is Mr. Sliverstone, with dishevelled hair, powdering away with pen, ink, and paper, at a rate which, if he has any power of sustaining it, would settle the longest sermon in no time. At first he is too much absorbed to be roused by this intrusion; but presently looking up, says faintly, "Ah!" and pointing to his desk with a weary and languid smile, extends his hand, and hopes you'll forgive him. Then Mrs. Sliverstone sits down beside him, and taking his hand in hers, tells you how that Mr. Sliverstone has been shut up there ever since nine o'clock in the morning (it is by this time twelve at noon), and how she knows it cannot be good for his health, and is very uneasy about it. Unto this Mr. Sliverstone replies firmly, that "It must be done;" which agonises Mrs. Sliverstone still more, and she goes on to tell you that such were Mr. Sliverstone's labours last week—what with the buryings, marryings, churchings, christenings, and all together,— that when he was going up the pulpit stairs on Sunday evening, he was obliged to hold on by the rails, or he would certainly have fallen over into his own pew. Mr Sliverstone, who has been listening and smiling meekly, says, "Not quite so bad as that, not quite so bad!" he admits though, on cross-examination, that he *was* very near falling upon the verger who was following him up to bolt the door; but adds, that it was his duty as a Christian to fall upon him, if need were, and that he, Mr. Sliverstone (and possibly the verger too) ought to glory in it.

This sentiment communicates new impulse to Mrs. Sliverstone, who launches into new praises of Mr. Sliverstone's worth and excellence, to which he listens in the same meek silence, save when he puts in a word of self-denial relative to some question of fact, as—"Not seventy-two christenings that week, my dear. Only seventy-one, only seventy-one." At length his lady has quite concluded, and then he says, Why should he repine, why should he give way, why should he suffer his heart to sink within him? Is it he alone who toils and suffers? What has she gone through, he should like to know? What does she go through every day for him and for society?

With such an exordium Mr. Sliverstone launches out into glowing praises of the conduct of Mrs. Sliverstone in the production of eight young children, and the subsequent rearing and fostering of the same and thus the husband magnifies the wife, and the wife the husband.

This would be well enough if Mr. and Mrs. Sliverstone kept it to themselves, or even to themselves and a friend or two; but they do not. The more hearers they have, the more egotistical the couple become, and the more anxious they are to make believers in their merits. Perhaps this is the worst kind of egotism. It has not even the poor excuse of being spontaneous but is the result of a deliberate system and malice aforethought. Mere empty-headed conceit excites our pity, but ostentatious hypocrisy awakens our disgust.

THE COUPLE WHO CODDLE THEMSELVES

Mrs. Merrywinkle's maiden name was Chopper. She was the only child of Mr. and Mrs. Chopper. Her father died when she was, as the play-books express it, "yet an infant"; and so old Mrs. Chopper, when her daughter married, made the house of her son-in-law her home from that time henceforth, and set up her staff of rest with Mr. and Mrs. Merrywinkle.

Mr. and Mrs. Merrywinkle are a couple who coddle themselves; and the venerable Mrs. Chopper is an aider and abetter in the same.

Mr Merrywinkle is a rather lean and long-necked gentleman, middle-aged and middle-sized, and usually troubled with a cold in the head. Mrs. Merrywinkle is a delicate-looking lady, with very light hair, and is exceedingly subject to the same unpleasant disorder. The venerable Mrs. Chopper—who is strictly entitled to the appellation, her daughter not being very young, otherwise than by courtesy, at the time of her marriage, which was some years ago—is a mysterious old lady who lurks behind a pair of spectacles, and is afflicted with a chronic disease, respecting which she has taken a vast deal of medical advice, and referred to a vast number of medical books, without meeting any definition of symptoms that at all suits her, or enables her to say, "That's my complaint." Indeed, the absence of authentic information upon the subject of this complaint would seem to be Mrs. Chopper's greatest ill, as in all other respects she is an uncommonly hale and hearty gentlewoman.

Both Mr. and Mrs. Chopper wear an extraordinary quantity of flannel, and have a habit of putting their feet in hot water to an unnatural extent. They likewise indulge in chamomile tea and such-like compounds, and rub themselves on the slightest provocation with camphorated spirits and other lotions applicable to mumps, sore-throat, rheumatism, or lumbago.

Mr. Merrywinkle's leaving home to go to business on a damp or wet morning is a very elaborate affair. He puts on wash-leather socks over his stockings, and India-rubber shoes above his boots, and wears under his waistcoat a cuirass of hare-skin. Besides these precautions, he winds a thick shawl round his throat, and blocks up his mouth with a large silk handkerchief. Thus accoutred, and furnished besides with a greatcoat and umbrella, he braves the dangers of the streets; travelling in severe weather at a gentle trot, the better to preserve the circulation, and bringing his mouth to the surface to take breath, but very seldom, and with the utmost caution. His office-door opened, he shoots past his clerk at the same pace, and diving into his own private room, closes the door, examines the window-fastenings, and gradually unrobes himself: hanging his pocket-handkerchief on the fender to air, and determining to write to the newspapers about the fog, which, he says, "has really got to that pitch that it is quite unbearable."

In this last opinion Mrs. Merrywinkle and her respected mother fully concur; for though not present, their thoughts and tongues are occupied with the same subject, which is their constant theme all day. If anybody happens to call, Mrs. Merrywinkle opines that they must assuredly be mad, and her first salutation is, "Why, what in the name of goodness can bring you out in such weather? You know you *must* catch your death." This assurance is corroborated by Mrs. Chopper, who adds, in further confirmation, a dismal legend concerning an individual of her acquaintance who, making a call under precisely parallel circumstances, and being then in the best health and spirits, expired in forty-eight hours afterwards, of a complication of inflammatory disorders. The visitor, rendered not altogether comfortable perhaps by this and other precedents, inquires very affectionately after Mr. Merrywinkle, but by so doing brings about

no change of the subject; for Mr. Merrywinkle's name is inseparably
connected with his complaints, and his complaints are inseparably
connected with Mrs. Merrywinkle's; and when these are done with,
Mrs. Chopper, who has been biding her time, cuts in with the chronic
disorder—a subject upon which the amiable old lady never leaves off
speaking until she is left alone, and very often not then.

But Mr. Merrywinkle comes home to dinner. He is received by Mrs.
Merrywinkle and Mrs. Chopper, who, on his remarking that he thinks
his feet are damp, turn pale as ashes and drag him up-stairs, imploring
him to have them rubbed directly with a dry coarse towel. Rubbed
they are, one by Mrs. Merrywinkle and one by Mrs. Chopper, until
the friction causes Mr. Merrywinkle to make horrible faces, and look
as if he had been smelling very powerful onions; when they desist,
and the patient, provided for his better security with thick worsted
stockings and list slippers, is borne down-stairs to dinner. Now the
dinner is always a good one, the appetites of the diners being delicate,
and requiring a little of what Mrs. Merrywinkle calls "tittivation"; the
secret of which is understood to lie in good cookery and tasteful spices,
and which process is so successfully performed in the present instance,
that both Mr. and Mrs. Merrywinkle eat a remarkably good dinner, and
even the afflicted Mrs. Chopper wields her knife and fork with much
of the spirit and elasticity of youth. But Mr. Merrywinkle, in his desire
to gratify his appetite, is not unmindful of his health, for he has a bottle
of carbonate of soda with which to qualify his porter, and a little pair
of scales in which to weigh it out. Neither in his anxiety to take care
of his body is he unmindful of the welfare of his immortal part, as he
always prays that for what he is going to receive he may be made truly
thankful; and in order that he may be as thankful as possible, eats and
drinks to the utmost.

Either from eating and drinking so much, or from being the victim
of this constitutional infirmity, among others, Mr. Merrywinkle, after
two or three glasses of wine, falls fast asleep; and he has scarcely closed
his eyes, when Mrs. Merrywinkle and Mrs. Chopper fall asleep likewise.

It is on awakening at tea-time that their most alarming symptoms prevail; for then Mr. Merrywinkle feels as if his temples were tightly bound round with the chain of the street-door, and Mrs. Merrywinkle as if she had made a hearty dinner of half-hundred weights, and Mrs. Chopper as if cold water were running down her back, and oyster-knives with sharp points were plunging of their own accord into her ribs. Symptoms like these are enough to make people peevish, and no wonder that they remain so until supper-time, doing little more than doze and complain, unless Mr. Merrywinkle calls out very loudly to a servant "to keep that draught out," or rushes into the passage to flourish his fist in the countenance of the twopenny-postman, for daring to give such a knock as he had just performed at the door of a private gentleman with nerves.

Supper, coming after dinner, should consist of some gentle provocative; and therefore the tittivating art is again in requisition, and again done honour to by Mr. and Mrs. Merrywinkle, still comforted and abetted by Mrs. Chopper. After supper, it is ten to one but the last-named old lady becomes worse, and is led off to bed with the chronic complaint in full vigour. Mr. and Mrs. Merrywinkle, having administered to her a warm cordial, which is something of the strongest, then repair to their own room, where Mr. Merrywinkle, with his legs and feet in hot water, superintends the mulling of some wine which he is to drink at the very moment he plunges into bed, while Mrs. Merrywinkle, in garments whose nature is unknown to and unimagined by all but married men, takes four small pills with a spasmodic look between each, and finally comes to something hot and fragrant out of another little saucepan, which serves as her composing-draught for the night.

There is another kind of couple who coddle themselves, and who do so at a cheaper rate and on more spare diet, because they are niggardly and parsimonious; for which reason they are kind enough to coddle their visitors too. It is unnecessary to describe them, for our readers may rest assured of the accuracy of these general principles:—that all couples who coddle themselves are selfish and slothful,—that they charge upon every wind that blows, every rain that falls, and every vapour that hangs in the air, the evils which arise from their own imprudence or the gloom which is engendered in their own tempers,—and that all men and women, in couples or otherwise, who fall into exclusive habits of self-indulgence, and forget their natural sympathy and close connection with everybody and everything in the world around them, not only neglect the first duty of life, but, by a happy retributive justice, deprive themselves of its truest and best enjoyment.

THE OLD COUPLE

They are grandfather and grandmother to a dozen grown people and have great-grandchildren besides; their bodies are bent, their hair is gray, their step tottering and infirm. Is this the lightsome pair whose wedding was so merry, and have the young couple indeed grown old so soon!

It seems but yesterday—and yet what a host of cares and griefs are crowded into the intervening time which, reckoned by them, lengthens out into a century! How many new associations have wreathed themselves about their hearts since then! The old time is gone, and a new time has come for others—not for them. They are but the rusting link that feebly joins the two, and is silently loosening its hold and dropping asunder.

It seems but yesterday—and yet three of their children have sunk into the grave, and the tree that shades it has grown quite old. One was an infant—they wept for him; the next a girl, a slight young thing too delicate for earth—her loss was hard indeed to bear. The third, a man. That was the worst of all, but even that grief is softened now.

It seems but yesterday—and yet how the gay and laughing faces of that bright morning have changed and vanished from above ground!

Faint likenesses of some remain about them yet, but they are very faint and scarcely to be traced. The rest are only seen in dreams, and even they are unlike what they were, in eyes so old and dim.

One or two dresses from the bridal wardrobe are yet preserved. They are of a quaint and antique fashion, and seldom seen except in pictures. White has turned yellow, and brighter hues have faded. Do you wonder, child? The wrinkled face was once as smooth as yours, the eyes as bright, the shrivelled skin as fair and delicate. It is the work of hands that have been dust these many years.

Where are the fairy lovers of that happy day whose annual return comes upon the old man and his wife like the echo of some village bell which has long been silent? Let yonder peevish bachelor, racked by rheumatic pains, and quarrelling with the world, let him answer to the question. He recollects something of a favourite playmate; her name was Lucy—so they tell him. He is not sure whether she was married, or went abroad, or died. It is a long while ago, and he don't remember.

Is nothing as it used to be; does no one feel, or think, or act, as in days of yore? Yes. There is an aged woman who once lived servant with the old lady's father, and is sheltered in an alms-house not far off. She is still attached to the family, and loves them all; she nursed the children in her lap, and tended in their sickness those who are no more. Her old mistress has still something of youth in her eyes; the young ladies are like what she was, but not quite so handsome, nor are the gentlemen as stately as Mr. Harvey used to be. She has seen a great deal of trouble; her husband and her son died long ago; but she has got over that, and is happy now—quite happy.

If ever her attachment to her old protectors were disturbed by fresher cares and hopes, it has long since resumed its former current. It has filled the void in the poor creature's heart, and replaced the love of kindred. Death has not left her alone, and this, with a roof above her head, and a warm hearth to sit by, makes her cheerful and contented. Does she remember the marriage of great-grandmamma? Ay, that she does, as well—as if it was only yesterday. You wouldn't think it to look at her now, and perhaps she ought not to say so of herself, but she was as smart a young girl then as you'd wish to see. She recollects she took a friend of hers up-stairs to see Miss Emma dressed for church; her name was—ah! she forgets the name, but she remembers that she was a very pretty girl, and that she married not long after wards, and lived—it has quite passed out of her mind where she lived, hut she knows she bad a bad husband who used her ill, and that she died in Lambeth workhouse. Dear, dear, in Lambeth workhouse!

And the old couple—have they no comfort or enjoyment of existence? See them among their grandchildren and great-grandchildren; how garrulous they are, how they compare one with another, and insist on likenesses which no one else can see; how gently the old lady lectures the girls on points of breeding and decorum, and points the moral by anecdotes of herself in her young days—how the old gentleman chuckles over boyish feats and roguish tricks, and tells long stories of a "barring-out" achieved at the school he went to: which was very wrong, he tells the boys, and never to be imitated of course, but which he cannot help letting them know was very pleasant too—especially when he kissed the master's niece. This last, however, is a point on which the old lady is very tender, for she considers it a shocking and indelicate thing to talk about, and always says so whenever it is mentioned, never failing to observe that he ought to be very penitent for having been so sinful. So the old gentleman gets no further, and what the schoolmaster's niece said afterwards (which he is always going to tell) is lost to posterity.

The old gentleman is eighty years old, to-day—"Eighty years old, Crofts, and never had a headache," he tells the barber who shaves him (the barber being a young fellow, and very subject to that complaint). "That's a great age, Crofts," says the old gentleman. "I don't think it's sich a wery great age, Sir," replied the barber. "Crofts," rejoins the old gentleman, "you're talking nonsense to me. Eighty not a great age?" "It's a wery great age, Sir, for a gentleman to be as healthy and active as you are," returns the barber; "but my grandfather, Sir, he was ninety-four." "You don't mean that, Crofts?" says the old gentleman. "I do indeed,

Sir," retorts the barber, "and as wiggerous as Julius Caesar my grandfather was." The old gentleman muses a little time, and then says, "What did he die of, Crofts?" "He died accidentally, Sir," returns the barber; "he didn't mean to do it. He always would go a-running about the streets— walking never satisfied *his* spirit—and he run against a post and died of a hurt in his chest." The old gentleman says no more until the shaving is concluded, and then he gives Crofts half-a-crown to drink his health. He is a little doubtful of the barber's veracity afterwards, and telling the anecdote to the old lady, affects to make very light of it—though to be sure (he adds) there was old Parr, and in some parts of England, ninety-five or so is a common age, quite a common age.

This morning the old couple are cheerful but serious, recalling old times as well as they can remember them, and dwelling upon many passages in their past lives which the day brings to mind. The old lady reads aloud, in a tremulous voice, out of a great Bible, and the old gentleman, with his hand to his ear, listens with profound respect. When the book is closed, they sit silent for a short space, and afterwards resume their conversation, with a reference perhaps to their dead children, as a subject not unsuited to that they have just left. By degrees they are led to consider which of those who survive are the most like those dearly-remembered objects, and so they fall into a less solemn strain, and become cheerful again.

How many people in all, grandchildren, great-grandchildren, and one or two intimate friends of the family, dine together to-day at the eldest son's to congratulate the old couple, and wish them many happy returns, is a calculation beyond our powers; but this we know, that the old couple no sooner present themselves, very sprucely and carefully attired, than there is a violent shouting and rushing forward of the younger branches with all manner of presents, such as pocket-books, pencil-cases, pen-wipers, watch-papers, pin-cushions, sleeve-buckles, worked-slippers, watch-guards, and even a nutmeg-grater: the latter article being presented by a very chubby and very little boy, who exhibits it in great triumph as an extraordinary variety. The old couple's emotion at these tokens of remembrance occasions quite a pathetic scene, of which the chief ingredients are a vast quantity of kissing and hugging, and repeated wipings of small eyes and noses with small square pocket-handkerchiefs, which don't come at all easily out of small pockets. Even the peevish bachelor is moved, and he says, as he presents the old gentleman with a queer sort of antique ring from his own finger, that he'll be de'ed if he doesn't think he looks younger than he did ten years ago.

But the great time is after dinner, when the dessert and wine are on the table, which is pushed back to make plenty of room, and they are all gathered in a large circle round the fire, for it is then—the glasses being filled, and everybody ready to drink the toast—that two great- grandchildren rush out at a given signal, and presently return, dragging in old Jane Adams leaning upon her crutched stick, and trembling with age and pleasure. Who so popular as poor old Jane, nurse and story-teller in ordinary to two generations; and who so happy as she, striving to bend her stiff limbs into a curtsey, while tears of pleasure steal down her withered cheeks!

The old couple sit side by side, and the old time seems like yesterday indeed. Looking back upon the path they have travelled, its dust and ashes disappear; the flowers that withered long ago show brightly again upon its borders, and they grow young once more in the youth of those about them.

CONCLUSION

We have taken for the subjects of the foregoing moral essays twelve samples of married couples, carefully selected from a large stock on hand, open to the inspection of all corners. These samples are intended for the benefit of the rising generation of both sexes, and, for their more easy and pleasant information, have been separately ticketed and labelled in the manner they have seen.

We have purposely excluded from consideration the couple in which the lady reigns paramount and supreme, holding such cases to be of a very unnatural kind, and, like hideous births and other monstrous deformities, only to be discreetly and sparingly exhibited.

And here our self-imposed task would have ended, but that to those young ladies and gentlemen who are yet revolving singly round the church, awaiting the advent of that time when the mysterious laws of attraction shall draw them towards it in couples, we are desirous of addressing a few last words.

Before marriage and afterwards, let them learn to centre all their hopes of real and lasting happiness in their own fireside; let them cherish the faith that in home, and all the English virtues which the love of home engenders, lies the only true source of domestic felicity; let them believe that round the household gods contentment and tranquillity cluster in their gentlest and most graceful forms ; and that many weary hunters of happiness through the noisy world have learnt this truth too late, and found a cheerful spirit and a quiet mind only at home at last.

How much may depend on the education of daughters and the conduct of mothers; how much of the brightest part of our old national character may be perpetuated by their wisdom or frittered away by their folly—how much of it may have been lost already, and how much more in danger of vanishing every day—are questions too weighty for discussion here, but well deserving a little serious consideration from all young couples nevertheless.

To that one young couple on whose bright destiny the thoughts of nations are fixed, may the youth of England look, and not in vain, for an example. From that one young couple, blessed and favoured as they are, may they learn that even the glare and glitter of a court, the splendour of a palace, and the pomp and glory of a throne yield, in their power of conferring happiness, to domestic worth and virtue. From that one young couple may they learn that the crown of a great empire, costly and jewelled though it be, gives place in the estimation of a Queen to the plain gold ring that links her woman's nature to that of tens of thousands of her humble subjects, and guards in her woman's heart one secret store of tenderness, whose proudest boast shall be that it knows no Royalty save Nature's own, and no pride of birth but being the child of heaven!

So shall the highest young couple in the land for once hear the truth, when men throw up their caps, and cry with loving shouts—

God bless them.

SUNDAY UNDER THREE HEADS

BY TIMOTHY SPARKS

DEDICATION

TO THE RIGHT REVEREND

THE BISHOP OF LONDON

MY LORD,

You were among the first, some years ago, to expatiate on the vicious addiction of the lower classes of society, to Sunday excursions; and were thus instrumental in calling forth occasional demonstrations of those extreme opinions on the subject, which are very generally received with derision, if not with contempt.

Your elevated station, my Lord, affords you countless opportunities of increasing the comforts and pleasures of the humbler classes of society—not by the expenditure of the smallest portion of your princely income, but by merely sanctioning with the influence of your example, their harmless pastimes, and innocent recreations.

That your Lordship would ever have contemplated Sunday recreations with so much horror, if you had been at all acquainted with the wants and necessities of the people who indulged in them, I cannot imagine possible. That a Prelate of your elevated rank, has the faintest conception of the extent of those wants, and the nature of those necessities, I do not believe.

For these reasons, I venture to address this little Pamphlet to your Lordship's consideration. I am quite conscious that the outlines I have drawn, afford but a very imperfect description of the feelings they are intended to illustrate; but I claim for them one merit—their truth and freedom from exaggeration. I may have fallen short of the mark, but I have never overshot it: and while I have pointed out what appears to me, to be injustice on the part of others, I hope I have carefully abstained from committing it myself.

> I am,
>> My Lord,
> Your Lordship's most obedient,
>>> Humble Servant,
>>> TIMOTHY SPARKS.

June, 1836.

Sunday under Three Heads

I

As it is

THERE ARE FEW THINGS FROM which I derive greater pleasure, than walking through some of the principal streets of London on a fine Sunday, in summer, and watching the cheerful faces of the lively groups with which they are thronged. There is something, to my eyes at least, exceedingly pleasing in the general desire evinced by the humbler classes of society, to appear neat and clean on this their only holiday. There are many grave old persons, I know, who shake their heads with an air of profound wisdom, and tell you that poor people dress too well now-a-days; that when they were children, folks knew their stations in life better; that you may depend upon it, no good will come of this sort of thing in the end,—and so forth: but I fancy I can discern in the fine bonnet of the working-man's wife, or the feather-bedizened hat of his child, no inconsiderable evidence of good feeling on the part of the man himself, and an affectionate desire to expend the few shillings he can spare from his week's wages, in improving the appearance and adding to the happiness of those who are nearest and dearest to him. This may be a very heinous and unbecoming degree of vanity, perhaps, and the money might possibly be applied to better uses: it must not be forgotten, however, that it might very easily be devoted to worse: and if two or three faces can be rendered happy and contented by a trifling improvement of outward appearance, I cannot help thinking that the object is very cheaply purchased, even at the expense of a smart gown, or a gaudy riband. There is a great deal of very unnecessary cant about the over-dressing of the common people. There is not a manufacturer or tradesman in existence, who would not employ a man who takes a reasonable degree of pride in the appearance of himself and those about him, in preference to a sullen slovenly fellow, who works doggedly on, regardless of his own clothing and that of his wife and children, and seeming to take pleasure or pride in nothing.

The pampered aristocrat, whose life is one continued round of licentious pleasures and sensual gratifications; or the gloomy enthusiast, who detests the cheerful amusements he can never enjoy, and envies the healthy feelings he can never know, and who would put down the one and suppress the other, until he made the minds of his fellow-beings as besotted and distorted as his own;—neither of these men can by possibility form an adequate notion of what Sunday really is, to those whose lives are spent in sedentary or laborious occupations, and who are accustomed to look forward to it through their whole existence, as their only day of rest from toil, and innocent enjoyment.

The sun that rises over the quiet streets of London on a bright Sunday morning, shines till his setting, on gay and happy faces. Here and there, so early as six o'clock, a young man and woman in their best attire, may be seen hurrying along on their way to the house of some acquaintance, who is included in their scheme of pleasure for the day; from whence, after stopping to take "a bit of breakfast", they sally forth, accompanied by several old people, and a whole crowd of young ones, bearing large hand-baskets full of provisions, and Belcher handkerchiefs done up in bundles, with the neck of a bottle sticking out at the top, and closely-packed apples bulging out at the sides,—and away they hurry along the streets leading to the steam-packet wharfs, which are already plentifully sprinkled with parties bound for the same destination. Their good humour and delight know no bounds—for it is a delightful morning, all blue over head, and nothing like a cloud in the whole sky; and even the air of the river at London Bridge is something to them, shut up as they have been, all the week, in close streets and heated rooms. There are dozens of steamers to all sorts of places—Gravesend, Greenwich, and Richmond; and such numbers of people, that when you have once sat down on the deck, it is all but a moral impossibility to get up again—to say nothing of walking about, which is entirely out of the question. Away they go, joking and laughing, and eating and drinking, and admiring every thing they see, and pleased with every thing they hear, to climb Windmill Hill, and catch a glimpse of the rich corn-fields and beautiful orchards of Kent; or to stroll among the fine old trees of Greenwich Park, and survey the wonders of Shooter's Hill and Lady James's Folly; or to glide past the beautiful meadows of Twickenham and Richmond, and to gaze with a delight which only people like them can know, on every lovely object in the fair prospect around. Boat follows boat, and coach succeeds coach, for the next three hours; but all are filled, and all with the same kind of people—neat and clean, cheerful and contented.

They reach their places of destination, and the taverns are crowded; but there is no drunkenness or brawling, for the class of men who commit the enormity of making Sunday excursions, take their families with them: and this in itself would be a check upon them, even if they were inclined to dissipation, which they really are not. Boisterous their mirth may be, for they have all the excitement of feeling that fresh air and green fields can impart to the dwellers in crowded cities, but it is innocent and harmless. The glass is circulated, and the joke goes round; but the one is free from excess, and the other from offence; and nothing but good humour and hilarity prevail.

In streets like Holborn and Tottenham Court Road, which form the central market of a large neighbourhood; inhabited by a vast number of mechanics and poor people, a few shops are open at an early hour of the morning; and a very poor man, with a thin and sickly woman by his side, may be seen with their little basket in hand, purchasing the scanty quantity of necessaries they can afford, which the time at which the man receives his wages, or his having a good deal of work to do, or

the woman's having been out charing till a late hour, prevented their
procuring over-night. The coffee-shops too, at which clerks and young
men employed in counting-houses can procure their breakfasts, are
also open. This class comprises, in a place like London, an enormous
number of people, whose limited means prevent their engaging for
their lodgings any other apartment than a bedroom, and who have
consequently no alternative but to take their breakfast at a coffee-shop,
or go without it altogether. All these places, however, are quickly closed;
and by the time the church bells begin to ring, all appearance of traffic
has ceased. And then, what are the signs of immorality that meet the
eye? Churches are well filled, and Dissenters' chapels are crowded to
suffocation. There is no preaching to empty benches, while the drunken
and dissolute populace run riot in the streets.

Here is a fashionable church, where the service commences
at a late hour, for the accommodation of such members of the
congregation—and they are not a few—as may happen to have
lingered at the Opera far into the morning of the Sabbath; an
excellent contrivance for poising the balance between God and
Mammon, and illustrating the ease with which a man's duties to both,
may be accommodated and adjusted. How the carriages rattle up,
and deposit their richly-dressed burdens beneath the lofty portico!
The powdered footmen glide along the aisle, place the richly-bound
prayer-books on the pew desks, slam the doors, and hurry away,
leaving the fashionable members of the congregation to inspect
each other through their glasses, and to dazzle and glitter in the eyes
of the few shabby people in the free seats. The organ peals forth,
the hired singers commence a short hymn, and the congregation
condescendingly rise, stare about them, and converse in whispers.
The clergyman enters the reading-desk,—a young man of noble
family and elegant demeanour, notorious at Cambridge for his
knowledge of horse-flesh and dancers, and celebrated at Eton for his
hopeless stupidity. The service commences. Mark the soft voice in
which he reads, and the impressive manner in which he applies his

white hand, studded with brilliants, to his perfumed hair. Observe the graceful emphasis with which he offers up the prayers for the King, the Royal Family, and all the Nobility; and the nonchalance with which he hurries over the more uncomfortable portions of the service, the seventh commandment for instance, with a studied regard for the taste and feeling of his auditors, only to be equalled by that displayed by the sleek divine who succeeds him, who murmurs, in a voice kept down by rich feeding, most comfortable doctrines for exactly twelve minutes, and then arrives at the anxiously expected "Now to God", which is the signal for the dismissal of the congregation. The organ is again heard; those who have been asleep wake up, and those who have kept awake, smile and seem greatly relieved; bows and congratulations are exchanged, the livery servants are all bustle and commotion, bang go the steps, up jump the footmen, and off rattle the carriages: the inmates discoursing on the dresses of the congregation, and congratulating themselves on having set so excellent an example to the community in general, and Sunday-pleasurers in particular.

Enter a less orthodox place of religious worship, and observe the contrast. A small close chapel with a white-washed wall, and plain deal pews and pulpit, contains a closely-packed congregation, as different in dress, as they are opposed in manner, to that we have just quitted. The hymn is sung—not by paid singers, but by the whole assembly at the loudest pitch of their voices, unaccompanied by any musical instrument, the words being given out, two lines at a time, by the clerk. There is something in the sonorous quavering of the harsh voices, in the lank and hollow faces of the men, and the sour solemnity of the women, which bespeaks this a stronghold of intolerant zeal and ignorant enthusiasm. The preacher enters the pulpit. He is a coarse, hard-faced man of forbidding aspect, clad in rusty black, and bearing in his hand a small plain Bible from which he selects some passage for his text, while the hymn is concluding. The congregation fall upon their knees, and are hushed into profound stillness as he delivers an extempore prayer, in which he calls upon the

Sacred Founder of the Christian faith to bless his ministry, in terms of disgusting and impious familiarity not to be described. He begins his oration in a drawling tone, and his hearers listen with silent attention. He grows warmer as he proceeds with his subject, and his gesticulation becomes proportionately violent. He clenches his fists, beats the book upon the desk before him, and swings his arms wildly about his head. The congregation murmur their acquiescence in his doctrines; and a short groan, occasionally bears testimony to the moving nature of his eloquence. Encouraged by these symptoms of approval, and working himself up to a pitch of enthusiasm amounting almost to frenzy, he denounces sabbath-breakers with the direst vengeance of offended Heaven. He stretches his body half out of the pulpit, thrusts forth his arms with frantic gestures, and blasphemously calls upon The Deity to visit with eternal torments, those who turn aside from the word, as interpreted and preached by—himself. A low moaning is heard, the women rock their bodies to and fro, and wring their hands; the preacher's fervour increases, the perspiration starts upon his brow, his face is flushed, and he clenches his hands convulsively, as he draws a hideous and appalling picture of the horrors preparing for the wicked in a future state. A great excitement is visible among his hearers, a scream is heard, and some young girl falls senseless on the floor. There is a momentary rustle, but it is only for a moment—all eyes are turned towards the preacher. He pauses, passes his handkerchief across his face, and looks complacently round. His voice resumes its natural tone, as with mock humility he offers up a thanksgiving for having been successful in his efforts, and having been permitted to rescue one sinner from the path of evil. He sinks back into his seat, exhausted with the violence of his ravings; the girl is removed, a hymn is sung, a petition for some measure for securing the better observance of the Sabbath, which has been prepared by the good man, is read; and his worshipping admirers, struggle who shall be the first to sign it.

But the morning service has concluded, and the streets are again crowded with people. Long rows of cleanly-dressed charity children, preceded by a portly beadle and a withered schoolmaster, are returning to their welcome dinner; and it is evident, from the number of men with beer-trays who are running from house to house, that no inconsiderable portion of the population are about to take theirs at this early hour. The bakers' shops in the humbler suburbs especially, are filled with men, women, and children, each anxiously waiting for the Sunday dinner. Look at the group of children who surround that working man who has just emerged from the baker's shop at the corner of the street, with the reeking dish, in which a diminutive joint of mutton simmers above a vast heap of half-browned potatoes. How the young rogues clap their hands, and dance round their father, for very joy at the prospect of the feast: and how anxiously the youngest and chubbiest of the lot, lingers on tiptoe by his side, trying to get a peep into the interior of the dish. They turn up the street, and the chubby-faced boy trots on as fast as his little legs will carry him, to herald the approach of the dinner to "Mother", who is standing with a baby in her arms on the doorstep, and who seems almost as pleased with the whole scene as the children themselves; whereupon "baby", not precisely understanding the importance of the business in hand, but clearly perceiving that it is something unusually lively, kicks and crows most lustily, to the unspeakable delight of all the children and both the parents: and the dinner is borne into the house amidst a shouting of small voices, and jumping of fat legs, which would fill Sir Andrew Agnew with astonishment; as well it might, seeing that Baronets, generally speaking, eat pretty comfortable dinners all the week through, and cannot be expected to understand what people feel, who only have a meat dinner on one day out of every seven.

The bakings being all duly consigned to their respective owners, and the beer-man having gone his rounds, the church bells ring for afternoon service, the shops are again closed, and the streets are more than ever thronged with people; some who have not been to church in the morning, going to it now; others who have been to church, going out for a walk; and others—let us admit the full measure of their guilt—going for a walk, who have not been to church at all. I am afraid the smart servant of all work, who has been loitering at the corner of the square for the last ten minutes, is one of the latter class. She is evidently waiting for somebody, and though she may have made up her mind to go to church with him one of these mornings, I don't think they have any such intention on this particular afternoon. Here he is, at last. The white trousers, blue coat, and yellow waistcoat—and more especially that cock of the hat—indicate, as surely as inanimate objects can, that Chalk Farm and not the parish church, is their destination. The girl colours up, and puts out her hand with a very awkward affectation of indifference. He gives it a gallant squeeze, and away they walk, arm in arm, the girl just looking back towards her "place" with an air of conscious self-importance, and nodding to her fellow-servant who has gone up to the two-pair-of-stairs window, to take a full view of "Mary's young man", which being communicated to William, he takes off his hat to the fellow-servant: a proceeding which affords unmitigated satisfaction to all parties, and impels the fellow-servant to inform Miss Emily confidentially, in the course of the evening, "that the young man as Mary keeps company with, is one of the most genteelest young men as ever she see."

The two young people who have just crossed the road, and are following this happy couple down the street, are a fair specimen of another class of Sunday-pleasurers. There is a dapper smartness, struggling through very limited means, about the young man, which induces one to set him down at once as a junior clerk to a tradesman or attorney. The girl no one could possibly mistake. You may tell a young woman in the employment of a large dress-maker, at any time, by a certain neatness of cheap finery and humble following of fashion, which pervade her whole attire; but unfortunately there are other tokens not to be misunderstood—the pale face with its hectic bloom, the slight distortion of form which no artifice of dress can wholly conceal, the unhealthy stoop, and the short cough—the effects of hard work and close application to a sedentary employment, upon a tender frame. They turn towards the fields. The girl's countenance brightens, and an unwonted glow rises in her face. They are going to Hampstead or Highgate, to spend their holiday afternoon in some place where they can see the sky, the fields, and trees, and breathe for an hour or two the pure air, which so seldom plays upon that poor girl's form, or exhilarates her spirits.

I would to God, that the iron-hearted man who would deprive such people as these of their only pleasures, could feel the sinking of heart and soul, the wasting exhaustion of mind and body, the utter prostration of present strength and future hope, attendant upon that incessant toil which lasts from day to day, and from month to month; that toil which is too often protracted until the silence of midnight, and resumed with the first stir of morning. How marvellously would his ardent zeal for other men's souls, diminish after a short probation, and how enlightened and comprehensive would his views of the real object and meaning of the institution of the Sabbath become!

The afternoon is far advanced—the parks and public drives are crowded. Carriages, gigs, phaetons, stanhopes and vehicles of every description, glide smoothly on. The promenades are filled with loungers on foot, and the road is thronged with loungers on horse back. Persons of every class are crowded together, here, in one dense mass. The plebeian, who takes his pleasure on no day but Sunday, jostles the patrician, who takes his, from year's end to year's end. You look in vain for any outward signs of profligacy or debauchery. You see nothing before you but a vast number of people, the denizens of a large and crowded city, in the needful and rational enjoyment of air and exercise.

It grows dusk. The roads leading from the different places of suburban resort, are crowded with people on their return home, and the sound of merry voices rings through the gradually darkening fields. The evening is hot and sultry. The rich man throws open the sashes of his spacious dining-room, and quaffs his iced wine in splendid luxury. The poor man, who has no room to take his meals in, but the close apartment to which he and his family have been confined throughout the week, sits in the tea-garden of some famous tavern, and drinks his beer in content and comfort. The fields and roads are gradually deserted, the crowd once more pour into the streets, and disperse to their several homes; and by midnight all is silent and quiet, save where a few stragglers linger beneath the window of some great man's house, to listen to the strains of music from within: or stop to gaze upon the splendid carriages which are waiting to convey the guests, from the dinner-party of an Earl.

There is a darker side to this picture, on which, so far from its being any part of my purpose to conceal it, I wish to lay particular stress. In some parts of London, and in many of the manufacturing towns of England, drunkenness and profligacy in their most disgusting forms, exhibit in the open streets on Sunday, a sad and a degrading spectacle. We need go no farther than St. Giles's, or Drury Lane, for sights and scenes of a most repulsive nature. Women with scarcely the articles of apparel which common decency requires, with forms bloated by disease, and faces rendered hideous by habitual drunkenness—men reeling and staggering along—children in rags and filth—whole streets of squalid and miserable appearance, whose inhabitants are lounging in the public road, fighting, screaming, and swearing—these are the common objects which present themselves in, these are the well-known characteristics of, that portion of London to which I have just referred.

And why is it, that all well-disposed persons are shocked, and public decency scandalised, by such exhibitions?

These people are poor—that is notorious. It may be said that they spend in liquor, money with which they might purchase necessaries, and there is no denying the fact; but let it be remembered that even if they applied every farthing of their earnings in the best possible way, they would still be very—very poor. Their dwellings are necessarily uncomfortable, and to a certain degree unhealthy. Cleanliness might do much, but they are too crowded together, the streets are too narrow, and the rooms too small, to admit of their ever being rendered desirable habitations. They work very hard all the week. We know that the effect of prolonged and arduous labour, is to produce, when a period of rest does arrive, a sensation of lassitude which it requires the application of some stimulus to overcome. What stimulus have they? Sunday comes, and with it a cessation of labour. How are they to employ the day, or what inducement have they to employ it, in recruiting their stock of health? They see little parties, on pleasure excursions, passing through the streets; but they cannot imitate their example, for they have not the means. They may walk, to be sure, but it is exactly the inducement to walk that they require. If every one of these men knew, that by taking the trouble to walk two or three miles he would be enabled to share in a good game of cricket, or some athletic sport, I very much question whether any of them would remain at home.

But you hold out no inducement, you offer no relief from listlessness, you provide nothing to amuse his mind, you afford him no means of exercising his body. Unwashed and unshaven, he saunters moodily about, weary and dejected. In lieu of the wholesome stimulus he might derive from nature, you drive him to the pernicious excitement to be gained from art. He flies to the gin-shop as his only resource; and when, reduced to a worse level than the lowest brute in the scale of creation, he lies wallowing in the kennel, your saintly lawgivers lift up their hands to heaven, and exclaim for a law which shall convert the day intended for rest and cheerfulness, into one of universal gloom, bigotry, and persecution.

II

AS SABBATH BILLS WOULD MAKE IT

The provisions of the bill introduced into the House of Commons by Sir Andrew Agnew, and thrown out by that House on the motion for the second reading, on the 18th of May in the present year, by a majority of 32, may very fairly be taken as a test of the length to which the fanatics, of which the honourable Baronet is the distinguished leader, are prepared to go. No test can be fairer; because while on the one hand this measure may be supposed to exhibit all that improvement which mature reflection and long deliberation may have suggested, so on the other it may very reasonably be inferred, that if it be quite as severe in its provisions, and to the full as partial in its operation, as those which have preceded it, and experienced a similar fate, the disease under which the honourable Baronet and his friends labour, is perfectly hopeless, and beyond the reach of cure.

The proposed enactments of the bill are briefly these:—All work is prohibited on the Lord's day, under heavy penalties, increasing with every repetition of the offence. There are penalties for keeping shops open—penalties for drunkenness—penalties for keeping open houses of entertainment—penalties for being present at any public meeting or assembly—penalties for letting carriages, and penalties for hiring them—penalties for travelling in steam-boats, and penalties for taking passengers—penalties on vessels commencing their voyage on Sunday—penalties on the owners of cattle who suffer them to be driven on the Lord's day—penalties on constables who refuse to act, and penalties for resisting them when they do. In addition to these trifles, the constables are invested with arbitrary, vexatious, and most extensive powers; and all this in a bill which sets out with a hypocritical and canting declaration that "nothing is more acceptable to God than the *true and sincere* worship of Him according to His holy will, and that it is the bounden duty of Parliament to promote the observance of the Lord's day, by protecting every class of society against being required to sacrifice their comfort, health, religious privileges, and conscience, for the convenience, enjoyment, or supposed advantage of any other class on the Lord's day"! The idea of making a man truly moral through the ministry of constables, and sincerely religious under the influence of penalties, is worthy of the mind which could form such a mass of monstrous absurdity as this bill is composed of.

The House of Commons threw the measure out certainly, and by so doing retrieved the disgrace—so far as it could be retrieved—of placing among the printed papers of Parliament, such an egregious specimen of legislative folly; but there was a degree of delicacy and forbearance about the debate that took place, which I cannot help thinking as unnecessary and uncalled for, as it is unusual in Parliamentary discussions. If it had been the first time of Sir Andrew Agnew's attempting to palm such a measure upon the country, we might well understand, and duly appreciate, the delicate and compassionate feeling due to the supposed weakness and imbecility of the man, which prevented his proposition being exposed in its true colours, and induced this Hon. Member to bear testimony to his excellent motives, and that Noble Lord to regret that he could not—although he had tried to do so—adopt any portion of the bill. But when these attempts have been repeated, again and again; when Sir Andrew Agnew has renewed them session after session, and when it has become palpably evident to the whole House that

> His impudence of proof in every trial,
> Kens no polite, and heeds no plain denial—

it really becomes high time to speak of him and his legislation, as they appear to deserve, without that gloss of politeness, which is all very well in an ordinary case, but rather out of place when the liberties and comforts of a whole people are at stake.

In the first place, it is by no means the worst characteristic of this bill, that it is a bill of blunders: it is, from beginning to end, a piece of deliberate cruelty, and crafty injustice. If the rich composed the whole population of this country, not a single comfort of one single man would be affected by it. It is directed exclusively, and without the exception of a solitary instance, against the amusements and recreations of the poor. This was the bait held out by the Hon. Baronet to a body of men, who cannot be supposed to have any very strong sympathies in common with the poor, because they cannot understand their sufferings or their struggles. This is the bait, which will in time prevail, unless public attention is awakened, and public feeling exerted, to prevent it.

Take the very first clause, the provision that no man shall be allowed to work on Sunday—"That no person, upon the Lord's day, shall do, or hire, or employ any person to do any manner of labour, or any work of his or her ordinary calling". What class of persons does this affect? The rich man? No. Menial servants, both male and female, are specially exempted from the operation of the bill. "Menial servants" are among the poor people. The bill has no regard for them. The Baronet's dinner must be cooked on Sunday, the Bishop's horses must be groomed, and the Peer's carriage must be driven. So the menial servants are put utterly beyond the pale of grace;—unless, indeed, they are to go to heaven through the sanctity of their masters, and possibly they might think even that, rather an uncertain passport.

There is a penalty for keeping open, houses of entertainment. Now, suppose the bill had passed, and that half-a-dozen adventurous licensed victuallers, relying upon the excitement of public feeling on the subject, and the consequent difficulty of conviction (this is by no means an improbable supposition), had determined to keep their houses and gardens open, through the whole Sunday afternoon, in defiance of the law. Every act of hiring or working, every act of buying or selling, or delivering, or causing anything to be bought or sold, is specifically made a separate offence—mark the effect. A party, a man and his wife and children, enter a tea-garden, and the informer stations himself in the next box, from whence he can see and hear everything that passes. "Waiter!" says the father. "Yes, Sir." ' "Pint of the best ale!" "Yes, Sir." Away runs the waiter to the: bar, and gets the ale from the landlord. Out comes the informer's note-book—penalty on the father for hiring, on the waiter for delivering, and on the landlord for selling, on the Lord's day. But it does not stop here. The waiter delivers the ale, and darts off, little suspecting the penalties in store for him. "Hollo," cries the father, "waiter!" "Yes, Sir." "Just get this little boy a biscuit, will you?" "Yes, Sir." Off runs the waiter again, and down goes another case of hiring, another case of delivering, and another case of selling; and so it would go on *ad infinitum*, the sum and substance of the matter being, that every time a man or woman cried, "Waiter!" on Sunday, he or she would be fined not less than forty shillings, nor more than a hundred; and every time a waiter replied, "Yes, Sir," he and his master would be fined in the same amount: with the addition of a new sort of window duty on the landlord, to wit, a tax of twenty shillings an hour for every hour beyond the first one during which he should have his shutters down on the Sabbath.

With one exception, there are perhaps no clauses in the whole bill, so strongly illustrative of its partial operation, and the intention of its framer, as those which relate to travelling on Sunday. Penalties of ten, twenty, and thirty pounds, are mercilessly imposed upon coach proprietors who shall run their coaches on the Sabbath; one, two, and ten pounds upon those who hire, or let to hire, horses and carriages upon the Lord's day, but not one syllable about those who have no necessity to hire, because they have carriages and horses of their own; not one word of a penalty on liveried coachmen and footmen. The whole of the saintly venom is directed against the hired cabriolet, the humble fly, or the rumbling hackney-coach, which enables a man of the poorer class to escape for a few hours from the smoke and dirt, in the midst of which he has been confined throughout the week: while the escutcheoned carriage and the dashing cab, may whirl their wealthy owners to Sunday feasts and private oratorios, setting constables, informers, and penalties, at defiance. Again, in the description of the places of public resort which it is rendered criminal to attend on Sunday, there are no words comprising a very fashionable promenade. Public discussions, public debates, public lectures and speeches, are cautiously guarded against; for it is by their means that the people become enlightened enough, to deride the last efforts of bigotry and superstition. There is a stringent provision for punishing the poor man who spends an hour in a news-room, but there is nothing to prevent the rich one, from lounging away the day in the Zoological Gardens.

There is, in four words, a mock proviso, which affects to forbid travelling "with any animal" on the Lord's day. This, however, is revoked, as relates to the rich man, by a subsequent provision. We have then a penalty of not less than fifty, nor more than one hundred pounds, upon any person participating in the control, or having the command of any vessel which shall commence her voyage on the Lord's day, should the wind prove favourable. The next time this bill is brought forward (which will no doubt be at an early period of the next session of Parliament) perhaps it will be better to amend this clause by declaring, that from and after the passing of the act, it shall he deemed unlawful for the wind to blow at all upon the Sabbath. It would remove a great deal of temptation from the owners and captains of vessels.

The reader is now in possession of the principal enacting clauses of Sir Andrew Agnew's bill, with the exception of one, for preventing the killing or taking of "*fish, or other wild animals*", and the ordinary provisions which are inserted for form's sake in all acts of Parliament. I now beg his attention to the clauses of exemption.

They are two in number. The first exempts menial servants from any rest, and all poor men from any recreation: outlaws a milkman after nine o'clock in the morning, and makes eating-houses lawful for only two hours in the afternoon; permits a medical man to use his carriage on Sunday, and declares that a clergyman may either use his own, or hire one.

The second is artful, cunning, and designing; shielding the rich man from the possibility of being entrapped, and affecting at the same time, to have a tender and scrupulous regard, for the interests of the whole community. It declares, "that nothing in this act contained, shall extend to works of piety, charity, or necessity".

What is meant by the word "necessity" in this clause? Simply this— that the rich man shall be at liberty to make use of all the splendid luxuries he has collected around him, on any day in the week, because habit and custom have rendered them "necessary" to his easy existence; but that the poor man who saves his money to provide some little pleasure for himself and family at lengthened intervals, shall not be permitted to enjoy it. It is not "necessary" to him:—Heaven knows, he very often goes long enough without it. This is the plain English of the clause. The carriage and pair of horses, the coachman, the footman, the helper, and the groom, are "necessary" on Sundays, as on other days, to the bishop and the nobleman; but the hackney-coach, the hired gig, or the taxed cart, cannot possibly be "necessary" to the working-man on Sunday, for he has it not at other times. The sumptuous dinner and the rich wines, are "necessaries" to a great man in his own mansion: but the pint of beer and the plate of meat, degrade the national character in an eating-house.

Such is the bill for promoting the true and sincere worship of God according to His Holy Will, and for protecting every class of society against being required to sacrifice their health and comfort on the Sabbath. Instances in which its operation would be unjust, as it would be absurd, might be multiplied to an endless amount; but it is sufficient to place its leading provisions before the reader. In doing so, I have purposely abstained from drawing upon the imagination for possible cases; the provisions to which I have referred, stand in so many words upon the bill as printed by order of the House of Commons; and they can neither be disowned, nor explained away.

Let us suppose such a bill as this, to have actually passed both branches of the legislature; to have received the royal assent; and to have come into operation. Imagine its effect in a great city like London.

Sunday comes, and brings with it a day of general gloom and austerity. The man who has been toiling hard all the week, has been looking towards the Sabbath, not as to a day of rest from labour, and healthy recreation, but as one of grievous tyranny and grinding oppression. The day which his Maker intended as a blessing, man has converted into a curse. Instead of being hailed by him as his period of relaxation, he finds it remarkable only as depriving him of every comfort and enjoyment. He has many children about him, all sent into the world at an early age, to struggle for a livelihood; one is kept in a warehouse all day, with an interval of rest too short to enable him to reach home, another walks four or five miles to his employment at the docks, a third earns a few shillings weekly, as an errand boy, or office messenger; and the employment of the man himself, detains him at some distance from his home from morning till night. Sunday is the only day on which they could all meet together, and enjoy a homely meal in social comfort; and now they sit down to a cold and cheerless dinner: the pious guardians of the man's salvation having, in their regard for the welfare of his precious soul, shut up the bakers' shops. The fire blazes high in the kitchen chimney of these well-fed hypocrites, and the rich steams of the savoury dinner scent the air. What care they to be told that this class of men have neither a place to cook in—nor means to bear the expense, if they had?

Look into your churches—diminished congregations, and scanty attendance. People have grown sullen and obstinate, and are becoming disgusted with the faith which condemns them to such a day as this, once in every seven. And as you cannot make people religious by Act of Parliament, or force them to church by constables, they display their feeling by staying away.

Turn into the streets, and mark the rigid gloom that reigns over everything around. The roads are empty, the fields are deserted, the houses of entertainment are closed. Groups of filthy and discontented-looking men, are idling about at the street corners, or sleeping in the sun; but there are no decently-dressed people of the poorer class, passing to and fro. Where should they walk to? It would take them an hour, at least, to get into the fields, and when they reached them, they could procure neither bite nor sup, without the informer and the penalty. Now and then, a carriage rolls smoothly on, or a well-mounted horseman, followed by a liveried attendant, canters by; but with these exceptions, all is as melancholy and quiet, as if a pestilence had fallen on the city.

Bend your steps through the narrow and thickly-inhabited streets, and observe the sallow faces of the men and women, who are lounging at the doors, or lolling from the windows. Regard well, the closeness of these crowded rooms, and the noisome exhalations that rise from the drains and kennels; and then laud the triumph of religion and morality, which condemns people to drag their lives out in such stews as these, and makes it criminal for them to eat or drink in the fresh air, or under the clear sky. Here and there, from some half-opened window, the loud shout of drunken revelry strikes upon the ear, and the noise of oaths and quarrelling—the effect of the close and heated atmosphere—is heard on all sides. See the men all rush to join the crowd that are making their way down the street, and how loud the execrations of the mob become as they draw nearer. They have assembled round a little knot of constables, who have seized the stock-in-trade, heinously exposed on Sunday, of some miserable walking-stick seller, who follows clamouring for his property. The dispute grows warmer and fiercer, until at last some of the more furious among the crowd, rush forward to restore the goods to their owner. A general conflict takes place; the sticks of the constables are exercised in all directions; fresh assistance is procured; and half a dozen of the assailants are conveyed to the station-house, struggling, bleeding, and cursing. The case is taken to the police-office on the following morning; and after a frightful amount of perjury on both sides, the men are sent to prison for resisting the officers, their families to the workhouse to keep them from starving: and there they both remain for a month afterwards, glorious trophies of the sanctified enforcement of the Christian Sabbath. Add to such scenes as these, the profligacy, idleness, drunkenness, and vice, that will be committed to an extent which no man can foresee, on Monday, as an atonement for the restraint of the preceding day; and you have a very faint and imperfect picture of the religious effects of this Sunday legislation, supposing it could ever be forced upon the people.

But let those who advocate the cause of fanaticism, reflect well, upon the probable issue of their endeavours. They may, by perseverance, succeed with Parliament. Let them ponder on the probability of succeeding with the people. You may deny the concession of a political question for a time, and a nation will bear it patiently. Strike home to the comforts of every man's fireside—tamper with every man's freedom and liberty—and one month, one week, may rouse a feeling abroad, which a king would gladly yield his crown to quell, and a peer would resign his coronet to allay.

It is the custom to affect a deference for the motives of those who advocate these measures, and a respect for the feelings by which they are actuated. They do not deserve it. If they legislate in ignorance, they are criminal and dishonest; if they do so with their eyes open, they commit wilful injustice; in either case, they bring religion into contempt. But they do NOT legislate in ignorance. Public prints, and public men, have pointed out to them again and again, the consequences of their proceedings. If they persist in thrusting themselves forward, let those consequences rest upon their own heads, and let them be content to stand upon their own merits.

It may be asked, what motives can actuate a man who has so little regard for the comfort of his fellow-beings, so little respect for their wants and necessities, and so distorted a notion of the beneficence of his Creator. I reply, an envious, heartless, ill-conditioned dislike, to seeing those whom fortune has placed below him, cheerful and happy—an intolerant confidence in his own high worthiness before God, and a lofty impression of the demerits of others—pride, selfish pride, as inconsistent with the spirit of Christianity itself, as opposed to the example of its Founder upon earth.

To these may be added another class of men—the stern and gloomy enthusiasts, who would make earth a hell, and religion a torment: men who, having wasted the earlier part of their lives in dissipation and depravity, find themselves when scarcely past its meridian, steeped to the neck in vice, and shunned like a loathsome disease. Abandoned by the world, having nothing to fall back upon, nothing to remember but time mis-spent, and energies misdirected, they turn their eyes and not their thoughts to Heaven, and delude themselves into the impious belief, that in denouncing the lightness of heart of which they cannot partake, and the rational pleasures from which they never derived enjoyment, they are more than remedying the sins of their old career, and—like the founders of monasteries and builders of churches, in ruder days—establishing a good set claim upon their Maker.

III

As it Might be Made

The supporters of Sabbath Bills, and more especially the extreme class of Dissenters, lay great stress upon the declarations occasionally made by criminals from the condemned cell or the scaffold, that to Sabbath-breaking they attribute their first deviation from the path of rectitude; and they point to these statements, as an incontestable proof of the evil consequences which await a departure from that strict and rigid observance of the Sabbath, which they uphold. I cannot help thinking that in this, as in almost every other respect connected with the subject, there is a considerable degree of cant, and a very great deal of wilful blindness. If a man be viciously disposed—and with very few exceptions, not a man dies by the executioner's hands, who has not been in one way or other a most abandoned and profligate character for many years—if a man be viciously disposed, there is no doubt that he will turn his Sunday to bad account, that he will take advantage of it, to dissipate with other bad characters as vile as himself; and that in this way, he may trace his first yielding to temptation, possibly his first commission of crime, to an infringement of the Sabbath. But this would be an argument against any holiday at all. If his holiday had been Wednesday instead of Sunday, and he had devoted it to the same improper uses, it would have been productive of the same results. It is too much to judge of the character of a whole people, by the confessions of the very worst members of society. It is not fair, to cry down things which are harmless in themselves, because evil-disposed men may turn them to bad account. Who ever thought of deprecating the teaching poor people to write, because some porter in a warehouse had committed forgery? Or into what man's head did it ever enter, to prevent the crowding of churches, because it afforded a temptation for the picking of pockets?

When the Book of Sports, for allowing the peasantry of England to divert themselves with certain games in the open air, on Sundays, after evening service, was published by Charles the First, it is needless to say the English people were comparatively rude and uncivilised. And yet it is extraordinary to how few excesses it gave rise, even in that day, when men's minds were not enlightened, or their passions moderated, by the influence of education and refinement. That some excesses were committed through its means, in the remoter parts of the country, and that it was discontinued in those places, in consequence, cannot be denied: but generally speaking, there is no proof whatever on record, of its having had any tendency to increase crime, or to lower the character of the people.

The Puritans of that time, were as much opposed to harmless recreations and healthful amusements as those of the present day, and it is amusing to observe that each in their generation, advance precisely the same description of arguments. In the British Museum, there is a curious pamphlet got up by the Agnews of Charles's time, entitled 'A Divine Tragedie lately acted, or a Collection of sundry memorable examples of God's Judgements upon Sabbath Breakers, and other like Libertines in their unlawful Sports, happening within the realme of England, in the compass only of two yeares last past, since the Booke (of Sports) was published, worthy to be knowne and considered of all men, especially such who are guilty of the sinne, or archpatrons thereof'. This amusing document, contains some fifty or sixty veritable accounts of balls of fire that fell into churchyards and upset the sporters, and sporters that quarrelled and upset one another, and so forth: and among them is one anecdote containing an example of a rather different kind, which I cannot resist the temptation of quoting, as strongly illustrative of the fact, that this blinking of the question has not even the recommendation of novelty.

"A woman about Northampton, the same day that she heard the booke for sports read, went immediately, and having 3. pence in her purse, hired a fellow to goe to the next towne to fetch a Minstrell, who coming, she with others fell a daucing, which continued within night; at which time shee was got with child, which at the birth shee murthering, was detected and apprehended, and being convented before the justice, shee confessed it, and withal told the occasion of it, saying it was her falling to sport on the Sabbath, upon the reading of the Booke, so as for this treble sinfull act, her presumptuous profaning of the Sabbath, w^h" brought her adultory and that murther. Shee was according to the Law both of God and man, put to death. Much sinne and misery followeth upon Sabbath-breaking."

It is needless to say, that if the young lady near Northampton had "fallen to sport" of such a dangerous description, on any other day but Sunday, the first result would probably have been the same: it never having been distinctly shown that Sunday is more favourable to the propagation of the human race than any other day in the week. The second result—the murder of the child—does not speak very highly for the amiability of her natural disposition; and the whole story, supposing it to have had any foundation at all, is about as much chargeable upon the Book of Sports, as upon the Book of Kings. Such "sports" have taken place in Dissenting Chapels before now; but religion has never been blamed in consequence; nor has it been proposed to shut up the chapels on that account.

The question, then, very fairly arises, whether we have any reason to suppose that allowing games in the open air on Sundays, or even providing the means of amusement for the humbler classes of society on that day, would be hurtful and injurious to the character and morals of the people.

I was travelling in the west of England a summer or two back, and was induced by the beauty of the scenery, and the seclusion of the spot, to remain for the night in a small village, distant about seventy miles from London. The next morning was Sunday; and I walked out, towards the church. Groups of people—the whole population of the little hamlet apparently—were hastening in the same direction. Cheerful and good-humoured congratulations were heard on all sides, as neighbours overtook each other, and walked on in company. Occasionally I passed an aged couple, whose married daughter and her husband were loitering by the side of the old people, accommodating their rate of walking to their feeble pace, while a little knot of children hurried on before; stout young labourers in clean round frocks; and buxom girls with healthy, laughing faces, were plentifully sprinkled about in couples, and the whole scene was one of quiet and tranquil contentment, irresistibly captivating. The morning was bright and pleasant, the hedges were green and blooming, and a thousand delicious scents were wafted on the air, from the wild flowers which blossomed on either side of the footpath. The little church was one of those venerable simple buildings which abound in the English counties: half overgrown with moss and ivy, and standing in the centre of a little plot of ground, which, but for the green mounds with which it was studded, might have passed for a lovely meadow. I fancied that the old clanking bell which was now summoning the congregation together, would seem less terrible when it rung out the knell of a departed soul, than I had ever deemed possible before—that the sound would tell only of a welcome to calmness and rest, amidst the most peaceful and tranquil scene in nature.

I followed into the church—a low-roofed building with small arched windows, through which the sun's rays streamed upon a plain tablet on the opposite wall, which had once recorded names, now as undistinguishable on its worn surface, as were the bones beneath, from the dust into which they had resolved. The impressive service of the Church of England was spoken—not merely *read*—by a grey headed minister, and the responses delivered by his auditors, with an air of sincere devotion as far removed from affectation or display, as from coldness or indifference. The psalms were accompanied by a few instrumental performers, who were stationed in a small gallery extending across the church at the lower end, over the door; and the voices were led by the clerk, who it was evident derived no slight pride and gratification from this portion of the service. The discourse was plain, unpretending, and well adapted to the comprehension of the hearers. At the conclusion of the service, the villagers waited in the churchyard, to salute the clergyman as he passed; and two or three, I observed, stepped aside, as if communicating some little difficulty, and asking his advice. This, to guess from the homely bows, and other rustic expressions of gratitude, the old gentleman readily conceded. He seemed intimately acquainted with the circumstances of all his parishioners; for I heard him inquire after one man's youngest child, another man's wife, and so forth; and that he was fond of his joke, I discovered from overhearing him ask a stout, fresh-coloured young fellow, with a very pretty bashful-looking girl on his arm, "when those banns were to be put up?"—an inquiry which made the young fellow more fresh-coloured, and the girl more bashful, and which, strange to say, caused a great many other girls who were standing round, to colour up also, and look anywhere but in the faces of their male companions.

As I approached this spot in the evening about half an hour before sunset, I was surprised to hear the hum of voices, and occasionally a shout of merriment from the meadow beyond the churchyard; which I found, when I reached the stile, to be occasioned by a very animated game of cricket, in which the boys and young men of the place were engaged, while the females and old people were scattered about: some seated on the grass watching the progress of the game, and others sauntering about in groups of two or three, gathering little nosegays of wild roses and hedge flowers. I could not but take notice of one old man in particular, with a bright-eyed granddaughter by his side, who was giving a sunburnt young fellow some instructions in the game, which he received with an air of profound deference, but with an occasional glance at the girl, which induced me to think that his attention was rather distracted from the old gentleman's narration of the fruits of his experience. When it was his turn at the wicket, too, there was a glance towards the pair every now and then, which the old grandfather very complacently considered as an appeal to his judgment of a particular hit, but which a certain blush in the girl's face, and a downcast look of the bright eye, led me to believe was intended for somebody else than the old man,—and understood by somebody else, too, or I am much mistaken.

I was in the very height of the pleasure which the contemplation of the scene afforded me, when I saw the old clergyman making his way towards us. I trembled for an angry interruption to the sport, and was almost on the point of crying out, to warn the cricketers of his approach; he was so close upon me, however, that I could do nothing but remain still, and anticipate the reproof that was preparing. What was my agreeable surprise to see the old gentleman standing at the stile, with his hands in his pockets, surveying the whole scene with evident satisfaction! And how dull I must have been, not to have known till my friend the grandfather (who, by-the-bye, said he had been a wonderful cricketer in his time) told me, that it was the clergyman himself who had established the whole thing: that it was his field they played in; and that it was he who had purchased stumps, bats, ball, and all!

It is such scenes as this, I would see near London, on a Sunday evening. It is such men as this, who would do more in one year, to make people properly religious, cheerful, and contented, than all the legislation of a century could ever accomplish.

It will be said—it has been very often—that it would be matter of perfect impossibility to make amusements and exercises succeed in large towns, which may be very well adapted to a country population. Here, again, we are called upon to yield to bare assertions on matters of belief and opinion, as if they were established and undoubted facts. That there is a wide difference between the two cases, no one will be prepared to dispute; that the difference is such as to prevent the application of the same principle to both, no reasonable man, I think, will be disposed to maintain. The great majority of the people who make holiday on Sunday now, are industrious, orderly, and well-behaved persons. It is not unreasonable to suppose that they would be no more inclined to an abuse of pleasures provided for them, than they are to an abuse of the pleasures they provide for themselves; and if any people, for want of something better to do, resort to criminal practices on the Sabbath as at present observed, no better remedy for the evil can be imagined, than giving them the opportunity of doing something which will amuse them, and hurt nobody else.

The propriety of opening the British Museum to respectable people on Sunday, has lately been the subject of some discussion. I think it would puzzle the most austere of the Sunday legislators to assign any valid reason for opposing so sensible a proposition. The Museum contains rich specimens from all the vast museums and repositories of Nature, and rare and curious fragments of the mighty works of art, in bygone ages: all calculated to awaken contemplation and inquiry, and to tend to the enlightenment and improvement of the people. But attendants would be necessary, and a few men would be employed upon the Sabbath. They certainly would; but how many? Why, if the British Museum, and the National Gallery, and the Gallery of Practical Science, and every other exhibition in London, from which knowledge is to be derived and information gained, were to be thrown open on a Sunday afternoon, not fifty people would be required to preside over the whole: and it would take treble the number to enforce a Sabbath bill in any three populous parishes.

I should like to see some large field, or open piece of ground, in every outskirt of London, exhibiting each Sunday evening on a larger scale, the scene of the little country meadow. I should like to see the time arrive, when a man's attendance to his religious duties might be left to that religious feeling which most men possess in a greater or less degree, but which was never forced into the breast of any man by menace or restraint. I should like to see the time when Sunday might be looked forward to, as a recognised day of relaxation and enjoyment, and when every man might feel, what few men do now, that religion is not incompatible with rational pleasure and needful recreation.

How different a picture would the streets and public places then present! The museums, and repositories of scientific and useful inventions, would be crowded with ingenious mechanics and industrious artisans, all anxious for information, and all unable to procure it at any other time. The spacious saloons would be swarming with practical men: humble in appearance, but destined, perhaps, to become the greatest inventors and philosophers of their age. The labourers who now lounge away the day in idleness and intoxication, would be seen hurrying along, with cheerful faces and clean attire, not to the close and smoky atmosphere of the public-house, but to the fresh and airy fields. Fancy the pleasant scene. Throngs of people, pouring out from the lanes and alleys of the metropolis, to various places of common resort at some short distance from the town, to join in the refreshing sports and exercises of the day—the children gambolling in crowds upon the grass, the mothers looking on, and enjoying themselves the little game they seem only to direct; other parties strolling along some pleasant walks, or reposing in the shade of the stately trees; others again intent upon their different amusements. Nothing should be heard on all sides, but the sharp stroke of the bat as it sent the ball skimming along the ground, the clear ring of the quoit as it struck upon the iron peg: the noisy murmur of many voices, and the loud shout of mirth and delight, which would awaken the echoes far and wide, till the fields rung with it. The day would pass away, in a series of enjoyments which would awaken no painful reflections when night arrived; for they would be calculated to bring with them, only health and contentment. The young would lose that dread of religion, which the sour austerity of its professors too often inculcates in youthful bosoms; and the old would find less difficulty in persuading them to respect its observances. The drunken and dissipated, deprived of any excuse for their misconduct, would no longer excite pity but disgust. Above all, the more ignorant and humble class of men, who now partake of many of the bitters of life, and taste but few of its sweets, would naturally feel attachment and respect for that code of morality, which, regarding the many hardships of their station, strove to alleviate its rigours, and endeavoured to soften its asperity.

This is what Sunday might be made, and what it might be made without impiety or profanation. The wise and beneficent Creator who places men upon earth, requires that they shall perform the duties of that station of life to which they are called, and He can never intend that the more a man strives to discharge those duties, the more he shall be debarred from happiness and enjoyment. Let those who have six days in the week for all the world's pleasures, appropriate the seventh to fasting and gloom, either for their own sins or those of other people, if they like to bewail them; but let those who employ their six days in a worthier manner, devote their seventh to a different purpose. Let divines set the example of true morality: preach it to their flocks in the morning, and dismiss them to enjoy true rest in the afternoon; and let them select for their text, and let Sunday legislators take for their motto, the words which fell from the lips of that Master, whose precepts they misconstrue, and whose lessons they pervert—"The Sabbath was made for man, and not man to serve the Sabbath".

Bentley's Miscellany "Extraordinary Gazette"

Bentley's Miscellany "Extraordinary Gazette"

by Boz. 1837

Speech of His Mightiness on opening the Second Number of Bentley's Miscellany, edited by "Boz"

On Wednesday, the first of February, "the House" (of Bentley) met for the despatch of business, in pursuance of the Proclamation inserted by authority in all the Morning, Evening, and Weekly Papers, appointing that day for the publication of the Second Number of the Miscellany, edited by "Boz".

His Mightiness the Editor, in his progress to New Burlington-street, received with the utmost affability the numerous petitions of the crossing-sweepers; and was repeatedly and loudly hailed by the cab men on the different stands in the line of road through which he passed. His Mightiness appeared in the highest possible spirits; and immediately after his arrival at the House, delivered himself of the following most gracious speech:—

"My Lords, Ladies, and Gentlemen,

"In calling upon you to deliberate on the various important matters which I have now to submit to your consideration, I rely with entire confidence on that spirit of good-will and kindness of which I have more than once taken occasion to express my sense; and which I am but too happy to acknowledge again.

"It has been the constant aim of my policy to preserve peace in your minds, and promote merriment in your hearts; to set before you the scenes and characters of real life in all their endless diversity; occasionally (I hope) to instruct, always to amuse, and never to offend. I trust I may refer you to my Pickwickian measures, already taken and still in progress, in confirmation of this assurance.

"In further proof of my sincere anxiety for the amusement and lightheartedness of the community, let me direct your particular attention to the volume I now lay before you, which contains no fewer than twenty-one reports, of greater or less extent, from most eminent, active, and intelligent commissioners. I cannot but anticipate that when you shall have given an attentive perusal to this general report on Periodical Literature, you will be seized with an eager and becoming desire to possess yourselves of all the succeeding numbers,—a desire on which too much praise and encouragement can never be bestowed.

"Gentlemen of the Reviews,

"I have directed the earliest copies of every monthly number to be laid before you. They shall be framed with the strictest regard to the taste and wishes of the people; and I am confident that I may rely on your zealous and impartial co-operation in the public service.

"The accounts and estimates of the first number have been made out; and I am happy to inform you that the state of the revenue as compared with the expenditure (great as the latter has been, and must necessarily continue to be) is most satisfactory; in fact, that a surplus of considerable extent has been already realised. It affords me much pleasure to reflect that not the smallest difficulty will arise, in the appropriation of it.

"My Lords, Ladies And Gentlemen,

"I continue to receive from Foreign Powers, undeniable assurances of their disinterested regard and esteem. The free and independent

States of America have done me the honour to reprint my Sketches, gratuitously; and to circulate them throughout the Possessions of the British Crown in India, without charging me anything at all. I think I shall recognize Don Carlos if I ever meet him in the street; and I am sure I shall at once know the King of the French, for I have seen him before.

"I deeply lament the ferment and agitation of the public mind in Ireland, which was occasioned by the inadequate supply of the first number of this Miscellany. I deplore the outrages which were committed by an irritated and disappointed populace on the shop of the agent; and the violent threats which were directed against him, personally, on his stating his inability to comply with their exorbitant demands. I derive great satisfaction from reflecting that the promptest and most vigorous measures were instantaneously taken to repress the tumult. A large detachment of Miscellanies was levied and shipped with all possible despatch; and I have it in my power to state, that, although the excitement has not yet wholly subsided, it has been, by these means, materially allayed. I have every reason to hope that the arrangements since made with my agent in the Port of Dublin, render any recurrence of the disturbances extremely improbable, and will effectually prevent their breaking out afresh.

"I view with heartfelt satisfaction, the loyal and peaceable demeanour of the people of Scotland; who, although they experienced a similar provocation to outrage and rebellion, were content to wait until fresh supplies could be forwarded per mail and steam.

"I feel unfeigned pleasure in bearing similar testimony to the forbearing disposition and patriotic feeling of the hardy mountaineers in the Principality of Wales.

"I have concluded treaties on the most advantageous terms, not only with the powers whose names are already known to you, but with others, to whom it might prove disadvantageous to the public service to make any more direct reference at present. I have laboured, and shall continue to labour, most earnestly and zealously for your pleasure and enjoyment; and, surrounded as I am, by talent and ability, I look most confidently to your approval and support."

NOTE OF THE REPORTER.

His Mightiness incorporated with his speech on general topics, some especial reference to one *Oliver Twist*. Not distinctly understanding the allusion, we have abstained from giving it.

THE MUDFOG PAPERS

THE MUDFOG PAPERS

PUBLIC LIFE OF MR. TULRUMBLE
ONCE MAYOR OF MUDFOG

MUDFOG IS A PLEASANT TOWN—a remarkably pleasant town—situated in a charming hollow by the side of a river, from which river, Mudfog derives an agreeable scent of pitch, tar, coals, and rope-yarn, a roving population in oilskin hats, a pretty steady influx of drunken barge-men, and a great many other maritime advantages. There is a good deal of water about Mudfog, and yet it is not exactly the sort of town for a watering-place, either. Water is a perverse sort of element at the best of times, and in Mudfog it is particularly so. In winter, it comes oozing down the streets and tumbling over the fields,—nay, rushes into the very cellars and kitchens of the houses, with a lavish prodigality that might well be dispensed with; but in the hot summer weather it *will* dry up, and turn green: and, although green is a very good colour in its way, especially in grass, still it certainly is not becoming to water; and it cannot be denied that the beauty of Mud- fog is rather impaired, even by this trifling circumstance. Mudfog is a healthy place—very healthy ;—damp, perhaps, but none the worse for that. It's quite a mistake to suppose that damp is unwholesome: plants thrive best in damp situations, and why shouldn't men? The inhabitants of Mudfog are unanimous in asserting that there exists not a finer race of people on the face of the earth; here we have an indisputable and veracious contradiction of the vulgar error at once. So, admitting Mudfog to be damp, we distinctly state that it is salubrious.

The town of Mudfog is extremely picturesque. Limehouse and Ratcliff Highway are both something like it, but they give you a very faint idea of Mudfog. There are a great many more public houses in Mudfog—more than in Ratcliff Highway and Limehouse put together. The public buildings, too, are very imposing. We consider the town-hall one of the finest specimens of shed architecture, extant: it is a combination of the pig-sty and tea-garden-box orders; and the simplicity of its design is of surpassing beauty. The idea of placing a large window on one side of the door, and a small one on the other, is particularly happy. There is a fine old Doric beauty, too, about the padlock and scraper, which is strictly in keeping with the general effect.

In this room do the mayor and corporation of Mudfog assemble together in solemn council for the public weal. Seated on the massive wooden benches, which, with the table in the centre, form the only furniture of the whitewashed apartment, the sage men of Mudfog spend hour after hour in grave deliberation. Here they settle at what hour of the night the public-houses shall be closed, at what hour of the morning they shall be permitted to open, how soon it shall be lawful for people to eat their dinner on church-days, and other great political questions; and sometimes, long after silence has fallen on the town, and the distant lights from the shops and houses have ceased to twinkle, like far-off stars, to the sight of the boatmen on the river, the illumination in the two unequal-sized windows of the town-hall, warns the inhabitants of Mudfog that its little body of legislators, like a larger and better-known body of the same genus, a great deal more noisy, and not a whit more profound, are patriotically dozing away in company, far into the night, for their country's good.

Among this knot of sage and learned men, no one was so eminently distinguished, during many years, for the quiet modesty of his appearance and demeanour, as Nicholas Tulrumble, the well-known coal-dealer. However exciting the subject of discussion, however animated the tone of the debate, or however warm the personalities exchanged, (and even in Mudfog we get personal sometimes,) Nicholas Tulrumble was always the same. To say truth, Nicholas, being an industrious man, and always up betimes, was apt to fall asleep when a debate began, and to remain asleep till it was over, when he would wake up very much refreshed, and give his vote with the greatest complacency. The fact was, that Nicholas Tulrumble, knowing that everybody there had made up his mind beforehand, considered the talking as just a long botheration about nothing at all; and to the present hour it remains a question, whether, on this point at all events, Nicholas Tulrumble was not pretty near right.

Time, which strews a man's head with silver, sometimes fills his pockets with gold. As he gradually performed one good office for Nicholas Tulrumble, he was obliging enough, not to omit the other. Nicholas began life in a wooden tenement of four feet square, with a capital of two and ninepence, and a stock in trade of three bushels and a-half of coals, exclusive of the large lump which hung, by way of sign-board, outside. Then he enlarged the shed, and kept a truck; then he left the shed, and the truck too, and started a donkey and a Mrs. Tulrumble; then he moved again and set up a cart; the cart was soon afterwards exchanged for a waggon; and so he went on like his great predecessor Whittington—only without a cat for a partner—increasing in wealth and fame, until at last he gave up business altogether, and retired with Mrs. Tulrumble and family to Mudfog Hall, which he had himself erected, on something which he attempted to delude himself into the belief was a hill, about a quarter of a mile distant from the town of Mudfog.

About this time, it began to be murmured in Mudfog that Nicholas Tulrumble was growing vain and haughty; that prosperity and success had corrupted the simplicity of his manners, and tainted the natural goodness of his heart; in short, that he was setting up for a public character, and a great gentleman, and affected to look down upon his old companions with compassion and contempt. Whether these reports were at the time well-founded, or not, certain it is that Mrs. Tulrumble very shortly afterwards started a four-wheel chaise, driven by a tall postilion in a yellow cap,—that Mr. Tulrumble junior took to smoking cigars, and calling the footman a "feller",—and that Mr. Tulrumble from that time forth, was no more seen in his old seat in the chimney-corner of the Lighterman's Arms at night. This looked bad; but, more than this, it began to be observed that Mr. Nicholas Tulrumble attended the corporation meetings more frequently than heretofore; and he no longer went to sleep as he had done for so many years, but propped his eyelids open with his two forefingers; that he read the newspapers by himself at home; and that he was in the habit of indulging abroad in distant and mysterious allusions to "masses of people", and "the property of the country", and "productive power", and "the monied interest": all of which denoted and proved that Nicholas Tulrumble was either mad, or worse; and it puzzled the good people of Mudfog amazingly.

At length, about the middle of the month of October, Mr. Tulrumble and family went up to London; the middle of October being, as Mrs. Tulrumble informed her acquaintance in Mudfog, the very height of the fashionable season.

Somehow or other, just about this time, despite the health-pre serving air of Mudfog, the Mayor died. It was a most extraordinary circumstance; he had lived in Mudfog for eighty-five years. The corporation didn't understand it at all; indeed it was with great difficulty that one old gentleman, who was a great stickler for forms, was dissuaded from proposing a vote of censure on such unaccountable conduct. Strange as it was, however, die he did, without taking the slightest notice of the corporation; and the corporation were imperatively called upon to elect his successor. So, they met for the purpose; and being very full of Nicholas Tulrumble just then, and Nicholas Tulrumble being a very important man, they elected him, and wrote off to London by the very next post to acquaint Nicholas Tulrumble with his new elevation.

Now, it being November time, and Mr. Nicholas Tulrumble being in the capital, it fell out that he was present at the Lord Mayor's show and dinner, at sight of the glory and splendour whereof, he, Mr. Tulrumble, was greatly mortified, inasmuch as the reflection would force itself on his mind, that, had he been born in London instead of in Mudfog, he might have been a Lord Mayor too, and have patronized the judges, and been affable to the Lord Chancellor, and friendly with the Premier, and coldly condescending to the Secretary to the Treasury, and have dined with a flag behind his back, and done a great many other acts and deeds which unto Lord Mayors of London peculiarly appertain. The more he thought of the Lord Mayor, the more enviable a personage he seemed. To be a King was all very well; but what was the King to the Lord Mayor! When the King made a speech, everybody knew it was somebody else's writing; whereas here was the Lord Mayor, talking away for half an hour—all out of his own head—amidst the enthusiastic applause of the whole company, while it was notorious that the King might talk to his parliament till he was black in the face without getting so much as a single cheer. As all these reflections passed through the mind of Mr. Nicholas Tulrumble, the Lord Mayor of London appeared to him the greatest sovereign on the face of the earth, beating the Emperor of Russia all to nothing, and leaving the Great Mogul immeasurably behind.

Mr. Nicholas Tulrumble was pondering over these things, and inwardly cursing the fate which had pitched his coal-shed in Mudfog, when the letter of the corporation was put into his hand. A crimson flush mantled over his face as he read it, for visions of brightness were already dancing before his imagination.

"My dear," said Mr. Tulrumble to his wife, "they have elected me, Mayor of Mudfog."

"Lor-a-mussy!" said Mrs. Tulrumble "why what's become of old Sniggs?"

"The late Mr. Sniggs, Mrs. Tulrumble," said Mr. Tulrumble sharply, for he by no means approved of the notion of unceremoniously designating a gentleman who filled the high office of Mayor, as "Old Sniggs",— "The late Mr. Sniggs, Mrs. Tulrumble, is dead."

The communication was very unexpected; but Mrs. Tulrumble only ejaculated "Lor-a-mussy!" once again, as if a Mayor were a mere ordinary Christian, at which Mr. Tulrumble frowned gloomily.

"What a pity 'tan't in London, ain't it?" said Mrs. Tulrumble after a short pause: "what a pity 'tan't in London, where you might have had a show."

"I *might* have a show in Mudfog, if I thought proper, I apprehend," said Mr. Tulrumble mysteriously.

"Lor! so you might, I declare," replied Mrs. Tulrumble.

"And a good one too," said Mr. Tulrumble.

"Delightful!" exclaimed Mrs. Tulrumble.

"One which would rather astonish the ignorant people down there," said Mr. Tulrumble.

"It would kill them with envy," said Mrs. Tulrumble.

So it was agreed that his Majesty's lieges in Mudfog should be astonished with splendour, and slaughtered with envy, and that such a show should take place as had never been seen in that town, or in any other town before,—no, not even in London itself.

On the very next day after the receipt of the letter, down came the tall postilion in a post-chaise,—not upon one of the horses, but inside— actually inside the chaise,—and, driving up to the very door of the town-hall, where the corporation were assembled, delivered a letter, written by the Lord knows who, and signed by Nicholas Tulrumble, in which Nicholas said, all through four sides of closely-written, gilt-edged, hot-pressed, Bath post letter paper, that he responded to the call of his fellow-townsmen with feelings of heartfelt delight; that he accepted the arduous office which their confidence had imposed upon him; that they would never find him shrinking from the discharge of his duty; that he would endeavour to execute his functions with all that dignity which their magnitude and importance demanded; and a great deal more to the same effect. But even this was not all. The tall postilion produced from his right-hand top-boot, a damp copy of that afternoon's number of the county paper; and there, in large type, running the whole length of the very first column, was a long address from Nicholas Tulrumble to the inhabitants of Mudfog, in which he said that he cheerfully complied with their requisition, and, in short, as if to prevent any mistake about the matter, told them over again what a grand fellow he meant to be, in very much the same terms as those in which he had already told them all about the matter in his letter.

The corporation stared at one another very hard at all this, and then looked as if for explanation to the tall postilion; but as the tall postilion was intently contemplating the gold tassel on the top of his yellow cap, and could have afforded no explanation whatever, even if his thoughts had been entirely disengaged, they contented themselves with coughing very dubiously, and looking very grave. The tall postilion then delivered another letter, in which Nicholas Tulrumble informed the corporation, that he intended repairing to the town-hall, in grand state and gorgeous procession, on the Monday afternoon next ensuing. At this the corporation looked still more solemn; but, as the epistle wound up with a formal invitation to the whole body to dine with the Mayor on that day, at Mudfog Hall, Mudfog Hill, Mudfog, they began to see the fun of the thing directly, and sent back their compliments, and they'd be sure to come.

Now there happened to be in Mudfog, as somehow or other there does happen to be, in almost every town in the British dominions, and perhaps in foreign dominions too—we think it very likely, but, being no great traveller, cannot distinctly say—there happened to be, in Mudfog, a merry-tempered, pleasant-faced, good-for-nothing sort of vagabond, with an invincible dislike to manual labour, and an unconquerable attachment to strong beer and spirits, whom everybody knew, and nobody, except his wife, took the trouble to quarrel with, who inherited from his ancestors the appellation of Edward Twigger, and rejoiced in the *sobriquet* of Bottle-nosed Ned. He was drunk upon the average once a day, and penitent upon an equally fair calculation once a month; and when he was penitent, he was invariably in the very last stage of maudlin intoxication. He was a ragged, roving, roaring kind of fellow, with a burly form, a sharp wit, and a ready head, and could turn his hand to anything when he chose to do it. He was by no means opposed to hard labour on principle, for he would work away at a cricket-match by the day together,— running, and catching, and batting, and bowling, and revelling in toil

which would exhaust a galley-slave. He would have been invaluable
to a fire-office; never was a man with such a natural taste for pumping
engines, running up ladders, and throwing furniture out of two-pair-
of-stairs' windows: nor was this the only element in which he was
at home; he was a humane society in himself, a portable drag, an
animated life-preserver, and had saved more people, in his time, from
drowning, than the Plymouth life-boat, or Captain Manby's apparatus.
With all these qualifications, notwithstanding his dissipation, Bottle-
nosed Ned was a general favourite; and the authorities of Mudfog,
remembering his numerous services to the population, allowed him
in return to get drunk in his own way, without the fear of stocks, fine,
or imprisonment. He had a general licence, and he showed his sense
of the compliment by making the most of it.

We have been thus particular in describing the character and avocations
of Bottle-nosed Ned, because it enables us to introduce a fact politely,
without hauling it into the reader's presence with indecent haste by the
head and shoulders, and brings us very naturally to relate, that on the very
same evening on which Mr. Nicholas Tulrumble and family returned to
Mudfog, Mr. Tulrumble's new secretary, just imported from London, with
a pale face and light whiskers, thrust his head down to the very bottom of
his neckcloth-tie, in at the taproom door of the Lighterman's Arms, and
inquiring whether one Ned Twigger was luxuriating within, announced
himself as the bearer of a message from Nicholas Tulrumble, Esquire,
requiring Mr. Twigger's immediate attendance at the hall, on private and
particular business. It being by no means Mr. Twigger's interest to affront
the Mayor, he rose from the fireplace with a slight sigh, and followed the
light-whiskered secretary through the dirt and wet of Mudfog streets, up
to Mudfog Hall, without further ado.

Mr. Nicholas Tulrumble was seated in a small cavern with a sky light,
which he called his library, sketching out a plan of the procession on
a large sheet of paper; and into the cavern the secretary ushered Ned
Twigger.

"Well, Twigger!" said Nicholas Tulrumble, condescendingly.

There was a time when Twigger would have replied, "Well, Nick!" but that was in the days of the truck, and a couple of years before the donkey; so, he only bowed.

"I want you to go into training, Twigger," said Mr. Tulrumble.

"What for, sir?" inquired Ned, with a stare.

"Hush, hush, Twigger!" said the Mayor. "Shut the door, Mr. Jennings. Look here, Twigger."

As the Mayor said this, he unlocked a high closet, and disclosed a complete suit of brass armour, of gigantic dimensions.

"I want you to wear this next Monday, Twigger," said the Mayor.

"Bless your heart and soul, sir!" replied Ned, "you might as well ask me to wear a seventy-four pounder, or a cast-iron boiler."

"Nonsense, Twigger, nonsense!" said the Mayor.

"I couldn't stand under it, sir," said Twigger; "it would make mashed potatoes of me, if I attempted it."

"Pooh, pooh, Twigger!" returned the Mayor. "I tell you I have seen it done with my own eyes, in London, and the man wasn't half such a man as you are, either."

"I should as soon have thought of a man's wearing the case of an eight-day clock to save his linen," said Twigger, casting a look of apprehension at the brass suit.

"It's the easiest thing in the world," rejoined the Mayor.

"It's nothing," said Mr. Jennings.

"When you're used to it," added Ned.

"You do it by degrees," said the Mayor. "You would begin with one piece to-morrow, and two the next day, and so on, till you had got it all on. Mr. Jennings, give Twigger a glass of rum. Just try the breast-plate, Twigger. Stay; take another glass of rum first. Help me to lift it, Mr. Jennings. Stand firm, Twigger! There!—it isn't half as heavy as it looks, is it?"

Twigger was a good strong, stout fellow; so, after a great deal of staggering, he managed to keep himself up, under the breast-plate, and even contrived, with the aid of another glass of rum, to walk about in it, and the gauntlets into the bargain. He made a trial of the helmet, but was not equally successful, inasmuch as he tipped over instantly,—an accident which Mr. Tulrumble clearly demonstrated to be occasioned by his not having a counteracting weight of brass on his legs.

"Now, wear that with grace and propriety on Monday next," said Tulrumble "and I'll make your fortune."

"I'll try what I can do, sir," said Twigger.

"It must be kept a profound secret," said Tulrumble.

"Of course, sir," replied Twigger.

"And you must be sober," said Tulrumble; "perfectly sober."

Mr. Twigger at once solemnly pledged himself to be as sober as a judge, and Nicholas Tulrumble was satisfied, although, had we been Nicholas, we should certainly have exacted some promise of a more specific nature; inasmuch as, having attended the Mudfog assizes in the evening more than once, we can solemnly testify to having seen judges with very strong symptoms of dinner under their wigs. However, that's neither here nor there.

The next day, and the day following, and the day after that, Ned Twigger was securely locked up in the small cavern with the skylight, hard at work at the armour. With every additional piece he could manage to stand upright in, he had an additional glass of rum; and at last, after many partial suffocations, he contrived to get on the whole suit, and to stagger up and down the room in it, like an intoxicated effigy from Westminster Abbey.

Never was man so delighted as Nicholas Tulrumble; never was woman so charmed as Nicholas Tulrumble's wife. Here was a sight for the common people of Mudfog! A live man in brass armour! Why, they would go wild with wonder!

The day—*the* Monday—arrived.

If the morning had been made to order, it couldn't have been better adapted to the purpose. They never showed a better fog in London on Lord Mayor's day, than enwrapped the town of Mudfog on that eventful occasion. It had risen slowly and surely from the green and stagnant water with the first light of morning, until it reached a little above the lamp-post tops; and there it had stopped, with a sleepy, sluggish obstinacy, which bade defiance to the sun, who had got up very blood-shot about the eyes, as if he had been at a drinking-party over-night, and was doing his day's work with the worst possible grace. The thick damp mist hung over the town like a huge gauze curtain. All was dim and dismal. The church steeples had bidden a temporary adieu to the world below; and every object of lesser importance—houses, barns, hedges, trees, and barges—had all taken the veil.

The church-clock struck one. A cracked trumpet from the front garden of Mudfog Hall produced a feeble flourish, as if some asthmatic person had coughed into it accidentally; the gate flew open, and out came a gentleman, on a moist-sugar coloured charger, intended to represent a herald, but bearing a much stronger resemblance to a court-card on horseback. This was one of the Circus people, who always came down to Mudfog at that time of the year, and who had been engaged by Nicholas Tulrumble expressly for the occasion. There was the horse, whisking his tail about, balancing himself on his hind-legs, and flourishing away with his fore-feet, in a manner which would have gone to the hearts and souls of any reasonable crowd. But a Mudfog crowd never was a reasonable one, and in all probability never will be. Instead of scattering the very fog with their shouts, as they ought most indubitably to have done, and were fully intended to do, by Nicholas Tulrumble, they no sooner recognised the herald, than they began to growl forth the most unqualified disapprobation at the bare notion of his riding like any other man. If he had come out on his head indeed, or jumping through a hoop, or flying through a red-hot drum, or even standing on one leg with his other foot in his mouth, they might have had something to say to him; but for a professional gentleman to sit astride in the saddle, with his feet in the stirrups, was rather too good a joke. So, the herald was a decided failure, and the crowd hooted with great energy, as he pranced in gloriously away.

On the procession came. We are afraid to say how many supernumeraries there were, in striped shirts and black velvet caps, to imitate the

London waterman, or how many base imitations of running-footmen, or how many banners, which, owing to the heaviness of the atmosphere, could by no means be prevailed on to display their inscriptions: still less do we feel disposed to relate how the men who played the wind instruments, looking up into the sky (we mean the fog) with musical fervour, walked through pools of water and hillocks of mud, till they covered the powdered heads of the running-footmen aforesaid with splashes, that looked curious, but not ornamental; or how the barrel-organ performer put on the wrong stop, and played one tune while the band played another; or how the horses, being used to the arena, and not to the streets, would stand still and dance, instead of going on and prancing;—all of which are matters which might be dilated upon to great advantage, but which we have not the least intention of dilating upon, not withstanding.

Oh! it was a grand and beautiful sight to behold a corporation in glass coaches, provided at the sole cost and charge of Nicholas Tulrumble, coming rolling along, like a funeral out of mourning, and to watch the attempts the corporation made to look great and solemn, when Nicholas Tulrumble himself, in the four-wheel chaise, with the tall postilion, rolled out after them, with Mr. Jennings on one side to look like a chaplain, and a supernumerary on the other, with an old life-guardsman's sabre, to imitate the sword-bearer; and to see the tears rolling down the faces of the mob as they screamed with merriment. This was beautiful! and so was the appearance of Mrs. Tulrumble and son, as they bowed with grave dignity out of their coach-window to all the dirty faces that were laughing around them: but it is not even with this that we have to do, but with the sudden stopping of the procession at another blast of the trumpet, whereat, and whereupon, a profound silence ensued, and all eyes were turned towards Mudfog Hall, in the confident anticipation of some new wonder.

"They won't laugh now, Mr. Jennings," said Nicholas Tulrumble.

"I think not, sir," said Mr. Jennings.

"See how eager they look," said Nicholas Tulrumble. "Aha! the laugh will be on our side now; eh, Mr. Jennings?"

"No doubt of that, sir," replied Mr. Jennings; and Nicholas Tulrumble, in a state of pleasurable excitement, stood up in the four-wheel chaise, and telegraphed gratification to the Mayoress behind.

While all this was going forward, Ned Twigger had descended into the kitchen of Mudfog Hall for the purpose of indulging the servants with a private view of the curiosity that was to burst upon the town; and, somehow or other, the footman was so companionable, and the housemaid so kind, and the cook so friendly, that he could not resist the offer of the first-mentioned to sit down and take something—just to drink success to master in.

So, down Ned Twigger sat himself in his brass livery on the top of the kitchen-table; and in a mug of something strong, paid for by the unconscious Nicholas Tulrumble, and provided by the companionable footman, drank success to the Mayor and his procession; and, as Ned laid by his helmet to imbibe the something strong, the companionable footman put it on his own head, to the immeasurable and unrecordable delight of the cook and housemaid. The companionable footman was very facetious to Ned, and Ned was very gallant to the cook and housemaid by turns. They were all very cosy and comfortable; and the something strong went briskly round.

At last Ned Twigger was loudly called for, by the procession people: and, having had his helmet fixed on, in a very complicated manner, by the companionable footman, and the kind housemaid, and the friendly cook, he walked gravely forth, and appeared before the multitude.

The crowd roared—it was not with wonder, it was not with surprise; it was most decidedly and unquestionably with laughter.

"What!" said Mr. Tulrumble, starting up in the four-wheel chaise. "Laughing? If they laugh at a man in real brass armour, they'd laugh when their own fathers were dying. Why doesn't he go into his place, Mr. Jennings? What's he rolling down towards us for? he has no business here!"

"I am afraid, sir—" faltered Mr. Jennings.

"Afraid of what, sir?" said Nicholas Tulrumble, looking up into the secretary's face.

"I am afraid he's drunk, sir," replied Mr. Jennings.

Nicholas Tulrumble took one look at the extraordinary figure that was bearing down upon them; and then, clasping his secretary by the arm, uttered an audible groan in anguish of spirit.

It is a melancholy fact that Mr. Twigger having full licence to demand a single glass of rum on the putting on of every piece of the armour, got, by some means or other, rather out of his calculation in the hurry and confusion of preparation, and drank about four glasses to a piece instead of one, not to mention the something strong which went on the top of it. Whether the brass armour checked the natural flow of perspiration, and thus prevented the spirit from evaporating, we are not scientific enough to know; but, whatever the cause was, Mr. Twigger no sooner found himself outside the gate of Mudfog Hall, than he also found himself in a very considerable state of intoxication; and hence his extraordinary style of progressing. This was bad enough, but, as if fate and fortune had conspired against Nicholas Tulrumble, Mr. Twigger, not having been penitent for a good calendar month, took it into his head to be most especially and particularly sentimental, just when his repentance could have been most conveniently dispensed with. Immense tears were rolling down his cheeks, and he was vainly endeavouring to conceal his grief by applying to his eyes a blue cotton pocket-handkerchief with white spots,—an article not strictly in keeping with a suit of armour some three hundred years old, or thereabouts.

"Twigger, you villain!" said Nicholas Tulrumble quite forgetting his dignity, "go back."

"Never," said Ned. "I'm a miserable wretch. I'll never leave you."

The by-standers of course received this declaration with acclamations of "That's right, Ned; don't."

"I don't intend it," said Ned, with all the obstinacy of a very tipsy man. "I'm very unhappy. I'm the wretched father of an unfortunate family; but I am very faithful, sir. I'll never leave you." Having reiterated this obliging promise, Ned proceeded in broken words to harangue the crowd upon the number of years he had lived in Mudfog, the excessive respectability of his character, and other topics of the like nature.

"Here! will anybody lead him away?" said Nicholas: "if they'll call on me afterwards, I'll reward them well."

Two or three men stepped forward, with the view of bearing Ned off, when the secretary interposed.

"Take care! take care!" said Mr. Jennings. "I beg your pardon, sir; but they'd better not go too near him, because, if he falls over, he'll certainly crush somebody."

At this hint the crowd retired on all sides to a very respectful distance, and left Ned, like the Duke of Devonshire, in a little circle of his own.

"But, Mr. Jennings," said Nicholas Tulrumble, "he'll be suffocated."

"I'm very sorry for it, sir," replied Mr. Jennings; "but nobody can get that armour off, without his own assistance. I'm quite certain of it from the way he put it on."

Here Ned wept dolefully, and shook his helmeted head, in a manner that might have touched a heart of stone; but the crowd had not hearts of stone, and they laughed heartily.

"Dear me, Mr. Jennings," said Nicholas, turning pale at the possibility of Ned's being smothered in his antique costume—"Dear me, Mr. Jennings, can nothing be done with him?"

"Nothing at all," replied Ned, "nothing at all. Gentlemen, I'm an unhappy wretch. I'm a body, gentlemen, in a brass coffin." At this poetical idea of his own conjuring up, Ned cried so much that the people began to get sympathetic, and to ask what Nicholas Tulrumble meant by putting a man into such a machine as that; and one individual in a hairy waistcoat like the top of a trunk, who had previously expressed his opinion that if Ned hadn't been a poor man, Nicholas wouldn't have dared do it, hinted at the propriety of breaking the four-wheel chaise, or Nicholas's head, or both, which last compound proposition the crowd seemed to consider a very good notion.

It was not acted upon, however, for it had hardly been, broached, when Ned Twigger's wife made her appearance abruptly in the little circle before noticed, and Ned no sooner caught a glimpse of her face and form, than from the mere force of habit he set off towards his home just as fast as his legs could carry him; and that was not very quick in the present instance either, for, however ready they might have been to carry *him*, they couldn't get on very well under the brass armour. So, Mrs. Twigger had plenty of time to denounce Nicholas Tulrumble to his face: to express her opinion that he was a decided monster; and to intimate that, if her ill-used husband sustained any personal damage from the brass armour, she would have the law of Nicholas Tulrumble for manslaughter. When she had said all this with due vehemence, she posted after Ned, who was dragging himself along as best he could, and deploring his unhappiness in most dismal tones.

What a wailing and screaming Ned's children raised when he got home at last! Mrs. Twigger tried to undo the armour, first in one place, and then in another, but she couldn't manage it; so she tumbled Ned into bed, helmet, armour, gauntlets, and all. Such a creaking as the bedstead made, under Ned's weight in his new suit! It didn't break down though; and there Ned lay, like the anonymous vessel in the Bay of Biscay, till next day, drinking barley-water, and looking miserable: and every time he groaned, his good lady said it served him right, which was all the consolation Ned Twigger got.

Nicholas Tulrumble and the gorgeous procession went on together to the town-hall, amid the hisses and groans of all the spectators, who had suddenly taken it into their heads to consider poor Ned a martyr. Nicholas was formally installed in his new office, in acknowledgment of which ceremony he delivered himself of a speech, composed by the secretary, which was very long, and no doubt very good, only the noise of the people outside prevented anybody from hearing it, but Nicholas Tulrumble himself. After which, the procession got back to Mudfog Hall any how it could; and Nicholas and the corporation sat down to dinner.

But the dinner was flat, and Nicholas was disappointed. They were such dull sleepy old fellows, that corporation. Nicholas made quite as long speeches as the Lord Mayor of London had done, nay, he said the very same things that the Lord Mayor of London had said, and the deuce a cheer the corporation gave him. There was only one man in the party who was thoroughly awake; and he was insolent, and called him Nick. Nick! What would be the consequence, thought Nicholas, of anybody presuming to call the Lord Mayor of London "Nick!" He should like to know what the sword-bearer would say to that; or the recorder, or the toast-master, or any other of the great officers of the city. They'd nick him.

But these were not the worst of Nicholas Tulrumble's doings. It they had been, he might have remained a Mayor to this day, and have talked till he lost his voice. He contracted a relish for statistics, and I got philosophical; and the statistics and the philosophy together, led him into an act which increased his unpopularity and hastened his downfall.

At the very end of the Mudfog High-street, and abutting on the river-side, stands the Jolly Boatmen, an old-fashioned low-roofed, bay-windowed house, with a bar, kitchen, and tap-room all in one, and a large fireplace with a kettle to correspond, round which the working men have congregated time out of mind on a winter's night, refreshed by draughts of good strong beer, and cheered by the sounds of a fiddle and tambourine: the Jolly Boatmen having been duly licensed by the Mayor and corporation, to scrape the fiddle and thumb the tambourine from time, whereof the memory of the oldest inhabitants goeth not to the contrary. Now Nicholas Tulrumble had been reading pamphlets on crime, and parliamentary reports,—or had made the secretary read them to him, which is the same thing in effect,—and he at once perceived that this fiddle and tambourine must have done more to demoralize Mudfog, than any other operating causes that ingenuity could imagine. So he read up for the subject, and determined to come out on the corporation with a burst, the very next time the licence was applied for.

The licensing day came, and the red-faced landlord of the Jolly Boatmen walked into the town-hall, looking as jolly as need be, having actually put on an extra fiddle for that night, to commemorate the anniversary of the Jolly Boatmen's music licence. It was applied for in due form, and was just about to be granted as a matter of course, when up rose Nicholas Tulrumble, and drowned the astonished corporation in a torrent of eloquence. He descanted in glowing terms upon the increasing depravity of his native town of Mudfog, and the excesses committed by its population. Then, he related how shocked he had been, to see barrels of beer sliding down into the cellar of the Jolly Boatmen week after week; and how he had sat at a window opposite the Jolly Boatmen for two days together, to count the people who went in for beer between the hours of twelve and one o'clock alone—which, by-the-bye, was the time at which the great majority of the Mudfog people dined. Then, he went on to state, how the number of people who came out with beer-jugs, averaged twenty-one in five minutes, which, being multiplied by twelve, gave two hundred and fifty-two people with beer-jugs in an hour, and multiplied again by fifteen (the number of hours during which the house was open daily) yielded three thousand seven hundred and eighty people with beer-jugs per day, or twenty-six thousand four hundred and sixty people with beer-jugs per week. Then he proceeded to show that a tambourine and moral degradation were synonymous terms, and a fiddle and vicious propensities wholly inseparable. All these arguments he strengthened and demonstrated by frequent references to a large book with a blue cover, and sundry quotations from the Middlesex magistrates; and in the end, the corporation, who were posed with the figures, and sleepy with the speech, and sadly in want of dinner into the bargain, yielded the palm to Nicholas Tulrumble, and refused the music licence to the Jolly Boatmen.

But although Nicholas triumphed, his triumph was short. He carried on the war against beer-jugs and fiddles, forgetting the time when he was glad to drink out of the one, and to dance to the other, till the people hated, and his old friends shunned him. He grew tired of the lonely magnificence of Mudfog Hall, and his heart yearned towards the Lighterman's Arms. He wished he had never set up as a public man, and sighed for the good old times of the coal-shop, and the chimney corner.

At length old Nicholas, being thoroughly miserable, took heart of grace, paid the secretary a quarter's wages in advance, and packed him off to London by the next coach. Having taken this step, he put his hat on his head, and his pride in his pocket, and walked down to the old room at the Lighterman's Arms. There were only two of the old fellows there, and they looked coldly on Nicholas as he proffered his hand.

"Are you going to put down pipes, Mr. Tulrumble?" said one.

"Or trace the progress of crime to 'bacca?" growled another.

"Neither," replied Nicholas Tulrumble, shaking hands with them both, whether they would or not. "I've come down to say that I'm very sorry for having made a fool of myself, and that I hope you'll give me up, the old chair, again."

The old fellows opened their eyes, and three or four more old fellows opened the door, to whom Nicholas, with tears in his eyes, thrust out his hand too, and told the same story. They raised a shout of joy, that made the bells in the ancient church-tower vibrate again, and wheeling the old chair into the warm corner, thrust old Nicholas down into it, and ordered in the very largest-sized bowl of hot punch, with an unlimited number of pipes, directly.

The next day, the Jolly Boatmen got the licence, and the next night, old Nicholas and Ned Twigger's wife led off a dance to the music of the fiddle and tambourine, the tone of which seemed mightily improved by a little rest, for they never had played so merrily before. Ned Twigger was in the very height of his glory, and he danced hornpipes, and balanced chairs on his chin, and straws on his nose, till the whole company, including the corporation, were in raptures of admiration at the brilliancy of his acquirements.

Mr. Tulrumble, junior, couldn't make up his mind to be anything but magnificent, so he went up to London and drew bills on his father; and when he had overdrawn, and got into debt, he grew penitent, and came home again.

As to old Nicholas, he kept his word, and having had six weeks of public life, never tried it any more. He went to sleep in the town-hall at the very next meeting; and, in full proof of his sincerity, has requested us to write this faithful narrative. We wish it could have the effect of reminding the Tulrumble of another sphere, that puffed-up conceit is not dignity, and that snarling at the little pleasures they were once glad to enjoy, because they would rather forget the times when they were of lower station, renders them objects of contempt and ridicule.

This is the first time we have published any of our gleanings from this particular source. Perhaps, at some future period, we may venture to open the chronicles of Mudfog.

Full Report of the First Meeting of the Mudfog Association

For the Advancement of Everything

We have made the most unparalleled and extraordinary exertions to place before our readers a complete and accurate account of the proceedings at the late grand meeting of the Mudfog Association, holden in the town of Mudfog; it affords us great happiness to lay the result before them, in the shape of various communications received from our able, talented, and graphic correspondent, expressly sent down for the purpose, who has immortalized us, himself, Mudfog, and the association, all at one and the same time. We have been, indeed, for some days unable to determine who will transmit the greatest name to posterity; ourselves, who sent our correspondent down; our correspondent, who wrote an account of the matter; or the association, who gave our correspondent something to write about. We rather incline to the opinion that we are the greatest man of the party, inasmuch as the notion of an exclusive and authentic report originated with us; this may be prejudice; it may arise from a prepossession on our part in our own favour. Be it so. We have no doubt that every gentleman concerned in this mighty assemblage is troubled with the same complaint in a greater or less degree; and it is a consolation to us to know that we have at least this feeling in common with the great scientific stars, the brilliant and extraordinary luminaries, whose speculations we record.

We give our correspondent's letters in the order in which they reached us. Any attempt at amalgamating them into one beautiful whole, would only destroy that glowing tone, that dash of wildness, and rich vein of picturesque interest, which pervade them throughout.

"*Mudfog, Monday night, seven o'clock.*

"We are in a state of great excitement here. Nothing is spoken of, but the approaching meeting of the association. The inn-doors are thronged with waiters anxiously looking for the expected arrivals; and the numerous bills which are wafered up in the windows of private houses, intimating that there are beds to let within, give the streets a very animated and cheerful appearance, the wafers being of a great variety of colours, and the monotony of printed inscriptions being relieved by every possible size and style of hand-writing. It is confidently rumoured that Professors Snore, Doze, and Wheezy have engaged three beds and a sitting-room at the Pig and Tinder-box. I give you the rumour as it has reached me; but I cannot, as yet, vouch for its accuracy. The moment I have been enabled to obtain any certain information upon this interesting point, you may depend upon receiving it."

"*Half-past seven.*

"I have just returned from a personal interview with the landlord of the Pig and Tinder-box. He speaks confidently of the probability of Professors Snore, Doze, and Wheezy taking up their residence at his house during the sitting of the association, but denies that the beds have been yet engaged; in which representation he is confirmed by the chambermaid—a girl of artless manners, and interesting appearance. The boots denies that it is at all likely that Professors Snore, Doze, and Wheezy will put up here; but I have reason to believe that this man has been suborned by the proprietor of the Original Pig, which is the opposition hotel. Amidst such conflicting testimony it is difficult to arrive at the real truth; but you may depend upon receiving authentic information upon this point the moment the fact is ascertained. The excitement still continues. A boy fell through the window of the pastrycook's shop at the corner of the High-street about half an hour ago, which has occasioned much confusion. The general impression is, that it was an accident. Pray heaven it may prove so!"

"*Tuesday, noon.*

"At an early hour this morning the bells of all the churches struck seven o'clock; the effect of which, in the present lively state of the town, was extremely singular. While I was at breakfast, a yellow gig, drawn by a dark grey horse, with a patch of white over his right eyelid, proceeded at a rapid pace in the direction of the Original Pig stables; it is currently reported that this gentleman has arrived here for the purpose of attending the association, and, from what I have heard, I consider it extremely probable, although nothing decisive is yet known regarding him. You may conceive the anxiety with which we are all looking forward to the arrival of the four o'clock coach this afternoon.

"Notwithstanding the excited state of the populace, no outrage has yet been committed, owing to the admirable discipline and discretion of the police, who are nowhere to be seen. A barrel-organ is playing opposite my window, and groups of people, offering fish and vegetables for sale, parade the streets. With these exceptions everything quiet, and I trust will continue so."

"*Five o'clock.*

"It is now ascertained, beyond all doubt, that Professors Snore, Doze, and Wheezy will *not* repair to the Pig and Tinder-box, but have actually engaged apartments at the Original Pig. This intelligence is *exclusive*; and I leave you and your readers to draw their own inferences from it. Why Professor Wheezy, of all people in the world, should repair to the Original Pig in preference to the Pig and Tinder-box, it is not easy to conceive. The professor is a man who should be above all such petty feelings. Some people here openly impute treachery, and a distinct breach of faith to Professors Snore and Doze; while others, again, are disposed to acquit them of any culpability in the transaction, and to insinuate that the blame rests solely with Professor Wheezy. I own that I incline to the latter opinion; and although it gives me great pain to speak in terms of censure or disapprobation of a man of such transcendent genius and acquirements, still I am bound to say that, if my suspicions be well founded, and if all the reports which have reached my ears be true, I really do not well know what to make of the matter.

"Mr. Slug, so celebrated for his statistical researches, arrived this afternoon by the four o'clock stage. His complexion is a dark purple, and he has a habit of sighing constantly. He looked extremely well, and appeared in high health and spirits. Mr. Woodensconce also came down in the same conveyance. The distinguished gentleman was fast asleep on his arrival, and I am informed by the guard that he had been so the whole way. He was, no doubt, preparing for his approaching fatigues; but what gigantic visions must those be that flit through the brain of such a man when his body is in a state of torpidity!

"The influx of visitors increases every moment. I am told (I know not how truly) that two post-chaises have arrived at the Original Pig within the last half-hour, and I myself observed a wheelbarrow, containing three carpet bags and a bundle, entering the yard of the Pig and Tinder-box no longer ago than five minutes since. The people are still quietly pursuing their ordinary occupations; but there is a wildness in their eyes, and an unwonted rigidity in the muscles of their countenances, which shows to the observant spectator that their expectations are strained to the very utmost pitch. I fear, unless some very extraordinary arrivals take place to-night, that consequences may arise from this popular ferment, which every man of sense and feeling would deplore."

"Twenty minutes past six.

"I have just heard that the boy who fell through the pastrycook's window last night has died of the fright. He was suddenly called upon to pay three and sixpence for the damage done, and his constitution, it seems, was not strong enough to bear up against the shock. The inquest, it is said, will be held to-morrow."

"Three-quarters past seven.

"Professors Muff and Nogo have just driven up to the hotel door; they at once ordered dinner with great condescension. We are all very much delighted with the urbanity of their manners, and the ease with which they adapt themselves to the forms and ceremonies of ordinary life. Immediately on their arrival they sent for the head waiter, and privately requested him to purchase a live dog,—as cheap a one as he could meet with,—and to send him up after dinner, with a pie-board, a knife and fork, and a clean plate. It is conjectured that some experiments will be tried upon the dog to-night; if any particulars should transpire, I will forward them by express."

"Half-past eight.

"The animal has been procured. He is a pug-dog, of rather intelligent appearance, in good condition, and with very short legs. He has been tied to a curtain-peg in a dark room, and is howling dreadfully."

"Ten minutes to nine.

"The dog has just been rung for. With an instinct which would appear almost the result of reason, the sagacious animal seized the waiter by the calf of the leg when he approached to take him, and made a desperate, though ineffectual resistance. I have not been able to procure admission to the apartment occupied by the scientific gentlemen; but, judging from the sounds which reached my ears when I stood upon the landing-place outside the door, just now, I should be disposed to say that the dog had retreated growling beneath some article of furniture, and was keeping the professors at bay. This conjecture is confirmed by the testimony of the ostler, who, after peeping through the keyhole, assures me that he distinctly saw Professor Nogo on his knees, holding forth a small bottle of prussic acid, to which the animal, who was crouched beneath an arm-chair, obstinately declined to smell. You cannot imagine the feverish state of irritation we are in, lest the interests of science should be sacrificed to the prejudices of a brute creature, who is not endowed with sufficient sense to foresee the incalculable benefits which the whole human race may derive from so very slight a concession on his part."

"Nine o'clock.

"The dog's tail and ears have been sent down-stairs to be washed; from which circumstance we infer that the animal is no more. His forelegs have been delivered to the boots to be brushed, which strengthens the supposition."

"Half after ten.

"My feelings are so overpowered by what has taken place in the course of the last hour and a half, that I have scarcely strength to detail the rapid succession of events which have quite bewildered all those who are cognizant of their occurrence. It appears that the pug-dog mentioned in my last was surreptitiously obtained,—stolen, in fact,—by some person attached to the stable department, from an unmarried lady resident in this town. Frantic on discovering the loss of her favourite, the lady rushed distractedly into the street, calling in the most heart-rending and pathetic manner upon the passengers to restore her, her Augustus,—for so the deceased was named, in affectionate remembrance of a former lover of his mistress, to whom he bore a striking personal resemblance, which renders the circumstances additionally affecting. I am not yet in a condition to inform you what circumstance induced the bereaved lady to direct her steps to the hotel which had witnessed the last struggles of her *protégé*. I can only state that she arrived there, at the very instant when his detached members were passing through the passage on a small tray. Her shrieks still reverberate in my ears! I grieve to say that the expressive features of Professor Muff were much scratched and lacerated by the injured lady; and that Professor Nogo, besides sustaining several severe bites, has lost some handfuls of hair from the same cause. It must be some consolation to these gentlemen to know that their ardent attachment to scientific pursuits has alone occasioned these unpleasant consequences; for which the sympathy of a grateful country will sufficiently reward them. The unfortunate lady remains at the Pig and Tinder-box, and up to this time is reported in a very precarious state.

"I need scarcely tell you that this unlooked-for catastrophe has cast a damp and gloom upon us in the midst of our exhilaration; natural in any case, but greatly enhanced in this, by the amiable qualities of the deceased animal, who appears to have been much and deservedly respected by the whole of his acquaintance."

"Twelve o'clock.

"I take the last opportunity before sealing my parcel to inform you that the boy who fell through the pastrycook's window is not dead, as was universally believed, but alive and well. The report appears to have had its origin in his mysterious disappearance. He was found half an hour since on the premises of a sweet-stuff maker, where a raffle had been announced for a second-hand seal-skin cap and a tambourine; and where—a sufficient number of members not having been obtained at first—he had patiently waited until the list was completed. This fortunate discovery has in some degree restored our gaiety and cheerfulness. It is proposed to get up a subscription for him without delay.

Everybody is nervously anxious to see what to-morrow will bring forth. If any one should arrive in the course of the night, I have left strict directions to be called immediately. I should have sat up, in deed, but the agitating events of this day have been too much for me.

"No news yet of either of the Professors Snore, Doze, or Wheezy. It is very strange!"

"Wednesday afternoon.

"All is now over; and, upon one point at least, I am at length enabled to set the minds of your readers at rest. The three professors arrived at ten minutes after two o'clock, and, instead of taking up their quarters at the Original Pig, as it was universally understood in the course of yesterday that they would assuredly have done, drove straight to the Pig and Tinder-box, where they threw off the mask at once, and openly announced their intention of remaining. Professor Wheezy *may* reconcile this very extraordinary conduct with *his* notions of fair and equitable dealing, but I would recommend Professor Wheezy to be cautious how he presumes too far upon his well-earned reputation. How such a man as Professor Snore, or, which is still more extraordinary, such an individual as Professor Doze, can quietly allow himself to be mixed up with such proceedings as these, you will naturally inquire. Upon this head, rumour is silent; I have my speculations, but forbear to give utterance to them just now."

"Four o'clock.

"The town is filling fast; eighteenpence has been offered for a bed and refused. Several gentlemen were under the necessity last night of sleeping in the brick fields, and on the steps of doors, for which they were taken before the magistrates in a body this morning, and committed to prison as vagrants for various terms. One of these persons I understand to be a highly-respectable tinker, of great practical skill, who had forwarded a paper to the President of Section D. Mechanical Science, on the construction of pipkins with copper bottoms and safety-valves, of which report speaks highly. The incarceration of this gentleman is greatly to be regretted, as his absence will preclude any discussion on the subject.

"The bills are being taken down in all directions, and lodgings are being secured on almost any terms. I have heard of fifteen shillings a week for two rooms, exclusive of coals and attendance, but I can scarcely believe it. The excitement is dreadful. I was informed this morning that the civil authorities, apprehensive of some outbreak of popular feeling, had commanded a recruiting sergeant and two corporals to be under arms; and that, with the view of not irritating the people unnecessarily by their presence, they had been requested to take up their position before daybreak in a turnpike, distant about a quarter of a mile from the town. The vigour and promptness of these measures cannot be too highly extolled.

"Intelligence has just been brought me, that an elderly female, in a state of inebriety, has declared in the open street her intention to 'do' for Mr. Slug. Some statistical returns compiled by that gentleman, relative to the consumption of raw spirituous liquors in this place, are supposed to be the cause of the wretch's animosity. It is added that this declaration was loudly cheered by a crowd of persons who had assembled on the spot; and that one man had the boldness to designate Mr. Slug aloud by the opprobrious epithet of 'Stick-in-the-mud'! It is earnestly to be hoped that now, when the moment has arrived for their interference, the magistrates will not shrink from the exercise of that power which is vested in them by the constitution of our common country."

"Half-past ten.

"The disturbance, I am happy to inform you, has been completely quelled, and the ringleader taken into custody. She had a pail of cold water thrown over her, previous to being locked up, and expresses great contrition and uneasiness. We are all in a fever of anticipation about to-morrow; but, now that we are within a few hours of the meeting of the association, and at last enjoy the proud consciousness of having its illustrious members amongst us, I trust and hope everything may go off peaceably. I shall send you a full report of to-morrow's proceedings by the night coach."

"Eleven o'clock.

"I open my letter to say that nothing whatever has occurred since I folded it up."

"*Thursday.*

"The sun rose this morning at the usual hour. I did not observe anything particular in the aspect of the glorious planet, except that he appeared to me (it might have been a delusion of my heightened fancy) to shine with more than common brilliancy, and to shed a refulgent lustre upon the town, such as I had never observed before. This is the more extraordinary, as the sky was perfectly cloudless, and the atmosphere peculiarly fine. At half-past nine o'clock the general committee assembled, with the last year's president in the chair. The report of the council was read; and one passage, which stated that the council had corresponded with no less than three thousand five hundred and seventy-one persons, (all of whom paid their own post age,) on no fewer than seven thousand two hundred and forty-three topics, was received with a degree of enthusiasm which no efforts could suppress. The various committees and sections having been appointed, and the more formal business transacted, the great proceedings of the meeting commenced at eleven o'clock precisely. I had the happiness of occupying a most eligible position at that time, in

"SECTION A.—ZOOLOGY AND BOTANY
GREAT ROOM, PIG AND TINDER-BOX

President—Professor Snore. *Vice-Presidents*—Professors Doze and Wheezy.

"The scene at this moment was particularly striking. The sun streamed through the windows of the apartments, and tinted the whole scene with its brilliant rays, bringing out in strong relief the noble visages of the professors and scientific gentlemen, who, some with bald heads, some with red heads, some with brown heads, some with grey heads, some with black heads, some with block heads, presented a coup d'oeil which no eye-witness will readily forget. In front of these gentlemen were papers and inkstands; and round the room, on elevated benches extending as far as the forms could reach, were assembled a brilliant concourse of those lovely and elegant women for which Mudfog is justly acknowledged to be without a rival in the whole world. The contrast between their fair faces and the dark coats and trousers of the scientific gentlemen I shall never cease to remember while Memory holds her seat.

"Time having been allowed for a slight confusion, occasioned by the falling down of the greater part of the platforms, to subside, the president called on one of the secretaries to read a communication entitled 'Some remarks on the industrious fleas, with considerations on the importance of establishing infant-schools among that numerous class of society; of directing their industry to useful and practical ends; and of applying the surplus fruits thereof, towards providing for them a comfortable and respectable maintenance in their old age'.

"The author stated, that, having long turned his attention to the moral and social condition of these interesting animals, he had been induced to visit an exhibition in Regent-street, London, commonly known by the designation of 'The Industrious Fleas'. He had there seen many fleas, occupied certainly in various pursuits and avocations, but occupied, he was bound to add, in a manner which no man of well-regulated mind could fail to regard with sorrow and regret. One flea, reduced to the level of a beast of burden, was drawing about a miniature gig, containing a particularly small effigy of His Grace the Duke of Wellington; while another was staggering beneath the weight of a golden model of his great adversary Napoleon Bonaparte. Some, brought up as mountebanks and ballet-dancers, were performing a figure-dance (he regretted to observe, that, of the fleas so employed, several were females); others were in training, in a small card-board box, for pedestrians,—mere sporting characters—and two were actually engaged in the cold-blooded and barbarous occupation of duelling; a pursuit from which humanity recoiled with horror and disgust. He suggested that measures should be immediately taken to employ the labour of these fleas as part and parcel of the productive power of the country, which might easily be done by the establishment among them of infant schools and houses of industry, in which a system of virtuous education, based upon sound principles, should be observed, and moral precepts strictly inculcated. He proposed that every flea who presumed to exhibit, for hire, music, or dancing, or any species of theatrical entertainment, without a licence, should be considered a vagabond, and treated accordingly; in which respect he only placed him upon a level with the rest of mankind. He would further suggest that their labour should be placed under the control and regulation of the state, who should set apart from the profits, a fund for the support of superannuated or disabled fleas, their widows and orphans. With this view, he proposed that liberal premiums should be offered for the three best designs for a general almshouse; from which—as insect architecture was well known to be in a very advanced and perfect state—we might possibly derive many valuable hints for the improvement of our metropolitan universities, national galleries, and other public edifices.

"THE PRESIDENT wished to be informed how the ingenious gentleman proposed to open a communication with fleas generally, in the first instance, so that they might be thoroughly imbued with a sense of the advantages they must necessarily derive from changing their mode of life, and applying themselves to honest labour. This appeared to him, the only difficulty.

"THE AUTHOR submitted that this difficulty was easily overcome, or rather that there was no difficulty at all in the case. Obviously the course to be pursued, if Her Majesty's government could be prevailed upon to take up the plan, would be, to secure at a remunerative salary the individual to whom he had alluded as presiding over the exhibition in Regent-street at the period of his visit. That gentleman would at once be able to put himself in communication with the mass of the fleas, and to instruct them in pursuance of some general plan of education, to be sanctioned by Parliament, until such time as the more intelligent among them were advanced enough to officiate as teachers to the rest.

"THE PRESIDENT and several members of the section highly complimented the author of the paper last read, on his most ingenious and important treatise. It was determined that the subject should be recommended to the immediate consideration of the council.

"MR. WIGSBY produced a cauliflower somewhat larger than a chaise-umbrella, which had been raised by no other artificial means than the simple application of highly carbonated soda-water as manure. He explained that by scooping out the head, which would afford a new and delicious species of nourishment for the poor, a parachute, in principle something similar to that constructed by M. Garnerin, was at once obtained; the stalk of course being kept downwards. He added that he was perfectly willing to make a descent from a height of not less than three miles and a quarter; and had in fact already proposed the same to the proprietors of Vauxhall Gardens, who in the handsomest manner at once consented to his wishes, and appointed an early day next summer for the undertaking; merely stipulating that the rim of the cauliflower should be previously broken in three or four places to ensure the safety of the descent.

"THE PRESIDENT congratulated the public on the *grand gala* in store for them, and warmly eulogised the proprietors of the establishment alluded to, for their love of science, and regard for the safety of human life, both of which did them the highest honour.

"A Member wished to know how many thousand additional lamps the royal property would be illuminated with, on the night after the descent.

"MR. WIGSBY replied that the point was not yet finally decided; but he believed it was proposed, over and above the ordinary illuminations, to exhibit in various devices eight millions and a-half of additional lamps.

"The Member expressed himself much gratified with this announcement.

"MR. BLUNDERUM delighted the section with a most interesting and valuable paper 'on the last moments of the learned pig' which produced a very strong impression on the assembly, the account being compiled from the personal recollections of his favourite attendant. The account stated in the most emphatic terms that the animal's name was not Toby, but Solomon; and distinctly proved that he could have no near relatives in the profession, as many designing persons had falsely stated, inasmuch as his father, mother, brothers and sisters, had all fallen victims to the butcher at different times. An uncle of his indeed, had with very great labour been traced to a sty in Somers Town; but as he was in a very infirm state at the time, being afflicted with measles, and shortly afterwards disappeared, there appeared too much reason to conjecture that he had been converted into sausages. The disorder of the learned pig was originally a severe cold, which, being aggravated by excessive trough indulgence, finally settled upon the lungs, and terminated in a general decay of the constitution. A melancholy instance of a presentiment entertained by the animal of his approaching dissolution was recorded. After gratifying a numerous and fashionable company with his performances, in which no falling off whatever was visible, he fixed his eyes on the biographer, and, turning to the watch which lay on the floor, and on which he was accustomed to point out the hour, deliberately passed his snout twice round the dial. In precisely four-and-twenty hours from that time he had ceased to exist!

"PROFESSOR WHEEZY inquired whether, previous to his demise, the animal had expressed, by signs or otherwise, any wishes regarding the disposal of his little property.

"MR. BLUNDERUM replied, that, when the biographer took up the pack of cards at the conclusion of the performance, the animal grunted several times in a significant manner, and nodding his head as he was accustomed to do, when gratified. From these gestures it was understood that he wished the attendant to keep the cards, which he had ever since done. He had not expressed any wish relative to his watch, which had accordingly been pawned by the same individual.

"THE PRESIDENT wished to know whether any Member of the Section had ever seen or conversed with the pig-faced lady, who was reported to have worn a black velvet mask, and to have taken her meals from a golden trough.

"After some hesitation a Member replied that the pig-faced lady was his mother-in-law, and that he trusted the President would not violate the sanctity of private life.

"THE PRESIDENT begged pardon. He had considered the pig-faced lady a public character. Would the honourable member object to state, with a view to the advancement of science, whether she was in any way connected with the learned pig?

"The Member replied in the same low tone, that, as the question appeared to involve a suspicion that the learned pig might be his half-brother, he must decline answering it.

"SECTION B.—ANATOMY AND MEDICINE
COACH-HOUSE, PIG AND TINDER-BOX

President—Dr. Toorell. *Vice-Presidents*—Professors Muff and Nogo.

"DR. KUTANKUMAGEN (of Moscow) read to the section a report of a case which had occurred within his own practice, strikingly illustrative of the power of medicine, as exemplified in his successful treatment of a virulent disorder. He had been called in to visit the patient on the 1st of April, 1837. He was then labouring under symptoms peculiarly alarming to any medical man. His frame was stout and muscular, his step firm and elastic, his cheeks plump and red, his voice loud, his appetite good, his pulse full and round. He was in the constant habit of eating three meals *per diem*, and of drinking at least one bottle of wine, and one glass of spirituous liquors diluted with water, in the course of the four hours. He laughed constantly, and in so hearty a manner that it was terrible to hear him. By dint of powerful medicine, low diet, and bleeding, the symptoms in the course of three days perceptibly decreased. A rigid perseverance in the same course of treatment for only one week, accompanied with small doses of water-gruel, weak broth, and barley-water, led to their entire disappearance. In the course of a month he was sufficiently recovered to be carried down-stairs by two nurses, and to enjoy an airing in a close carriage, supported by soft pillows. At the present moment he was restored so far as to walk about, with the slight assistance of a crutch and a boy. It would perhaps be gratifying to the section to learn that he ate little, drank little, slept little, and was never heard to laugh by any accident whatever.

"DR. W. R. FEE, in complimenting the honourable member upon the triumphant cure he had effected, begged to ask whether the patient still bled freely?

"DR KUTANKUMAGEN replied in the affirmative.

"DR. W. R. FEE.—And you found that he bled freely during the whole course of the disorder?

"DR. KUTANKUMAGEN—Oh dear, yes; most freely.

"DR. NEESHAWTS supposed, that if the patient had not submitted to be bled with great readiness and perseverance, so extraordinary a cure could never, in fact, have been accomplished. Dr. Kutankumagen rejoined, certainly not.

"MR. KNIGHT BELL (M.R.C.S.) exhibited a wax preparation of the interior of a gentleman who in early life had inadvertently swallowed a door-key. It was a curious fact that a medical student of dissipated habits, being present at the *post mortem* examination, found means to escape unobserved from the room, with that portion of the coats of the stomach upon which an exact model of the instrument was distinctly impressed, with which he hastened to a locksmith of doubtful character, who made a new key from the pattern so shown to him. With this key the medical student entered the house of the deceased gentleman, and committed a burglary to a large amount, for which he was subsequently tried and executed.

"THE PRESIDENT wished to know what became of the original key after the lapse of years. Mr. Knight Bell replied that the gentleman was always much accustomed to punch, and it was supposed the acid had gradually devoured it.

"Dr. Neeshawts and several of the members were of opinion that the key must have lain very cold and heavy upon the gentleman's stomach.

"Mr. Knight Bell believed it did at first. It was worthy of remark, perhaps, that for some years the gentleman was troubled with a nightmare, under the influence of which he always imagined himself a wine-cellar door.

"Professor Muff related a very extraordinary and convincing proof of the wonderful efficacy of the system of infinitesimal doses, which the section were doubtless aware was based upon the theory that the very minutest amount of any given drug, properly dispersed through the human frame, would be productive of precisely the same result as a very large dose administered in the usual manner. Thus, the fortieth part of a grain of calomel was supposed to be equal to a five-grain calomel pill, and so on in proportion throughout the whole range of medicine. He had tried the experiment in a curious manner upon a publican who had been brought into the hospital with a broken head, and was cured upon the infinitesimal system in the incredibly short space of three months. This man was a hard drinker. He (Professor Muff) had dispersed three drops of rum through a bucket of water, and requested the man to drink the whole. What was the result? Before he had drunk a quart, he was in a state of beastly intoxication; and five other men were made dead drunk with the remainder.

"The President wished to know whether an infinitesimal dose of soda-water would have recovered them? Professor Muff replied that the twenty-fifth part of a teaspoonful, properly administered to each patient, would have sobered him immediately. The President remarked that this was a most important discovery, and he hoped the Lord Mayor and Court of Aldermen would patronize it immediately.

"A Member begged to be informed whether it would be possible to administer—say, the twentieth part of a grain of bread and cheese to all grown-up paupers, and the fortieth part to children, with the same satisfying effect as their present allowance.

"PROFESSOR MUFF was willing to stake his professional reputation on the perfect adequacy of such a quantity of food to the support of human life—in workhouses; the addition of the fifteenth part of a grain of pudding twice a week would render it a high diet.

"PROFESSOR NOGO called the attention of the section to a very extraordinary case of animal magnetism. A private watchman, being merely looked at by the operator from the opposite side of a wide street, was at once observed to be in a very drowsy and languid state. He was followed to his box, and being once slightly rubbed on the palms of the hands, fell into a sound sleep, in which he continued without intermission for ten hours.

"SECTION C.—STATISTICS
HAY-LOFT, ORIGINAL PIG

President—Mr. Woodensconce. *Vice-Presidents*—Mr. Ledbrain and Mr. Timbered.

"Mr. Slug stated to the section the result of some calculations he had made with great difficulty and labour, regarding the state of infant education among the middle classes of London. He found that, within a circle of three miles from the Elephant and Castle, the following were the names and numbers of children's books principally in circulation:—

Jack the Giant-killer	7,943
Ditto and Bean-stalk	8,625
Ditto and Eleven Brothers	2,845
Ditto and Jill	1,998
Total	21,407

"He found that the proportion of Robinson Crusoes to Philip Quarlls was as four and a half to one; and that the preponderance of Valentine and Orsons over Goody Two Shoeses was as three and an eighth of the former to half a one of the latter; a comparison of Seven Champions with Simple Simons gave the same result. The ignorance that prevailed, was lamentable. One child, on being asked whether he would rather be Saint George of England or a respectable tallow-chandler, instantly replied, 'Taint George of Ingling'. Another, a little boy of eight years old, was found to be firmly impressed with a belief in the existence of dragons, and openly stated that it was his intention when he grew up, to rush forth sword in hand for the deliverance of captive princesses, and the promiscuous slaughter of giants. Not one child among the number interrogated had ever heard of Mungo Park,—some inquiring whether he was at all connected with the black man that swept the crossing; and others whether he was in any way related to the Regent's Park. They had not the slightest conception of the commonest principles of mathematics, and considered Sindbad the Sailor the most enterprising voyager that the world had ever produced.

"A Member, strongly deprecating the use of all the other books mentioned, suggested that Jack and Jill might perhaps be exempted from the general censure, inasmuch as the hero and heroine, in the very outset of the tale, were depicted as going *up* a hill to fetch a pail of water, which was a laborious and useful occupation,—supposing   t h e family linen was being washed, for instance.

"Mr. Slug feared that the moral effect of this passage was more than counterbalanced by another in a subsequent part of the poem, in which very gross allusion was made to the mode in which the heroine was personally chastised by her mother

   "'For laughing at Jack's disaster';

besides, the whole work had this one great fault, *it was not true*.

"The President complimented the honourable member on the excellent distinction he had drawn. Several other Members, too, dwelt upon the immense and urgent necessity of storing the minds of children with nothing but facts and figures; which process the President very forcibly remarked, had made them (the section) the men they were.

"MR. SLUG then stated some curious calculations respecting the dogs'-meat barrows of London. He found that the total number of small carts and barrows engaged in dispensing provision to the cats and dogs of the metropolis was one thousand seven hundred and forty- three. The average number of skewers delivered daily with the provender, by each dogs'-meat cart or barrow, was thirty-six. Now, multiplying the number of skewers so delivered by the number of harrows, a total of sixty-two thousand seven hundred and forty-eight skewers daily would be obtained. Allowing that, of these sixty-two thousand seven hundred and forty-eight skewers, the odd two thousand seven hundred and forty-eight were accidentally devoured with the meat, by the most voracious of the animals supplied, it followed that sixty thousand skewers per day, or the enormous number of twenty-one millions nine hundred thousand skewers annually, were wasted in the kennels and dustholes of London; which, if collected and warehoused, would in ten years' time afford a mass of timber more than sufficient for the construction of a first-rate vessel of war for the use of her Majesty's navy, to be called 'The Royal Skewer', and to become under that name the terror of all the enemies of this island.

"MR. X. LEDBRAIN read a very ingenious communication, from which it appeared that the total number of legs belonging to the manufacturing population of one great town in Yorkshire was, in round numbers, forty thousand, while the total number of chair and stool legs in their houses was only thirty thousand, which, upon the very favourable average of three legs to a seat, yielded only ten thousand seats in all. From this calculation it would appear,—not taking wooden or cork legs into the account, but allowing two legs to every person,—that ten thousand individuals (one-half of the whole population) were either destitute of any rest for their legs at all, or passed the whole of their leisure time in sitting upon boxes.

"Section D.—Mechanical Science
Coach-House, Original Pig

President—Mr. Carter. *Vice-Presidents*—Mr. Truck and Mr. Waghorn.

"Professor Queerspeck exhibited an elegant model of a portable railway, neatly mounted in a green case, for the waistcoat pocket. By attaching this beautiful instrument to his boots, any Bank or public-office clerk could transport himself from his place of residence to his place of business, at the easy rate of sixty-five miles an hour, which, to gentlemen of sedentary pursuits, would be an incalculable advantage.

"The President was desirous of knowing whether it was necessary to have a level surface on which the gentleman was to run.

"Professor Queerspeck explained that City gentlemen would run in trains, being handcuffed together to prevent confusion or unpleasantness. For instance, trains would start every morning at eight, nine, and ten o'clock, from Camden Town, Islington, Camberwell, Hackney, and various other places in which City gentlemen are accustomed to reside. It would be necessary to have a level, but he had provided for this difficulty by proposing that the best line that the circumstances would admit of, should be taken through the sewers which undermine the streets of the metropolis, and which, well lighted by jets from the gas pipes which run immediately above them, would form a pleasant and commodious arcade, especially in winter-time, when the inconvenient custom of carrying umbrellas, now so general, could be wholly dispensed with. In reply to another question, Professor Queerspeck stated that no substitute for the purposes to which these arcades were at present devoted had yet occurred to him, but he hoped no fanciful objection on this head would be allowed to interfere with so great an undertaking.

"Mr. Jobba produced a forcing-machine on a novel plan, for bringing joint-stock railway shares prematurely to a premium. The instrument was in the form of an elegant gilt weather-glass, of most dazzling appearance, and was worked behind, by strings, after the manner of a pantomime trick, the strings being always pulled by the directors of the company to which the machine belonged. The quicksilver was so ingeniously placed, that when the acting directors held shares in their pockets, figures denoting very small expenses and very large returns appeared upon the glass; but the moment the directors parted with these pieces of paper, the estimate of needful expenditure suddenly increased itself to an immense extent, while the statements of certain profits became reduced in the same proportion. Mr. Jobba stated that the machine had been in constant requisition for some months past, and he had never once known it to fail.

"A Member expressed his opinion that it was extremely neat and pretty. He wished to know whether it was not liable to accidental derangement? Mr. Jobba said that the whole machine was undoubtedly liable to be blown up, but that was the only objection to it.

"PROFESSOR NOGO arrived from the anatomical section to exhibit a model of a safety fire-escape, which could be fixed at any time, in less than half an hour, and by means of which, the youngest or most infirm persons (successfully resisting the progress of the flames until it was quite ready) could be preserved if they merely balanced themselves for a few minutes on the sill of their bedroom window, and got into the escape without falling into the street. The Professor stated that the number of boys who had been rescued in the daytime by this machine from houses which were not on fire, was almost incredible. Not a conflagration had occurred in the whole of London for many months past to which the escape had not been carried on the very next day, and put in action before a concourse of persons.

"THE PRESIDENT inquired whether there was not some difficulty in ascertaining which was the top of the machine, and which the bottom, in cases of pressing emergency.

"PROFESSOR NOGO explained that of course it could not be expected to act quite as well when there was a fire, as when there was not a fire;

but in the former case he thought it would be of equal service whether the top were up or down."

With the last section our correspondent concludes his most able and faithful Report, which will never cease to reflect credit upon him for his scientific attainments, and upon us for our enterprising spirit. It is needless to take a review of the subjects which have been discussed; of the mode in which they have been examined; of the great truths which they have elicited. They are now before the world, and we leave them to read, to consider, and to profit.

The place of meeting for next year has undergone discussion, and has at length been decided, regard being had to, and evidence being taken upon, the goodness of its wines, the supply of its markets, the hospitality of its inhabitants, and the quality of its hotels. We hope at this next meeting our correspondent may again he present, and that we may be once more the means of placing his communications before the world. Until that period we have been prevailed upon to allow this number of our Miscellany to be retailed to the public, or wholesaled to the trade, without any advance upon our usual price.

We have only to add, that the committees are now broken up, and that Mudfog is once again restored to its accustomed tranquillity,—that Professors and Members have had balls, and *soirées*, and suppers, and great mutual complimentations, and have at length dispersed to their several homes,—whither all good wishes and joys attend them, until next year!

Signed Boz.

Full Report of the Second Meeting of the Mudfog Association

For the Advancement of Everything

In October last, we did ourselves the immortal credit of recording, at an enormous expense, and by dint of exertions unparalleled in the history of periodical publication, the proceedings of the Mudfog Association for the Advancement of Everything, which in that month held its first great half-yearly meeting, to the wonder and delight of the whole empire. We announced at the conclusion of that extraordinary and most remarkable Report, that when the Second Meeting of the Society should take place, we should be found again at our post, renewing our gigantic and spirited endeavours, and once more making the world ring with the accuracy, authenticity, immeasurable superiority, and intense remarkability of our account of its proceedings. In redemption of this pledge, we caused to be despatched per steam to Oldcastle (at which place this second meeting of the Society was held on the 20th instant), the same superhumanly-endowed gentleman who furnished the former report, and who,—gifted by nature with transcendent abilities, and furnished by us with a body of assistants scarcely inferior to himself,—has forwarded a series of letters, which, for faithfulness of description, power of language, fervour of thought, happiness of expression, and importance of subject-matter, have no equal in the epistolary literature of any age or country. We give this gentleman's correspondence entire, and in the order in which it reached our office.

"*Saloon of Steamer, Thursday night, half-past eight.*
"When I left New Burlington Street this evening in the hackney cabriolet, number four thousand two hundred and eighty-five, I experienced sensations as novel as they were oppressive. A sense of the

importance of the task I had undertaken, a consciousness that I was leaving London, and, stranger still, going somewhere else, a feeling of loneliness and a sensation of jolting, quite bewildered my thoughts, and for a time rendered me even insensible to the presence of my carpet-bag and hat-box. I shall ever feel grateful to the driver of a Blackwall omnibus who, by thrusting the pole of his vehicle through the small door of the cabriolet, awakened me from a tumult of imaginings that are wholly indescribable. But of such materials is our imperfect nature composed!

"I am happy to say that I am the first passenger on board, and shall thus be enabled to give you an account of all that happens in the order of its occurrence. The chimney is smoking a good deal, and so are the crew; and the captain, I am informed, is very drunk in a little house upon deck, something like a black turnpike. I should infer from all I hear that he has got the steam up.

"You will readily guess with what feelings I have just made the discovery that my berth is in the same closet with those engaged by Professor Woodensconce, Mr. Slug, and Professor Grime. Professor Woodensconce has taken the shelf above me, and Mr. Slug and Professor Grime the two shelves opposite. Their luggage has already arrived. On Mr. Slug's bed is a long tin tube of about three inches in diameter, carefully closed at both ends. What can this contain? Some powerful instrument of a new construction, doubtless."

"Ten minutes past nine

"Nobody has yet arrived, nor has anything fresh come in my way except several joints of beef and mutton, from which I conclude that a good plain dinner has been provided for to-morrow. There is a singular smell below, which gave me some uneasiness at first; but as the steward says it is always there, and never goes away, I am quite comfortable again. I learn from this man that the different sections will be distributed at the Black Boy and Stomach-ache, and the Boot-jack and Countenance. If this intelligence be true (and I have no reason to doubt it), your readers will draw such conclusions as their different opinions may suggest.

"I write down these remarks as they occur to me, or as the facts come to my knowledge, in order that my first impressions may lose nothing of their original vividness. I shall despatch them in small packets as opportunities arise."

"*Half-past nine.*

"Some dark object has just appeared upon the wharf. I think it is a travelling carriage."

"*A quarter to ten.*

"No, it isn't."

"*Half past ten.*

"The passengers are pouring in every instant. Four omnibuses full have just arrived upon the wharf, and all is bustle and activity. The noise and confusion are very great. Cloths are laid in the cabins, and the steward is placing blue plates-full of knobs of cheese at equal distances down the centre of the tables. He drops a great many knobs; but, being used to it, picks them up again with great dexterity, and, after wiping them on his sleeve, throws them back into the plates. He is a young man of exceedingly prepossessing appearance—either dirty or a mulatto, but I think the former.

"An interesting old gentleman, who came to the wharf in an omnibus, has just quarrelled violently with the porters, and is staggering towards the vessel with a large trunk in his arms. I trust and hope that he may reach it in safety; but the board he has to cross is narrow and slippery. Was that a splash? Gracious powers!

"I have just returned from the deck. The trunk is standing upon the extreme brink of the wharf, but the old gentleman is nowhere to be seen. The watchman is not sure whether he went down or not, but promises to drag for him the first thing to-morrow morning. May his humane efforts prove successful!

"Professor Nogo has this moment arrived with his nightcap on under his hat. He has ordered a glass of cold brandy and water, with a hard biscuit and a bason, and has gone straight to bed. What can this mean?

"The three other scientific gentlemen to whom I have already alluded have come on board, and have all tried their beds, with the exception of Professor Woodensconce, who sleeps in one of the top ones, and can't get into it. Mr. Slug, who sleeps in the other top one, is unable to get out of his, and is to have his supper handed up by a boy. I have had the honour to introduce myself to these gentlemen, and we have amicably arranged the order in which we shall retire to rest; which it is necessary to agree upon, because, although the cabin is very comfortable, there is not room for more than one gentleman to be out of bed at a time, and even he must take his boots off in the passage.

"As I anticipated, the knobs of cheese were provided for the passengers' supper, and are now in course of consumption. Your readers will be surprised to hear that Professor Woodensconce has abstained from cheese for eight years, although he takes butter in considerable quantities. Professor Grime having lost several teeth, is unable, I observe, to eat his crusts without previously soaking them in his bottled porter. How interesting are these peculiarities!"

"Half-past eleven.

"Professors Woodensconce and Grime, with a degree of good humour that delights us all, have just arranged to toss for a bottle of mulled port. There has been some discussion whether the payment should be decided by the first toss or the best out of three. Eventually the latter course has been determined on. Deeply do I wish that both gentlemen could win; but that being impossible, I own that my personal aspirations (I speak as an individual, and do not compromise either you or your readers by this expression of feeling) are with Professor Woodensconce. I have backed that gentleman to the amount of eighteenpence."

"*Twenty minutes to twelve.*

"Professor Grime has inadvertently tossed his half-crown out of one of the cabin-windows, and it has been arranged that the steward shall toss for him. Bets are offered on any side to any amount, but there are no takers.

"Professor Woodensconce has just called 'woman'; but the coin having lodged in a beam, is a long time coming down again. The interest and suspense of this one moment are beyond anything that can be imagined."

"*Twelve o'clock.*

"The mulled port is smoking on the table before me, and Professor Grime has won. Tossing is a game of chance; but on every ground, whether of public or private character, intellectual endowments, or scientific attainments, I cannot help expressing my opinion that Professor Woodensconce *ought* to have come off victorious. There is an exultation about Professor Grime incompatible, I fear, with true greatness."

"*A quarter past twelve.*

"Professor Grime continues to exult, and to boast of his victory in no very measured terms, observing that he always does win, and that he knew it would be a 'head' beforehand, with many other remarks of a similar nature. Surely this gentleman is not so lost to every feeling of decency and propriety as not to feel and know the superiority of Professor Woodensconce? Is Professor Grime insane? or does he wish to be reminded in plain language of his true position in society, and the precise level of his acquirements and abilities? Professor Grime will do well to look to this."

"*One o'clock.*

"I am writing in bed. The small cabin is illuminated by the feeble light of a flickering lamp suspended from the ceiling; Professor Grime is lying on the opposite shelf on the broad of his back, with his mouth wide open. The scene is indescribably solemn. The rippling of the tide, the noise of the sailors' feet overhead, the gruff voices on the river, the dogs on the shore, the snoring of the passengers, and a constant creaking of every plank in the vessel, are the only sounds that meet the ear. With these exceptions, all is profound silence.

"My curiosity has been within the last moment very much excited. Mr. Slug, who lies above Professor Grime, has cautiously withdrawn the curtains of his berth, and, after looking anxiously out, as if to satisfy himself that his companions are asleep, has taken up the tin tube of which I have before spoken, and is regarding it with great interest. What rare mechanical combination can be contained in that mysterious case? It is evidently a profound secret to all."

"A quarter past one.

"The behaviour of Mr. Slug grows more and more mysterious. He has unscrewed the top of the tube, and now renews his observations upon his companions, evidently to make sure that he is wholly unobserved. He is clearly on the eve of some great experiment. Pray heaven that it be not a dangerous one; but the interests of science must be promoted, and I am prepared for the worst."

"Five minutes later.

"He has produced a large pair of scissors, and drawn a roll of some substance, not unlike parchment in appearance, from the tin case. The experiment is about to begin. I must strain my eyes to the utmost, in the attempt to follow its minutest operation."

Twenty minutes before two.

"I have at length been enabled to ascertain that the tin tube contains a few yards of some celebrated plaster, recommended—as I discover on regarding the label attentively through my eye-glass—as a preservative against sea-sickness. Mr. Slug has cut it up into small portions, and is now sticking it over himself in every direction."

"Three o'clock.

"Precisely a quarter of an hour ago we weighed anchor, and the machinery was suddenly put in motion with a noise so appalling, that Professor Woodensconce (who had ascended to his berth by means of a platform of carpet-bags arranged by himself on geometrical principles) darted from his shelf head foremost, and, gaining his feet with all the rapidity of extreme terror, ran wildly into the ladies' cabin, under the impression that we were sinking, and uttering loud cries for aid. I am assured that the scene which ensued baffles all description. There were one hundred and forty-seven ladies in their respective berths at the time.

"Mr. Slug has remarked, as an additional instance of the extreme ingenuity of the steam-engine as applied to purposes of navigation, that in whatever part of the vessel a passenger's berth may be situated, the machinery always appears to be exactly under his pillow. He intends stating this very beautiful, though simple discovery, to the association."

"Half-past three.

"We are still in smooth water; that is to say, in as smooth water as a steam-vessel ever can be, for, as Professor Woodensconce (who has just woke up) learnedly remarks, another great point of ingenuity about a steamer is, that it always carries a little storm with it. You can scarcely conceive how exciting the jerking pulsation of the ship becomes. It is a matter of positive difficulty to get to sleep."

"Friday afternoon, six o'clock.

"I regret to inform you that Mr. Slug's plaster has proved of no avail. He is in great agony, but has applied several large, additional pieces notwithstanding. How affecting is this extreme devotion to science and pursuit of knowledge under the most trying circumstances!

"We were extremely happy this morning, and the breakfast was one of the most animated description. Nothing unpleasant occurred until noon, with the exception of Doctor Foxey's brown silk umbrella and white hat becoming entangled in the machinery while he was explaining to a knot of ladies the construction of the steam-engine. I fear the gravy soup for lunch was injudicious. We lost a great many passengers almost immediately afterwards."

"*Half-past six.*
"I am again in bed. Anything so heart-rending as Mr. Slug's sufferings it has never yet been my lot to witness."

"*Seven o'clock.*
"A messenger has just come down for a clean pocket-handkerchief from Professor Woodenscone's bag, that unfortunate gentleman being quite unable to leave the deck, and imploring constantly to be thrown overboard. From this man I understand that Professor Nogo, though in a state of utter exhaustion, clings feebly to the hard biscuit and cold brandy and water, under the impression that they will yet restore him. Such is the triumph of mind over matter.

"Professor Grime is in bed, to all appearance quite well; but he *will* eat, and it is disagreeable to see him. Has this gentleman no sympathy with the sufferings of his fellow-creatures? If he has, on what principle can he call for mutton-chops—and smile?"

"*Black Boy and Stomach-ache,*
Oldcastle, Saturday noon.
"You will be happy to learn that I have at length arrived here in safety. The town is excessively crowded, and all the private lodgings and hotels are filled with *savans* of both sexes. The tremendous assemblage of intellect that one encounters in every street is in the last degree overwhelming.

"Notwithstanding the throng of people here, I have been fortunate enough to meet with very comfortable accommodation on very reasonable terms, having secured a sofa in the first-floor passage at one guinea per night, which includes permission to take my meals in the bar, on condition that I walk about the streets at all other times, to make room for other gentlemen similarly situated. I have been over the outhouses intended to be devoted to the reception of the various sections, both here and at the Boot-jack and Countenance, and am much delighted with the arrangements. Nothing can exceed the fresh appearance of the saw-dust with which the floors are sprinkled. The forms are of unplaned deal, and the general effect, as you can well imagine, is extremely beautiful."

"*Half-past nine.*

"The number and rapidity of the arrivals are quite bewildering. Within the last ten minutes a stage-coach has driven up to the door, filled inside and out with distinguished characters, comprising Mr. Muddlebranes, Mr. Drawley, Professor Muff, Mr. X. Misty, Mr. X.X. Misty, Mr. Purblind, Professor Rummun, The Honourable and Reverend Mr. Long Eers, Professor John Ketch, Sir William Joltered, Doctor Buffer, Mr. Smith (of London), Mr. Brown (of Edinburgh), Sir Hookham Snivey, and Professor Pumpkinskull. The ten last-named gentlemen were wet through, and looked extremely intelligent."

"*Sunday, two o'clock, p.m.*

"The Honourable and Reverend Mr. Long Eers, accompanied by Sir William Joltered, walked and drove this morning. They accomplished the former feat in boots, and the latter in a hired fly. This has naturally given rise to much discussion.

"I have just learnt that an interview has taken place at the Boot-jack and Countenance between Sowster, the active and intelligent beadle of this place, and Professor Pumpkinskull, who, as your readers are doubtless aware, is an influential member of the council. I forbear to communicate any of the rumours to which this very extraordinary proceeding has given rise until I have seen Sowster, and endeavoured to ascertain the truth from him."

"Half-past six.

"I engaged a donkey-chaise shortly after writing the above, and proceeded at a brisk trot in the direction of Sowster's residence, passing through a beautiful expanse of country, with red brick buildings on either side, and stopping in the market-place to observe the spot where Mr. Kwakley's hat was blown off yesterday. It is an uneven piece of paving, but has certainly no appearance which would lead one to suppose that any such event had recently occurred there. From this point I proceeded—passing the gas-works and tallow-melter's—to a lane which had been pointed out to me as the beadle's place of residence; and before I had driven a dozen yards further, I had the good fortune to meet Sowster himself advancing towards me.

"Sowster is a fat man, with a more enlarged development of that peculiar conformation of countenance which is vulgarly termed a double chin than I remember to have ever seen before. He has also a very red nose, which he attributes to a habit of early rising—so red, indeed, that but for this explanation I should have supposed it to proceed from occasional inebriety. He informed me that he did not feel himself at libe-rty to relate what had passed between himself and Professor Pumpkinskull, but had no objection to state that it was connected with a matter of police regulation, and added with peculiar significance 'Never wos sitch times!'

"You will easily believe that this intelligence gave me considerable surprise, not wholly unmixed with anxiety, and that I lost no time in waiting on Professor Pumpkinskull, and stating the object of my visit. After a few moments' reflection, the Professor, who, I am bound to say, behaved with the utmost politeness, openly avowed (I mark the passage in italics) *that he had requested Sowster to attend on the Monday morning at the Boot-jack and Countenance, to keep off the boys; and that he had further desired that the under-beadle might be stationed, with the same object, at the Black Boy and Stomach-ache*!

"Now I leave this unconstitutional proceeding to your comments and the consideration of your readers. I have yet to learn that a beadle, without the precincts of a church, churchyard, or workhouse, and acting otherwise than under the express orders of churchwardens and overseers in council assembled, to enforce the law against people who come upon the parish, and other offenders, has any lawful authority whatever over the rising youth of this country. I have yet to learn that a beadle can he called out by any civilian to exercise a domination and despotism over the boys of Britain. I have yet to learn that a beadle will be permitted by the commissioners of poor law regulation to wear out the soles and heels of his boots in illegal interference with the liberties of people not proved poor or otherwise criminal. I have yet to learn that a beadle has power to stop up the Queen's highway at his will and pleasure, or that the whole width of the street is not free and open to any man, boy, or woman in existence, up to the very walls of the houses—ay, be they Black Boys and Stomach-aches, or Boot-jacks and Countenances, I care not."

"*Nine o'clock.*

"I have procured a local artist to make a faithful sketch of the tyrant Sowster, which, as he has acquired this infamous celebrity, you will no doubt wish to have engraved for the purpose of presenting a copy with every copy of your next number. I enclose it. The under-beadle has consented to write his life, but it is to be strictly anonymous.

"The accompanying likeness is of course from the life, and complete in every respect. Even if I had been totally ignorant of the man's real character, and it had been placed before me without remark, I should have shuddered involuntarily. There is an intense malignity of expression in the features, and a baleful ferocity of purpose in the ruffian's eye, which appals and sickens. His whole air is rampant with cruelty, nor is the stomach less characteristic of his demoniac propensities."

"*Monday*.

"The great day has at length arrived. I have neither eyes, nor ears, nor pens, nor ink, nor paper, for anything but the wonderful proceedings that have astounded my senses. Let me collect my energies and proceed to the account.

"Section A.—Zoology and Botany
Front Parlour, Black Boy and Stomach-Ache

President—Sir William Joltered. *Vice-Presidents*—Mr. Muddlebranes and Mr. Drawley.

"Mr. X. X. Misty communicated some remarks on the disappearance of dancing-bears from the streets of London, with observations on the exhibition of monkeys as connected with barrel-organs. The writer had observed, with feelings of the utmost pain and regret, that some years ago a sudden and unaccountable change in the public taste took place with reference to itinerant bears, who, being discountenanced by the populace, gradually fell off one by one from the streets of the metropolis, until not one remained to create a taste for natural history in the breasts of the poor and uninstructed. One bear, indeed,—a brown and ragged animal,—had lingered about the haunts of his former triumphs, with a worn and dejected visage and feeble limbs, and had essayed to wield his quarter-staff for the amusement of the multitude; but hunger, and an utter want of any due recompense for his abilities, had at length driven him from the field, and it was only too probable that he had fallen a sacrifice to the rising taste for grease. He regretted to add that a similar, and no less lamentable, change had taken place with reference to monkeys. These delightful animals had formerly been almost as plentiful as the organs on the tops of which they were accustomed to sit; the proportion in the year 1829 (it appeared by the parliamentary return) being as one monkey to three

The Tyrant Sowster

organs. Owing, however, to an altered taste in musical instruments, and the substitution, in a great measure, of narrow boxes of music for organs, which left the monkeys nothing to sit upon, this source of public amusement was wholly dried up. Considering it a matter of the deepest importance, in connection with national education, that the people should not lose such opportunities of making themselves acquainted with the manners and customs of two most interesting species of animals, the author submitted that some measures should be immediately taken for the restoration of these pleasing and truly intellectual amusements.

"THE PRESIDENT inquired by what means the honourable member proposed to attain this most desirable end?

"THE AUTHOR submitted that it could be most fully and satisfactorily accomplished, if Her Majesty's Government would cause to be brought over to England, and maintained at the public expense, and for the public amusement, such a number of bears as would enable every quarter of the town to be visited—say at least by three bears a week. No difficulty whatever need be experienced in providing a fitting place for the reception of these animals, as a commodious bear-garden could be erected in the immediate neighbourhood of both Houses of Parliament; obviously the most proper and eligible spot for such an establishment.

"PROFESSOR MULL doubted very much whether any correct ideas of natural history were propagated by the means to which the honourable member had so ably adverted. On the contrary, he believed that they had been the means of diffusing very incorrect and imperfect notions on the subject. He spoke from personal observation and personal experience, when he said that many children of great abilities had been induced to believe, from what they had observed in the streets, at and before the period to which the honourable gentleman had referred, that all monkeys were born in red coats and spangles, and that their hats and feathers also came by nature. He wished to know distinctly whether the honourable gentleman attributed the want of encouragement the bears had met with to the decline of public taste in that respect, or to a want of ability on the part of the bears themselves?

"MR. X. X. MISTY replied, that he could not bring himself to believe but that there must be a great deal of floating talent among the bears and monkeys generally; which, in the absence of any proper encouragement, was dispersed in other directions.

"PROFESSOR PUMPKINSKULL wished to take that opportunity of calling the attention of the section to a most important and serious point. The author of the treatise just read had alluded to the prevalent taste for bears'-grease as a means of promoting the growth of hair, which undoubtedly was diffused to a very great and (as it appeared to him) very alarming extent. No gentleman attending that section could fail to be aware of the fact that the youth of the present age evinced, by their behaviour in the streets, and at all places of public resort, a considerable lack of that gallantry and gentlemanly feeling which, in more ignorant times, had been thought becoming. He wished to know whether it were possible that a constant outward application of bears'-grease by the young gentlemen about town had imperceptibly infused into those unhappy persons something of the nature and quality of the bear. He shuddered as he threw out the remark; but if this theory, on inquiry, should prove to be well founded, it would at once explain a great deal of unpleasant eccentricity of behaviour, which, without some such discovery, was wholly unaccountable.

"THE PRESIDENT highly complimented the learned gentleman on his most valuable suggestion, which produced the greatest effect upon the assembly; and remarked that only a week previous he had seen some young gentlemen at a theatre eyeing a box of ladies with a fierce intensity, which nothing but the influence of some brutish appetite could possibly explain. It was dreadful to reflect that our youth were so rapidly verging into a generation of bears.

"After a scene of scientific enthusiasm it was resolved that this important question should be immediately submitted to the consideration of the council.

"THE PRESIDENT wished to know whether any gentlemen could inform the section what had become of the dancing-dogs?

"A MEMBER replied, after some hesitation, that on the day after three glee-singers had been committed to prison as criminals by a late most zealous police-magistrate of the metropolis, the dogs had abandoned their professional duties, and dispersed themselves in different quarters of the town to gain a livelihood by less dangerous means. He was given to understand that since that period they had supported themselves by lying in wait for and robbing blind men's poodles.

"MR. FLUMMERY exhibited a twig, claiming to be a veritable branch of that noble tree known to naturalists as the Shakspeare, which has taken root in every land and climate, and gathered under the shade of its broad green boughs the great family of mankind. The learned gentleman remarked that the twig had been undoubtedly called by other names in its time; but that it had been pointed out to him by an old lady in Warwickshire, where the great tree had grown, as a shoot of the genuine Shakspeare, by which name he begged to introduce it to his countrymen.

"THE PRESIDENT wished to know what botanical definition the honourable gentleman could afford of the curiosity.

"MR. FLUMMERY expressed his opinion that it was A Decided Plant.

"SECTION B.—DISPLAY OF MODELS AND MECHANICAL SCIENCE LARGE
ROOM, BOOT-JACK AND COUNTENANCE

President—Mr. Mallett. *Vice-Presidents*—Messrs. Leaver and Scroo.

"MR. CRINKLES exhibited a most beautiful and delicate machine, of little larger size than an ordinary snuff-box, manufactured entirely by himself, and composed exclusively of steel, by the aid of which more pockets could be picked in one hour than by the present slow and tedious process in four-and-twenty. The inventor remarked that it had been put into active operation in Fleet Street, the Strand, and other thoroughfares, and had never been once known to fail.

"After some slight delay, occasioned by the various members of the section buttoning their pockets,

"THE PRESIDENT narrowly inspected the invention, and declared that he had never seen a machine of more beautiful or exquisite construction. Would the inventor be good enough to inform the section whether he had taken any and what means for bringing it into general operation?

"MR. CRINKLES stated that, after encountering some preliminary difficulties, he had succeeded in putting himself in communication with Mr. Fogle Hunter, and other gentlemen connected with the swell mob, who had awarded the invention the very highest and most unqualified approbation. He regretted to say, however, that these distinguished practitioners, in common with a gentleman of the name of Gimlet-eyed Tommy, and other members of a secondary grade of the profession whom he was understood to represent, entertained an insuperable objection to its being brought into general use, on the ground that it would have the inevitable effect of almost entirely superseding manual labour, and throwing a great number of highly-deserving persons out of employment.

"THE PRESIDENT hoped that no such fanciful objections would be allowed to stand in the way of such a great public improvement.

"MR. CRINKLES hoped so too; but he feared that if the gentlemen of the swell mob persevered in their objection, nothing could be done.

"PROFESSOR GRIME suggested, that surely, in that case, Her Majesty's Government might be prevailed upon to take it up.

"MR. CRINKLES said, that if the objection were found to be insuperable he should apply to Parliament, which he thought could not fail to recognise the utility of the invention.

"THE PRESIDENT observed that, up to this time Parliament had certainly got on very well without it; but, as they did their business on a very large scale, he had no doubt they would gladly adopt the improvement. His only fear was that the machine might be worn out by constant working.

"Mr. Coppernose called the attention of the section to a proposition of great magnitude and interest, illustrated by a vast number of models, and stated with much clearness and perspicuity in a treatise entitled 'Practical Suggestions on the necessity of providing some harmless and wholesome relaxation for the young noblemen of England'. His proposition was, that a space of ground of not less than ten miles in length and four in breadth should be purchased by a new company, to be incorporated by Act of Parliament, and inclosed by a brick wall of not less than twelve feet in height. He proposed that it should be laid out with highway roads, turnpikes, bridges, miniature villages, and every object that could conduce to the comfort and glory of Four-in-hand Clubs, so that they might be fairly presumed to require no drive beyond it. This delightful retreat would be fitted up with most commodious and extensive stables, for the convenience of such of the nobility and gentry as had a taste for ostling, and with houses of entertainment furnished in the most expensive and handsome style. It would be further provided with whole streets of door-knockers and bell-handles of extra size, so constructed that they could be easily wrenched off at night, and regularly screwed on again, by attendants provided for the purpose, every day. There would also be gas lamps of real glass, which could be broken at a comparatively small expense per dozen, and a broad and handsome foot pavement for gentlemen to drive their cabriolets upon when they were humorously disposed—for the full enjoyment of which feat live pedestrians would be procured from the workhouse at a very small charge per head. The place being inclosed, and carefully screened from the intrusion of the public, there would be no objection to gentlemen laying aside any article of their costume that was considered to interfere with a pleasant frolic, or, indeed, to their walking about without any costume at all, if they liked that better. In short, every facility of enjoyment would be afforded that the most gentlemanly person could possibly desire. But as even these advantages would be incomplete unless there were some means provided of enabling the nobility and gentry to display their prowess when they sallied forth after dinner, and as some inconvenience might be experienced in the event of their being reduced to the necessity of pummelling each other, the inventor had turned his attention to the construction of an entirely new police force, composed exclusively of automaton figures, which, with the assistance of the ingenious Signor Gagliardi, of Windmill-street, in the Haymarket, he had succeeded in making with such nicety, that a policeman, cab-driver, or old woman, made upon the principle of the models exhibited, would walk about until knocked down like any real man; nay, more, if set upon and beaten by six or eight noblemen and gentlemen, after it was down, the figure would utter divers groans, mingled with entreaties for mercy, thus rendering the illusion complete, and the enjoyment perfect. But the invention did not stop even here; for station-houses would be built, containing good beds for noblemen and gentlemen during the night, and in the morning they would repair to a commodious police office, where a pantomimic investigation would take place before the automaton magistrates,—quite equal to life,—who would fine them in so many counters, with which they would be previously provided for the purpose. This office would be furnished with an inclined plane, for the convenience of any nobleman or gentleman who might wish to brings in his horse as a witness; and the prisoners would be at perfect liberty, as they were now, to interrupt the complainants as much as they pleased, and to make any remarks that they thought proper. The charge for these amusements would amount to very little more than they already cost, and the inventor submitted that the public would be much benefited and comforted by the proposed arrangement.

"PROFESSOR NOGO wished to be informed what amount of automaton police force it was proposed to raise in the first instance.

"Mr. Coppernose replied, that it was proposed to begin with seven divisions of police of a score each, lettered from A to G inclusive. It was proposed that not more than half this number should be placed on active duty, and that the remainder should be kept on shelves in the police office ready to be called out at a moment's notice.

"The President, awarding the utmost merit to the ingenious gentleman who had originated the idea, doubted whether the automaton police would quite answer the purpose. He feared that noblemen and gentlemen would perhaps require the excitement of threshing living subjects.

"Mr. Coppernose submitted, that as the usual odds in such cases were ten noblemen or gentlemen to one policeman or cab-driver, it could make very little difference in point of excitement whether the policeman or cab-driver were a man or a block. The great advantage would be, that a policeman's limbs might be all knocked off, and yet he would be in a condition to do duty next day. He might even give his evidence next morning with his head in his hand, and give it equally well.

"Professor Muff.—Will you allow me to ask you, sir, of what materials it is intended that the magistrates' heads shall be composed?

"Mr. Coppernose.—The magistrates will have wooden heads of course, and they will be made of the toughest and thickest materials that can possibly be obtained.

"Professor Muff.—I am quite satisfied. This is a great invention.

"Professor Nogo.—I see but one objection to it. It appears to me that the magistrates ought to talk.

"Mr. Coppernose no sooner heard this suggestion than he touched a small spring in each of the two models of magistrates which were placed upon the table; one of the figures immediately began to exclaim with great volubility that he was sorry to see gentlemen in such a situation, and the other to express a fear that the policeman was intoxicated.

"The section, as with one accord, declared with a shout of applause that the invention was complete; and the President, much excited, retired with Mr. Coppernose to lay it before the council. On his return,

"MR. TICKLE displayed his newly-invented spectacles, which enabled the wearer to discern, in very bright colours, objects at a great distance, and rendered him wholly blind to those immediately before him. It was, he said, a most valuable and useful invention, based strictly upon the principle of the human eye.

"THE PRESIDENT required some information upon this point. He had yet to learn that the human eye was remarkable for the peculiarities of which the honourable gentleman had spoken.

"MR. TICKLE was rather astonished to hear this, when the President could not fail to be aware that a large number of most excellent persons and great statesmen could see, with the naked eye, most marvellous horrors on West India plantations, while they could discern nothing whatever in the interior of Manchester cotton mills. He must know, too, with what quickness of perception most people could discover their neighbours' faults, and how very blind they were to their own. If the President differed from the great majority of men in this respect, his eye was a defective one, and it was to assist his vision that these glasses were made.

"MR. BLANK exhibited a model of a fashionable annual, composed of copper-plates, gold leaf, and silk boards, and worked entirely by milk and water.

"MR. PROSEE, after examining the machine, declared it to be so ingeniously composed, that he was wholly unable to discover how it went on at all.

"MR. BLANK.—Nobody can, and that is the beauty of it.

"Section C.—Anatomy and Medicine
Bar Room, Black Boy And Stomach-Ache

President—Dr. Soemup. *Vice-Presidents*—Messrs. Pessell and Mortair.

"Dr. Grummidge stated to the section a most interesting case of monomania, and described the course of treatment he had pursued with perfect success. The patient was a married lady in the middle rank of life, who, having seen another lady at an evening party in a full suit of pearls, was suddenly seized with a desire to possess a similar equipment, although her husband's finances were by no means equal to the necessary outlay. Finding her wish ungratified, she fell sick, and the symptoms soon became so alarming, that he (Dr. Grummidge) was called in. At this period the prominent tokens of the disorder were sullenness, a total indisposition to perform domestic duties, great peevishness, and extreme languor, except when pearls were mentioned, at which times the pulse quickened, the eyes grew brighter, the pupils dilated, and the patient, after various incoherent exclamations, burst into a passion of tears, and exclaimed that nobody cared for her, and that she wished herself dead. Finding that the patient's appetite was affected in the presence of company, he began by ordering a total abstinence from all stimulants, and forbidding any sustenance but weak gruel; he then took twenty ounces of blood, applied a blister under each ear, one upon the chest, and another on the back; having done which, and administered five grains of calomel, he left the patient to her repose. The next day she was somewhat low, but decidedly better, and all appearances of irritation were removed. The next day she improved still further, and on the next again. On the fourth there was some appearance of a return of the old symptoms, which no sooner developed themselves, than he administered another dose of calomel, and left strict orders that, unless a decidedly favourable change occurred within two hours, the patient's head should be immediately shaved to the very last curl. From that moment she began to mend, and, in less than four-and-twenty hours was perfectly restored. She did not now betray the least emotion at the sight or mention of pearls or any other ornaments. She was cheerful and good-humoured, and a most beneficial change had been effected in her whole temperament and condition.

"MR. PIPKIN (M.R.C.S.) read a short but most interesting communication in which he sought to prove the complete belief of Sir William Courtenay, otherwise Thom, recently shot at Canterbury, in the Homœopathic system. The section would bear in mind that one of the Homœopathic doctrines was, that infinitesimal doses of any medicine which would occasion the disease under which the patient laboured, supposing him to be in a healthy state, would cure it. Now, it was a remarkable circumstance—proved in the evidence— that the deceased Thom employed a woman to follow him about all day with a pail of water, assuring her that one drop (a purely Homœopathic remedy, the section would observe), placed upon his tongue, after death, would restore him. What was the obvious inference? That Thom, who was marching and counter-marching in osier beds, and other swampy places, was impressed with a presentiment that he should be drowned; in which case, had his instructions been complied with, he could not fail to have been brought to life again instantly by his own prescription. As it was, if this woman, or any other person, had administered an infinitesimal dose of lead and gunpowder immediately after he fell, he would have recovered forthwith. But unhappily the woman concerned did not possess the power of reasoning by analogy, or carrying out a principle, and thus the unfortunate gentleman had been sacrificed to the ignorance of the peasantry.

"Section D.—Statistics
Out-House, Black Boy and Stomach-Ache

President—Mr. Slug. *Vice-Presidents*—Messrs. Noakes and Styles

"Mr. Kwakley stated the result of some most ingenious statistical inquiries relative to the difference between the value of the qualification of several members of Parliament as published to the world, and its real nature and amount. After reminding the section that every member of Parliament for a town or borough was supposed to possess a clear freehold estate of three hundred pounds per annum, the honourable gentleman excited great amusement and laughter by stating the exact amount of freehold property possessed by a column of legislators, in which he had included himself. It appeared from this table, that the amount of such income possessed by each was o pounds, o shillings, and o pence, yielding an average of the same. (Great laughter.) It was pretty well known that there were accommodating gentlemen in the habit of furnishing new members with temporary qualifications, to the ownership of which they swore solemnly—of course as a mere matter of form. He argued from these *data* that it was wholly unnecessary for members of Parliament to possess any property at all, especially as when they had none the public could get them so much cheaper.

"Supplementary Section, E.—Umbugology and Ditchwaterisics

President—Mr. Grub. *Vice-Presidents*—Messrs. Dull and Dummy

"A paper was read by the secretary descriptive of a bay pony with one eye, which had been seen by the author standing in a butcher's cart at the corner of Newgate Market. The communication described the author of the paper as having, in the prosecution of a mercantile pursuit, betaken himself one Saturday morning last summer from Somers Town to Cheapside; in the course of which expedition he had beheld the extraordinary appearance above described. The pony had one distinct eye, and it had been pointed out to him by his friend Captain Blunderbore, of the Horse Marines, who assisted the author in his search, that whenever he winked this eye he whisked his tail (possibly to drive the flies off), but that he always winked and whisked at the same time. The animal was lean, spavined, and tottering; and the author proposed to constitute it of the family of *Fitfordogsmeataurious*. It certainly did occur to him that there was no case on record of a pony with one clearly-defined and distinct organ of vision, winking and whisking at the same moment.

"MR. Q. J. SNUFFLETOFFLE had heard of a pony winking his eye, and likewise of a pony whisking his tail, but whether they were two ponies or the same pony he could not undertake positively to say. At all events, he was acquainted with no authenticated instance of a simultaneous winking and whisking, and he really could not but doubt the existence of such a marvellous pony in opposition to all those natural laws by which ponies were governed. Referring, however, to the mere question of his one organ of vision, might he suggest the possibility of this pony having been literally half asleep at the time he was seen, and having closed only one eye.

"THE PRESIDENT observed that, whether the pony was half asleep or fast asleep, there could be no doubt that the association was wide awake, and therefore that they had better get the business over, and go to dinner. He had certainly never seen anything analogous to this pony, but he was not prepared to doubt its existence; for he had seen many queerer ponies in his time, though he did not pretend to have seen any more remarkable donkeys than the other gentlemen around him.

"PROFESSOR JOHN KETCH was then called upon to exhibit the skull of the late Mr. Greenacre, which he produced from a blue bag, remarking, on being invited to make any observations that occurred to him, 'that he'd pound it as that 'ere 'spectable section had never seed a more gamerer cove nor he vos'.

"A most animated discussion upon this interesting relic ensued; and, some difference of opinion arising respecting the real character of the deceased gentleman, Mr. Blubb delivered a lecture upon the cranium before him, clearly showing that Mr. Greenacre possessed the organ of destructiveness to a most unusual extent, with a most remarkable development of the organ of carveativeness. Sir Hookham Snivey was proceeding to combat this opinion, when Professor Ketch suddenly interrupted the proceedings by exclaiming, with great excitement of manner, 'Walker!'

"The President begged to call the learned gentleman to order.

"Professor Ketch.—'Order be blowed! you've got the wrong un, I tell you. It ain't no 'ed at all; it's a coker-nut as my brother-in-law has been a-carvin', to hornament his new baked tatur-stall wots a-comin' down 'ere vile the 'sociation's in the town. Hand over, vill you?'

"With these words, Professor Ketch hastily repossessed himself of the cocoa-nut, and drew forth the skull, in mistake for which he had exhibited it. A most interesting conversation ensued; but as there appeared some doubt ultimately whether the skull was Mr. Greenacre's, or a hospital patient's, or a pauper's, or a man's, or a woman's, or a monkey's, no particular result was obtained."

"I cannot," says our talented correspondent in conclusion, "I cannot close my account of these gigantic researches and sublime and noble triumphs without repeating a *bon mot* of Professor Woodensconce's, which shows how the greatest minds may occasionally unbend when truth can be presented to listening ears, clothed in an attractive and playful form. I was standing by, when, after a week of feasting and feeding, that learned gentleman, accompanied by the whole body of wonderful men, entered the hail yesterday, where a sumptuous dinner was prepared; where the richest wines sparkled on the board, and fat bucks—propitiatory sacrifices to learning—sent forth their savoury odours. 'Ah!' said Professor Woodensconce, rubbing his hands, 'this is what we meet for; this is what inspires us; this is what keeps us together, and beckons us onward; this is the *spread* of science, and a glorious spread it is.'"

THE PANTOMIME OF LIFE

THE PANTOMIME OF LIFE

BEFORE WE PLUNGE HEADLONG INTO this paper, let us at once confess to a fondness for pantomimes—to a gentle sympathy with clowns and pantaloons—to an unqualified admiration of harlequins and columbines—to a chaste delight in every action of their brief existence, varied and many-coloured as those actions are, and inconsistent though they occasionally be with those rigid and formal rules of propriety which regulate the proceedings of meaner and less comprehensive minds. We revel in pantomimes—not because they dazzle one's eyes with tinsel and gold leaf; not because they present to us, once again, the well-beloved chalked faces, and goggle eyes of our childhood; not even because, like Christmas-day, and Twelfth-night, and Shrove-Tuesday, and one's own birthday, they come to us but once a year ;—our attachment is founded on a graver and a very different reason. A pantomime is to us, a mirror of life; nay more, we maintain that it is so to audiences generally, although they are not aware of it, and that this very circumstance is the secret cause of their amusement and delight.

Let us take a slight example. The scene is a street: an elderly gentleman, with a large face and strongly marked features, appears. His countenance beams with a sunny smile, and a perpetual dimple is on his broad, red cheek. He is evidently an opulent elderly gentleman, comfortable in circumstances, and well-to-do in the world. He is not unmindful of the adornment of his person, for he is richly, not to say gaudily, dressed; and that he indulges to a reasonable extent in the pleasures of the table may be inferred from the joyous and oily manner in which he rubs his stomach, by way of informing the audience that he is going home to dinner. In the fulness of his heart, in the fancied security of wealth, in the possession and enjoyment of all the good things of life, the elderly gentleman suddenly loses his footing, and stumbles. How the audience

roar! He is set upon by a noisy and officious crowd, who buffet and
cuff him unmercifully. They scream with delight! Every time the elderly
gentleman struggles to get up, his relentless persecutors knock him
down again. The spectators are convulsed with merriment! And when
at last the elderly gentleman does get up, and staggers away, despoiled
of hat, wig, and clothing, himself battered to pieces, and his watch
and money gone, they are exhausted with laughter, and express their
merriment and admiration in rounds of applause.

Is this like life? Change the scene to any real street;—to the Stock
Exchange, or the City banker's; the merchant's counting-house, or
even the tradesman's shop. See any one of these men fall,—the more
suddenly, and the nearer the zenith of his pride and riches, the better.
What a wild hallo is raised over his prostrate carcase by the shouting
mob; how they whoop and yell as he lies humbled beneath them! Mark
how eagerly they set upon him when he is down; and how they mock
and deride him as he slinks away. Why, it is the pantomime to the very
letter.

Of all the pantomimic *dramatis personæ*, we consider the pantaloon
the most worthless and debauched. Independent of the dislike one
naturally feels at seeing a gentleman of his years engaged in pursuits
highly unbecoming his gravity and time of life, we cannot conceal
from ourselves the fact that he is a treacherous, worldly-minded old
villain, constantly enticing his younger companion, the clown, into
acts of fraud or petty larceny, and generally standing aside to watch
the result of the enterprise. If it be successful, he never forgets to
return for his share of the spoil; but if it turn out a failure, he generally
retires with remarkable caution and expedition, and keeps carefully
aloof until the affair has blown over. His amorous propensities, too, are
eminently disagreeable; and his mode of addressing ladies in the open
street at noon-day is downright improper, being usually neither more
nor less than a perceptible tickling of the aforesaid ladies in the waist,
after committing which, he starts back, manifestly ashamed (as well he
may be) of his own indecorum and temerity; continuing, nevertheless,

to ogle and beckon to them from a distance in a very unpleasant and immoral manner.

Is there any man who cannot count a dozen pantaloons in his own social circle? Is there any man who has not seen them swarming at the west end of the town on a sunshiny day or a summer's evening, going through the last-named pantomimic feats with as much liquorish energy, and as total an absence of reserve, as if they were on the very stage itself? We can tell upon our fingers a dozen pantaloons of our acquaintance at this moment—capital pantaloons, who have been performing all kinds of strange freaks, to the great amusement of their friends and acquaintance, for years past; and who to this day are making such comical and ineffectual attempts to be young and dissolute, that all beholders are like to die with laughter.

Take that old gentleman who has just emerged from the *Café de l' Europe* in the Haymarket, where he has been dining at the expense of the young man upon town with whom he shakes hands as they part at the door of the tavern. The affected warmth of that shake of the hand, the courteous nod, the obvious recollection of the dinner, the savoury flavour of which still hangs upon his lips, are all characteristics of his great prototype. He hobbles away humming an opera tune, and twirling his cane to and fro, with affected carelessness. Suddenly he stops—'tis at the milliner's window. He peeps through one of the large panes of glass; and, his view of the ladies within being obstructed by the India shawls, directs his attentions to the young girl with the band-box in her hand, who is gazing in at the window also. See! he draws beside her. He coughs; she turns away from him. He draws near her again; she disregards him. He gleefully chucks her under the chin, and, retreating a few steps, nods and beckons with fantastic grimaces, while the girl bestows a contemptuous and supercilious look upon his wrinkled visage. She turns away with a flounce, and the old gentleman trots after her with a toothless chuckle. The pantaloon to the life!

But the close resemblance which the clowns of the stage bear to those of every-day life is perfectly extraordinary. Some people talk with a sigh of the decline of pantomime, and murmur in low and dismal tones the name of Grimaldi. We mean no disparagement to the worthy and excellent old man when we say that this is downright nonsense. Clowns that beat Grimaldi all to nothing turn up every day, and nobody patronises them—more's the pity!

"I know who you mean," says so dirty-faced patron of Mr. Osbaldistone's, laying down the Miscellany when he has got thus far, and bestowing upon vacancy a most knowing glance; "you mean C. J. Smith as did Guy Fawkes and George Barnwell at the Garden." The dirty-faced gentleman has hardly uttered the words, when he is interrupted by a young gentleman in no shirt-collar and a Petersham coat. "No, no," says the young gentleman; "he means Brown, King, and Gibson, at the 'Delphi." Now, with great deference both to the first-named gentleman with the dirty face, and the last-named gentleman in the non-existing shirt-collar, we do *not* mean either the performer who so grotesquely burlesqued the Popish conspirator, or the three unchangeables who have been dancing the same dance under different imposing titles, and doing the same thing under various high-sounding names for some five or six years last past. We have no sooner made this avowal, than the public, who have hitherto been silent witnesses of the dispute, inquire what on earth it is we *do* mean; and, with becoming respect, we proceed to tell them.

It is very well known to all playgoers and pantomime-seers, that the scenes in which a theatrical clown is at the very height of his glory are those which are described in the play-bills as "Cheese-monger's shop and Crockery warehouse ", or "Tailor's shop, and Mrs. Queertable's boarding-house", or places bearing some such title, where the great fun of the thing consists in the hero's taking lodgings which he has not the slightest intention of paying for, or obtaining goods under false pretences, or abstracting the stock-in-trade of the respectable shopkeeper next door, or robbing warehouse porters as they pass under his window, or, to shorten the catalogue, in his swindling everybody he possibly can, it only remaining to be observed that, the more extensive the swindling is, and the more barefaced the impudence of the swindler, the greater the rapture and ecstasy of the audience. Now it is a most remarkable fact that precisely this sort of thing occurs in real life day after day, and nobody sees the humour of it. Let us illustrate our position by detailing the plot of this portion of the pantomime—not of the theatre, but of life.

The Honourable Captain Fitz-Whisker Fiercy, attended by his livery servant Do'em—a most respectable servant to look at, who has grown grey in the service of the captain's family—views, treats for, and ultimately obtains possession of, the unfurnished house, such a number, such a street. All the tradesmen in the neighbourhood are in agonies of competition for the captain's custom; the captain is a good-natured, kind-hearted, easy man, and, to avoid being the cause of disappointment to any, he most handsomely gives orders to all. Hampers of wine, baskets of provisions, cart-loads of furniture, boxes of jewellery, supplies of luxuries of the costliest description, flock to the house of the Honourable Captain Fitz-Whisker Fiercy, where they are received with the utmost readiness by the highly respectable Do'em; while the captain himself struts and swaggers about with that compound air of conscious superiority and general blood-thirstiness which a military captain should always, and does most times, wear, to the admiration and terror of plebeian men. But the tradesmen's backs are no sooner turned, than the captain, with all the eccentricity of a mighty mind, and assisted by the faithful Do'em, whose devoted fidelity is not the least touching part of his character, disposes of everything to great advantage; for, although the articles fetch small sums, still they are sold considerably above cost price, the cost to the captain having been nothing at all. After various manœuvres, the imposture is discovered, Fitz-Fiercy and Do'em are recognised as confederates, and the police-office to which they are both taken is thronged with their dupes.

Who can fail to recognise in this, the exact counterpart of the best portion of a theatrical pantomime—Fitz-Whisker Fiercy by the clown;

Do'em by the pantaloon; and supernumeraries by the tradesmen? The best of the joke, too, is, that the very coal-merchant who is loudest in his complaints against the person who defrauded him, is the identical man who sat in the centre of the very front row of the pit last night and laughed the most boisterously at this very same thing,—and not so well done either. Talk of Grimaldi, we say again! Did Grimaldi, in his best days, ever do anything in this way equal to Da Costa?

The mention of this latter justly celebrated clown reminds us of his last piece of humour, the fraudulently obtaining certain stamped acceptances from a young gentleman in the army. We had scarcely laid down our pen to contemplate for a few moments this admirable actor's performance of that exquisite practical joke, than a new branch of our subject flashed suddenly upon us. So we take it up again at once.

All people who have been behind the scenes, and most people who have been before them, know, that in the representation of a pantomime, a good many men are sent upon the stage for the express purpose of being cheated, or knocked down, or both. Now, down to a moment ago, we had never been able to understand for what possible purpose a great number of odd, lazy, large-headed men, whom one is in the habit of meeting here, and there, and everywhere, could ever have been created. We see it all, now. They are the supernumeraries in the pantomime of life; the men who have been thrust into it, with no other view than to be constantly tumbling over each other, and running their heads against all sorts of strange things. We sat opposite to one of these men at a supper-table, only last week. Now we think of it, he was exactly like the gentlemen with the pasteboard heads and faces, who do the corresponding business in the theatrical pantomimes; there was the same broad stolid simper—the same dull leaden eye—the same unmeaning, vacant stare; and whatever was said, or whatever was done, he always came in at precisely the wrong place, or jostled against something that he had not the slightest business with. We looked at the man across the table again and again; and could not satisfy ourselves what race of beings to class him with. How very odd that this never occurred to us before!

We will frankly own that we have been much troubled with the harlequin. We see harlequins of so many kinds in the real living pantomime, that we hardly know which to select as the proper fellow of him of the theatres. At one time we were disposed to think that the harlequin was neither more nor less than a young man of family and independent property, who had run away with an opera-dancer, and was fooling his life and his means away in light and trivial amusements. On reflection, however, we remembered that harlequins are occasionally guilty of witty, and even clever acts, and we are rather disposed to acquit our young men of family and independent property, generally speaking, of any such misdemeanours. On a more mature consideration of the subject, we have arrived at the conclusion that the harlequins of life are just ordinary men, to be found in no particular walk or degree, on whom a certain station, or particular conjunction of circumstances, confers the magic wand. And this brings us to a few words on the pantomime of public and political life, which we shall say at once, and then conclude—merely premising in this place that we decline any reference whatever to the columbine, being in no wise satisfied of the nature of her connection with her parti-coloured lover, and not feeling by any means clear that we should be justified in introducing her to the virtuous and respectable ladies who peruse our lucubrations.

We take it that the commencement of a Session of Parliament is neither more nor less than the drawing up of the curtain for a grand comic pantomime, and that his Majesty's most gracious speech on the opening thereof may be not inaptly compared to the clown's opening speech of "Here we are!" "My lords and gentlemen, here we are!" appears, to our mind at least, to be a very good abstract of the point and meaning of the propitiatory address of the ministry. When we remember how frequently this speech is made, immediately after *the change* too, the parallel is quite perfect, and still more singular.

Perhaps the cast of our political pantomime never was richer than at this day. We are particularly strong in clowns. At no former time, we should say, have we had such astonishing tumblers, or performers so ready to go through the whole of their feats for the amusement of an admiring throng. Their extreme readiness to exhibit, indeed, has given rise to some ill-natured reflections; it having been objected that by exhibiting gratuitously through the country when the theatre is closed, they reduce themselves to the level of mountebanks, and thereby tend to degrade the respectability of the profession. Certainly Grimaldi never did this sort of thing; and though Brown, King, and Gibson have gone to the Surrey in vacation time, and Mr. C. J. Smith has ruralised at Sadler's Wells, we find no theatrical precedent for a general tumbling through the country, except in the gentleman, name unknown, who threw summersets on behalf of the late Mr. Richardson, and who is no authority either, because he had never been on the regular boards.

But, laying aside this question, which after all is a mere matter of taste, we may reflect with pride and gratification of heart on the proficiency of our clowns as exhibited in the season. Night after night will they twist and tumble about, till two, three, and four o'clock in the morning; playing the strangest antics, and giving each other the funniest slaps on the face that can possibly be imagined, without evincing the smallest tokens of fatigue. The strange noises, the confusion, the shouting and roaring, amid which all this is done, too, would put to shame the most turbulent sixpenny gallery that ever yelled through a boxing-night.

It is especially curious to behold one of these clowns compelled to go through the most surprising contortions by the irresistible influence of the wand of office, which his leader or harlequin holds above his head. Acted upon by this wonderful charm he will become perfectly motionless, moving neither hand, foot, nor finger, and will even lose the faculty of speech at an instant's notice; or on the other hand, he will become all life and animation if required, pouring forth a torrent of words without sense or meaning, throwing himself into the wildest and most fantastic contortions, and even grovelling on the earth and licking up the dust. These exhibitions are more curious than pleasing; indeed, they are rather disgusting than otherwise, except to the admirers of such things, with whom we confess we have no fellow-feeling.

Strange tricks——very strange tricks——are also performed by the harlequin who holds for the time being the magic wand which we have just mentioned. The mere waving it before a man's eyes will dispossess his brains of all the notions previously stored there, and fill it with an entirely new set of ideas; one gentle tap on the back will alter the colour of a man's coat completely; and there are some expert performers, who, having this wand held first on one side and then on the other, will change from side to side, turning their coats at every evolution, with so much rapidity and dexterity, that the quickest eye can scarcely detect their motions. Occasionally, the genius who confers the wand, wrests it from the hand of the temporary possessor, and consigns it to some new performer; on which occasions all the characters change sides, and then the race and the hard knocks begin anew.

We might have extended this chapter to a much greater length—we might have carried the comparison into the liberal professions—we might have shown, as was in fact our original purpose, that each is in itself a little pantomime with scenes and characters of its own, complete; but, as we fear we have been quite lengthy enough already, we shall leave this chapter just where it is. A gentleman, not altogether unknown as a dramatic poet, wrote thus a year or two ago—

> "All the world's a stage,
> And all the men and women merely players":

and we, tracking out his footsteps at the scarcely-worth-mentioning little distance of a few millions of leagues behind, venture to add, by way of new reading, that he meant a Pantomime, and that we are all actors in The Pantomime of Life.

Some Particulars
Concerning a Lion

SOME PARTICULARS CONCERNING A LION

WE HAVE A GREAT RESPECT for lions in the abstract. In common with most other people, we have heard and read of many instances of their bravery and generosity. We have duly admired that heroic self-denial and charming philanthropy which prompts them never to eat people except when they are hungry, and we have been deeply impressed with a becoming sense of the politeness they are said to display towards unmarried ladies of a certain state. All natural histories teem with anecdotes illustrative of their excellent qualities; and one old spelling-book in particular recounts a touching instance of an old lion, of high moral dignity and stern principle, who felt it his imperative duty to devour a young man who had contracted a habit of swearing, as a striking example to the rising generation.

All this is extremely pleasant to reflect upon, and, indeed, says a very great deal in favour of lions as a mass. We are bound to state, however, that such individual lions as we have happened to fall in with have not put forth any very striking characteristics, and have not acted up to the chivalrous character assigned them by their chroniclers. We never saw a lion in what is called his natural state, certainly; that is to say, we have never met a lion out walking in a forest, or crouching in his lair under a tropical sun, waiting till his dinner should happen to come by, hot from the baker's. But we have seen some under the influence of captivity, and the pressure of misfortune; and we must say that they appeared to us very apathetic, heavy-headed fellows.

The lion at the Zoological Gardens, for instance. He is all very well; he has an undeniable mane, and looks very fierce; but, Lord bless us! what of that? The lions of the fashionable world look just as ferocious, and are the most harmless creatures breathing. A box-lobby lion or a Regent-street animal will put on a most terrible aspect, and roar fearfully, if you affront him; but he will never bite, and, if you offer to attack him manfully, will fairly turn tail and sneak off. Doubtless these creatures roam about sometimes in herds, and, if they meet any especially meek-looking and peaceably-disposed fellow, will endeavour to frighten him; but the faintest show of a vigorous resistance is sufficient to scare them even then. These are pleasant characteristics, whereas we make it matter of distinct charge against the Zoological lion and his brethren at the fairs, that they are sleepy, dreamy, sluggish quadrupeds.

We do not remember to have ever seen one of them perfectly awake, except at feeding-time. In every respect we uphold the biped lions against their four-footed namesakes, and we boldly challenge controversy upon the subject.

With these opinions it may be easily imagined that our curiosity and interest were very much excited the other day, when a lady of our acquaintance called on us and resolutely declined to accept our refusal of her invitation to an evening party; "for", said she, "I have got a lion coming". We at once retracted our plea of a prior engagement, and became as anxious to go, as we had previously been to stay away.

We went early, and posted ourselves in an eligible part of the drawing-room, from whence we could hope to obtain a full view of the interesting animal. Two or three hours passed, the quadrilles began, the room filled; but no lion appeared. The lady of the house became inconsolable,—for it is one of the peculiar privileges of these lions to make solemn appointments and never keep them,—when all of a sudden there came a tremendous double rap at the street-door, and the master of the house, after gliding out (unobserved as he flattered himself) to peep over the banisters, came into the room, rubbing his hands together with great glee, and cried out in a very important voice, "My dear, Mr. — (naming the lion) has this moment arrived."

Upon this all eyes were turned towards the door, and we observed several young ladies, who had been laughing and conversing previously with great gaiety and good humour, grow extremely quiet and sentimental; while some young gentlemen, who had been cutting great figures in the facetious and small-talk way, suddenly sank very obviously in the estimation of the company, and were looked upon with great coldness and indifference. Even the young man who had been ordered from the music shop to play the pianoforte was visibly affected, and struck several false notes in the excess of his excitement.

All this time there was a great talking outside, more than once accompanied by a loud laugh, and a cry of "Oh! capital! excellent!" from which we inferred that the lion was jocose, and that these exclamations were occasioned by the transports of his keeper and our host. Nor were we deceived; for when the lion at last appeared, we overheard his keeper, who was a little prim man, whisper to several gentlemen of his acquaintance, with uplifted hands, and every expression of half-suppressed admiration, that—(naming the lion again) was in *such* cue to-night!

The lion was a literary one. Of course, there were a vast number of people present who had admired his roarings, and were anxious to be introduced to him; and very pleasant it was to see them brought up for the purpose, and to observe the patient dignity with which he received all their patting and caressing. This brought forcibly to our mind what we had so often witnessed at country fairs, where the other lions are compelled to go through as many forms of courtesy as they chance to be acquainted with, just as often as admiring parties happen to drop in upon them.

While the lion was exhibiting in this way, his keeper was not idle, for he mingled among the crowd, and spread his praises most industriously. To one gentleman he whispered some very choice thing that the noble animal had said in the very act of coming up stairs, which, of course, rendered the mental effort still more astonishing; to another he murmured a hasty account of a grand dinner that had taken place the day before, where twenty-seven gentlemen had got up all at once to demand an extra cheer for the lion; and to the ladies he made sundry promises of interceding to procure the majestic brute's sign-manual for their albums. Then, there were little private consultations in different corners, relative to the personal appearance and stature of the lion; whether he was shorter than they had expected to see him, or taller, or thinner, or fatter, or younger, or older; whether he was like his portrait, or unlike it; and whether the particular shade of his eyes was black, or blue, or hazel, or green, or yellow, or mixture. At all these consultations the keeper assisted; and, in short, the lion was the sole and single subject of discussion till they sat him down to whist, and then the people relapsed into their old topics of conversation—themselves and each other.

We must confess that we looked forward with no slight impatience to the announcement of supper; for if you wish to see a tame lion under particularly favourable circumstances, feeding-time is the period of all others to pitch upon. We were therefore very much delighted to observe a sensation among the guests, which we well knew how to interpret, and immediately afterwards to behold the lion escorting the lady of the house down-stairs. We offered our arm to an elderly female of our acquaintance, who—dear old soul!—is the very best person that ever lived, to lead down to any meal; for, be the room ever so small, or the party ever so large, she is sure, by some intuitive perception of the eligible, to push and pull herself and conductor close to the best dishes on the table ;—we say we offered our arm to this elderly female, and, descending the stairs shortly after the lion, were fortunate enough to obtain a seat nearly opposite him.

Of course the keeper was there already. He had planted himself at precisely that distance from his charge which afforded him a decent pretext for raising his voice, when he addressed him, to so loud a key, as could not fail to attract the attention of the whole company, and immediately began to apply himself seriously to the task of bringing the lion out, and putting him through the whole of his manoeuvres Such flashes of wit as he elicited from the lion! First of all, they began to make puns upon a salt-cellar, and then upon the breast of a fowl, and then upon the trifle; but the best jokes of all were decidedly on the lobster salad, upon which latter subject the lion came out most vigorously, and, in the opinion of the most competent authorities, quite outshone himself. This is a very excellent mode of shining in society, and is founded, we humbly conceive, upon the classic model of the dialogues between Mr Punch and his friend the proprietor, wherein the latter takes all the up-hill work, and is content to pioneer to the jokes and repartees of Mr. P. himself, who never fails to gain great credit and excite much laughter thereby. Whatever it be founded on, however, we recommend it to all lions, present and to come; for in this instance it succeeded to admiration, and perfectly dazzled the whole body of hearers.

When the salt-cellar, and the fowl's breast, and the trifle, and the lobster salad were all exhausted, and could not afford standing-room for another solitary witticism, the keeper performed that very dangerous feat which is still done with some of the caravan lions, although in one instance it terminated fatally, of putting his head in the animal's mouth, and placing himself entirely at its mercy. Boswell frequently presents a melancholy instance of the lamentable results of this achievement, and other keepers and jackals have been terribly lacerated for their daring. It is due to our lion to state, that he condescended to be trifled with, in the most gentle manner, and finally went home with the showman in a hack cab; perfectly peaceable, but slightly fuddled.

Being in a contemplative mood, we were led to make some reflections upon the character and conduct of this genus of lions as we walked homewards, and we were not long in arriving at the conclusion that our former impression in their favour was very much strengthened and confirmed by what we had recently seen. While the other lions receive company and compliments in a sullen, moody, not to say snarling manner, these appear flattered by the attentions that are paid them; while those conceal themselves to the utmost of their power from the vulgar gaze, these court the popular eye, and, unlike their brethren, whom nothing short of compulsion will move to exertion, are ever ready to display their acquirements to the wondering throng. We have known bears of undoubted ability who, when the expectations of a large audience have been wound up to the utmost pitch, have peremptorily refused to dance; well-taught monkeys, who have unaccountably objected to exhibit on the slack wire; and elephants of unquestioned genius, who have suddenly declined to turn the barrel-organ; but we never once knew or heard of a biped lion, literary or otherwise,—and we state it as a fact which is highly creditable to the whole species,—who, occasion offering, did not seize with avidity on any opportunity which was afforded him, of performing to his heart's content on the first violin.

MR. ROBERT BOLTON

MR. ROBERT BOLTON

In the parlour of the Green Dragon, a public-house in the immediate neighbourhood of Westminster Bridge, everybody talks politics, every evening, the great political authority being Mr. Robert Bolton, an individual who defines himself as "a gentleman connected with the press", which is a definition of peculiar indefiniteness. Mr. Robert Bolton's regular circle of admirers and listeners are an undertaker, a greengrocer, a hairdresser, a baker, a large stomach surmounted by a man's head, and placed on the top of two particularly short legs, and a thin man in black, name, profession, and pursuit unknown, who always sits in the same position, always displays the same long, vacant face, and never opens his lips, surrounded as he is by most enthusiastic conversation, except to puff forth a volume of tobacco smoke, or give vent to a very snappy, loud, and shrill *hem*! The conversation sometimes turns upon literature, Mr. Bolton being a literary character, and always upon such news of the day as is exclusively possessed by that talented individual. I found myself (of course, accidentally) in the Green Dragon the other evening, and, being somewhat amused by the following conversation, preserved it.

"Can you lend me a ten-pound note till Christmas?" inquired the hairdresser of the stomach.

"Where's your security, Mr. Clip?"

"My stock in trade,—there's enough of it, I'm thinking, Mr. Thicknesse. Some fifty wigs, two poles, half-a-dozen head blocks, and a dead Bruin."

"No, I won't, then," growled out Thicknesse. "I lends nothing on the security of the whigs or the Poles either. As for whigs, they're cheats;

as for the Poles, they've got no cash. I never have nothing to do with blockheads, unless I can't awoid it (ironically), and a dead bear's about as much use to me as I could be to a dead bear."

"Well, then," urged the other, "there's a book as belonged to Pope, Byron's Poems, valued at forty pounds, because it's got Pope's identical scratch on the back; what do you think of that for security?"

"Well, to be sure!". cried the baker. "But how d'ye mean, Mr. Clip?"

"Mean! why, that it's got the *hottergruff* of Pope.

'Steal not this book, for fear of hangman's rope;
For it belongs to Alexander Pope.'

All that's written on the inside of the binding of the book; so, as my son says, we're *bound* to believe it."

"Well, sir," observed the undertaker, deferentially, and in a half-whisper, leaning over the table, and knocking over the hairdresser's grog as he spoke, "that argument's very easy upset."

"Perhaps, sir," said Clip, a little flurried, "you'll pay for the first upset afore you thinks of another."

"Now," said the undertaker, bowing amicably to the hairdresser, "I *think*, I says I *think*—you'll excuse me, Mr. Clip, I *think*, you see, that won't go down with the present company—unfortunately, my master had the honour of making the coffin of that ere Lord's housemaid, not no more nor twenty year ago. Don't think I'm proud on it, gentlemen; others might be; but I hate rank of any sort. I've no more respect for a Lord's footman than I have for any respectable tradesman in this room. I may say no more nor I have for Mr. Clip! (bowing). Therefore, that ere Lord must have been born long after Pope died. And it's a logical interference to defer, that they neither of them lived at the same time. So what I mean is this here, that Pope never had no book, never seed, felt, never smelt no book (triumphantly) as belonged to that ere Lord. And, gentlemen, when I consider how patiently you have 'eared the ideas what I have expressed, I feel bound, as the best way to reward you for the kindness you have exhibited, to sit down without saying anything more—partickler as I perceive a worthier visitor nor myself is just entered. I am not in the habit of paying compliments, gentlemen; when I do, therefore, I hope I strikes with double force."

"Ah, Mr. Murgatroyd! what's all this about striking with double force?" said the object of the above remark, as he entered. "I never excuse a man's getting into a rage during winter, even when he's seated so close to the fire as you are. It is very injudicious to put yourself into such a perspiration. What is the cause of this extreme physical and mental excitement, sir?"

Such was the very philosophical address of Mr. Robert Bolton, a shorthand-writer, as he termed himself—a bit of equivoque passing current among his fraternity, which must give the uninitiated a vast idea of the establishment of the ministerial organ, while to the initiated it signifies that no one paper can lay claim to the enjoyment of their services. Mr. Bolton was a young man, with a somewhat sickly and very dissipated expression of countenance. His habiliments were composed of an exquisite union of gentility, slovenliness, assumption, simplicity, *newness*, and old age. Half of him was dressed for the winter, the other half for the summer. His hat was of the newest cut, the D'Orsay; his trousers had been white, but the inroads of mud and ink, etc., had given them a piebald appearance; round his throat he wore a very high black cravat, of the most tyrannical stiffness: while his *tout ensemble* was hidden beneath the enormous folds of an old brown poodle-collared great-coat, which was closely buttoned up to the aforesaid cravat. His fingers peeped through the ends of his black kid gloves, and two of the toes of each foot took a similar view of society through the extremities of his highlows. Sacred to the bare walls of his garret be the mysteries of his interior dress! He was a short, spare, man, of a somewhat inferior deportment. Everybody seemed influenced by his entry into the room, and his salutation of each member partook of the patronising. The hairdresser made way for him between himself and the stomach. A minute afterwards he had taken possession of his pint and pipe. A pause in the conversation took place. Everybody was waiting, anxious for his first observation.

"Horrid murder in Westminster this morning," observed Mr. Bolton.

Everybody changed their positions. All eyes were fixed upon the man of paragraphs.

"A baker murdered his son by boiling him in a copper," said Mr. Bolton.

"Good heavens!" exclaimed everybody, in simultaneous horror.

"Boiled him, gentlemen I" added Mr. Bolton, with the most effective emphasis; "*boiled* him!"

"And the particulars, Mr. B.," inquired the hairdresser, "the particulars?"

Mr. Bolton took a very long draught of porter, and some two or three dozen whiffs of tobacco, doubtless to instil into the commercial capacities of the company the superiority of a gentleman connected with the press, and then said—

"The man was a baker, gentlemen. (Every one looked at the baker present, who stared at Bolton.) His victim, being his son, also was necessarily the son of a baker. The wretched murderer had a wife, whom he was frequently in the habit, while in an intoxicated state, of kicking, pummelling, flinging mugs at, knocking down, and half-killing while in bed, by inserting in her mouth a considerable portion of a sheet or blanket."

The speaker took another draught, everybody looked at everybody else, and exclaimed "Horrid!"

"It appears in evidence, gentlemen," continued Mr. Bolton, "that, on the evening of yesterday, Sawyer the baker came home in a reprehensible state of beer. Mrs. S., connubially considerate, carried him in that condition up-stairs into his chamber, and consigned him to their mutual couch. In a minute or two she lay sleeping beside the man whom the morrow's dawn beheld a murderer! (Entire silence informed the reporter that his picture had attained the awful effect he desired.) The son came home about an hour afterwards, opened the door, and went up to bed. Scarcely (gentlemen, conceive his feelings of alarm), scarcely had he taken off his indescribables, when shrieks(to his experienced ear *maternal* shrieks) scared the silence of surrounding night. He put his indescribables on again, and ran down-stairs. He opened the door of the parental bed-chamber. His father was dancing upon his mother. What must have been his feelings! In the agony of the minute he rushed at his male parent as he was about to plunge a knife into the side of his female. The mother shrieked. The father caught the son (who had wrested the knife from the paternal grasp) up in his arms, carried him down-stairs, shoved him into a copper of boiling water among some linen, closed the lid, and jumped upon the top of it, in which position he was, found with a ferocious countenance by the mother, who arrived in the melancholy wash-house just as he had so settled himself.

"'Where's my boy?' shrieked the mother.

"'In that copper, boiling,' coolly replied the benign father.

"Struck by the awful intelligence, the mother rushed from the house, and alarmed the neighbourhood. The police entered a minute afterwards. The father, having bolted the wash-house door, had bolted himself. They dragged the lifeless body of the boiled baker from the cauldron, and, with a promptitude commendable in men of their station, they immediately carried it to the station-house. Subsequently, the baker was apprehended while seated on the top of a lamp-post in Parliament Street, lighting his pipe."

The whole horrible ideality of the Mysteries of Udolpho, condensed into the pithy effect of a ten-line paragraph, could not possibly have so affected the narrator's auditory. Silence, the purest and most noble of all kinds of applause, bore ample testimony to the barbarity of the baker, as well as to Bolton's knack of narration; and it was only broken after some minutes had elapsed by interjectional expressions, of the intense indignation of every man present. The baker wondered how a British baker could so disgrace himself and the highly honour-able calling to which he belonged; and the others indulged in a variety of wonderments connected with the subject; among which not the least wonderment was that which was awakened by the genius and information of Mr. Robert Bolton, who, after a glowing eulogium on himself, and his unspeakable influence with the daily press, was proceeding, with a most solemn countenance, to hear the pros and cons of the Pope autograph question, when I took up my hat, and left.

FAMILIAR EPISTLE FROM A PARENT TO A CHILD

FAMILIAR EPISTLE FROM A PARENT TO A CHILD

AGED TWO YEARS AND TWO MONTHS

My Child,

To recount with what trouble I have brought you up—with what an anxious eye I have regarded your progress,—how late and how often I have sat up at night working for you,—and how many thousand letters I have received from, and written to your various relations and friends, many of whom have been of a querulous and irritable turn,—to dwell on the anxiety and tenderness with which I have (a far as I possessed the power) inspected and chosen your food; rejecting the indigestible and heavy matter which some injudicious but well-meaning old ladies would have had you swallow, and retaining only those light and pleasant articles which I deemed calculated to keep you free from all gross humours, and to render you an agreeable child, and one who might be popular with society in general,—to dilate on the steadiness with which I have prevented your annoying any company by talking politics—always assuring you that you would thank me for it yourself some day when you grew older,—to expatiate, in short, upon my own assiduity as a parent, is beside my present purpose, though I cannot but contemplate your fair appearance—your robust health, and unimpeded circulation (which I take to be the great secret of your good looks) without the liveliest satisfaction and delight.

It is a trite observation, and one which, young as you are, I have no doubt you have often heard repeated, that we have fallen upon strange times, and live in days of constant shiftings and changes. I had a melancholy instance of this only a week or two since. I was returning from Manchester to London by the Mail Train, when I suddenly fell into another train—a mixed train—of reflection, occasioned by the dejected and disconsolate demeanour of the Post-Office Guard. We were stopping at some station where they take in water, when he dismounted slowly from the little box in which he sits in ghastly mockery of his old condition with pistol and blunderbuss beside him, ready to shoot the first highwayman (or railwayman) who shall attempt to stop the horses, which now travel (when they travel at all) *inside* and in a portable stable invented for the purpose,— he dismounted, I say, slowly and sadly, from his post, and looking mournfully about him as if in dismal recollection of the old roadside public-house——the blazing fire—the glass of foaming ale—the buxom handmaid and admiring hangers-on of tap-room and stable, all honoured by his notice; and, retiring a little apart, stood leaning against a signal-post, surveying the engine with a look of combined affliction and disgust which no words can describe. His scarlet coat and golden lace were tarnished with ignoble smoke; flakes of soot had fallen on his bright green shawl—his pride in days of yore— the steam condensed in the tunnel from which we had just emerged, shone upon his hat like rain. His eye betokened that he was thinking of the coachman; and as it wandered to his own seat and his own fast-fading garb, it was plain to see that he felt his office and himself had alike no business there, and were nothing but an elaborate practical joke.

As we whirled away, I was led insensibly into an anticipation of those days to come, when mail-coach guards shall no longer be judges of horse-flesh—when a mail-coach guard shall never even have seen a horse—when stations shall have superseded stables, and corn shall have given place to coke. "In those dawning times," thought I, "exhibition-rooms shall teem with portraits of Her Majesty's favourite engine, with boilers after Nature by future Landseers. Some Amburgh, yet unborn, shall break wild horses by his magic power; and in the dress of a mail-coach guard exhibit his TRAINED ANIMALS in a mock mail-coach. Then, shall wondering crowds observe how that, with the exception of his whip, it is all his eye; and crowned heads shall see them fed on oats, and stand alone unmoved and undismayed, while courtiers flee affrighted when the coursers neigh!"

Such, my child, were the reflections from which I was only awakened then, as I am now, by the necessity of attending to matters of present though minor importance. I offer no apology to you for the digression, for it brings me very naturally to the subject of change, which is the very subject of which I desire to treat.

In fact, my child, you have changed hands. Henceforth I resign you to the guardianship and protection of one of my most intimate and valued friends, Mr. Ainsworth, with whom, and with you, my best wishes and warmest feelings will ever remain. I reap no gain or profit by parting from you, nor will any conveyance of your property be required, for, in this respect, you have always been literally "Bentley's" Miscellany, and never mine.

Unlike the driver of the old Manchester mail, I regard this altered state of things with feelings of unmingled pleasure and satisfaction. Unlike the guard of the new Manchester mail, *your* guard is at home in his new place, and has roystering highwaymen and gallant desperadoes ever within call. And if I might compare you, coy child, to an engine; (not a Tory engine, nor a Whig engine, but a brisk and rapid locomotive;) your friends and patrons to passengers; and he who now stands towards you *in loco parentis* as the skilful engineer and supervisor of the whole, I would humbly crave leave to postpone the departure of the train on its new and auspicious course for one brief instant, while, with hat in hand, I approach side by side with the friend who travelled with me on the old road, and presume to solicit favour and kindness in behalf of him and his new charge, both for their sakes and that of the old coachman,

Boz.

THE LAMPLIGHTER

THE LAMPLIGHTER

"IF YOU TALK OF MURPHY and Francis Moore, gentlemen," said the lamplighter who was in the chair, "I mean to say that neither of 'em ever had any more to do with the stars than Tom Grig had."

"And what had *he* to do with 'em?" asked the lamplighter who officiated as vice.

"Nothing at all," replied the other; "just exactly nothing at all."

"Do you mean to say you don't believe in Murphy, then?" demanded the lamplighter who had opened the discussion.

"I mean to say I believe in Tom Grig," replied the chairman. "Whether I believe in Murphy, or not, is a matter between me and my conscience; and whether Murphy believes in himself, or not, is a matter between him and his conscience. Gentlemen, I drink your healths."

The lamplighter who did the company this honour, was seated in the chimney-corner of a certain tavern, which has been, time out of mind, the Lamplighters' House of Call. He sat in the midst of a circle of lamplighters, and was the cacique, or chief of the tribe.

If any of our readers have had the good fortune to behold a lamplighter's funeral, they will not be surprised to learn that lamplighters are a very strange and primitive people; that they rigidly adhere to old ceremonies and customs which have been handed down among them from father to son since the first public lamp was lighted out of doors; that they intermarry, and betroth their children in infancy; that they enter into no plots or conspiracies (for who ever heard of a traitorous lamplighter?); that they commit no crimes against the laws of their country (there being no instance of a murderous or burglarious lamplighter); that they are, in short, notwithstanding their apparently volatile and restless character, a highly moral and reflective people: having among themselves as many traditional observances as the Jews, and being, as a body, if not as old as the hills, at least as old as the streets. It is an article of their creed that the first faint glimmering of true civilisation shone in the first street-light maintained at the public expense. They trace their existence and high position in the public esteem, in a direct line to the heathen mythology; and hold that the history of Prometheus himself is but a pleasant fable, whereof the true hero is a lamplighter.

"Gentlemen," said the lamplighter in the chair, "I drink your healths."

"And perhaps, Sir," said the vice, holding up his glass, and rising a little way off his seat and sitting down again, in token that he recognised and returned the compliment, "perhaps you will add to that condescension by telling us who Tom Grig was, and how he came to be connected in your mind with Francis Moore, Physician."

"Hear, hear, hear!" cried the lamplighters generally.

"Tom Grig, gentlemen," said the chairman, "was one of us; and it happened to him, as it don't often happen to a public character in our line, that he had his what-you-may-call-it cast."

"His head?" said the vice.

"No," replied the chairman, "not his head."

"His face, perhaps?" said the vice. "No, not his face." "His legs?" "No, not his legs." Nor yet his arms, nor his hands, nor his feet, nor his chest, all of which were severally suggested.

"His nativity, perhaps?"

"That's it," said the chairman, awakening from his thoughtful attitude at the suggestion. "His nativity. That's what Tom had cast, gentlemen."

"In plaister?" asked the vice.

"I don't rightly know how it's done," returned the chairman. "But I suppose it was."

And there he stopped as if that were all he had to say; whereupon there arose a murmur among the company, which at length resolved itself into a request, conveyed through the vice, that he would go on. This being exactly what the chairman wanted, he mused for a little

time, performed that agreeable ceremony which is popularly termed
wetting one's whistle, and went on thus:

"Tom Grig, gentlemen, was, as I have said, one of us; and I may go
further, and say he was an ornament to us, and such a one as only the
good old times of oil and cotton could have produced. Tom's family,
gentlemen, were all lamplighters."

"Not the ladies, I hope?" asked the vice.

"They had talent enough for it, Sir," rejoined the chairman, "and
would have been, but for the prejudices of society. Let women have
ther rights, Sir, and the females of Tom's family would have been every
one of 'em in office. But that emancipation hasn't come yet, and hadn't
then, and consequently they confined themselves to the bosoms of their
families, cooked the dinners, mended the clothes, minded the children,
comforted their husbands, and attended to the house-keeping generally.
It's a hard thing upon the women, gentlemen, that they are limited to
such a sphere of action as this; very hard.

"I happen to know all about Tom, gentlemen, from the circumstance
of his uncle by his mother's side, having been my particular friend. His
(that's Tom's uncle's) fate was a melancholy one. Gas was the death
of him. When it was first talked of, he laughed. He wasn't angry; he
laughed at the credulity of human nature. 'They might as well talk,' he
says, 'of laying on an everlasting succession of glow-worms;' and then he
laughed again, partly at his joke, and partly at poor humanity.

"In course of time, however, the thing got ground, the experiment was
made, and they lighted up Pall Mall. Tom's uncle went to see it. I've heard
that he fell off his ladder fourteen times that night, from weakness, and
that he would certainly have gone on falling till he killed himself, if his
last tumble hadn't been into a wheelbarrow which was going his way, and
humanely took him home. 'I foresee in this,' says Tom's uncle faintly, and
taking to his bed as he spoke—' I foresee in this,' he says, 'the breaking up
of our profession. There's no more going the rounds to trim by daylight,
no more dribbling down of the oil on the hats and bonnets of ladies and
gentlemen when one feels in spirits. Any low fellow can light a gas-lamp.

And it's all up.' In this state of mind, he petitioned the government for—I want a word again, gentlemen—what do you call that which they give to people when it's found out, at last, that they've never been of any use, and have been paid too much for doing nothing?"

"Compensation?" suggested the vice.

"That's it," said the chairman. "Compensation. They didn't give it to him, though, and then he got very fond of his country all at once, and went about saying that gas was a death-blow to his native land, and that it was a plot of the radicals to ruin the country and destroy the oil and cotton trade for ever, and that the whales would go and kill themselves privately, out of sheer spite and vexation at not being caught. At last he got right-down cracked; called his tobacco-pipe a gas-pipe; thought his tears were lamp-oil; and went on with all manner of nonsense of that sort till one night he hung himself on a lamp-iron in Saint Martin's Lane, and there was an end of *him*.

"Tom loved him, gentlemen, but he survived it. He shed a tear over his grave, got very drunk, spoke a funeral oration that night in the watch-house, and was fined five shillings for it, in the morning. Some men are none the worse for this sort of thing. Tom was one of 'em. He went that very afternoon on a new beat: as clear in his head, and as free from fever as Father Mathew himself.

" Tom's new beat, gentlemen, was—I can't exactly say where, for that he'd never tell; but I know it was in a quiet part of town, where there were some queer old houses. I have always had it in my head that it must have been somewhere near Canonbury Tower in Islington, but that's a matter of opinion. Wherever it was, he went upon it, with a bran-new ladder, a white hat, a brown holland jacket and trousers, a blue neck-kerchief, and a sprig of full-grown double wallflower in his button-hole. Tom was always genteel in his appearance, and I have heard from the best judges, that if he had left his ladder at home that afternoon, you might have took him for a lord.

"He was always merry, was Tom, and such a singer, that if there was any encouragement for native talent, he'd have been at the opera.

He was on his ladder, lighting his first lamp, and singing to himself in a manner more easily to be conceived than described, when he hears the clock strike five, and suddenly sees an old gentleman with a telescope in his hand, throw up a window and look at him very hard.

"Tom didn't know what could be passing in this old gentleman's mind. He thought it likely enough that he might be saying within himself, 'Here's a new lamplighter—a good-looking young fellow— shall I stand something to drink?' Thinking this possible, he keeps quite still, pretending to be very particular about the wick, and looks at the old gentleman sideways, seeming to take no notice of him.

"Gentlemen, he was one of the strangest and most mysterious-looking files that ever Tom clapped his eyes on. He was dressed all slovenly and untidy, in a great gown of a kind of bed-furniture pattern, with a cap of the same on his head; and a long old flapped waistcoat; with no braces, no strings, very few buttons—in short, with hardly any of those artificial contrivances that hold society together. Tom knew by these signs, and by his not being shaved, and by his not being over-clean, and by a sort of wisdom not quite awake, in his face, that he was a scientific old gentleman. He often told me that if he could have conceived the possibility of the whole Royal Society being boiled down into one man, he should have said the old gentleman's body was that Body.

"The old gentleman clasps the telescope to his eye, looks all round, sees nobody else in sight, stares at Tom again, and cries out very loud:

"'Hal-loa!'

"'Halloa, Sir,' says Tom from the ladder; 'and halloa again, if you come to that.'

"'Here's an extraordinary fulfilment,' says the old gentleman, 'of a prediction of the planets.'

"'Is there?' says Tom. 'I'm very glad to hear it.'

"'Young man,' says the old gentleman, 'you don't know me.'

"'Sir,' says Tom, 'I have not that honour; but I shall be happy to drink your health, notwithstanding.'

"'I read,' cries the old gentleman, without taking any notice of this politeness on Tom's part—'I read what's going to happen, in the stars.'

"Tom thanked him for the information, and begged to know if anything particular was going to happen in the stars, in the course of a week or so; but the old gentleman, correcting him, explained that he read in the stars what was going to happen on dry land, and that he was acquainted with all the celestial bodies.

"'I hope they're all well, Sir,' says Tom—'everybody.'

"'Hush!' cries the old gentleman. 'I have consulted the book of Fate with rare and wonderful success. I am versed in the great sciences of astrology and astronomy. In my house here, I have every description of apparatus for observing the course and motion of the planets. Six months ago, I derived from this source, the knowledge that precisely as the clock struck five this afternoon a stranger would present himself— the destined husband of my young and lovely niece—in reality of illustrious and high descent, but whose birth would be enveloped in uncertainty and mystery. Don't tell me yours isn't,' says the old gentleman, who was in such a hurry to speak that he couldn't get the words out fast enough, 'for I know better.'

"Gentlemen, Tom was so astonished when he heard him say this, that he could hardly keep his footing on the ladder, and found it necessary to hold on by the lamp-post. There *was* a mystery about his birth. His mother had always admitted it. Tom had never known who was his father, and some people had gone so far as to say that even *she* was in doubt.

"While he was in this state of amazement, the old gentleman leaves the window, bursts out of the house-door, shakes the ladder, and Tom, like a ripe pumpkin, comes sliding down into his arms. -

"'Let me embrace you,' he says, folding his arms about him, and nearly lighting up his old bed-furniture gown at Tom's link. 'You're a man of noble aspect. Everything combines to prove the accuracy of my observations. You have had mysterious promptings within you,' he says; 'I know you have had whisperings of greatness, eh?' he says.

"'I think I have,' says Tom—Tom was one of those who can persuade themselves to anything they like—'I've often thought I wasn't the small beer I was taken for.'

"'You were right,' cries the old gentleman, hugging him again. 'Come in. My niece awaits us.'

"'Is the young lady tolerable good-looking, Sir?' says Tom, hanging fire rather, as he thought of her playing the piano, and knowing French, and being up to all manner of accomplishments.

"'She's beautiful!' cries the old gentleman, who was in such a terrible bustle that he was all in a perspiration. 'She has a graceful carriage, an exquisite shape, a sweet voice, a countenance beaming with animation and expression; and the eye,' he says, rubbing his hands, 'of a startled fawn.'

"Tom supposed this might mean, what was called among his circle of acquaintance, 'a game eye'; and, with a view to this defect, inquired whether the young lady had any cash.

"'She has five thousand pounds,' cries the old gentleman. 'But what of that? what of that? A word in your ear. I'm in search of the philosopher's stone. I have very nearly found it—not quite. It turns everything to gold; that's its property.'

"Tom naturally thought it must have a deal of property; and said that when the old gentleman did get it, he hoped he'd be careful to keep it in the family.

"'Certainly,' he says, 'of course. Five thousand pounds! What's five thousand pounds to us? What's five million?' he says. 'What's five thousand million? Money will be nothing to us. We shall never be able to spend it fast enough.'

"'We'll try what we can do, Sir,' says Tom.

"'We will,' says the old gentleman. 'Your name?'

"'Grig,' says Tom.

"The old gentleman embraced him again, very tight; and without speaking another word, dragged him into the house in such an excited manner, that it was as much as Tom could do to take his link and ladder with him, and put them down in the passage.

"Gentlemen, if Tom hadn't been always remarkable for his love of truth, I think you would still have believed him when he said that all this was like a dream. There is no better way for a man to find out whether he is really asleep or awake, than calling for something to eat. If he's in a dream, gentlemen, he'll find something wanting in the flavour, depend upon it.

"Tom explained his doubts to the old gentleman, and said that if there was any cold meat in the house, it would ease his mind very much to test himself at once. The old gentleman ordered up a venison pie, a small ham, and a bottle of very old Madeira. At the first mouthful of pie and the first glass of wine, Tom smacks his lips and cries out, 'I'm awake—wide awake;' and to prove that he was so, gentlemen, he made an end of 'em both.

"When Tom had finished his meal (which he never spoke of afterwards without tears in his eyes), the old gentleman hugs him again, and says, 'Noble stranger! let us visit my young and lovely niece.' Tom, who was a little elevated with the wine, replies, 'The noble stranger is agreeable!' At which words the old gentleman took him by the hand, and led him to the parlour; crying as he opened the door, 'Here is Mr. Grig, the favourite of the planets!'

"I will not attempt a description of female beauty, gentlemen, for every one of us has a model of his own that suits his own taste best. In this parlour that I'm speaking of, there were two young ladies; and if every gentleman present, will imagine two models of his own in their places, and will be kind enough to polish 'em up to the very highest pitch of perfection, he will then have a faint conception of their uncommon radiance.

"Besides these two young ladies, there was their waiting-woman, that under any other circumstances Tom would have looked upon as a Venus; and besides her, there was a tall, thin, dismal-faced young gentleman, half man and half boy, dressed in a childish suit of clothes very much too short in the legs and arms; and looking, according to Tom's comparison, like one of the wax juveniles from a tailor's door, grown up and run to seed. Now, this youngster stamped his foot upon the ground and looked very fierce at Tom, and Tom looked fierce at him—for to tell the truth, gentlemen, Tom more than half suspected that when they entered the room he was kissing one of the young ladies; and for anything Tom knew, you observe, it might be *his* young lady—which was not pleasant.

"'Sir,' says Tom, 'before we proceed any further, will you have the goodness to inform me who this young Salamander'—Tom called him that for aggravation, you perceive, gentlemen—' who this young Salamander may be?'

"'That, Mr. Grig,' says the old gentleman, 'is my little boy. He was christened Galileo Isaac Newton Flamstead. Don't mind him. He's a mere child.'

"'And a very fine child too,' says Tom—still aggravating, you'll observe—'of his age, and as good as fine, I have no doubt. How do you do, my man?' with which kind and patronising expressions, Tom reached up to pat him on the head, and quoted two lines about little boys, from Doctor Watts's Hymns, which he had learnt at a Sunday School.

"It was very easy to see, gentlemen, by this youngster's frowning and by the waiting-maid's tossing her head and turning up her nose, and by the young ladies turning their backs and talking together at the other end of the room, that nobody but the old gentleman took very kindly to the noble stranger. Indeed, Tom plainly heard the waiting-woman say of her master, that so far from being able to read the stars as he pretended, she didn't believe he knew his letters in 'em, or at best that he had got further than words in one syllable; but Tom, not minding this (for he was in spirits after the Madeira), looks with an agreeable air towards the young ladies, and, kissing his hand to both, says to the old gentleman, 'Which is which?'

"'This,' says the old gentleman, leading out the handsomest, if one of 'em could possibly be said to be handsomer than the other—'this is my niece, Miss Fanny Barker.'

"'If you'll permit me, Miss,' says Tom, 'being a noble stranger and a favourite of the planets, I will conduct myself as such.' With these words, he kisses the young lady in a very affable way, turns to the old gentleman, slaps him on the back, and says, 'When's it to come off, my buck?'

"The young lady coloured so deep, and her lip trembled so much, gentlemen, that Tom really thought she was going to cry. But she kept her feelings down, and turning to the old gentleman, says, 'Dear uncle, though you have the absolute disposal of my hand and fortune, and though you mean well in disposing of 'em thus, I ask you whether you don't think this is a mistake? Don't you think, dear uncle,' she says, 'that the stars must be in error? Is it not possible that the comet may have put 'em out?'

"'The stars,' says the old gentleman, 'couldn't make a mistake if they tried. Emma,' he says to the other young lady.

"'Yes, papa,' says she.

"'The same day that makes your cousin Mrs. Grig will unite you to the gifted Mooney. No remonstrance—no tears. Now, Mr. Grig, let me conduct you to that hallowed ground, that philosophical retreat, where my friend and partner, the gifted Mooney of whom I have just now spoken, is even now pursuing those discoveries which shall enrich us with the precious metal, and make us masters of the world. Come, Mr. Grig,' he says.

"'With all my heart, Sir,' replies Tom; 'and luck to the gifted Mooney, say I—not so much on his account as for our worthy selves!' With this sentiment, Tom kissed his hand to the ladies again, and followed him out; having the gratification to perceive, as he looked back, that they were all hanging on by the arms and legs of Galileo Isaac Newton Flamstead, to prevent him from following the noble stranger, and tearing him to pieces.

"Gentlemen, Tom's father-in-law that was to be, took him by the hand, and having lighted a little lamp, led him across a paved courtyard at the back of the house, into a very large, dark, gloomy room: filled with all manner of bottles, globes, books, telescopes, crocodiles, alligators, and other scientific instruments of every kind. In the centre of this room was a stove or furnace, with what Tom called a pot, but which in my opinion was a crucible, in full boil. In one corner was a sort of ladder leading through the roof; and up this ladder the old gentleman pointed, as he said in a whisper:

"'The observatory. Mr. Mooney is even now watching for the precise time at which we are to come into all the riches of the earth. It will be necessary for he and I, alone in that silent place, to cast your nativity before the hour arrives. Put the day and minute of your birth on this piece of paper, and leave the rest to me.'

"'You don't mean to say,' says Tom, doing as he was told and giving him back the paper, 'that I'm to wait here long, do you? It's a precious dismal place.'

"'Hush!' says the old gentleman. 'It's hallowed ground. Farewell!'

"'Stop a minute,' says Tom. 'What a hurry you're in! What's in that large bottle yonder?'

"'It's a child with three heads,' says the old gentleman; 'and everything else in proportion.'

"'Why don't you throw him away?' says Tom. 'What do you keep such unpleasant things here for?'

"'Throw him away!' cries the old gentleman. 'We use him constantly in astrology. He's a charm.'

"'I shouldn't have thought it,' says Tom, 'from his appearance. *Must* you go, I say?'

"The old gentleman makes him no answer, but climbs up the ladder in a greater bustle than ever. Tom looked after his legs till there was nothing of him left, and then sat down to wait; feeling (so he used to say) as comfortable as if he was going to be made a freemason, and they were heating the pokers.

"Tom waited so long, gentlemen, that he began to think it must be getting on for midnight at least, and felt more dismal and lonely than ever he had done in all his life. He tried every means of whiling away the time, but it never had seemed to move so slow. First, he took a nearer view of the child with three heads, and thought what a comfort it must have been to his parents. Then he looked up a long telescope which was pointed out of the window, but saw nothing particular, in consequence of the stopper being on at the other end. Then he came to a skeleton in a glass case, labelled, 'Skeleton of a Gentleman—prepared by Mr. Mooney',—which made him hope that Mr. Mooney might not be in the habit of preparing gentlemen that way without their own consent. A hundred times, at least, he looked into the pot where they were boiling the philosopher's stone down to the proper consistency, and wondered whether it was nearly done. 'When it is,' thinks Tom, 'I'll send out for sixpenn'orth of sprats, and turn 'em into gold fish for a first experiment.' Besides which, he made up his mind, gentlemen, to have a country-house and a park; and to plant a bit of it with a double row of gas-lamps a mile long, and go out every night with a French-polished mahogany ladder, and two servants in livery behind him, to light 'em for his own pleasure.

"'At length and at last, the old gentleman's legs appeared upon the steps leading through the roof, and he came slowly down: bringing along with him, the gifted Mooney. This Mooney, gentlemen, was even more scientific in appearance than his friend; and had, as Tom often declared upon his word and honour, the dirtiest face we can possibly know of, in this imperfect state of existence.

"Gentlemen, you are all aware that if a scientific man isn't absent in his mind, he's of no good at all. Mr. Mooney was so absent, that when the old gentleman said to him, 'Shake hands with Mr. Grig,' he put out his leg. 'Here's a mind, Mr. Grig!' cries the old gentleman in a rapture. 'Here's philosophy! Here's rumination! Don't disturb him,' he says, 'for this is amazing!'

"Tom had no wish to disturb him, having nothing particular to say; but he was so uncommonly amazing, that the old gentleman got impatient, and determined to give him an electric shock to bring him to—' for you must know, Mr. Grig,' he says, 'that we always keep a strongly charged battery, ready for that purpose.' These means being resorted to, gentlemen, the gifted Mooney revived with a loud roar, and he no sooner came to himself than both he and the old gentleman looked at Tom with compassion, and shed tears abundantly.

"'My dear friend,' says the old gentleman to the Gifted, 'prepare him.'

"'I say,' cries Tom, falling back, 'none of that, you know. No preparing by Mr. Mooney if you please.'

"'Alas!' replies the old gentleman, 'you don't understand us. My friend, inform him of his fate.—I can't.'

"The Gifted mustered up his voice, after many efforts, and informed Tom that his nativity had been carefully cast, and he would expire at exactly thirty-five minutes, twenty-seven seconds, and five-sixths of a second past nine o'clock, a.m., on that day two months.

"Gentlemen, I leave you to judge what were Tom's feelings at this announcement, on the eve of matrimony and endless riches. 'I think,' he says in a trembling voice, 'there must be a mistake in the working of that sum. Will you do me the favour to cast it up again?'—'There is no mistake,' replies the old gentleman, 'it is confirmed by Francis Moore, Physician. Here is the prediction for to-morrow two months.' And he showed him the page, where sure enough were these words,—'The decease of a great person may be looked for, about this time'.

"'Which,' says the old gentleman, 'is clearly you, Mr. Grig.'

"'Too clearly,' cries Tom, sinking into a chair, and giving one hand to the old gentleman, and one to the Gifted. 'The orb of day has set on Thomas Grig for ever!'

"At this affecting remark, the Gifted shed tears again, and the other two mingled their tears with his, in a kind—if I may use the expression—of Mooney and Co.'s entire. But the old gentleman recovering first, observed that this was only a reason for hastening the marriage, in order that Tom's distinguished race might be transmitted to posterity; and requesting the Gifted to console Mr. Grig during his temporary absence, he withdrew to settle the preliminaries with his niece immediately.

"And now, gentlemen, a very extraordinary and remarkable occurrence took place; for as Tom sat in a melancholy way in one chair, and the Gifted sat in a melancholy way in another, a couple of doors were thrown violently open, the two young ladies rushed in, and one knelt down in a loving attitude at Tom's feet, and the other at the Gifted's. So far, perhaps, as Tom was concerned—as he used to say—you will say there was nothing strange in this: but you will be of a different opinion when you understand that Tom's young lady was kneeling to the Gifted, and the Gifted's young lady was kneeling to Tom.

"'Halloa! stop a minute!' cries Tom; 'here's a mistake. I need condoling with by sympathising woman, under my afflicting circumstances; but we're out in the figure. Change partners, Mooney.'

"'Monster!' cries Tom's young lady, clinging to the Gifted.

"'Miss!' says Tom. 'Is *that* your manners?'

"'I abjure thee!' cries Tom's young lady. 'I renounce thee. I never will be thine. Thou,' she says to the Gifted, 'art the object of my first and all-engrossing passion. Wrapt in thy sublime visions, thou hast not perceived my love; but, driven to despair, I now shake off the woman and avow it. Oh, cruel, cruel man!' With which reproach she laid her head upon the Gifted's breast, and put her arms about him in the tenderest manner possible, gentlemen.

"'And I,' says the other young lady, in a sort of ecstasy, that made Tom start—'I hereby abjure my chosen husband too. Hear me, Goblin!'—this was to the Gifted—'Hear me! I hold thee in the deepest detestation. The maddening interview of this one night has filled my soul with love—but not for thee. It is for thee, for thee, young man,' she cries to Tom. 'As Monk Lewis finely observes, Thomas, Thomas, I am thine, Thomas, Thomas, thou art mine: thine for ever, mine for ever!' with which words, she became very tender likewise.

"Tom and the Gifted, gentlemen, as you may believe, looked at each other in a very awkward manner, and with thoughts not at all complimentary to the two young ladies. As to the Gifted, I have heard Tom say often, that he was certain he was in a fit, and had it inwardly.

"'Speak to me! Oh, speak to me!' cries Tom's young lady to the Gifted.

"'I don't want to speak to anybody,' he says, finding his voice at last, and trying to push her away. 'I think I had better go. I'm— I'm frightened,' he says, looking about as if he had lost something.

"'Not one look of love!' she cries. 'Hear me while I declare—'

"'I don't know how to look a look of love,' he says, all in a maze. 'Don't declare anything. I don't want to hear anybody.'

"'That's right!' cries the old gentleman (who it seems had been listening). 'That's right! Don't hear her. Emma shall marry you to-morrow, my friend, whether she likes it or not, and *she* shall marry Mr. Grig.'

"Gentlemen, these words were no sooner out of his mouth than Galileo Isaac Newton Flamstead (who it seems had been listening too) darts in, and spinning round and round, like a young giant's top, cries, 'Let her. Let her. I'm fierce; I'm furious. I give her leave. I'll never marry anybody after this—never. It isn't safe. She is the falsest of the false,' he cries, tearing his hair and gnashing his teeth; 'and I'll live and die a bachelor!'

"'The little boy,' observed the Gifted gravely, 'albeit of tender years, has spoken wisdom. I have been led to the contemplation of woman-kind, and will not adventure on the troubled waters of matrimony.'

"'What!' says the old gentleman, 'not marry my daughter! Won't you, Mooney? Not if I make her? Won't you? Won't you?'

"'No,' says Mooney, 'I won't. And if anybody asks me any more, I'll run away, and never come back again.'

"'Mr. Grig,' says the old gentleman, 'the stars must be obeyed. You have not changed your mind because of a little girlish folly—eh, Mr. Grig?'

"Tom, gentlemen, had had his eyes about him, and was pretty sure that all this was a device and trick of the waiting-maid, to put him off his inclination. He had seen her hiding and skipping about the two doors, and had observed that a very little whispering from her pacified the Salamander directly. 'So,' thinks Tom, 'this is a plot—but it won't fit.'

"'Eh, Mr. Grig?' says the old gentleman.

"'Why, Sir,' says Tom, pointing to the crucible, 'if the soup's nearly ready—'

"'Another hour beholds the consummation of our labours,' returned the old gentleman.

"'Very good,' says Tom, with a mournful air. 'It's only for two months, but I may as well be the richest man in the world even for that time. I'm not particular, I'll take her, Sir. I'll take her.'

"The old gentleman was in a rapture to find Tom still in the same mind, and drawing the young lady towards him by little and little, was joining their hands by main force, when all of a sudden, gentlemen, the crucible blows up, with a great crash; everybody screams; the room is filled with smoke; and Tom, not knowing what may happen next, throws himself into a Fancy attitude, and says, 'Come on, if you're a man!' without addressing himself to anybody in particular.

"'The labours of fifteen years!' says the old gentleman, clasping his hands and looking down upon the Gifted, who was saving the pieces, 'are destroyed in an instant!'—And I am told, gentlemen, by-the-bye, that this same philosopher's stone would have been discovered a hundred times at least, to speak within bounds, if it wasn't for the one unfortunate circumstance that the apparatus always blows up, when it's on the very point of succeeding.

"Tom turns pale when he hears the old gentleman expressing himself to this unpleasant effect, and stammers out that if it's quite agreeable to all parties, he would like to know exactly what has happened, and what change has really taken place in the prospects of that company.

"'We have failed for the present, Mr. Grig,' says the old gentleman, wiping his forehead. 'And I regret it the more, because I have in fact invested my niece's five thousand pounds in this glorious speculation. But don't be cast down,' he says, anxiously—'in another fifteen years, Mr. Grig—'

"'Oh!' cries Tom, letting the young lady's hand fall. 'Were the stars very positive about this union, Sir?'

"'They were,' says the old gentleman.

"'I am sorry to hear it,' Tom makes answer, 'for it's no go, Sir.'

"'No what!' cries the old gentleman.

"'Go, Sir,' says Tom, fiercely. 'I forbid the banns.' And with these words—which are the very words he used—he sat himself down in a chair, and, laying his head upon the table, thought with a secret grief of what was to come to pass on that day two months.

"Tom always said, gentlemen, that that waiting-maid was the artfullest minx he had ever seen; and he left it in writing in this country when he went to colonize abroad, that he was certain in his own mind she and the Salamander had blown up the philosopher's stone on purpose, and to cut him out of his property. I believe Tom was in the right, gentlemen; but whether or no, she comes forward at this point, and says, 'May I speak, Sir?' and the old gentleman answering, 'Yes, you may,' she goes on to say that 'the stars are no doubt quite right in every respect, but Tom is not the man.' And she says, 'Don't you remember, Sir, that when the clock struck five this afternoon, you gave Master Galileo a rap on the head with your telescope, and told him to get out of the way?' 'Yes, I do,' says the old gentleman. 'Then,' says the waiting-maid, 'I say he's the man, and the prophecy is fulfilled.' The old gentleman staggers at this, as if somebody had hit him a blow on the chest, and cries, 'He! why he's a boy!' Upon that, gentlemen, the Salamander cries out that he'll be twenty-one next Lady-day; and complains that his father has always been so busy with the sun round which the earth revolves, that he has never taken any notice of the son that revolves round him; and that he hasn't had a new suit of clothes since he was fourteen; and that he wasn't even taken out of nankeen frocks and trousers till he was quite unpleasant in 'em; and touches on a good many more family matters to the same purpose. To make short of a long story, gentlemen, they all talk together, and cry together, and remind the old gentleman that as to the noble family, his own grandfather would have been lord mayor if he hadn't died at a dinner the year before; and they show him by all kinds of arguments that if the cousins are married, the prediction comes true every way. At last, the old gentleman being quite convinced, gives in; and joins their hands; and leaves his daughter to marry anybody she likes; and they are all well pleased; and the Gifted as well as any of them.

"In the middle of this little family party, gentlemen, sits Tom all the while, as miserable as you like. But, when everything else is arranged, the old gentleman's daughter says, that their strange conduct was a little device of the waiting-maid's to disgust the lovers he had chosen for 'em, and will he forgive her? and if he will, perhaps he might even find her a husband—and when she says that, she looks uncommon hard at Tom. Then the waiting-maid says that, oh dear! she couldn't abear Mr. Grig should think she wanted him to marry her; and that she had even gone so far as to refuse the last lamplighter, who was now a literary character (having set up as a bill-sticker); and that she hoped Mr. Grig would not suppose she was on her last legs by any means, for the baker was very strong in his attentions at that moment, and as to the butcher, he was frantic. And I don't know how much more she might have said, gentlemen (for, as you know, this kind of young women are rare ones to talk), if the old gentleman hadn't cut in suddenly, and asked Tom if he'd have her, with ten pounds to recompense him for his loss of time and disappointment, and as a kind of bribe to keep the story secret.

"'It don't much matter, Sir,' says Tom, 'I ain't long for this world. Eight weeks of marriage, especially with this young woman, might reconcile me to my fate. I think,' he says, 'I could go off easy after that.' With which he embraces her with a very dismal face, and groans in a way that might move a heart of stone—even of philosopher's stone.

"'Egad,' says the old gentleman, 'that reminds me—this bustle put it out of my head—there was a figure wrong. He'll live to a green old age—eighty-seven at least!'

"'How much, Sir?' cries Tom.

"'Eighty-seven!' says the old gentleman.

"Without another word, Tom flings himself on the old gentleman's neck; throws up his hat; cuts a caper; defies the waiting-maid; and refers her to the butcher.

"'You won't marry her!' says the old gentleman, angrily.

"'And live after it!' says Tom. 'I'd sooner marry a mermaid with a small-tooth comb and looking-glass.'

"'Then take the consequences,' says the other.

"With those words—I beg your kind attention here, gentlemen, for it's worth your notice—the old gentleman wetted the forefinger of his right hand in some of the liquor from the crucible that was spilt on the floor, and drew a small triangle on Tom's forehead. The room swam before his eyes, and he found himself in the watch-house."

"Found himself *where*?" cried the vice, on behalf of the company generally.

"In the watch-house," said the chairman. "It was late at night, and he found himself in the very watch-house from which he had been let out that morning."

"Did he go home?" asked the vice.

"The watch-house people rather objected to that," said the chairman; "so he stopped there that night, and went before the magistrate in the morning. 'Why, you're here again, are you?' says the magistrate, adding insult to injury; 'we'll trouble you for five shillings more, if you can conveniently spare the money.' Tom told him he had been enchanted, but it was of no use. He told the contractors the same, but they wouldn't believe him. It was very hard upon him, gentlemen, as he often said, for was it likely he'd go and invent such a tale? They shook their heads and told him he'd say anything but his prayers—as indeed he would; there's no doubt about that. It was the only imputation on his moral character that ever *I* heard of."

TO BE READ AT DUSK

To be Read at Dusk

ONE, TWO, THREE, FOUR, FIVE. There were five of them.

Five couriers, sitting on a bench outside the convent on the summit of the Great St. Bernard in Switzerland, looking at the remote heights, stained by the setting sun, as if a mighty quantity of red wine had been broached upon the mountain top, and had not yet had time to sink into the snow.

This is not my simile. It was made for the occasion by the stoutest courier, who was a German. None of the others took any more notice of it than they took of me, sitting on another bench on the other side of the convent door, smoking my cigar, like them, and—also like them—looking at the reddened snow, and at the lonely shed hard by, where the bodies of belated travellers, dug out of it, slowly wither away, knowing no corruption in that cold region.

The wine upon the mountain top soaked in as we looked; the mountain became white; the sky, a very dark blue; the wind rose; and the air turned piercing cold. The five couriers buttoned their rough coats. There being no safer man to imitate in all such proceedings than a courier, I buttoned mine.

The mountain in the sunset had stopped the five couriers in a conversation. It is a sublime sight, likely to stop conversation. The mountain being now out of the sunset, they resumed. Not that I had heard any part of their previous discourse; for indeed, I had not then broken away from the American gentleman, in the travellers' parlour of the convent, who, sitting with his face to the fire, had undertaken to realise to me the whole progress of events which had led to the accumulation by the Honourable Ananias Dodger of one of the largest acquisitions of dollars ever made in our country.

"My God!" said the Swiss courier, speaking in French, which I do not hold (as some authors appear to do) to be such an all-sufficient excuse for a naughty word, that I have only to write it in that language to make it innocent; "if you talk of ghosts—"

"But I *don't* talk of ghosts," said the German.

"Of what then?" asked the Swiss.

"If I knew of what then," said the German, " I should probably know a great deal more."

It was a good answer, I thought, and it made me curious. So, I moved my position to that corner of my bench which was nearest to them, and leaning my back against the convent wall, heard perfectly, without appearing to attend.

"Thunder and lightning!" said the German, warming, "when a certain man is coming to see you, unexpectedly; and, without his own knowledge, sends some invisible messenger to put the idea of him into your head all day, what do you call that? When you walk along a crowded street—at Frankfort, Milan, London, Paris—and think that a passing stranger is like your friend Heinrich, and then that another passing stranger is like your friend Heinrich, and so begin to have a strange foreknowledge that presently you'll meet your friend Heinrich—which you do, though you believed him at Trieste— what do you call that?"

"It's not uncommon, either," murmured the Swiss and the other three.

"Uncommon!" said the German. "It's as common as cherries in the Black Forest. It's as common as maccaroni at Naples. And Naples reminds me! When the old Marchesa Senzanima shrieks at a card-party on the Chiaja—I heard and saw her, for it happened in a Bavarian family of mine, and I was overlooking the service that evening—I say, when the old Marchesa starts up at the card-table, white through her rouge, and cries, 'My sister in Spain is dead! I felt her cold touch on my back!'—and when that sister *is* dead at the moment—what do you call that?"

"Or when the blood of San Gennaro liquefies at the request of the clergy—as all the world knows that it does regularly once a-year, in my native city," said the Neapolitan courier after a pause, with a comical look, "what do you call that?"

"*That!*" cried the German. "Well, I think I know a name for that."

"Miracle?" said the Neapolitan, with the same sly face.

The German merely smoked and laughed; and they all smoked and laughed.

"Bah!" said the German, presently. "I speak of things that really do happen. When I want to see the conjurer, I pay to see a professed one, and have my money's worth. Very strange things do happen without ghosts. Ghosts! Giovanni Baptista, tell your story of the English bride. There's no ghost in that, but something full as strange. Will any man tell me what?"

As there was a silence among them, I glanced around. He whom I took to be Baptista was lighting a fresh cigar. He presently went on to speak. He was a Genoese, as I judged.

"The story of the English bride?" said he. "Basta! one ought not to call so slight a thing a story. Well, it's all one. But it's true. Observe me well, gentlemen, it's true. That which glitters is not always gold; but what I am going to tell, is true."

He repeated this more than once.

Ten years ago, I took my credentials to an English gentleman at Long's Hotel, in Bond Street, London, who was about to travel—it might be for one year, it might be for two. He approved of them; likewise of me. He was pleased to make inquiry. The testimony that he received was favourable He engaged me by the six months, and my entertainment was generous.

He was young, handsome, very happy. He was enamoured of a fair young English lady, with a sufficient fortune, and they were going to be married. It was the wedding-trip, in short, that we were going to take. For three months' rest in the hot weather (it was early summer then) he had hired an old place on the Riviera, at an easy distance from my city, Genoa, on the road to Nice. Did I know that place? Yes; I told him I knew it well. It was an old palace with great gardens.

It was a little bare, and it was a little dark and gloomy, being close surrounded by trees; but it was spacious, ancient, grand, and on the seashore. He said it had been so described to him exactly, and he was well pleased that I knew it. For its being a little bare of furniture, all such places were. For its being a little gloomy, he had hired it principally for the gardens, and he and my mistress would pass the summer weather in their shade.

"So all goes well, Baptista?" said he.

"Indubitably, signore; very well."

We had a travelling chariot for our journey, newly built for us, and in all respects complete. All we had was complete; we wanted for nothing. The marriage took place. They were happy. *I* was happy, seeing all so bright, being so well situated, going to my own city, teaching my language in the rumble to the maid, la bella Carolina, whose heart was gay with laughter: who was young and rosy.

The time flew. But I observed—listen to this, I pray! (and here the courier dropped his voice)—observed my mistress sometimes brooding in a manner very strange; in a frightened manner; in an unhappy manner; with a cloudy, uncertain alarm upon her. I think that I began to notice this when I was walking up hills by the carriage side, and master had gone on in front. At any rate, I remember that it impressed itself upon my mind one evening in the South of France, when she called to me to call master back; and when he came back, and walked for a long way, talking encouragingly and affectionately to her, with his hand upon the open window, and hers in it. Now and then, he laughed in a merry way, as if he were bantering her out of something. By-and-by, she laughed, and then all went well again.

It was curious. I asked la bella Carolina, the pretty little one, Was mistress unwell?—No.—Out of spirits?—No.—Fearful of bad roads, or brigands?—No. And what made it more mysterious was, pretty little one would not look at me in giving answer, but *would* look at the view.

But, one day she told me the secret.

"If you must know," said Carolina, "I find, from what I have overheard, that mistress is haunted."

"How haunted?"

"By a dream."

"What dream?"

"By a dream of a face. For three nights before her marriage, she saw a face in a dream—always the same face, and only One."

"A terrible face?"

"No. The face of a dark, remarkable-looking man, in black, with black hair and a grey moustache—a handsome man except for a reserved and secret air. Not a face she ever saw, or at all like a face she ever saw. Doing nothing in the dream but looking at her fixedly, out of darkness."

"Does the dream come back?"

"Never. The recollection of it, is all her trouble."

"And why does it trouble her?"

Carolina shook her head.

"That's master's question," said la bella. "She don't know. She wonders why, herself. But I heard her tell him, only last night, that if she was to find a picture of that face in our Italian house (which she is afraid she will) she did not know how she could ever bear it."

Upon my word I was fearful after this (said the Genoese courier) of our coming to the old palazzo, lest some such ill-starred picture should happen to be there. I knew there were many there; and, as we got nearer and nearer to the place, I wished the whole gallery in the crater of Vesuvius. To mend the matter, it was a stormy dismal evening when we, at last, approached that part of the Riviera. It thundered; and the thunder of my city and its environs, rolling among the high hills, is very loud. The lizards ran in and out of the chinks in the broken stone wall of the garden, as if they were frightened; the frogs bubbled and croaked their loudest; the sea-wind moaned, and the wet trees dripped; and the lightning—body of San Lorenzo, how it lightened!

We all know what an old palace in or near Genoa is—how time and the sea air have blotted it—how the drapery painted on the outer walls has peeled off in great flakes of plaster—how the lower windows are darkened with rusty bars of iron—how the courtyard is overgrown with grass—how the outer buildings are dilapidated—how the whole pile seems devoted to ruin. Our palazzo was one of the true kind. It had been shut up close for months. Months ?—years!—it had an earthy smell, like a tomb. The scent of the orange trees on the broad back terrace, and of the lemons ripening on the wall, and of some shrubs that grew around a broken fountain, had got into the house somehow, and had never been able to get out again. There was, in every room, an aged smell, grown faint with confinement. It pined in all the cupboards and drawers. In the little rooms of communication, between great rooms, it was stifling. If you turned a picture—to come back to the pictures—there it still was, clinging to the wall behind the frame, like a sort of bat.

The lattice-blinds were close shut, all over the house. There were two ugly grey old women in the house, to take care of it; one of them with a spindle, who stood winding and mumbling in the doorway, and who would as soon have let in the devil as the air. Master, mistress, la bella Carolina, and I, went all through the palazzo. I went first, though I have named myself last, opening the windows and the lattice blinds, and shaking down on myself splashes of rain, and scraps of mortar, and now and then a dozing mosquito, or a monstrous, fat, blotchy, Genoese spider.

When I had let the evening light into a room, master, mistress, and la bella Carolina, entered. Then, we looked round at all the pictures, and I went forward again into another room. Mistress secretly had great fear of meeting with the likeness of that face—we all had; but there was no such thing. The Madonna and Bambino, San Francisco, San Sebastiano, Venus, Santa Caterina, Angels, Brigands, Friars, Temples at Sunset, Battles, White Horses, Forests, Apostles, Doges, all my old acquaintances many times repeated ?—yes. Dark handsome man in black, reserved and secret, with black hair and grey moustache, looking fixedly at mistress out of darkness?—no.

At last we got through all the rooms and all the pictures, and came out into the gardens. They were pretty well kept, being rented by a gardener, and were large and shady. in one place there was a rustic theatre, open to the sky; the stage a green slope; the coulisses, three entrances upon a side, sweet-smelling, leafy screens. Mistress moved her bright eyes, even there, as if she looked to see the face come in upon the scene; but all was well.

"Now, Clara," master said, in a low voice, "you see that it is nothing? You are happy."

Mistress was much encouraged. She soon accustomed herself to that grim palazzo, and would sing, and play the harp, and copy the old pictures, and stroll with master under the green trees and vines all day. She was beautiful. He was happy. He would laugh and say to me, mounting his horse for his morning ride before the heat:

"All goes well, Baptista!"

"Yes, signore, thank God, very well."

We kept no company. I took la bella to the Duomo and Annunciata, to the Café, to the Opera, to the village Festa, to the Public Garden, to the Day Theatre, to the Marionetti. The pretty little one was charmed with all she saw. She learnt Italian—heavens! miraculously! Was mistress quite forgetful of that dream? I asked Carolina sometimes. Nearly, said la bella—almost. It was wearing out.

One day master received a letter, and called me.

"Baptista!"

"Signore!"

"A gentleman who is presented to me will dine here to-day. He is called the Signor Dellombra. Let me dine like a prince."

It was an odd name. I did not know that name. But, there had been many noblemen and gentlemen pursued by Austria on political suspicions, lately, and some names had changed. Perhaps this was one. Altro! Dellombra was as good a name to me as another.

When the Signor Dellombra came to dinner (said the Genoese courier in the low voice, into which he had subsided once before), I showed him into the reception-room, the great sala of the old palazzo. Master received him with cordiality, and presented him to mistress. As she rose, her face changed, she gave a cry, and fell upon the marble floor.

Then, I turned my head to the Signor Dellombra, and saw that he was dressed in black, and had a reserved and secret air, and was a dark remarkable-looking man, with black hair and a grey moustache.

Master raised mistress in his arms, and carried her to her own room, where I sent la bella Carolina straight. La bella told me afterwards that mistress was nearly terrified to death, and that she wandered in her mind about her dream all night.

Master was vexed and anxious—almost angry, and yet full of solicitude. The Signor Dellombra was a courtly gentleman, and spoke with great respect and sympathy of mistress's being so ill. The African wind had been blowing for some days (they had told him at his hotel of the Maltese Cross), and he knew that it was often hurtful. He hoped the beautiful lady would recover soon. He begged permission to retire, and to renew his visit when he should have the happiness of hearing that she was better. Master would not allow of this, and they dined alone.

He withdrew early. Next day he called at the gate, on horse back, to inquire for mistress. He did so two or three times in that week.

What I observed myself, and what la bella Carolina told me, united to explain to me that master had now set his mind on curing mistress of her fanciful terror. He was all kindness, but he was sensible and firm. He reasoned with her, that to encourage such fancies was to invite melancholy, if not madness. That it rested with herself to be herself. That if she once resisted her strange weakness, so successfully as to receive the Signor Dellombra as an English lady would receive any other guest, it was for ever conquered. To make an end, the signore came again, and mistress received him without marked distress (though with constraint and apprehension still), and the evening passed serenely. Master was so delighted with this change, and so anxious to confirm it, that the Signor Dellombra became a constant guest. He was accomplished in pictures, books, and music; and his society, in any grim palazzo, would have been welcome.

I used to notice, many times, that mistress was not quite recovered. She would cast down her eyes and droop her head, before the Signor Dellombra, or would look at him with a terrified and fascinated glance, as if his presence had some evil influence or power upon her. Turning from her to him, I used to see him in the shaded gardens, or the large half-lighted sala, looking, as I might say, "fixedly upon her out of darkness". But, truly, I had not forgotten la bella Carolina's words describing the face in the dream.

After his second visit I heard master say:

"Now, see, my dear Clara, it's over! Dellombra has come and gone, and your apprehension is broken like glass."

"Will he—will he ever come again?" asked mistress.

"Again? Why, surely, over and over again! Are you cold?" (she shivered).

"No, dear—but—he terrifies me: are you sure that he need come again?"

"The surer for the question, Clara!" replied master, cheerfully.

But, he was very hopeful of her complete recovery now, and grew more and more so every day. She was beautiful. He was happy.

"All goes well, Baptista?" he would say to me again.

"Yes, signore, thank God; very well."

We were all (said the Genoese courier, constraining himself to speak a little louder), we were all at Rome for the Carnival. I had been out, all day, with a Sicilian, a friend of mine, and a courier, who was there with an English family. As I returned at night to our hotel, I met the little Carolina, who never stirred from home alone, running distractedly along the Corso.

"Carolina! What's the matter?"

"O Baptista! O, for the Lord's sake! where is my mistress?"

"Mistress, Carolina?"

"Gone since morning—told me, when master went out on his day's journey, not to call her, for she was tired with not resting in the night (having been in pain), and would lie in bed until the evening; then get up refreshed. She is gone!—she is gone! Master has come back, broken down the door, and she is gone! My beautiful, my good, my innocent mistress!"

The pretty little one so cried, and raved, and tore herself that I could not have held her, but for her swooning on my arm as if she had been shot. Master came up—in manner, face, or voice, no more the master that I knew, than I was he. He took me (I laid the little one upon her bed in the hotel, and left her with the chamber-women), in a carriage, furiously through the darkness, across the desolate Campagna. When it was day, and we stopped at a miserable posthouse, all the horses had been hired twelve hours ago, and sent away in different directions. Mark me! by the Signor Dellombra, who had passed there in a carriage, with a frightened English lady crouching in one corner.

I never heard (said the Genoese courier, drawing a long breath) that she was ever traced beyond that spot. All I know is, that she vanished into infamous oblivion, with the dreaded face beside her that she had seen in her dream.

"What do you call *that*?" said the German courier, triumphantly. "Ghosts! There are no ghosts *there*! What do you call this, that I am going to tell you? Ghosts! There are no ghosts *here*!"

I took an engagement once (pursued the German courier) with an English gentleman, elderly and a bachelor, to travel through my country, my Fatherland. He was a merchant who traded with my country and knew the language, but who had never been there since he was a boy—as I judge, some sixty years before.

His name was James, and he had a twin-brother, John, also a bachelor. Between these brothers there was a great affection. They were in business together, at Goodman's Fields, but they did not live together. Mr. James dwelt in Poland Street, turning out of Oxford Street, London; Mr. John resided by Epping Forest.

Mr. James and I were to start for Germany in about a week. The exact day depended on business. Mr. John came to Poland Street (where I was staying in the house), to pass that week with Mr. James. But, he said to his brother on the second day, "I don't feel very well, James. There's not much the matter with me; but I think I am a little gouty. I'll go home and put myself under the care of my old housekeeper, who understands my ways. If I get quite better, I'll come back and see you before you go. If I don't feel well enough to resume my visit where I leave it off, why *you* will come and see *me* before you go." Mr. James, of course, said he would, and they shook hands—both hands, as they always did—and Mr. John ordered out his old-fashioned chariot and rumbled home.

It was on the second night after that—that is to say, the fourth in the week—when I was awoke out of my sound sleep by Mr. James coming into my bedroom in his flannel-gown, with a lighted candle. He sat upon the side of my bed, and looking at me, said:

"Wilhelm, I have reason to think I have got some strange illness upon me."

I then perceived that there was a very unusual expression in his face.

"Wilhelm," said he, " I am not afraid or ashamed to tell you what I might be afraid or ashamed to tell another man. You come from a sensible country, where mysterious things are inquired into and are not settled to have been weighed and measured—or to have been unweighable and unmeasurable—or in either case to have been completely disposed of, for all time—ever so many years ago. I have just now seen the phantom of my brother."

I confess (said the German courier) that it gave me a little tingling of the blood to hear it.

"I have just now seen," Mr. James repeated, looking full at me, that I might see how collected he was, "the phantom of my brother John. I was sitting up in bed, unable to sleep, when it came into my room, in a white dress, and regarding me earnestly, passed up to the end of the room, glanced at some papers on my writing-desk, turned, and, still looking earnestly at me as it passed the bed, went out at the door. Now, I am not in the least mad, and am not in the least disposed to invest that phantom with any external existence out of myself. I think it is a warning to me that I am ill; and I think I had better be bled."

I got out of bed directly (said the German courier) and began to get on my clothes, begging him not to be alarmed, and telling him that I would go myself to the doctor. I was just ready, when we heard a loud knocking and ringing at the street door. My room being an attic at the back, and Mr. James's being the second-floor room in the front, we went down to his room, and put up the window, to see what was the matter.

"Is that Mr. James?" said a man below, falling back to the opposite side of the way to look up.

"It is," said Mr. James, "and you are my brother's man, Robert."

"Yes, Sir. I am sorry to say, Sir, that Mr. John is ill. He is very bad, Sir. It is even feared that he may be lying at the point of death. He wants to see you, Sir. I have a chaise here. Pray come to him. Pray lose no time."

Mr. James and I looked at one another. "Wilhelm," said he, "this is strange. I wish you to come with me!" I helped him to dress, partly there and partly in the chaise; and no grass grew under the horses' iron shoes between Poland Street and the Forest.

Now, mind! (said the German courier) I went with Mr. James into his brother's room, and I saw and heard myself what follows.

His brother lay upon his bed, at the upper end of a long bed chamber. His old housekeeper was there, and others were there: I think three others were there, if not four, and they had been with him since early in the afternoon. He was in white, like the figure—necessarily so, because he had his night-dress on. He looked like the figure—necessarily so, because he looked earnestly at his brother when he saw him come into the room.

But, when his brother reached the bed-side, he slowly raised himself in bed, and looking full upon him, said these words:

"JAMES, YOU HAVE SEEN ME BEFORE, TO-NIGHT—AND YOU KNOW IT!'"' And so died!

I waited, when the German courier ceased, to hear something said of this strange story. The silence was unbroken. I looked round, and the five couriers were gone: so noiselessly that the ghostly mountain might have absorbed them into its eternal snows. By this time, I was by no means in a mood to sit alone in that awful scene, with the chill air coming solemnly upon me—or, if I may tell the truth, to sit alone anywhere. So I went back into the convent parlour, and, finding the American gentleman still disposed to relate the biography of the Honourable Ananias Dodger, heard it all out.

Joseph Grimaldi

Joseph Grimaldi

Introductory Chapter to
"Memoirs of Joseph Grimaldi"

It is some years now since we first conceived a strong veneration for Clowns, and an intense anxiety to know what they did with them selves out of pantomime time and off the stage. As a child, we were accustomed to pester our relations and friends with questions out of number concerning these gentry;—whether their appetite for sausages and such like wares was always the same, and if so, at whose expense they were maintained; whether they were ever taken up for pilfering other people's goods, or were forgiven by everybody because it was only done in fun; how it was they got such beautiful complexions, and where they lived; and whether they were born Clowns, or gradually turned into Clowns as they grew up. On these and a thousand other points our curiosity was insatiable. Nor were our speculations confined to Clowns alone; they extended to Harlequins, Pantaloons, and Columbines, all of whom we believed to be real and veritable personages, existing in the same forms and characters all the year round. How often have we wished that the Pantaloon were our godfather! and how often thought that to marry a Columbine would be to attain the highest pitch of all human felicity!

The delights—the ten thousand million delights—of a pantomime come streaming upon us now, even of the pantomime which came lumbering down in Richardson's waggons at fair time to the dull little town in which we had the honour to be brought up, and which a long row of small boys, with frills as white as they could be washed, and hands as clean as they would come, were taken to behold the glories of in fair daylight.

We feel again all the pride of standing in a body on the platform, the observed of all observers in the crowd below, while the junior usher pays away twenty-four ninepences to a stout gentleman under a Gothic arch, with a hoop of variegated lamps swinging over his head. Again we catch a glimpse (too brief, alas!) of the lady with a green parasol in her hand, on the outside stage of the next show but one, who supports herself on one foot on the back of a majestic horse, blotting-paper coloured and white; and once again our eyes open wide with wonder and our hearts throb with emotion as we deliver our cardboard check into the very hands of the Harlequin himself, who, all glittering with spangles and dazzling with many colours, deigns to give us a word of encouragement and commendation as we pass into the booth!

But what was this—even this—to the glories of the inside, where, amid the smell of sawdust and orange-peel, sweeter far than violets to youthful noses, the first play being over, the lovers united, the Ghost appeased, the Baron killed, and everything made comfortable and pleasant, the pantomime itself began! What words can describe the deep gloom of the opening scene where a crafty Magician holding a young lady in bondage was discovered studying an enchanted book to the soft music of a gong! or in what terms can we express the thrill of ecstasy with which, his magic power opposed by superior art, we beheld the monster himself converted into Clown! What mattered it that the stage was three yards wide and four deep? *we* never saw it. We had no eyes, ears, or corporeal senses but for the pantomime. And when its short career was run, and the Baron previously slaughtered, coming forward with his hand upon his heart, announced that for that favour Mr. Richardson returned his most sincere thanks, and the performances would commence again in a quarter of an hour, what jest could equal the effects of the Baron's indignation and surprise when the Clown, unexpectedly peeping from behind the curtain, requested the audience "not to believe it, for it was all gammon"! Who but a Clown could have called forth the roar of laughter that succeeded! and what witchery but a Clown's could have caused the junior usher himself to declare aloud, as he shook his sides and smote his knee in a moment of irrepressible joy, that that was the very best thing he had ever heard said!

We have lost that Clown now ;—he is still alive though, for we saw him only the day before last Bartholomew Fair eating a real saveloy, and we are sorry to say he had deserted to the illegitimate drama, for he was seated on one of "Clark's Circus" waggons ;—we have lost that Clown and that pantomime, but our relish for the entertainment still remains unimpaired. Each successive Boxing Day finds us in the same state of high excitement and expectation. On that eventful day, when new pantomimes are played for the first time at the two great theatres, and at twenty or thirty of the little ones, we still gloat as formerly upon the bills which set forth tempting descriptions of the scenery in staring red and black letters, and still fall down upon our knees, with other men and boys, upon the pavement by shop-doors, to read them down to the very last line. Nay, we still peruse with all eagerness and avidity the exclusive accounts of the coming wonders in the theatrical newspapers of the Sunday before, and still believe them as devoutly as we did before twenty years' experience had shown us that they are always wrong.

With these feelings upon the subject of pantomimes, it is no matter of surprise that when we first heard that Grimaldi had left some memoirs of his life behind him, we were in a perfect fever until we had perused the manuscript. It was no sooner placed in our hands by "the adventurous and spirited Publisher"—(if our recollection serve us, this is the customary style of the complimentary little paragraphs regarding new books which usually precede advertisements about Savory's clocks in the newspapers)—than we sat down at once and read it every word.

See how pleasantly things come about, if you let them take their own course! This mention of the manuscript brings us at once to the very point we are anxious to reach, and which we should have gained long ago, if we had not travelled into those irrelevant remarks concerning pantomimic representations.

For about a year before his death Grimaldi was employed in writing a full account of his life and adventures. It was his chief occupation and amusement; and as people who write their own lives, even in the midst of very many occupations, often find time to extend them to a most inordinate length, it is no wonder that his account of himself was exceedingly voluminous.

This manuscript was confided to Mr. Thomas Egerton Wilks, to alter and revise, with a view to its publication. Mr. Wilks, who was well acquainted with Grimaldi and his connections, applied himself to the task of condensing it throughout, and wholly expunging considerable portions, which, so far as the public were concerned, possessed neither interest nor amusement: he likewise interspersed here and there the substance of such personal anecdotes as he had gleaned from the writer in desultory conversation. While he was thus engaged, Grimaldi died.

Mr. Wilks having by the commencement of September concluded his labours, offered the manuscript to the present publisher, by whom it was shortly afterwards purchased unconditionally, with the full consent and concurrence of Mr. Richard Hughes, Grimaldi's executor.

The present Editor of these volumes has felt it necessary to say thus much in explanation of their origin, in order to establish beyond doubt the unquestionable authenticity of the memoirs they contain.

His own share in them is stated in a few words. Being much struck by several incidents in the manuscript—such as the description of Grimaldi's infancy, the burglary, the brother's return from sea under the extraordinary circumstances detailed, the adventure of the man with the two fingers on his left hand, the account of Mackintosh and his friends, and many other passages—and thinking that they might be related in a more attractive manner (they were at that time told in the first person, as if by Grimaldi himself, although they had necessarily lost any original manner which his recital might have imparted to them); he accepted a proposal from the publisher to edit the book, and *has* edited it to the best of his ability, altering its form throughout, and making such other alterations as he conceived would improve the narration of the facts, without any departure from the facts themselves.

He has merely to add that there has been no *book-making* in this case. He has not swelled the quantity of matter, but materially abridged it. The account of Grimaldi's first courtship may appear lengthy in its present form; but it has undergone a double and most comprehensive process of abridgment. The old man was garrulous upon a subject on which the youth had felt so keenly; and as the feeling did him honour in both stages of life, the Editor has not had the heart to reduce it further.

Here is the book, then, at last. After so much pains from so many hands—including the good right hand of George Cruikshank, which has seldom been better exercised—he humbly hopes it may find favour with the public.

DOUGHTY STREET, *February*, 1838.

JOHN OVERS

JOHN OVERS

PREFACE TO "EVENINGS OF A WORKING MAN"

The indulgent reader of this little book*—not called indulgent, I may hope, by courtesy alone, but with some reference also to its title and pretensions—may very naturally inquire bow it comes to have a preface to which my name is attached, nor is the reader's right or inclination to be satisfied on this head, likely to be much diminished, when I state in the outset, that I do not recommend it as a book of surpassing originality or transcendent merit. That I do not claim to have discovered, in humble life, an extraordinary and brilliant genius. That I cannot charge mankind in general, with having entered into a conspiracy to neglect the author of this volume, or to leave him pining in obscurity. That I have not the smallest intention of comparing him with Burns, the exciseman; or with Bloomfield, the shoemaker; or with Ebenezer Elliott, the worker in iron; or with James Hogg, the shepherd. That I see no reason to be hot, or bitter, or lowering, or sarcastic, or indignant, or fierce, or sour, or sharp, in his behalf. That I have nothing to rail at; nothing to exalt; nothing to flourish in the face of a stony-hearted world; and have but a very short and simple tale to tell.

But, such as it is, it has interested me: and I hope it may interest the reader too, if I state it, unaffectedly and plainly.

John Overs, the writer of the following pages, is, as is set forth in the title-page, a working man. A man who earns his weekly wages (or who did when he was strong enough) by plying of the hammer, plane, and chisel.

---

*   "Evenings of a Working Man": being the occupation of his scanty leisure. By John Overs.

He became known to me, to the best of my recollection, nearly six years ago, when he sent me some songs, appropriate to the different months of the year, with a letter, stating under what circumstances they had been composed, and in what manner he was occupied from morning until night I was, just then, relinquishing the conduct of a monthly periodical: or I would gladly have published them. As it was, I returned them to him, with a private expression of the interest I felt in such productions. They were afterwards accepted, with much readiness and consideration, by Mr. Tait, of Edinburgh; and were printed in his Magazine.

Finding, after some further correspondence with my new friend, that his authorship had not ceased with these verses, but that he still occupied his leisure moments in writing, I took occasion to remonstrate with him seriously against his pursuing that course. I pointed out to him a few of the uncertainties, anxieties, and difficulties of such a life, at the best. I entreated him to remember the position of heavy disadvantage in which he stood, by reason of his self education, and imperfect attainments; and I besought him to consider whether, having one or two of his pieces accepted occasionally, here and there, after long suspense and many refusals, it was probable that he would find himself, in the end, a happier or a more contented man. On all these grounds, I told him, his persistence in his new calling made me uneasy; and I advised him to abandon it, as strongly as I could.

In answer to this dissuasion of mine, he wrote me as manly and straightforward, but withal, as modest a letter, as ever I read in my life. He explained to me how limited his ambition was: soaring no higher than the establishment of his wife in some light business, and the better education of his children. He set before me, the difference between his evening and holiday studies, such as they were; and the having no better resource than an alehouse or a skittle-ground. He told me, how every small addition to his stock of knowledge, made his Sunday walks the pleasanter; the hedge-flowers sweeter; everything more full of interest and meaning to him. He assured me, that his daily work was not neglected for his self-imposed pursuits; but was faithfully and honestly performed; and so, indeed, it was.

He hinted to me, that his greater self-respect was some inducement and reward; supposing every other to elude his grasp; and showed me, how the fancy that he would turn this or that acquisition from his books to account, by and by, in writing, made him more fresh and eager to peruse and profit by them, when his long day's work was done.

I would not, if I could, have offered one solitary objection more, to arguments so unpretending and so true.

From that time to the present, I have seen him frequently. It has been a pleasure to me to put a few books in his way; to give him a word or two of counsel in his little projects and difficulties; and to read his compositions with him, when he has had an hour, or so, to spare. I have never altered them, otherwise than by recommending condensation now and then; nor have I, in looking over these sheets, made any emendation in them, beyond the ordinary corrections of the press; desiring them to be his genuine work, as they have been his sober and rational amusement.

The latter observation brings me to the origin of the present volume, and of this my slight share in it. The reader will soon comprehend why I touch the subject lightly, and with a sorrowful and faltering hand.

In all the knowledge I have had of John Overs, and in all the many conversations I have held with him, I have invariably found him, in every essential particular, but one, the same. I have found him from first to last a simple, frugal, steady, upright, honourable man; especially to be noted for the unobtrusive independence of his character, the instinctive propriety of his manner, and the perfect neatness of his appearance. The extent of his information: regard being had to his opportunities of acquiring it: is very remarkable; and the discrimination with which he has risen superior to the mere prejudices of the class with which he is associated, without losing his sympathy for all their real wrongs and grievances—they have a few—impressed me, in the beginning of our acquaintance, strongly in his favour.

The one respect in which he is not what he was, is in his hold on life.

He is very ill; the faintest shadow of the man who came into my little study for the first time half a dozen years ago, after the correspondence I have mentioned. He has been very ill for a long, long period; his disease is a severe and wasting affection of the lungs, which has incapacitated him, these many months, for every kind of occupation. "If I could only do a hard day's work," he said to me the other day, "how happy I should be!"

Having these papers by him, amongst others, he bethought himself that if he could get a bookseller to purchase them for publication in a volume, they would enable him to make some temporary provision for his sick wife and very young family. We talked the matter over together, and that it might be easier of accomplishment I promised him that I would write an introduction to his book.

I would to Heaven that I could do him better service! I would to Heaven it were an introduction to a long, and vigorous, and useful life! But Hope will not trim her lamp the less brightly for him and his, because of this impulse to their struggling fortunes; and trust me, reader, they deserve her light, and need it sorely.

He has inscribed this book to one whose skill will help him, under Providence, in all that human skill can do. To one who never could have recognised in any potentate on earth, a higher claim to constant kindness and attention, than he has recognised in him.

I have little more to say of it. While I do not commend it, on the one hand, as a prodigy, I do sincerely believe it, on the other, to possess some points of real interest, however considered; but which, if considered with reference to its title and origin, are of great interest.

If any delicate readers should approach the perusal of these "Evenings of a Working Man", with a genteel distaste to the principle of a workingman turning author at all, I may perhaps be permitted to suggest that the best protection against such an offence will be found in the Universal Education of the people; for the enlightenment of the many will effectually swamp any interest that may now attach in vulgar minds, to the few among them who are enabled, in any degree, to over come the great difficulties of their position.

And if such readers should deny the immense importance of communicating to this class, at this time, every possible means of know ledge, refinement and recreation; or the cause we have to hail with delight the least token that may arise among them of a desire to be wiser, better, and more gentle; I earnestly entreat them to educate themselves in this neglected branch of their own learning without delay; promising them that it is the easiest in its acquisition of any: requiring only open eyes and ears, and six easy lessons of an hour each in a working town. Which will render them perfect for the rest of their lives.

LONDON, *June* 1844.

ALSO AVAILABLE IN THE NONSUCH CLASSICS SERIES

For forthcoming titles and sales information see
www.nonsuch-publishing.com